The C

Kings

Book Two in:
'The Legends of Kalnay'
Series

By
Aaron Phillip Redditt

Table of Contents

Dedications

This book is dedicated to my metal family, who have shown me that support and encouragement go both ways in the most profound sense.

I would also like to dedicate this installment to Taylor McNallie, who told me what I needed to hear to reignite the fire in my writing and renew faith in myself and the passion I have for this series.

"You have found these things of the abyss hard to believe," he said, "but you will find the tangible and material things ahead still harder. That is the way of our minds. Marvels are doubly incredible when brought into three dimensions from the vague regions of possible dream. I shall not try to tell you much- that would be another and very different story. I will only tell you what you absolutely have to know."- H.P. Lovecraft, 'Through the Gates of the Silver Key'

Wendaros the Mighty: A Legend of Kalnay

In the ancient days of Kalnay, lived a mighty hunter; a tribal chief of Lec'tair Forest, named Wendaros. One day whilst hunting food for his people, Wendaros spotted the mightiest, largest stag ever beheld; four times the size of a grown man. The stag's pelt was the color of polished silver. Wendaros was so stunned by the beast's magnificence the stag fled before he could react.

With a full quiver of arrows and his fabled bow Ham'Gra, Wendaros diligently tracked the stag through Lec'tair Forest three days and nights. On the third night, after failing to yet overtake the creature, he hid in the high branches of a pine tree near a remote lake. He knew all beasts must drink and waited patiently within the treetop for his shot. After several hours of moonlit silence, the stag emerged from the belt of trees, drawing near the lake to drink. Wendaros readied his bow, nocking a thick oaken arrow with a deadly steel tip, waiting for the right moment. The stag searched cautiously for signs of peril. Seeing none- for Wendaros had camouflaged himself in the treetop- the beast began drinking crystal-clear water from the lake. By degrees, the full moon emerged through the veil of clouds, shining in splendor upon the stag.

Clearly beholding the stag's silver eye glinting in the moonlight Wendaros knew his moment had come. Drawing his bow, Wendaros uttered a quick prayer to Hannibal, God of the Hunt, and let fly his arrow. His aim was true; the arrow struck the stag through the eye from fifty feet away, piercing its brain. The stag uttered a shocked bellow, shattering the silence of the night before toppling to the ground, slain. Descending the tree to fetch his prize, Wendaros marked a radiant woman in a pure white shift emerging from the lake. The mysterious, pale beauty knelt over the fallen stag, weeping and wailing loudly. The still lake water rippled intensely at her cries. Nested birds scattered into the night sky, chirruping loudly; echoing and intensifying the woman's cries.

Wendaros approached the distraught figure, attempting to console her. "Tis simply a beast, lady; the meat will feed my starving tribe for a month. Its silver hide will fetch two dozen golden dragons, further aiding my people by providing us with warm blankets and material to construct new huts."

The mystery woman wheeled on Wendaros, scratching him savagely across the face. In an inhuman voice she shrieked, "This was no simple stag! This was my eldest son, Marten! I am Bloomaya, goddess of nature, o foolish mortal! You have slain an innocent creature for selfish gains! I curse *you*, oh mighty Wendaros, and *all* your tribe for this unprovoked slaughter! I curse you and your people to *always* know hunger! Never more will the soil of Kalnay yield fruit or vegetable to *your* kind! You and your kin will forever bear insatiable hunger for human flesh alone! It will *sicken* you to consume flesh- man, woman and child alike- but you will be helpless to crave it!" Bloomaya raised her right hand, splaying her fingers, moonbeams shooting twixt the shadows cast by her hand. "Evermore, your people will bear my mark on your countenance, so all will know the *hatred* I bear you! You and your kin shalt grow antlers: an everlasting reminder of the foul murder committed this day! There is *no* cure! There will be *no* forgiveness! Now and forever, I stand as thine *enemy*! Should you or your kin call upon my name, I will turn a deaf ear to your supplication!"

As Bloomaya pronounced the curse, Wendaros transformed into a grotesque parody of a man. His skin began to grey- the color of necrotizing flesh; his teeth grew hideously long and sharp. His fingers lengthened, ending in a set of ferocious, hooked claws. His bones broke and painfully lengthened, as he grew over twelve feet tall from head to toe. Where his feet had been, there transformed instead a large pair of cloven hooves. Silver fur clothed him from his hooves to his waist. Atop his skull grew a large, twisted set of many pronged antlers. The scratch across Wendaros' face blazed a ghostly white upon his grey face. During these mortifying changes Wendaros pleaded, shrieked in deep-seeded agony and begged in pained gasps for Bloomaya's forgiveness.

The goddess was thoroughly enveloped in hatred and wretched grief over her son's death; unmoved by Wendaros' pleas for mercy. As the horrific transformation finished, Bloomaya unleashed a peal of grief-induced laughter. Seizing Marten's body, the goddess dove into the lake. After she disappeared beneath the surface, Wendaros crawled weakly to the waterfront to gaze upon his reflection. Beholding his monstrous appearance, the former hero of Lec'tair Forest unleashed a cry of rage, sorrow and hunger, that sounded human and elk all at once. Thus, Wendaros the Mighty became Wendygo: the first and fiercest stag man and devourer of human flesh. Rising unsteadily to his newly transformed feet, Wendygo scented the night air, his overloaded senses keener than ever. He scented on that breeze the smell of his tribe, wafting in the air like a king's feast. The fading, human part of his nature was mortified at the love of, and desire for, that smell. With a mix of reluctance and desire, he turned from the lake to Lec'tair Forest behind him, galloping toward the scent of his new prey: mankind. Thus has the Wendygo dwelt, cursed, within the realm of Kalnay since; devouring any mortal men who stray into the domain of Lec'tair Forest, turning still others into one of their kind that their defiance of Bloomaya's curse may thrive forever, awaiting the day they may devour all of mankind and claim the realm of Kalnay for themselves.

Wagnar the Bloodstained: A Legend of Kalnay

In the ancient days of Kalnay- after the cursing of Baron Gareth Landis, but prior to the fall of the huntsman Wendaros- there came across the sea a man known as Wagnar the Bloodstained. He fled a nation whose name and memory have passed beyond recollection and which laid north of the Black Water Sea. His flight from unfriendly shores forced him to steal a small skiff and sparse supplies; for he had fled desperately for his life. When his skiff beached in Northern Kalnay after untold weeks adrift at sea, Wagnar was on the verge of death; his food ran out the previous week, and his fresh water two days prior to that. Through force of will, he abandoned the skiff, frantically ensnaring several rats dining on a seal carcass. One rat Wagnar ate raw, for he relished the taste of fresh blood and the juiciness of raw meat. His razor-sharp, filed teeth ripped and shredded at the tough rat meat. The other rats he sacrificed over a small fire built from his beached skiff as the sun sank beyond the horizon. With a small fileting knife he withdrew from his belt, he sliced the rodents' throats, dangling them over the meager fire. The rat blood sizzled and spattered into the greedily licking flames. As the blood dripped, Wagnar muttered a handful words in his foreign tongue, rocking to and fro on his knees before the growing tendrils of flame. As he offered his strange prayers, the flames grew larger, consuming the rats directly from his hands. The flames were those of Morgethel: a fire demon of old which Wagnar worshipped, who demanded blood sacrifice in exchange for blessings. Morgethel was still exalted in secret by strange people of the far north, such as Wagnar.

Once the rats were consumed- flesh, blood and bone- by Morgethel's unholy flames, Wagnar arose. His countenance was healthier and stronger than before; for in exchange for blood, Morgethel may grant a waning mortal rejuvenation and temporary longevity. Wagnar snuffed the fire upon attaining Morgethel's blessing, wending his way south in aimless solitude, reflecting upon the possibilities awaiting him in this new land. Before traveling half a league, Wagnar marked a bright light suddenly appear in the heavens. It plummeted like a falling star, impacting the ground mere feet before him with a clamor and quaking of the earth. When his eyes readjusted to the night's darkness, he beheld a radiant woman in a simple gray dress with a white lace veil upon her head standing before him. Wagnar was surprised by her sudden appearance and inquired of the woman who she was; hoping perhaps she was his spirit guide in this alien land.

With fire in her eyes and thunder in her voice she proclaimed, "I am Bronwyn-Aetha; goddess of the white and justice in this realm of Kalnay."

Wagnar bowed prostrate on the ground, splaying his bloodstained hands before him. "Hail to you, Bronwyn-Aetha. Forgive my harsh appearance. I have journeyed far, amidst strife, to reach this land. I did not expect to meet a goddess in my travels here."

Bronwyn-Aetha shouted over Wagnar's words, ignoring his platitudes. "You are a trespasser in this realm Wagnar, son of Ulthar! The blood of those slain by you in your distant homeland of Moorwyn; the life blood of your brother, his wife, and their two daughters, as well as the rodents sacrificed on the beach to the Pit Demon Morgethel, are offenses both to *me* and the realm of

Kalnay! For these offenses, I curse you, Wagnar the Bloodstained. From this night forth until the end of all nights, I confine you to the realm of darkness; as the darkness of Morgethel is your master. I curse you to know boundless hunger for the blood you have so freely spilt abroad and bring now unto Kalnay. Sunlight- the light of white, goodness and justice- shall *ever* be your enemy. The sharp and splintery edge of wood shall you fear as if 'twere death; for so it shall be unto you and your ilk for all time. Know that this fear shall prevent you from returning by ship to Moorwyn and the temples of Morgethel. Finally, I curse you with life eternal that you may never again commune with Morgethel; for the Pit Demon will nary recognize you as mortal again. Your soul shall be driven mad watching time march to the end of nights. Know too, Wagnar: *never* will I allow your savagery to be unleashed upon the rest of Kalnay. Should your travels lead you South to the Shavatnu Mountains, you shall be compelled in your bones to turn north, east or west. *Never* shall you find sympathetic shelter amongst men, for you will be abhorrent and nightmarish to the eye. This I promise. I, Bronwyn-Aetha have spoken; so shall it be." Then the goddess laid a fingertip upon Wagnar's brow, and he screamed in deep agony.

        Wagnar's heart slowed to a standstill, blood no longer coursing through his veins; yet he did not die. His finely honed, serrated teeth burst into a crooked shelf of needle-like fangs, contorting his jaw into a grotesque mask barely resembling that of a man. His hearing and sense of smell erupted to life; he could hear the very bracken and shrub roots growing and shifting in the soil below his feet. His eyesight became keener than a hawk's. He was forced to avert his gaze from Bronwyn-Aetha, as her supernatural radiance pierced him to his damned soul's core. Wagnar's dismay increased upon observing his hands; protruding roughly from his fingertips were three-inch-long, razor-sharp claws. Then Bronwyn-Aetha vanished and Wagnar was alone.

In fury and agony, the newly cursed Wagnar tracked and slaughtered a grown doe, gorging himself on its hot, thick blood. Before finishing his bloody feast, he was alerted by his newly heightened instincts of impending danger. Glancing worriedly to the horizon he marked the first, fiery sliver of sunlight climbing into the sky. Fear mingled with deep-seated hatred gripped his dead heart. With inhuman speed, he burrowed into the earth escaping the threat of death in the sunlight above. There he remained until sunset- sleeping, dreaming nightmares and churning anew the hatred he bore both gods and the rest of mankind. Thus, as the sun set, did Wagnar the Bloodstained arise as the first and most powerful of Nightstalkers which have plagued the Kalnayan Wastes of the North from the ancient times to the present day.

Prologue: Wrath of the Screech Owl

High within Lilith's black tower, there issued forth horrendous shrieks (which passersby far below could not properly distinguish as the cries of either man or beast). They were, in fact, the tortured cries of Straker, a Wildman tracker formerly of the Nightstalker Wastes. What now seemed to him centuries ago, Straker had embarked with his two brothers-in-arms, Levitt Long Knives and Nevar the Patchwork Knight, to capture an old wizard and his pretty young female apprentice. Not once, nor twice, had the trio of mercenaries failed, but *three* times.

At the skillful hands of Talon, the mute chief torturer of Regalias, Straker revealed the existence of the other two targets Nevar had pursued alone: a young boy- brother to the Prezla girl- and a stately blond woman who was a fabled dyre bear of myth. Lilith was perturbed that this unknown boy and bear woman had escaped the trio of sell-swords. She was further outraged to learn they had privately decided to separate and pursue the two refugee parties without first consulting, or even informing, her of their intentions. Her wrath was stoked to such extremes that she requisitioned Talon to torture Straker slowly for the first three weeks after his mewling, empty-handed return.

After those three weeks, word reached Lilith of Nevar's massive dead carcass discovered on a dirt road north of Bogdan. By all accounts, Nevar's left arm had been severed just below the elbow, his throat torn out by an animal- a bear, if the rumors were to be believed. The Screech Owl was furious to learn that this mysterious boy and dyre bear svanth had passed into the Nightstalker

Wastes via the Voshkarna; for they were now essentially beyond her reach. Lilith took charge of Straker's torture personally, at that point. She called upon the darkest, vilest spells to wreak havoc upon his entire being- body, mind and soul. She summoned fire to burn within the marrow of his bones. She twisted, contorted and constricted the man's internal organs. She trapped his mind within nightmares of being hunted by nightstalkers, mauled by a grymwulf, or being consumed alive by the cannibalistic wendygos of Lec'tair Forest. It was understandable to Lilith that Nevar fought and lost to a dyre bear and the boy; fighting a wild bear is a foolhardy endeavour; combatting a dyre bear is all but suicide. At *least,* she reflected, the Patchwork Knight went down fighting. In Straker's case, Lilith was downright perplexed how a man of his reputation had been vanquished by gnomes. Freckaying *gnomes*! Had she been in Straker's shoes, she would rather have perished attempting to fight, than live with the knowledge of being bested by folk no larger than children.

On one of the rare occasions during that hellish final weeks' time, Talon became occupied with the Overlord's business. Lilith strove to locate the escaped Prezla fugitives with her gift of Ravensight. In that reprieve from the relentless torture at both Lilith and Talon's hands, Straker reflected in desperation at his predicament. *I should have let the gnomes kill me. A quick slice across my throat; gods below, a severed vein in my leg would have been sweet release compared to* this *endless torment. Curse me for thinking this Screech Owl* svanth *would be grateful for any news I delivered. Levitt is dead. Nevar is dead. Soon, when Lilith grows bored of torturing me, I too will be dead.* The Wildman glanced weakly to his right, then to his left on the angled slab he was bound to. With each turn of his head, he held his gaze for a long, painful moment on the macabre spectacle which *used* to be his hands. Talon had methodically removed all five digits on both hands a week ago. Mere days ago, Talon just as deliberately removed his toes, plumbing for information on Lilith's behalf.

Lilith had suspiciously assumed that, Straker withholding vital information in the field- such as the true value of the girl, the existence of the she-bear and the possible Prezla boy fleeing north- meant there may be *other* things the Northerner had kept from her. After three solid weeks of pain, Lilith finally determined there was indeed nothing new to be learned. The Northman prayed blindly that the suffering would cease then. Sadly, his frantic prayers went unanswered. The fourth week of being locked within the black tower, Lilith relieved Talon of his duties, informing him, "You may, if you so desire, return to Lord Malikh's dungeons, Master Talon. If you do, I thank you kindly for your service these past weeks. They have been......entertaining *and* educational all at once.... On the other hand," Lilith hinted sinisterly, "you *could* stay and observe *my* work. The choice is yours, Master Torturer."

Talon folded his muscular arms across his broad, sinewy chest releasing a measured breath, staring intently into Lilith's face.

Smiling devilishly, Lilith hissed, "I suspected you would stay, Master Talon. Truly, you have a *rare* appreciation for the fine art of torture. I *like* that in a man. Watch. Perhaps *you* will learn something new for later." Like a viper, Lilith turned gracefully, slithering across the room, halting beside Straker. She raised her right hand, causing him to flinch, involuntarily turning his head to the left, feebly attempting to avoid her touch.

Lilith chuckled softly. "Straker," Lilith chided, "surely you know there is *no* evading me. I am everywhere....and I am nowhere. I think you are still cogent enough to grasp that. You failed *miserably* in your task. You failed me *worse* when you and that clod of a companion, Nevar, decided to be greedy, simple *sptoches.*" Here, Lilith paused, holding the tip of her forefinger to the man's temple. The northerner sucked in an involuntary breath, waiting, fearful of what the dark witch would do.

Smiling cruelly, she leaned close, hissing, "*Burtsa despat rysa*" in Straker's ear. Without warning, he howled like a coyote caught in a wire trap. As Lilith uttered her spell, the Wildman felt a white-hot needle of pain slowly digging into his skull where she placed her fingertip. Inward it burrowed: hot, intense and relentless; until he felt he must go mad or die.

"*Etsa,*" Lilith stated flatly. As immediately as it had begun, the unseen needle ceased burrowing into his skull.

Straker gasped, whimpering, "*Please,* Lady Lilith. I made a *mistake.* My compatriots and I *all* did. I can make this right. Grant me one more chance, I *beg* you. I will track the old man and girl....free of charge, of course. I will drag them before you, set them at your feet, to do with as your ladyship sees fit. Just....*please*....I beg you....spare me...."

Lilith smiled, stroking his sweaty, stubble-covered cheek. "Oh Straker," she cooed falsely, "I *wish* I could believe you. Regrettably, you have proven yourself a coward *and* a liar. I have no use for a lying coward. You are as likely to flee over the Chakti as you are to honor your word. No....I fear you will remain my plaything." As Lilith turned to walk away, the man croaked something inarticulate. Pausing, Lilith smiled, asking, "I'm sorry Straker....did you say something? I'm afraid I didn't hear you."

Straker raised his head, cleared his parched throat and seethed, "I said, I hope the dyre bear guts you like a *pig* for everyone to see. I hope you rot in the Nether-Realm, you crazy, freckaying *svanth*!"

Lilith's black eyes shot open in shock and rage. Raising her hands, she parted them in opposite directions in the air before Straker; as if opening a pair of curtains. As she did thus, Lilith shrieked, "*Corva*!"

With a horrible rending sound, like fabric composed of meat, Straker's chest split open. His eyes started widely, he uttered a faint grunt, coughing a jet of blood in Lilith's face. Staring in disbelief as his innards splashed all over the stone floor and his hot blood splattered all over Lilith's pale skin and black raiment, the Northman struggled to summon a final breath. His lungs, however, had been expelled by Lilith's savage spell. A moment later, his head lolled limply to his chest and Straker was no more.

With an evil smile, Lilith yanked his hair, lifting his limp head. The Screech Owl hissed in the dead man's face, "The dyre bear has *no* chance to gut me, if I gut her *first*." Whirling about, Lilith strode through the carnage of innards and blood, drenching the hem of her raven black dress in the Wildman's blood. Gazing sharply at the unmoving, unfazed Talon, Lilith declared, "Be a good man, and clean up this mess, Master Talon. I'm done playing....for now."

Bowing faintly, Talon grunted, nodding. Then Lilith exited, smearing a fading red trail of footprints and a swath of blood, like a doused paint brush, as she went. Talon fetched a bucket, filling it by hand with Straker's scattered entrails. As he did so, Talon marveled at how perfectly precise and succinct Lilith's magic was. The torturer swore in his mind, he would strive to learn the Dark Arts. Only then could Talon become the best torturer in all Kalnay.

Chapter One: The Limitations of Magic

Their journey east had been less difficult than Isabel first feared it might be. There were no towns or cities to speak of to the north of Regalias. This put the young Prezla's mind a bit more at ease, as traversing through even small towns could be difficult with the unique presence of Eimar and Tibelde- her, and Master Sarto's newfound friends. She and Sarto already had bounties on their heads; adding a pair of gnomes would draw more attention than they wanted. On occasion, the company was forced to evade small ranging parties of Red Guards dispatched by Overlord Malikh. Since the loss of Pallas and their subsequent, though brief, capture by Straker, Isabel was far warier of people in general. Avoiding patrols was simple. Any time they noted one nearing, Isabel used a concealment spell (*'Cofraith numa philas'*) and they silently moved past the patrols.

In the week and a half since departing the gnomish city of Mydoth in Othros, Sarto was impressed with how rapidly Isabel grasped the array of spells he taught her. With little effort, she mastered most intermediate spells he presented her. Isabel's appetite for knowledge was insatiable. Sarto knew this was largely due to her natural skills and keen wits. He also knew she sought this knowledge so voraciously because of lingering guilt over Pallas' death. Isabel all but demanded to learn an abundance of healing and mending spells; also dedicating herself to concocting healing potions and salves. That was when Sarto knew for certain she still blamed herself for Pallas' death. He strove to guide her to a happier path, but she clutched her unspoken grief deep in her heart. He knew better than to rebuke her openly, as he had done after Pallas' funeral. Sarto understood Isabel was pouring herself into healing magic as her form of grief processing. He understood that feeling well. Sarto had demonstrated the same determination after his re-naming ceremony; striving to make good on his promise to the gods, the diviners, and his friend Pallas. Therefore, rather than dissuade her, Sarto encouraged her whole-heartedly in the way she desired to learn. He compromised with her that, for every two healing spells he taught her, she must learn one defense spell. After some half-hearted arguing, Sarto convinced her that one superb defense spell was better by far than two good healing spells. Together, they worked on improving her rapidly growing skills as they sojourned across the Kalnayan grasslands.

On several occasions, Eimar and Tibelde stole a shiny trinket from roving bandits, or one of the Regalias patrols. Most times, the men who'd been robbed didn't even know that they'd been targeted by the pickpocketing gnomes. Occasionally, one might catch a passing glance of them and assume Eimar or Tibelde were ghosts; causing the superstitious patrol men to press on faster, hoping to avoid the alleged phantoms.

Early on their travels together, Isabel concernedly asked Tibelde, "Aren't you two afraid of discovery? The confirmed existence of gnomes in Kalnay could spell trouble for you and your people. Never mind the more immediate trouble *we* could be in if you're spotted."

Eimar beamed up at Isabel, patting her hand comfortingly and cooing, "Have no fear, Lady Isabel. My sister Tibelde and I aren't called '*Un Riveth Duallis*' for nothing you know."

With a puzzled look, Isabel queried, "What does '*Un Riveth Duallis*' mean, Eimar?"

Smacking his forehead with one palm, Eimar replied, "Oh, I beg your pardon, Lady Isabel. I forgot you aren't quite as fluent in ancient Kalnese as Master Sarto, here. '*Un Riveth Duallis*' means: 'The Shadow Twins'. It is the title we are known by amongst our kin."

"I see," Isabel replied. "What is the significance of the title, if I may ask?"

Beaming broader still, Eimar boasted, "It signifies praise for our skill at stealing from the dunkla men who pass through Othros. It is a high honor among gnomish folk to be recognized for one's skills in thievery." Pausing briefly, a thought occurred to Eimar. "What of you and your brother, Abel? Do *you* bear a title praising your skill at thievery too?"

Isabel giggled and shook her head. "No Eimar, we do *not*. Among mankind, stealing is a *crime*. It was something my mother would have tanned my hide for. The people of Gwenovair know Abel and I simply as the Farthen Twins, nothing more."

Eimar gave Isabel a puzzled look of his own. "Why would you go by your family surname? Are the people of Gwenovair *simpletons*, requiring constant reminder of whose children you are, or what house you descended from?"

Out of nowhere, Tibelde appeared, cuffing Eimar hard upside the head. "Hold your tongue, Eimar! By the *ancestors*, sometimes your head is thicker than a woodpecker's!" Turning to Isabel, Tibelde quickly touched her forehead, and then her lips, holding her hand up to the young sorceress with her head bowed. "My apologies, Lady Isabel. Eimar did *not* mean to infer the people of Gwenovair are addle-brained fools...." Here, she paused, throwing a venomous sidelong glance at her brother. "*Did* you, Eimar?"

Bowing swifter than Tibelde had done, Eimar sputtered, "Of course *not*! My *deepest* apologies, Lady Isabel. I cry your *sincerest* pardon for the unintended offense."

Watching the Shadow Twins bowing and apologizing awkwardly, caused Isabel to burst into unintended bouts of laughter. The Shadow Twins stood, staring confusedly at Isabel; struggling to determine the cause of her outburst. Isabel regained her composure, wiping tears of joy from her cheeks, explaining, "Forgive me, my friends, I am not laughing *at* you.... seeing you fuss over each other, apologizing for one another....it reminds me of Abel and myself. We behave thus as well....at least we did on Gwenovair. Your antics were a pleasant reminder of a happier time. Thank you, *both* of you, from the bottom of my heart. Know too, I took *no* offence at Eimar's words. To most humans, a family name is often an honor; my family is no exception. My father....was Sir Aldrich Farthen: a knight in service to the former king, Alaster, in his youth. He died....almost nine years ago now, on the shores of Igraine. He defended mine and other families against an attack by the Overlord's men....though I only learned this truth recently, from Abel. Many children were saved by *my* father's courageous sacrifice that night. I am *proud* to be a daughter of house Farthen." As she finished, tears sprung anew, and Isabel covered her face.

Sarto appeared at her side, drawing her wordlessly into his arms, allowing her to shed her grief upon his shoulder. Soothingly stroking her mouse brown hair, Sarto mumbled, "'Tis alright lass. There's no shame in grieving your father; so long as we honor his memory and celebrate his deeds."

They stopped shortly thereafter on the western bank of the lesser Inaratu River. There were no patrols nearby just then, so they rested by the shallow tributary. Before continuing, Sarto outlined the next leg of their journey. "Once we cross the lesser Inaratu, we must then cross the greater Inaratu. That will be another half day's travel east. Between the lesser and greater Inaratu, is a sizeable patch of land called the Marsh Plains. We'll camp on this side tonight, traversing the Marsh Plain at first light tomorrow. Unfortunately, because of our visibility here on the grasslands, we cannot light a fire tonight, lest we be spotted."

Eimar interjected, "Tibelde and I shall be fine, for gnome folk sleep underground. We can sense the vibrations of footsteps through the soil, so we will keep watch underground."

Sarto smiled wanly at Eimar, responding, "Thank you, Eimar." With his thoughts shielded, Sarto pondered, *did Pallas ever perceive me, like I do Eimar? The chap will simply* not *shut up....*

Isabel piped up then. "Master Sarto, perhaps our fireless night will give me the chance to try my hand at the bone warming spell you taught me the other day. I'd like to stay warm; as I'm sure you would too."

Sarto answered, "Of course Isabel. That's a *splendid* idea. If we can't have light, we can at least be warm in the dark. Let's make a shelter to shield us from the wind, should it arise." They ate a quiet supper of jerky and apples- which the Shadow Twins had plundered from a small farmstead a couple of days previous- watching the sunlight dwindle away. True to their word the Shadow Twins kept watch all night, allowing both Isabel and Sarto a rare evening of thorough rest. The next day the company forded the lesser Inaratu, before slogging for half the day through the Marsh Plains and finally crossing the thick, fast flowing vein of the greater Inaratu River. With the aid of Sarto's water-parting spell ('*Corva aquitane imor het*'), they managed to ford the greater Inaratu without incident. After crossing, the four companions were extremely fatigued from their trek. Sarto halted the journey for the remainder of the day so that all may dry their soggy boots and trousers around a fire. None of them complained, for all were weary, cold and damp.

Isabel asked Sarto, "Why do we not simply use magic to dry our boots and trousers, Master? Wouldn't it be faster?"

Sarto nodded. "Aye, Isabel; *'tis* faster. Consider this though: would you spend your magical energy on hastily dried boots and clean trousers, but leave yourself defenseless? Or, would you suffer soggy boots, but have more energy to repel arrows....or retain a deeper store of healing magic?"

Isabel's eyes bugged as she pondered Sarto's questions. "Do you mean to say, Master Sarto, that magical energy is *limited*? In *all* this time....never *once* was this limitation mentioned. Not *once*!"

Sarto stared at her quizzically, answering, "I cry your pardon, Isabel. I felt *certain* you gleaned that aspect of your abilities by now. How do you suppose it is, that you were able to tap unknown reserves of power within yourself when you aided me in boosting the strength of our distress call in Othros? Magic is *not* limitless. It is all around us, replenishing within a Prezla's skin, blood and bone; borrowing from the world around us....but there is only so much energy any one Prezla can call on, or handle, at once. To exceed those restrictions can have certain....*unpredictable* side effects on a Prezla. For example: the permanent change of your eye color; 'tis a minor change- albeit with peculiar consequences, but 'tis a *consequence* all the same. Had you not been strong enough to bolster the message's strength, your eyes could have burst into flames within their sockets, rather than change color. That is a *physical* change, your new eye color. There are also....*subconscious* changes. I didn't become who I was in Ackreth...." Here Sarto paused, rubbing his hands together nervously, subconsciously licking his lips.

Placing a comforting hand over Sarto's, Isabel voiced the name her master feared to utter. "*Apollos.* That's who you mean, isn't it Master Sarto?"

Nodding quickly, Sarto rasped, "Aye....*that* blackguard. I did not become....*him*, by learning magic the practical way. I stretched, pushed and outright *broke* the boundaries of magic *every* chance I got." Pausing briefly, Sarto looked deep into Isabel's Iolite eyes, continuing, "Now, do not think I am telling you *not* to test the limits of your skills. No wizard or witch, whether they serve the Light *or* the Dark, ever became a better Prezla by playing it safe. If *that* is what you wish to achieve, you should take up fortune-telling or a sleight-of-hand artistry in Marister. If you desire to become the *best* sorceress you can be Isabel, you *must* push the bounds of your skills. However, you must push with care. Push too hard, you may destroy yourself entirely, or fall to Pimedus....as *I* once did; as my....as *Lilith* has done. Do you understand my meaning, child?"

Isabel stared intently at Sarto as he spoke. It was as if, by staring, she could eat the words leaving his mouth. There was much to process in these words; their implications staggering. Rather than bombard him further, Isabel responded, "Aye Master Sarto, I understand. You have given me *much* to consider. I cry your pardon for my prior outburst."

Waving her apology off, Sarto answered, "Think nothing of it, Isabel. 'Tis *my* fault for not teaching you that earlier. Though I wish to believe it to the contrary, there are....*gaps*....in my knowledge. I cry your pardon now *and* later, for anything I neglect to mention. I cry your patience if there are things I forget. You are as good for me, as I for you. With Pallas gone, you are *truly* my anchor in this world. The last thing I wish is for you to be opposed to me. *That* is how Lilith and Pimedus win......I don't know quite what I'm saying. Forgive my rambling, child....I need rest."

Taking her cue, Isabel arose replying, "Aye Master Sarto, you rest. I will ensure the Shadow Twins are guarding the perimeter. You have nothing to fret about."

Hearing thus, Sarto settled into a weary bundle in the corner of the lightless shelter, falling solidly asleep. Isabel stared at him a moment longer, many questions and thoughts swirling in her mind. Forefront in her mind was him saying, *'fall to Pimedus....as* I *once did; as my....as* Lilith *has done.'* As she pondered this, Isabel had a shocking, pitiful realization: *Gods above......*Lilith *was Sarto's master! How did such a sweet man fall servant to one so....so* evil? She knew intrinsically she could *never* ask him; 'twas part of a past he feared and regretted. Knowing now, she realized the degree to which she must protect him; both from himself and the outside world. *Why didn't Pallas just* tell *me, that night beneath the apple tree?* She realized then it was something she had needed to discover herself. If she had been told, she may not have fully grasped the weight of her station; or her responsibility to be there for Sarto in Pallas' absence. Try as she might, Isabel could not shake the truth: *Sarto had once been a thrall to the Screech Owl.* As she finally lay down to sleep, the question that kept churning in her mind was: *Pallas,* why *didn't you tell me?*

Chapter Two: Domain of the Grey Men

Shortly after resuming their journey eastward the next morning, the travelers sensed a faint rumble in the earth. The Shadow Twins noticed first, stopping mid-pace, listening to, and feeling the earth. Sarto noticed their halt, inquiring, "What is it, my friends? What's wrong?"

"Riders approaching....from the south," Tibelde spoke.

Gripping his staff tightly, Sarto asked, "How many?"

"I detect....two dozen," Eimar answered.

"Aye," Tibelde confirmed, "at least four Northerners with them as well."

"*Sptoch*," hissed Sarto.

Isabel knelt, asking, "How close are they, Tibelde?"

Eimar and Tibelde answered in unison, "Less than three hundred yards south, closing fast."

Recalling Straker's uncanny scenting and tracking abilities, Isabel cast Sarto a worried look, asking, "Will our concealment spells cover our scent from these Northerners, Master Sarto?"

With a grim look on his face, Sarto shook his head. "No. Concealment spells only obstruct *sight*. As you well know Isabel, Northerners do not need to see you to track you."

Isabel queried, "Should we make a stand and fight them here, Master Sarto? My powers have grown vastly since encountering Straker and...."

"*No*," Sarto interrupted, "Right now, we are hidden from Lilith's Ravensight. If we kill these men, or are captured, we will draw Lilith's foul gaze. After that, who knows if we will evade it again? No; our *only* answer is flight."

With a curious expression, Eimar asked, "Where would we go, Master Wizard? There is naught but grasslands here, and Regalias to the south."

Staring hard to the east, Sarto pointed with his staff. "We must enter Lec'tair Forest. Be they Northerners, or servants to the Overlord, they are superstitious creatures. They will not enter the domain of the Grey Men."

Isabel glanced from Sarto to the nearby treeline of Lec'tair Forest in trepidation. "Master, you would have us enter the forest of the wendygos; of the *flesh-eaters*? Wouldn't it be less risky to engage these men directly and...."

"I will *not* risk drawing Lilith's attention by openly engaging these men, Isabel" Sarto spat. "Even if they see us fleeing at a distance, they do not know us. I would rather chance encountering wendygos than fleeing Lilith's persistent wrath and magical wiles. It is *decided*, my pupil. I will hear no more on the matter!" Turning to the gnomes, Sarto stated, "My friends, I fear we head into unknown peril. You have pledged your service on this quest. If this is too much to ask of you, we may part ways now. You may return proudly to your queen, Elissa and tell her you fulfilled your oath to us. *Or,* you may follow us into Lec'tair Forest to greet whatever dangers await us there. The choice is yours, Master Eimar and Lady Tibelde."

Without even a look twixt one another, Eimar and Tibelde replied in unison, "Master Sarto, we swore to follow you two on your quest. Through *all* dangers, we swore to stand by your sides. Gnomes do *not* run from oaths sworn, seeking safety. Rather, we embrace danger with heads held high, knives out, and war paint on. *This* is what it means to be a gnome." Saying thus, they bowed their heads quickly, hands over their hearts in renewed pledges of fealty.

Sarto smiled at the Shadow Twins, glanced apologetically at Isabel, then gazed in the direction of the approaching riders. Turning to face the steadfast gloom of Lec'tair Forest, Sarto barked over his shoulder, "Let us depart then. *Quickly.*"

The travelers had a decent head start on the riders but were spotted by the two scouting Northerners when the horsemen were seventy yards away. By then, Sarto's company were a hundred yards from the gloomy boundary of Lec'tair Forest. The fugitives laid on an extra burst of speed, as the riders altered course in rapid pursuit. The patrol closed hard from the south, spurring their horses, to catch the fleeing company.

Sarto began falling behind, so Isabel slowed her pace as well. Sarto shook his head once. "Don't *worry* about me, Isabel! Get to the forest! I'll hold these fools at bay!"

Isabel renewed her speed, closing the distance with the gnomes and the looming forest. Sarto stopped wearily in his tracks, facing the swiftly approaching horsemen. He heaved several breaths, watching them close the distance with a steely gaze. Fifty yards became forty. Forty became thirty. Thirty became twenty. As the horsemen closed the distance, Sarto thought, *closer, closer, closer......* When they were but twenty yards away, Sarto glanced passingly over his shoulder, pleased to see no sign of either Isabel or the Shadow Twins. *Amazing,* Sarto mused in wonderment, *they* listened *to me. I half expected to see them standing behind me.*

The horsemen were now a mere ten yards away, swords drawn, shouting for Sarto to identify himself. He slammed his staff firmly into the earth, crying, "*Reksla terra!*" With a loud, earthen rent, the ground he stood on shot forty feet into the air. The ground where the approaching horsemen rode upon remained below. Curses and cries arose from the horsemen, as they rode into a newly appeared cliff of earth. Those closer to the rear reined in their horses before it was too late. Others reined in their horses but were flung free. The men at the front ran full speed into the suddenly appeared earthen cliff. The wizard gazed down amusedly upon the disarrayed men below. None were dead; some had broken arms, or dazed beasts, but none had come to permanent harm. This was as Sarto desired. Resuming a decent jog towards the treeline where his company anxiously awaited him, Sarto thought to himself, *Pallas would be proud of that little spell, I think. I* do *have control, old friend. I hope this makes you happy, wherever you are.* Over his right shoulder, Sarto thought he heard a whisper. When he spun about, there was naught there. He paused a moment, puzzledly looking for the source of the whisper. Finding nothing, he shrugged, heading into the treeline.

        The company stuck close to the treeline of Lec'tair Forest. They were far enough beyond the sight of potential search parties, but not so far as to lose sight of the sun. It was oppressively dark within Lec'tair, despite the beauteous rays of early morning sunshine that shone parallel to the cursed forest. The thick canopy of branches wove together perfectly, obstructing the sunlight from above entirely. When Tibelde questioned Sarto as to why this was, he replied, "The wendygos are one of the *first* peoples of Kalnay. They were cursed by the foolishness and pride of the mighty hunter Wendaros eons ago. They are creatures of Pimedus: half-demon cannibals with no love for the gods. As creatures of Pimedus, they do not willingly abide the Light, preferring to dwell deep in the heart of these cursed woods."

        Isabel spoke next, saying, "Master Sarto, if they are so dangerous, perhaps we should leave *now*. We have evaded the riders. Blessedly, we have seen no sign of these monsters......maybe *now* is the time to count our blessings and depart."

        Sarto shook his head once. "*No,* Isabel. It is true; we evaded the patrols for now. However, the further south we venture, the closer we draw to Regalias. If we follow the edge of the forest, within sight of light, we can bypass Regalias and the Riverland towns without further incident. Before you know it, we will be in Hesketh and closer to Morgana. Do you trust me, Isabel?"

Though she bore reservations about being here, she did not wish to argue. Nodding, Isabel answered, "Aye, Master Sarto. I trust your judgment."

Smiling wearily, Sarto replied, "Excellent. Let us continue then. There are plenty hours of sunlight left. Let us use them to our advantage, shall we?"

Eimar, Isabel and Tibelde nodded their eager and uneasy consent. They proceeded silently and alertly along the treeline. Sarto and Eimar surveyed the grasslands to their right for pursuing parties, while Isabel and Tibelde watched their left flank, probing the eerie darkness of Lec'tair Forest pressing in about them for any sign of danger.

Before mid-afternoon, the skies beyond Lec'tair Forest were overcast; by sunset, a hard rain was falling. Isabel gazed out at the downpour, oddly surprised to find not a single drop fell within Lec'tair. When she asked Sarto about the phenomenon, he shrugged. "There is much about the world that I do not know....that, or I have forgotten. Why it does not rain within Lec'tair Forest is unknown to me."

Isabel wasn't ready to let the issue lie, so she prodded, "If you *had* to guess Master Sarto, for what reason do you suppose it isn't raining within the forest?"

Sarto heaved a sigh, rubbed his temples and leant back on the tree he had taken a seat against. "If I absolutely *had* to guess....it *could* be an extension of the curse by Bloomaya. Wendaros the mighty accidentally slew Bloomaya's son, if you recall the legend. She cursed him to consume human flesh. As the goddess of nature, Bloomaya withheld the fruits of the earth to further reinforce the curse against Wendaros......it could also be that the wendygos dislike rain, the same way they dislike sun. Creatures of Pimedus abhor all things associated with the Light. That includes the sun, rain- as rain works with the sun, growing fruit and vegetables.......perhaps a dark wizard once passed through here, desired not to get wet and enchanted the canopy to keep from getting wet......These are *all* suppositions though. Truthfully, I do not know exactly why these woods are dry; though I am certainly not going to gripe about it."

A thought occurred to Isabel, and she hunkered down in front of her master. "Master Sarto?"

His eyes closed in fatigue, Sarto answered, "Aye Isabel, what is it?"

"If I recall right, you mentioned to....to Pallas earlier on our journey, that you once encountered wendygos.... something about them setting you adrift on a raft to the east?"

His eyes still closed, Sarto nodded, replying, "Aye, Isabel, I did. Very good memory you have there."

Isabel asked, "How did *you* beat them?"

Opening his right eye, Sarto asked, "What makes you think I *beat* them, Isabel?"

"Well," she fumbled, "you are still here. The stories go that all entering Lec'tair Forest never leave....yet *you* are still alive. So....I assumed you somehow defeated them before...."

"Well, Isabel....as with the reason for there being no rain here, I don't rightly recall. Believe me: if I remembered how I avoided ending up over a cooking fire surrounded by horned, grey-skinned, half-human, demon cannibals, I would *assuredly* share my insights. If I had to hazard a guess....I would venture 'twas the gods who saved me....though the exact 'how' remains a mystery, even to me."

Isabel fell silent, running a hand absently in the dust to her left, thinking hard. Sarto noticed this with his peeped open eye, stating, "Don't fret so much, Isabel. All will be fine. We are quite near the treeline. The twins will sense anyone, or *anything*, moving nearby. For now, rest; we resume our trek southward tomorrow. If it is sunny and safe out....we'll exit Lec'tair and travel parallel to the treeline tomorrow. Does that compromise meet with your approval, young lady?"

Glancing furtively to her left, Isabel scanned the forest. Lec'tair made her uncomfortable in a way she couldn't pinpoint. She couldn't deny her master had a good point regarding the shelter of the trees. Additionally, she had already observed the twins demonstrate their worth as guardians and scouts. With a reluctant nod, Isabel answered, "Aye, Master Sarto. Spend the night here and depart for the grasslands if it isn't still raining, tomorrow. 'Tis a *good* plan; just as *you* are a good leader. Pallas would be proud of you, Master."

Sarto smiled wanly, replying, "My thanks, Isabel. You are *truly* the best pupil a master could have. Now, let us light a fire, and set about making supper. Eimar hasn't ceased mentioning his hunger since we departed Othros."

Isabel chuckled, answering, "Aye. Eimar certainly does like his food, doesn't he?"

As the sun set beyond the forest's edge, the company enjoyed a small feast of squirrel and the last of their apples roasted over a crackling fire. All was well in the world.

Just before midnight, Isabel was woken abruptly by rude hands seizing her tightly. She shot awake, struggling to fight back. She heard grunting and chuffing, as one would hear from an elk fighting a fellow stag over a contested doe. When Isabel locked eyes with her assailant, her blood ran cold and her breath hitched in her throat. Staring her maliciously in the eyes was a creature that was half man, half buck. The creature had a massive set of multi-pronged antlers, which appeared black in the dying light of the fire. Its silver eyes shone eerily in the flame's reflection. It had grey, human flesh from its head to its waist. From the waist down, it was coated in silver-grey fur and had a pair of cloven hooves. An overlarge set of human teeth protruded frighteningly from its face. The face itself bore a vertical set of four scratch marks from its forehead to just below its left eye that stood out pale white against the grey flesh. Many of its teeth appeared sharp, like wulf fangs. The hands grabbing her bore overlong fingers, ending in mid-length, sharp claws. It was also inhumanly strong; stronger than any normal man. Isabel had her first terrifying look at the fabled wendygos of Lec'tair Forest.

Jerking her rudely to her feet, the wendygo hoisted her high into the air with a single hand wrapped firmly about her throat. Isabel's panicked mind tried conjuring a spell; however, pronouncing words was impossible with the beast's hand clutching her throat. *Avia rysa*, Isabel thought, recalling her knives in her belt. The blades didn't budge an inch. Isabel realized with dismay she was not yet strong enough to summon spells with only her mind.

Realizing what she was attempting, the wendygo drew her close to his foul maw, grating, "No spells *witch*. Otherwise we *kill* your master." With one powerful twist, he whipped Isabel about to see Sarto already bound and gagged; his staff lying uselessly on the ground. Three wendygos held him as he struggled futilely against his captors. When Sarto saw the other wendygo holding Isabel by the neck, he stilled instantly.

Isabel darted her eyes about in fear. *Where are Eimar and Tibelde? Did these beasts kill them? Did they flee? Why didn't we receive warning about these creatures' presence in the camp? Gods above, keep us safe.*

The wendygo gripping Isabel, rasped, "Your *gnome* friends fled, if that is what you wonder, daughter of man." He dropped her rudely to the ground, grunting a deer-like noise to his companions. Before she could even roll over, two more wendygos seized her hands, bound them quickly in rope, dragging her to her feet, gagging her as they did so.

The lead wendygo laughed. To Isabel's ears, it sounded like an eerie moose call. The lead wendygo chuffed in his grating voice, "You are *lucky*, daughter of man. My king wishes to see you and your master, *Apollos,* before you are....*prepared.*" To Sarto, the lead wendygo taunted, "You should have let that raft carry you east on the Nevartane, ancient one. Now King Fenyang will not be as....*lenient* as the last time you trespassed in this domain. This is the problem with you Prezla: you never learn from your mistakes." Then the leader raised his head to the sky, bellowing like a moose. The three smaller wendygos hoisted Sarto and Isabel to their feet easily, one of them grabbing the wizard's staff. The remaining supplies, they left.

With fear thundering through her heart, Isabel prayed silently, desperately to the gods, *please....help us.* Then a crude burlap bag was thrown over her head; all disappeared into darkness.

Chapter Three: Fangs in the Dark

Abel was grateful to Nairadj for bringing the satchel full of Ulgnar's spare teeth these two and a half weeks now past. The first four days of their journey beyond the eastern shores of Voshkarna were relatively peaceful. They kept a wary eye out- Nairadj keeping a wary nose out as well- but encountered no problems. At first, Abel thought perhaps Nairadj had exaggerated the danger of nightstalkers. On the fourth night, he discovered she had indeed spoken true. The duo marched across a great, barren patch of hardpan with the quarter moon shining faintly down upon them. A faint breeze stirred a breath of dust off the ground. Suddenly Nairadj stood stalk still, drawing her dragon tooth dagger, warily scenting the air.

Abel froze as well, glancing about cautiously but spotting nothing unusual. Silently, Nairadj seized Abel's left arm, spinning him about slowly to face where she pointed, forty feet to the west. Abel wordlessly searched where Nairadj indicated, struggling to see what she saw with her animal-like night vision. All he beheld was a black mass; what appeared to be a shadow, standing free of a person. A moment later, he marked two fierce, red pinpoints appear near the top of the shadowy mass. He was startled, taking two reflexive steps backwards. Nairadj gripped his arm tighter, holding him in place. In a savage voice, Nairadj hissed, "*Don't* move, Abel. Fleeing will make it attack for *certain*. Right now, it's merely ascertaining the threat we pose. Stay where you are."

Abel grunted confirmation to Nairadj. Meanwhile, his mind whirled furiously. *Gods above, nightstalkers are real! The tale of Wagnar the*

Bloodstained and his demonic kin are true. *Whatever happens, I must be brave and smart. I have naught to fear for my cause is just.* For another moment the nightstalker stood motionless, sizing them up. Then, Abel blinked. The creature had disappeared when he reopened his eyes. He sucked in a short, terrified breath, hissing to Nairadj, "Where did it go?"

Scanning the dim night around her, Nairadj calmly responded, "It's out there, watching us. Keep your guard up, your dagger out and stay close to me. We are going to press onward. If it seizes you, remember this: stab it through the *heart*. That is the *only* way to kill them. Know this too: once we kill even one, *more* will be drawn by its death. Do *not* kill it, unless you are in mortal peril. Do you understand my meaning Abel?"

"Aye Master Nairadj; I understand you perfectly."

They continued through the night watchfully minding their surroundings, dragon tooth daggers at the ready. Nothing occurred. They slept undisturbed during the day. That night, the sole nightstalker returned. It was closer than the previous night: only thirty feet away now. This time, it openly shadowed them as they journeyed northeastward. Just before dawn, it darted off, seeking shelter against the day. As Nairadj and Abel continued in the early afternoon on their sixth day of walking, Abel queried, "Should we not simply track it to where it sleeps during the day and kill it, Master Nairadj?"

Striding ahead of him, Nairadj shook her head curtly once. "*No*. Here in the Nightstalker Wastes, there is no shortage of hiding places for these creatures to disappear to. Nightstalkers are like the gnomes of Othros, dwelling underground during the daytime as they sleep. They are fast, abundant in number, and deadly whether alone or in a pack. The one pursuing us could be *anywhere* underground. To search for a single nightstalker in daylight is to waste one's precious time. The best thing is to delay killing *any* nightstalkers until we must, press on to Djintani Lake, and secure a boat."

A thought occurred to Abel then. "Master Nairadj....if it's not too impertinent of me, might I ask how you know so much about nightstalkers?"

Without stopping, Nairadj stated flatly, "I have not *always* dwelt in the Southern Sand Flats, Abel. Let us leave it at that for now and press on."

Casting his eyes down, embarrassed, Abel muttered, "Of...of course Master. Forgive me."

With a stony voice, Nairadj responded, "It's not your fault Abel. The Wastes and I have....*history*. History which, being here again, is a painful reminder of...." Nairadj paused, cutting herself short. Measuring her words, she corrected, "When I am ready, I will reveal *all* to you. You have my *word*, Abel. Now, let us forge on. We will encamp soon. When dealing with nightstalkers, you must remember this absolute: besides your dagger, the *sun* is your best defense against nightstalkers. The sun is the true light of Bronwyn-Aetha, who cursed Wagnar the Bloodstained for his bloody deeds across the Black Water Sea to the north. All nightstalkers hate and fear the goddess, and her sentinel in the sky. If ever caught in daylight, the goddess would burn them in judgment for their bloody deeds. So, we camp in the day, and travel at night."

That night, the evening of their seventh day of travel in the Wastes, the nightstalker tracking them was now a mere twenty feet away.

Nairadj whispered to Abel as they traveled, "It will be soon now. If it doesn't attack tonight, it will be tomorrow."

"Why does it continue following? Doesn't it fear us?"

"No, it has no fear. Nightstalkers are fearless; the perfect predator. They only know hunger and the savage urge to quench it. Unless this beast has found other sustenance in the past several nights, he is *deliberately* starving himself."

"Why would he do that, Master Nairadj?"

"By building its hunger, it is also building its need for victory. It is creating a hunger large enough to be sated by feasting upon *both* of us. This makes it *more* dangerous, for it will not cease attacking until it feasts....or we kill it, and its demonic brethren are alerted to our presence."

"So, you're saying it wins regardless, Master? That's not very encouraging, if I may say so."

Glancing quickly at Abel, Nairadj countered, "The creature only wins entirely if we surrender; be that physical *or* mental. If we *believe* we will reach Volcros, we can defeat this creature's will. Do *you* believe we can make it, Abel?"

Pondering this a moment, Abel responded, "Aye, Master. I *do* believe we can make it."

"There's a good lad. Now, let us forge ahead."

The nightstalker did not attack that night. It gave Abel and Nairadj time to prepare themselves for the impending attack next evening. Abel prayed to the gods as he fell asleep beneath the mid-day sun. *Lady Bronwyn-Aetha, hear my prayer. Let us emerge victorious this night against the fiend that would have our lives. Lend our feet speed to reach Volcros swiftly and unscathed. Guide my sword and dagger in battle this night.......*

That night, beneath the sliver of moon, the nightstalker attacked. Abel and Nairadj had been on the move three hours prior to sunset. As the sun set, Abel drew his sword and dagger. Nairadj stayed his hand. "Your sword will be too cumbersome with these creatures; it's as likely to get you killed as not. Rely on the dragon tooth dagger and your hunting knife. These beasts will draw close to kill you; smaller, lighter weapons are better choices. One last thing: if you can, sever the head from the body. It's not as effective as the dragon's tooth to the heart, but it *does* work."

Abel sheathed his sword, drawing the hunting dagger his father, Sir Aldrich Farthen, had gifted him on his seventh celebration day. Looking at it, Abel reflected, *I bet father never thought I'd be using this to kill nightstalkers.* Abel looked at his dragon tooth dagger, with Nairadj's hand-carved inscription *'Drakt'vansh'* in the blade. Before the sun fell completely, Abel inquired, "What if I get the creature's blood in my mouth, or on my face, Master Nairadj? Will I become one of them?"

Drawing her own dagger, Nairadj placed a hand on her apprentice's shoulder, gazing reassuringly into his eyes. "No lad, you will *not* turn. It will be revolting in smell and taste, for they are creatures of the night and *dead* besides; but you will *not* turn. There is......a *ritual* to a turning. That is when you should *most* fear these devils: if they try and take you alive. That means they want to turn you. You must ensure that *never* happens. I have seen first-hand what turning looks like....it is *nothing* I would wish upon my worst nemesis. Now, prepare yourself and let us move on."

Once the sun sank below the horizon, their stalker appeared from beneath the ground, a mere ten feet from where they tread. At this proximity, Abel could, regrettably, better distinguish the features of their predator. The creature stood just over six feet tall. It was lanky. Its skin was fish belly white. It wore the tatters of a pair of leather trousers, but no shirt, for it did not feel the cold. It had wisps of black hair atop its white skull. Its eyes burned red, like coals. Its long, bony hands ended in slashing, mid-length claws. The part that scared Abel most though, were its fangs. The nightstalker's teeth were abnormally large; as large as the wendygo's teeth recorded in legend (which Isabel would have personally attested to, had she been present just then). The large teeth were jagged, jutting at terrifying, abnormal angles: as if swords and knives had been piled haphazardly within a weapon rack.

Abel felt his blood pump faster in his veins. He could hear his own heartbeat thudding wildly in his ears. The nightstalker turned its red-eyed gaze upon him, cocking its head curiously as if to say, '*Ah, so* you *are the weak one. I'm coming for you, mortal-child.*"

Nairadj whispered, "Control your heartbeat Abel. These things thrive on the fear they generate. They seek to disarm their prey by unnerving them. Remember who you are, Abel Drakt'vansh and be *courageous.*"

Abel nodded to his master, staring steadily at the nightstalker. Under his breath he whispered, "*I am Abel 'Drakt'vansh' of house Farthen. I have naught to fear, for my cause is just.*" Then he exhaled a long, slow breath, calming his racing heart. He closed his eyes momentarily. When he opened them, the creature was almost upon him. He ducked, spinning, as the stalker slashed at his face with his claws. When Abel rose, he planted his dragon's tooth dagger in the creature's shoulder. The abomination shrieked an unearthly sound: a mix of a man's wounded cry and the chittering call of a large bat. In a flash, the creature whirled about, batting Abel aside; hurling him several feet through the air. Abel clutched his hunting knife as he landed, ensuring he held it away from himself. He did not want to be unarmed if the stalker struck again; nor did he want to impale himself upon landing. With a harsh grunt, Abel found his feet.

He marked it circling Nairadj; she with her dragon's tooth dagger up. Abel dashed towards Nairadj as the stalker leapt. It attempted leaping over her, but she anticipated this move. Reaching up, she clamped her left hand firmly around its throat and with a fierce cry,

slamming the beast full force onto the dusty hardpan.
The beast cried in pain as Abel's dagger- which was still
embedded in its shoulder- was shoved through by the
force of impact. The stalker kicked upwards savagely
with both feet, sending Nairadj flying. Abel closed with it
as Nairadj flew backwards. His hunting knife shanked the
nightstalker low in the side, as he engaged. The monster
unleashed another unearthly, man-bat shriek at the fresh
pain. Grabbing Abel by the waist, it spun, throwing him
hard to the right. Abel's dragon tooth dagger still
protruded through its right chest, and it tore a bit as he
threw the boy. With a cry the stalker yanked it out
roughly, black blood trickling down his pale, bony chest.

Nairadj was on its left, rising painfully to her
feet. Abel was at its right, striving to suck in a breath as
he connected solidly with the unyielding hardpan. The
stalker turned on Nairadj, for she was the greater threat.
With Abel's dragon tooth blade in hand- the ivory faintly
singeing its pale, dead flesh- the nightmarish being closed
the short distance to Nairadj, knocking her solidly to the
ground. Then it was atop Nairadj, bearing Abel's blade
down fast- meaning to skewer her through the face.
Though she was pinned, she read its attack. As the
horror plunged the blade downward, Nairadj jerked her
head hard left, simultaneously drawing her left hand
across her chest. The dagger punched clean through the
center of her left hand, burying itself in her right
shoulder; pinning her hand to her shoulder. She barked
loudly in pain; her right hand clutched tightly about the
hilt of her dagger.

Suddenly, the stalker howled in pain as, from
behind, Abel buried his hunting knife straight down into
the creature's left shoulder. It lashed out, knocking Abel
back again, the blade buried in its shoulder. As the beast

knocked Abel backward, Nairadj acted. Sitting upright swiftly, she head-butted the stalker hard in the nose, her forehead erupting in a thick veil of pain. The creature was dazed momentarily, for it didn't expect such an attack from the wounded dyre bear. Nairadj swung the dagger in her right hand towards the stalker's exposed ribs. With a dry crack, like kindling broken sharply underfoot, Nairadj drove home her blade through the nightstalker's left ribs, puncturing its dead heart. The stalker tumbled backwards off Nairadj, feebly clutching its side, shrieking that unearthly, piercing man-bat cry. With her left hand still pinned to her chest, Nairadj rose with a pained grunt. She knelt, yanking Abel's hunting knife rudely from the stalker's shoulder with her free right hand. It shrilled weakly, staring at her with its hateful red eyes. Leaning close to its monstrous face, she whispered, "*Vish mor Rivaith, gotsmer*" (which in the ancient tongue, means, "Return to the Shadow, demon"). In one swift, horizontal slash, she beheaded the stalker with Abel's hunting knife. All was suddenly silent.

Abel staggered towards Nairadj, drawing a torch from his pack, igniting it quickly. When it was lit, he drew closer to the dead stalker, gazing at his master in shock. "Master Nairadj......by the gods, you are badly injured." Dropping the torch to the ground, Abel rooted in his pack for bandages and salve.

Dazedly, Nairadj stared at her pinned hand, chuckling mirthlessly. "I've had worse injuries, young Abel." Then her legs buckled. The she-bear crumpled to a sitting position, grunting as the dagger pinning her hand and shoulder together jarred roughly at the impact.

Rushing worriedly to her side, Abel lifted the torch to inspect the wound. "Alright Master....it doesn't appear the dagger pierced anything significant. The blade has punctured your shoulder; cleanly, thank the gods. First, I must remove the dagger. It's going to hurt, but I need you to keep as still as you can. Then, I need to remove your shirt on the right side, so I can apply the salves and bandages. Are you ready?"

Nairadj looked dazedly at Abel, replying sarcastically, "Aye, Abel. I'm as ready as someone whose hand is pinned to their own shoulder can be. Proceed."

"Okay." Abel placed his left hand firmly on Nairadj's shoulder, his right hand on the dagger's hilt, and exhaled a long breath. "Here we go." As swiftly as he dared, he withdrew the dagger from Nairadj's shoulder.

Nairadj bellowed in pain, clutching Abel's left forearm with her right hand, but remained as still as possible. When the blade was free of both her shoulder and her hand, Nairadj's left hand slumped into her lap. Frowning at her mangled left hand, Nairadj wheezed, "I'm afraid I will require your assistance getting this tunic off Abel....my left hand is going to be, regrettably, *quite* useless for awhile."

With a lump in his throat, Abel responded dryly, "Of course Master. Just....sit still. I will take care of you." With his jaw set, he hurriedly unstrung the laces up the front of Nairadj's tunic, tenderly removing it on the right side, exposing her wounded right shoulder and her right breast. Sucking in a measured breath, Abel rose, circling behind Nairadj with the salves and bandages. He was about to place the salve on the wound in back, when Nairadj croaked, "Wait a moment, Abel."

"What is it Master? Is something wrong?"

Nodding at Abel's bag, Nairadj asked, "Is there any alcohol in your satchel?"

"Aye, Master. Do you need a drink?"

Nairadj shook her head. "No....leastways not *yet*....no, you should pour some alcohol over the wound, front and backside to sterilize the wound."

Abel riffled through his bag and asked, "Won't alcohol sting?"

Nairadj chuckled mirthlessly. "Aye, it *will*. That's how you know the wound is clean, *because* it stings. If you're worried, you needn't be. As I said, I've been hurt worse than this."

Focusing deliberately on her back wound, Abel heaved a breath, answering, "Alright....if you say so master Nairadj. Brace yourself." Then Abel poured a dollop of mead onto Nairadj's back wound.

The bear lady cringed, hissing between gritted teeth, but remained still despite the stinging pain. Abel did likewise on the entry wound, watching distractedly as the mead washed a thin trail of blood down over Nairadj's milky white, exposed breast. Then, Abel returned to himself, placing the last salve carefully over the entry wound at the front of her shoulder. "Lady Nairadj, you must press on the front salve while I wrap bandages over the wound. Can you do that?"

Placing her right hand firmly over the salve in the front, she nodded faintly. "Aye, Abel. Proceed."

As Abel wrapped the bandage over her shoulder and under her right arm, he couldn't help but marvel yet again at how smooth Nairadj's skin was. *No....focus on the task at hand. Master Nairadj needs your help. This is no time for distraction.* When Abel finished bandaging her shoulder, he helped Nairadj lace up her shirt strings, though slightly looser than before, so as not to cause her further discomfort. As he did so, Nairadj chuckled to herself.

Looking up, Abel asked, "What's so funny Master Nairadj?"

Smiling faintly through her mask of pain, Nairadj replied, "You don't know?"

Abel pondered a moment, then shook his head. "I can't think of anything amusing about this situation right now."

Staring intently into Abel's sea green eyes, Nairadj stated, "You didn't blush when you saw me naked this time. You grow more mature every day, my young warrior."

At the mention of her nakedness, Abel blushed red hot, but held her emerald green gaze as he finished bandaging Nairadj's left hand. "You were injured. There was no *time* to be childish about your nakedness. Besides," he smirked, "it was *only* your right breast and shoulder that were naked....*technically.*"

This caused Nairadj to laugh, then grimace, as she involuntarily clutched her injured shoulder. "Well, aren't *you* the logical one tonight. *Please*, don't make me laugh again. It *really* hurts to laugh right now."

"As you wish, Master Nairadj, so I shall oblige."
Then Abel rose, gathered their bags, picked up his torch,
extending his hand to his master. "Shall we put some
distance twixt ourselves and this abomination, Nairadj
'*Vaith'vansh*'?"

Nairadj took Abel's hand, rising to her feet,
grimacing at the pain in her shoulder and her bandaged
left hand. "Aye, Abel '*Drakt'vansh*', let's make haste.
Djintani Lake is still quite a way off. Nightstalkers will be
more closely on our trail now and in greater numbers.
We'll need to move for longer periods now to avoid being
overrun."

Abel replied, "Then what are we waiting for?
Let's move."

Another five days of hard travel brought Nairadj
and Abel to the southern shores of Djintani Lake. In that
time they picked up a pack of four nightstalkers. Nairadj
was grateful that she and Abel had avoided picking up
any more during the first three nights after slaying the
first stalker. Her gratitude turned to ashes in her mouth
as they approached the lakeshore in the early afternoon
of their thirteenth day of travel since bypassing the
Voshkarna. She searched, desperate and angry, up and
down Djintani Lake's shore. "By the ancestors, where are
the *freckaying*, gods' damned boats?!"

Scattered to the north, she and Abel spotted
numerous wrecks of different size boats. The weary duo
searched frantically for a whole boat. The closest they
found was a longboat with several holes in the bottom.

Abel suggested, "Maybe.... maybe we could piece together the longboat with scraps from some of these wrecks?"

Nairadj shook her head in frustration. "There's not enough *time* before sunset to adequately salvage it as a water worthy vessel. We have no tools or means to plug the holes in the lifeboat." Nairadj dropped the sack of dragon teeth with a frustrated sigh, sinking to her knees, exhausted and out of ideas. A small pile of Ulgnar's teeth spilled from the bag onto the gritty shore, clanking and clattering together. Gazing curiously at the scattered teeth, Abel got a peculiar idea. Without a word, he snatched up half a dozen teeth of differing sizes and dashed to the longboat with the holes in it. Dragging the boat as far ashore as he could, Abel jumped into it, inspecting the holes in the bottom. To him, they appeared to be knotholes in the lumber, circular in shape. Abel examined the width of each tooth looking for one roughly the same size as the first hole. When Abel found the right one, he raised it up, point down. He exhaled a single, measured breath before plunging the tooth into the knot hole. There was a sharp squeak as the tooth plunged into the wood. To Abel, it reminded him of freeing the axe head from a particularly stubborn stump of firewood back home. He released the base of the tooth, inspecting his handiwork. The tooth was wedged firmly into the larger knot hole. Aside from the root jutting up, his work held. Abel smiled to himself, following suit with the other two knotholes: finding a tooth that would fit snugly. As Abel finished with the final tooth, Nairadj came over to see what he was doing. She was pleasantly surprised at Abel's ingenuity, and told him as much.

Abel looked up happily, asking, "Do you think it will hold, Master Nairadj?"

For a long moment, Nairadj didn't speak. She stared at the interior, looking from tooth to tooth in wondrous frustration at the simplicity of Abel's solution. *Why didn't I think of that? Such a simple solution, and I nearly gave up like a cub who can't climb a tree.* When Nairadj spoke, she smiled wanly and shrugged. "I suppose the only way to know for certain is to test it out." Together, they lifted the longboat, walking it the few feet back to the water's edge. They avoided dragging it, lest they dislodge the teeth, or further wreck the old vessel on stray rocks. When they set it in the water, they did so delicately. They both stared with bated breath at the bottom of the boat, observing no immediate leaks sprout from around the three teeth lodged there. They glanced at each other for a long, silent moment. Then Nairadj sighed and muttered, "Well, we know it floats. Now we need to see if it floats with weight inside it." Abel began to climb in, until Nairadj held up her good hand. "I had better get in first Abel. I weigh more than you. If it buckles beneath *me*, then we are back to the beginning."

Abel nodded, holding the boat steady from his side. Releasing a long breath, Nairadj lifted one of her lengthy legs, tilted the boat towards her slightly and stepped into the longboat. The boat groaned like an old oak door whose hinges had not been oiled in some time. Nairadj balanced on one foot, leaning against Abel's side of the boat, nervously holding her breath for a long moment. Abel glanced at her with a smirk, coaxing, "You need to *sit*, Master. Boats make noises when they haven't been used in awhile. It's nothing to worry about."

Nairadj released a pent-up breath, replying, "Aye, as you say Abel. You have been around more boats than I, so I trust you." She swung her other leg fully into the boat, sitting on the plank seat. Abel steadied the boat as Nairadj got settled. Once she did, they both stared intently at the jutting dragon teeth plugging the bottom of the boat. Nairadj half expected them to shoot up like corks from shaken bottles of ale. She was relieved to note they did not budge. Abel wasn't worried the teeth would pop out; rather he worried about hissing jets of water forcing through the holes beneath the lodged teeth. To his deep relief, that did not happen. The companions glanced gratefully at each other, unleashing a bout of relieved laughter. They had *finally* found a break in these tiresome Wastes.

Nairadj remained in the boat, fearing to jinx their good fortune by leaving it; in addition, her injuries in her hand and shoulder were flaring in pain again, and she was grateful for the break. Abel quickly found two paddles amongst the dead boat husks littering the shore, setting them in the boat. Nairadj jammed hers firmly in the muck beneath the water so the boat could not drift away without Abel. Swiftly, Abel rounded up their packs, plus the bag of dragon's teeth. Like the seasoned fisherman he was, Abel vaulted from the shallows into the boat. This startled Nairadj as the boat canted terribly to one side when he jumped in. Then, she passed Abel his paddle, pulling hers free of the muck in the shallows. They rowed from shore; free, for the time being, from the scourge of nightstalkers.

As night fell, Abel and Nairadj heard the man-bat cries and chirrups of the nightstalkers following them doggedly north along the shore, seventy feet to their left. It sent a chill up Abel's back. "It sounds like there are more now," he stated nervously.

Nairadj nodded faintly in the light of the quarter moon, rummaging through her pack for more salted jerky and the last two of their apples. "Aye, Abel. The deadliest thing about nightstalkers is their relentlessness. Until we reach Volcros, these creatures will pursue us, increasing in number until there is a swarm. If that becomes the case prior to safely passing within the walls of Volcros......well, let's just say we will attain legendary Shade slayer status by then."

Listening to the continued eerie shrieks from shore, Abel asked, "Does Djintani Lake go all the way north to Volcros, Master Nairadj?"

Taking a bite of her apple, Nairadj answered, "*Mostly*, yes it does Abel. Eventually we will abandon the boat. For now, we can enjoy a safe night's rest."

Finishing her apple in several quick bites, Nairadj wiped her right hand on her trousers, mindful of her injured left. She motioned for Abel's paddle. "Here, I will paddle for now. You should get some rest."

Abel firmly shook his head. "*No*, master; your hand is still mending. In truth, I shouldn't have let you row earlier. *I* will row for the night. *You* get some sleep. We are safe on the water, are we not?"

Sighing, Nairadj answered, "Aye Abel, we are. Nightstalkers cannot swim. Water is of the gods; a conduit of life....and death. Nightstalkers fear the water, so we will be fine."

"Very well then master; you get your rest. I will continue rowing us north."

As Nairadj wrapped her blanket about her shoulders, slouching on her seat, she mumbled, "My thanks, Abel. You are a *true* knight and a gentleman. I wish you a peaceful eve." Then she slouched forward, leaning on her knees and fell fast asleep. Abel kept rowing; listening unwillingly to the stalkers' eerie, frustrated calls along the shoreline.

They rowed and drifted northwards on Djintani Lake another two days before encountering any problems. Trouble arose as they drew near where the shoreline seemed to draw closer to them. Abel was rowing in the warm sunlight of dawn. Nairadj was fileting and preparing several fish she caught as they sailed. Suddenly, the water grew shallow. The longboat screeched and splintered on the bow side. Nairadj lurched forward, dropping her fileting knife and fish. Abel fell backwards, bashing his skull on the floor behind his seat, barking in pain. Nairadj looked worriedly over the side, asking, "What did we hit?"

Cradling his bruised skull, Abel spun awkwardly to look over the prow of the ship. When he looked, he saw thick, black rocks clearly on the water's surface. The boat slowly began taking on water. Abel replied, "We've hit a shoal of rocks. The boat is *sinking*. We have to get the boat to shore quickly."

Abel's fisherman instincts kicked in. Jumping from the ship, he pushed the longboat back gently off the rocks before hopping back in. Nairadj scooped up Abel's oars, holding them ready when he resumed his seat. With one paddle, he turned the longboat to shore. Then he pumped his arms in long, powerful strokes, launching the crippled craft towards the shore. It was just after sunrise when they beached the damaged craft.

Abel leapt out, grabbed their supply bags and waded to shore, depositing them on the ground. He returned a moment later to walk the water-laden craft closer to shore, so Nairadj could easier exit the vessel. When they were near enough, Nairadj jumped over the side, planting her feet firmly on the ground beneath the water. Together she and Abel heaved the ruined craft ashore. Before they departed, Nairadj yanked the three dragon teeth from the boat. They stood a moment, staring at the useless vessel, watching the rising sun glint off the clear water of the lake. Abel squinted at his master, asking, "How far are we from Volcros, Master Nairadj?"

Nairadj gazed northward a long moment, then answered, "It is yet another two days walk.... possibly *three*."

Abel crossed his arms, asking the question neither of them wanted to know, but *needed* to. "How many nightstalkers follow us now?"

Nairadj grunted, replying, "Based on the noises last night....probably a dozen now. Even if it's another two days walk....there could be another six or eight stalkers pursuing us by then."

Abel started visibly. "You mean to tell me, Master Nairadj, we may be pursued by up to *twenty* nightstalkers before we reach Volcros?"

With a weary sigh, Nairadj nodded, "Aye, Abel. Regrettably, that *is* what I'm telling you."

Setting his jaw, Abel stared northward. "Alright....we stick to the lake shore. You mentioned they abhor water, so they will not flank us on the waterfront. We have torches lit all night, and dragon's teeth lining our belts, in case they get past the torches. We press north. Do you concur with that plan of action, Master Nairadj?"

Nairadj gazed at her apprentice in wonderment. *My, how he has grown as a warrior. Gone is the meek, little boy who set out to play hero. The person standing before me now, is a man in* full. To Abel, she said, "Aye, it's a solid plan. It will not be easy....but when were legends ever written about anything easy?"

Abel smiled faintly, answering, "Aye, Master Nairadj. The minstrels never sang about chicken-livered warriors, or craven dyre bears. Let us press on and *earn* ourselves those praises. We have a Queen to parley with."

On the second night after beaching the wrecked boat, Abel had already killed six nightstalkers. As he planted yet another dragon's tooth in the last creature's dead heart, Abel thought sardonically, *well....I can certainly add the title of* Vaith'vansh' *to my own name now.* Both Abel and Nairadj brandished lit torches back and forth as they pressed onward. Around them crowded a dozen nightstalkers, chittering their cursed bat-like calls. As Abel brandished his torch at three stalkers pressing in from the rear, Abel called to Nairadj, "Master, are we within sight of Volcros yet? It's getting rather *crowded* back here."

Ahead, Nairadj was yanking her '*Vaith'vansh*' carved dagger from the chest of her eighth felled nightstalker since yester night. Squinting against the torchlight, she called to Abel, "The city is within sight, young Abel. I cannot gauge how close it is with these beasts pressed in so closely. We simply have to keep pressing onward."

Another nightstalker darted towards Abel; its clawed hands extended out, its horrible maw of jagged teeth searching for Abel's neck. In one fluid motion, Abel side-stepped the monster's attack, planting his dragon tooth dagger in its heart, then drew his hunting knife from his belt, beheading the beast in one fell strike. Its pale, headless body toppled dead at Abel's feet. He quickly sheathed his hunting knife, plucking his dragon tooth dagger from the stalker's chest all while brandishing his torch at the pressing pack of nightstalkers. *There are* far *more than twenty of these accursed creatures gathered about us. It appears Master Nairadj was right: these things sense when one of them dies, rushing to replace their fallen comrades. Gods above, hear me: deliver us safely to Volcros, please.*

Up ahead, Nairadj slew another. A second pressed in immediately, and the spare dragon tooth dagger Nairadj had used was lost as she retreated several paces from the advancing nightstalkers. *Ancestors of old, please grant us safe passage. Do not punish this boy for my sins and errors of old. I seek to set right my mistakes by aiding this young man on his quest. I cannot bear him turning into this* evil, *pressing in foully about us. Please, grant us mercy and deliver us from this trial.* Within three more paces, Nairadj was back to back with Abel. They had tossed their torches at their feet, to free their other hands to wield another dagger. As they stood there, back to back, Nairadj stated, "I am sorry, Abel. It seems I could not deliver you safely to Sigourney. I have failed you as your master."

Abel nudged Nairadj, countering, "Master Nairadj, make no apologies. This was *my* choice as much as yours to venture north. We are alive yet. The gods do *not* ignore their champions in time of need. We may *yet* triumph. What a song *that* will be for the minstrels, eh?"

Nairadj's faltering courage was bolstered by Abel's words, and she adjusted her stance to counter an attacking nightstalker. "Aye, Abel. You are right, of course. Let's give these demons a reason to remember our names, shall we?"

They fought hard- tired as they were- slaying another three nightstalkers a piece. Then, the horde pressed in hard. Abel and Nairadj were knocked to the ground, daggers flying from their hands. As the swarm was poised to descend upon them, chaos erupted at the rear. Distracted, the swarming beasts turned to see what the commotion was. From where Abel and Nairadj lay, they could not discern what was happening; but they knew it boded in their favor, whatever it was. Rolling to opposite sides, they scooped up their weapons, resuming the slaughter. In moments the remaining nightstalkers, numbering three dozen, were piled three high on the ground in a swath of a dozen feet. Standing over the felled creatures was a band of a dozen people, dressed in an assortment of furs and leather. Their faces and hands were painted black- with dead stalker blood (Abel later learned) to mask their scent. In the center of their saviors, stood a very tall man, atop one of the fallen stalkers.

Even in his state of battle fatigue, Abel couldn't help but be impressed by the man's stature. The man in the center of the dead stalker swarm stood over seven feet tall. He had long blonde hair tied in a braided ponytail and even in the dark of night, Abel registered his piercing blue eyes. In one hand was a short sword, a hatchet gripped in the other. The tall man also had a long fur cloak hanging from his shoulders. He was clearly in charge, for the rest of the group looked to him to speak or act. Staring from Nairadj to Abel, the tall man sheathed his weapons on his belt. After another moment, he spoke. "I am Hearn. Captain of the Night Patrol and loyal servant to Sigourney, Queen of the Wastes. The Queen has heard of your journey and greatly desires an audience with you Nairadj '*Vaith'vansh*', of the Red-Ditch bear tribe; and you, Abel '*Drakt'vansh*' of house Farthen." Hearne then waved his followers forward, stating flatly, "Seize them. We return to Volcros to present the prisoners to our Queen."

Chapter Four: Hann'Lec- City of Skulls

Eimar silently cursed himself for a fool. When the wendygos invaded their camp two days ago, neither he nor Tibelde had sensed them until it was too late. As the Shadow Twins hurried after the kidnappers, Eimar reflected on the events leading to this moment....

The big wendygo touched his great hooves down on the earth at the far side of the thick elm Eimar leant against as he kept watch. Feeling the tremors of the beast's hooves touch down so near him, Eimar was seized with a sudden burst of panic. Hastily, he cast a mental warning to Tibelde. *Sister! There are* wendygos *all around us! There is no time to warn Isabel or Sarto! What should we do?*

Tibelde sent back a quick, level reply. *Remain calm Eimar. We must burrow. If we are caught, we cannot help either of them. If we hide, we can follow and mount a rescue.*

Eimar countered, *Sister, will not our Prezla companions think us slain or fled? I want no stain of dishonor on our name....*

Dishonor can be atoned for, brother. If we are killed or captured, we are less than useless to our friends. Now, burrow; we will follow these monsters to their dwelling.

So, the Shadow Twins swiftly burrowed below the forest soil, leaving no trace they had been there, evading the wendygo raiders. After a brief exchange above ground, the wendygos' hooves receded to the east. Eimar and Tibelde could not discern Sarto or Isabel's footprints as the wendygos departed, leading them to believe the Prezla were being carried. When it was safe, the Shadow Twins emerged from the earth. All their supplies were still there, untouched and unspoiled. "Why leave behind the supplies?" Eimar queried.

With a note of disgust in her voice, Tibelde replied, "They have no *use* for our supplies, brother. Remember, wendygos eat but one thing: human flesh. Come; let us be after our friends." In a flash, they doused the fire, repacked their rucksacks, grabbed Isabel and Sarto's satchels and dashed off like quicksilver in pursuit of their captured friends.

Through the burlap sack over her head, Isabel detected nothing that might aid her or Sarto in escaping these devils. There was no sun to gauge direction by through the thickly knit forest canopy. All she knew was they *weren't* heading west. This realization brought little comfort to Isabel. She was aware they traveled swiftly, for she felt a wisp of breeze through the burlap. Isabel could also hear the '*whoosh*' of her captor racing hard past knotted, dead trees, with her strapped tight to its back. Despite her disdain at being taken captive, she was mildly impressed by the wendygos' manner of prisoner transport. Her hands were bound with coarse rope, to the wendygo's sizeable antlers. Her feet were bound at the ankle, around the wendygo's waist. Had she not been in bonds, it would have appeared to others as if she were on a piggyback ride. Isabel felt the wendygo's slender, strong, clawed hands digging uncomfortably into the meat of her lower thighs, as it effortlessly bore her weight. By slinging her over its back, the beast ensured ease of mobility, running no risk of his captive escaping.

After another day of hard running, the wendygos slowed their pace. Where once had been an unearthly quiet, Isabel was increasingly bombarded by blood-curdling bellows, cries and calls of men amalgamated with moose, elk, caribou, and deer. Before too long, Isabel's hearing was fully immersed in the day to day sounds of the wendygo people. Her disorientation increased as she registered other, more familiar, noises: the hammering of steel on a smithy's anvil; the sounds of haggling merchants; even a bell chiming- albeit a poorly crafted one. To Isabel's ears, it sounded hauntingly like the town square in Birosh. Still, there was the chillingly eerie animal calls co-mingled overtop the otherwise familiar sounds. Within minutes, the marketplace sounds faded. The silence closed mercifully in, save for her captor's hooves clopping on a stone floor in a large hall (she discerned this by the echo around her). Despite her racing heart, she kept a firm grip on her mind. *If I show fear, it could mean death.*

Moments later, her captor knelt. Isabel felt claws slice the rope around her ankles effortlessly. She felt a second pair of clawed hands slice the ropes binding her wrists. Her feet fumbled as they touched ground. Isabel reached down to steady herself from toppling to the ground. *Great,* she fumed to herself, *my legs are like jelly. Running away is no option any time soon.* Finding her feet, she stood tall, the sack still over her head. *Do not show fear. I have naught to fear for my cause is just.*

Regrettably, as the burlap sack was yanked roughly off her head, Isabel found she *did* have something to fear. Before her, on an elevated platform with stone steps running up it, was a throne. The throne was composed entirely of human skulls and a variety of interlaced, magnificent antlers from all sorts of woodland beasts: moose, caribou, elk and deer. Seated upon the bone and antler throne was the largest wendygo Isabel had yet seen. The nightmare creature upon the throne was at least as tall as Nairadj in bear form- twelve feet, possibly more, in height. He had the single largest pair of caribou antlers atop his skull in the hall. His eyes were blank silver orbs within their sockets; like a pile of silver grymwulf coins melted into perfect circles. The wendygo cracked a repulsive grin, revealing the same horrifying, sharp, oversized teeth as her captors. In a gravelly voice that raised gooseflesh all over Isabel's body, the great wendygo stated, "Welcome daughter of man....and Apollos the *Meddler*, to my city; Hann'Lec- the city of skulls. I fear you will never leave it alive."

All through the painfully uncomfortable journey eastward, Sarto was thinking. He thought of how he might free Isabel from these monsters. He reflected upon the chances of the *same* sptoch happening to the *same* person a second time in the *same* gods' forsaken forest, with the *same* gods' damned cannibalistic demon people. He pondered the odd absence of the gnomes at the camp. *The Shadow Twins are fabled for sensing trouble before it happens....how did they miss* this*? They can sense vibrations in the soil. They told us as much; unless....unless the wendygos came in by the trees. Yes....yes, that's probable. It* would *explain the lack of warning. What happened to them then? There are* three *possibilities. The first, and worst, is they were killed. Second and least likely, is they were pompous windbags who fled at the first sign of trouble. Thirdly, they sensed* *trouble at the last minute, hid and are following in hopes of rescuing us. They would not flee. If they were dead, our captors would have boasted of their kills; for gnomes and wendygos are well-known ancient foes. They* must *be following....elsewise Isabel and I are doomed.*

Conversely......we could be doomed already. It never bodes well when your enemies already *know your name; not ever. Worse, I can't recall what I did to offend the wendygos....or why I was set adrift on that raft all those years ago. Gods above, I hate getting old. Memory just isn't as reliable as it was....especially since my last encounter with wendygos was prior to becoming Sarto. Good luck explaining that the wizard they think they have captured is no longer the same person. Wendygos believe the proof of sight and smell....I'm certain I don't smell like....like the* other *one, anymore. I guess there's nothing for it....I must wait and see what transpires. For all I know, the king wishes to grant me a pardon...."*

As his burlap hood was removed, Sarto *knew* he was not receiving a pardon. He knew it with certainty when the king declared, "Welcome daughter of man....and Apollos the *Meddler,* to my city; Hann'Lec- the city of skulls. I fear you will never leave it alive."

Must be a new king, Sarto mused, *I don't remember the last one being such a sizeable brute.*

The wendygo who had borne him hence struck both Sarto and Isabel across the calves with Sarto's own staff, grating, "*Kneel,* longpig Prezla! You are being addressed by King Fenyang! Show the respect owed to him!"

Casually raising his hand to stay his enthusiastic minion's hand, Fenyang growled, "It's alright Shomari. Our honored guest doesn't know me *personally*. This longpig wizard knew my *father*, Laran the Savage."

In his mind, Sarto noted, *Oh. There it is: family grudge. How* wonderful.

"Does that name....how do you *longpigs* say it again......ring a bell? *Yes*! That's it, exactly! Does the name Laran the Savage, ring a bell, *Apollos* the Wrathful?"

Sarto flinched at the mention of his old name. *I am going to be the death of me.* Always*, that other bastard and his misdeeds follow me. I remember now* exactly *why I stayed on Gwenovair all those years: the* other *never existed there.* Composing himself, Sarto spoke. "King Fenyang, son of Laran the Savage," he began with a bow of the head, "long have been my years upon Kalnay; many more before that in Ackreth. I have seen and done many things. Most of those things done have been cruel in varying degrees. Regrettably, I remember but a *fraction* of those with any certainty or clarity."

Fenyang's horrendous smile dropped away, his silver eyes swirling with ire. "Are you saying," Fenyang rumbled, "you do not recall the *grief* you caused my father, Laran, all those years ago, Apollos the Meddler?"

As levelly as he could, Sarto gazed Fenyang in the eye, declaring, "I am afraid, my lord, it is much more....*complicated* than that. The man your father knew....*Apollos*, as I was once called, he....he *died*. I stand in his place, bearing his likeness, but neither his heart *nor* mind. I am known now, liege, as Sarto the Mender.

Though I do not recall the exact nature of the wrongdoing done to your father....or you, I *would* make amends. Tell me how I may satisfy your grace regarding your father. Anything you would ask, I will do; if it be within my powers to do so."

Fenyang stared intently at Sarto, incredulous that a man with such a reputation for evil could become the pathetic, silver-tongued fool kneeling before him. After a long moment's silence, Fenyang rose to his full height, staring down on the puny longpig wizard with contempt. "There is *one* thing you can do for me, Sarto the *Fool*. You and your apprentice can *die* for the effrontery against my father's mighty name, remembered or otherwise."

Sarto's eyes flared in anger. He would not fight his own death, for his misdeeds were many. The death of Isabel, however, was more than he would tolerate. Sarto hissed, "*Vish mor het tass.*" His staff flew from Shomari's hands, to his own. Pivoting on his left knee, Sarto aimed the staff at Fenyang, shouting, "*Avia Briesa!*" A large fireball erupted from the end of Sarto's staff, flying towards the startled Fenyang, who stumbled back into his throne. A guard to the king's right leapt twixt Fenyang and the fireball, taking it full in the chest. The guard toppled to the ground, burning, writhing and shrieking like a wounded elk.

Shomari leapt onto Sarto's back, knocking the wizard onto his stomach, the staff flying from his grasp. Sarto rolled over as Shomari struggled for a better grip on the wriggling wizard. Sarto grabbed the wendygo by the throat with his right hand, bellowing, "*Burtsa rysa!*" Shomari grunted, collapsing on his side. The wendygo clutched weakly at his throat, where an invisible knife ran

him through the gullet, killing him instantly. Sarto rose
swiftly to his feet, holding his hand out for his staff,
barking, "*Vish mor het tass*" again. When it contacted his
hand, he wrapped his fingers around it tightly, spinning
to his left. Mid-turn he halted in horror at what he saw.
Another wendygo had Isabel on her feet, gripping her
throat; two of the beast's claws lightly piercing the tender
flesh on Isabel's neck. The wendygo clutching Isabel
hissed fiercely, "Drop the staff *wizard*, or I rip your
longpig pupil's throat out! Do it!"

      The fire in Sarto's steely eyes dimmed. He
dropped his staff, the solid wooden sound clacking loudly
in the hall. The wendygo gripping Isabel held his ground,
looking to his king. Fenyang rose from his throne,
striding towards Sarto, stepping over the immolated
guard who smelt strongly of both singed fur and burning
flesh. Sarto sighed, turned to face Fenyang and waited
resignedly for whatever would happen next. The
wendygo king loomed high over Sarto, looking down with
a terrifying mask of rage spread across his animal face.
For a moment they simply stared at one another.
Fenyang broke the silence. "You shouldn't have done
that, *longpig*." Lifting his gaze to the guard holding
Isabel, he declared, "We will serve these two for breaking
fast on the morrow, Abrafo. We begin with the *girl*, I
think. I want Apollos to watch his student die. I want
him to know how *horribly* he has failed her." With
lightning fast reflexes, Fenyang raised one massive hoofed
foot, kicking Sarto squarely in the chest.

      Sarto felt at least five of his ribs break as he
flew across the hall. The wizard connected hard with the
stone wall, falling to the ground unconscious. Before he
struck the wall, Sarto thought, *Pallas, my old friend....I*

have failed you....I have failed all *of you.* Then darkness consumed him whole.

High above the great hall, Eimar and Tibelde observed through a grimy, broken window as the scenario unfolded below. Through their mind link, they asked, *what are we going to do?* They saw Sarto get kicked clear across the hall. They listened as Fenyang bellowed, "Take these longpigs to the pen! Ready the cooking fires! I want them white hot by sunrise. Then, we feast! Now get out, *all* of you!"

Eimar and Tibelde watched the wendygos scatter, carrying out their orders. In unison, Tibelde and Eimar thought, *we follow Isabel and Sarto.* Quietly as mice, they raced along the narrow ledge, following the wendygos dragging their friends away: two of them carrying Sarto, while the third, Abrafo, dragged Isabel along.

I don't like the sound of these pens, *brother of mine*, Tibelde thought.

What's to like, sister of mine? These devils are cannibals, Eimar returned.

True. Let us have a closer look.

Leaping flawlessly twixt the close-knit rooftops, Eimar and Tibelde kept low, following Abrafo and his comrades. Thankfully there were no guards atop the roofs, so Eimar and Tibelde proceeded without trouble. The trouble became when they beheld the pens. The pens were a maze of wrought-iron bars, zigging and

zagging forward and back three times after the gate.
Across the narrow passages that went forward and back,
were iron crossbars at chest and knee height (by human
reckoning). They saw Isabel shoved through. When she
tried to turn back to help her master, the bar would not
reverse. The two carrying Sarto hoisted him overhead,
passing through the iron crossbars. Once they traversed
the maze, they came to a secondary gate, leading into the
open pen. In the pen was only one other prisoner, oddly
out of place. The prisoner was a younger wendygo with
a short set of buck antlers who appeared skinnier than
any wendygo the Shadow Twins had yet seen. Glancing
at each other, they mentally queried: *what do you make
of* that *?*

Once the two carrying Sarto entered the main
pen, they dropped the injured wizard unceremoniously to
the ground. Isabel protested, struggling to fight back.
The sorceress was shoved backwards by one oppressor,
landing painfully on her back. She opened her mouth to
cast a spell, but the wendygo who knocked her down
slapped her hard across the face, jolting her head hard to
the right. The second wendygo meanwhile, picked up a
pair of iron hand shackles, attached to an iron muzzle.
The first grabbed Isabel rudely by the hair, jerking her
head back. The second one clamped the evil looking
device over her lower face, locking it at the back. The
first one grabbed her hands, jerking them viciously
together as the other shackled her wrists. When they
finished, Isabel was forced to prop her knees up to rest
her hands on- for the mask only had a foot-long chain
connected to her wrist shackles. Satisfied that she was
properly bound, the guards turned their attention to the
unconscious Sarto. They drug him across the pen from
Isabel. The young, emaciated wendygo sat in the corner
between the two of them. The two guards threw Sarto

harshly against the wall, cuffing and masking him in moments. When they finished, they strode to a third gate at the far end of the pen, where another guard let them out.

Sitting back on their elevated perch, the Shadow Twins held mental conference. *This is not going to be easy,* Eimar thought.

Who said it was going to be easy, *brother? These are* wendygos, *after all,* Tibelde reminded.

Alright, Eimar continued, *what are we going to need to make this jailbreak work?*

Firstly, we need lock picks....or better yet, keys, Tibelde replied.

How much are you willing to bet the guard at the third gate has both the key for the gate, the shackles and those monstrous masks?

I'd bet you my amethyst necklace at home brother, that he will have all *the keys we need.*

Okay then....next we need to observe the guards' patrol patterns twixt now and sunset....or our rough approximation of when sunset is. I hate *not being able to see the sun....*

Focus Eimar. Our friends' lives are at stake.

Aye....sorry Tibelde. We need medical supplies for Sarto....probably a stick for him to bite down on. I'm certain I heard several of his ribs break when that brute kicked him in the chest.

Tibelde winced as she recalled the noise. *Aye brother, that would be a safe assumption. Most importantly, we do this quietly, quickly and perfectly. If we are spotted or heard, the wendygos will run us down.*

By the goddess, *sister, what a* mean *thing to say; those brutes could never run us down.*

I was referring to Sarto and Isabel. You forget, Eimar, people *cannot run as fast as gnomes.*

True. I can't think of anything else we need before then. I'll scrounge the medical supplies from our goods. You keep an eye on the patrols and see whose hands exchange those keys.

Aye brother, I will. Now we wait.

Within two hours it was sunset (approximately). The majority of wendygos bustling in the streets below returned to their homes. Tibelde and Eimar watched with keen eyes as the keys to the iron-gated pen were passed at the changing of the guards. Once the new guard was alone, Eimar and Tibelde dashed down from the roofs. When they reached the street, the Shadow Twins burrowed unseen into the earth, propelling silently towards the unawares guard. When they were below him, they rose in unison through the earth to attack. Grabbing hold of his ankles, the gnomes pulled the oblivious guard soundlessly into the earth. Eimar filched the keys as they tugged the doomed wendygo down, as Tibelde slit the guard's throat. In another moment, they emerged exactly where he had been moments before, dashing to the pen where their friends were being held.

Tibelde climbed onto Eimar's shoulders, unlocking the gate. It creaked faintly on its old hinges as it swung inward. Eimar held the gate open, watching out for trouble. Meanwhile, Tibelde dashed silently across the pen with the keys to free her friends. Isabel looked up as she heard the key clink faintly in her manacles, a look of relieved joy flashing across her masked face. Once the mask and shackles were off, Isabel threw her arms around the gnome, wrapping her in a fierce hug. Tibelde hugged her back, helping the young Prezla to her feet.

"I am so *glad* you're alive," Isabel whispered as they crept to Sarto. She spotted Eimar manning the gate. Her heart was doubly overjoyed, and Isabel threw Eimar a cautious wave hello. As Tibelde undid the manacles on Sarto's hands, Isabel placed both hands delicately on Sarto's torso. In a hushed voice, she whispered, "*Vas marsane.*"

Within Sarto's chest came a flurry of grinding noises as his broken ribs instantly reset. The pain of the process jolted the wizard awake. He firmly grasped Isabel's upper arm in a vice-like grip, groaning horribly through the iron muzzle Tibelde was unlocking. Sarto sounded to Isabel like a furious, injured tomcat. Tibelde and Isabel froze, glancing about for trouble. Eimar did likewise, his knife at the ready should guards arrive to investigate. After a tense minute they relaxed, satisfied they were still safe for now. When Sarto noticed Isabel's iolite eyes concernedly staring at him, he blinked, releasing his talon-like grip on her arms. Tibelde found the key to Sarto's mask, freeing him from its iron grip. Once the mask was removed, Sarto rasped, "Thank you Isabel....and you too Tibelde. Truly, you two are angels sent by the gods."

Reflexively, Isabel wrapped her master in a strong hug. He sucked in a pained breath through gritted teeth as she brushed against his reset ribs. Wrapping his left arm loosely around Isabel in a reciprocal hug, Sarto wheezed, "I'm happy to see you too, child."

Isabel whispered in his ear, "I thought I'd *lost* you, Master."

Chuckling faintly, Sarto whispered back, "You'll find, Isabel, I'm rather like an unlucky bronze wendygo: I *always* turn up again. Now, help me up please."

Isabel delicately helped her master up off the ground. The old wizard stood in a place a moment, getting his bearings. Looking to Tibelde, Sarto asked, "What's the plan, Lady Tibelde?"

"My brother and I free you. We sneak out of the city. We hope no one notes your absence till morning."

Sarto stared dumbly at the gnome before shrugging. "That's more of a plan than I have. What about patrols along the city walls, or in the streets?"

It was Tibelde's turn to shrug. "Truthfully, Master Wizard....Eimar and I only planned how to break you two out of the pen. The rest we're making up as we go."

Behind Sarto, a treble voice interjected, "*I* can help you escape Hann'Lec."

Whirling about, the trio of companions searched for the source of the voice. The voice belonged to the bound, emaciated wendygo in the corner. Isabel glanced at the curled up wendygo with suspicion, sneering, "How can *you* help us, *monster?* You're chained up."

Pointing towards Tibelde with a clawed hand, the captive wendygo countered, "The gnome female has the keys, does she not? Free me. I will guide you safely from this wretched city."

Tibelde took a single step forward, dangling the keys. "Why should I release you, *flesh-eater?* You're one of the very *things* that kidnapped my friends in the first place."

The wendygo snorted weakly, "I may be a wendygo in appearance, but I am *nothing* like the rest of my....*people*. I am sentenced to die at sunrise; same as your Prezla friends were." Here he raised his manacled, claw-tipped hands and finished, "So, free me, or *don't*. Escape *with* me or perish *without* me in the attempt. The choice is yours."

Tibelde and Isabel looked to Sarto. He took the keys from Tibelde, knelt before the golden-eyed young wendygo, and stared at him for a quiet moment. Sarto broke the silence, asking, "What is your name lad?"

The young wendygo replied, "My name is Khalon, Master Wizard."

Sarto held his hand out, palm up. Khalon leaned forward. The wizard unshackled the buck's chafed wrists. "How do we escape then, young Khalon?"

Rising slowly to his feet, Khalon unwittingly grunted in pain, as he rose to his full height for the first time in several weeks. He towered above both Sarto and Isabel at over seven and a half feet. Looking around, he did not observe anyone approaching. The four of them moved towards the gate. Once they all exited, Eimar quietly shut the gate. "In order to escape, you must look, and *smell*, like us. My people's sense of smell is extraordinary," Khalon explained.

Eimar gazed at Khalon, remarking disdainfully, "Does it matter if the subject is deceased or not?"

Khalon looked perplexedly at the gnome, replying warily, "*No*, it doesn't. Wendygos smell the same alive or dead."

Eimar smiled mischievously, replying, "Be right back. Sister of mine, would you help me with this?" Together, they dug up the dead guard, splaying him on the ground up to his knees out of the hole.

Khalon grunted faintly at the sight of the body lying before him. "This was Damerley. We were part of the same, converted brood." Eimar moved back cautiously, not liking the implication of Khalon's words. Khalon knelt over Damerley's corpse, running his clawed hand from his head to his stomach. "Forgive me for what I must do now, Damerley." With a sickening, wet, ripping noise, Khalon plunged his hand deep into Damerley's innards. Withdrawing his hand, he held the dead wendygo's liver up. "Here, rub this over any exposed flesh to mask your scent."

Without a word, Sarto took the offered liver, smearing it all over Isabel's neck, face, hands and feet.

Passing her the liver, he muttered, "Do it Isabel. We have no time to waste." Sucking in a breath, she smeared the liver on Sarto's exposed skin. In another moment, they were both a ruddy color, and smelled positively foul.

While they smeared the liver on themselves, Khalon attempted to yank off Damerley's antlers. He grunted, sinking back on his haunches, panting heavily. "I'm too weak. I haven't eaten for days. It was part of my punishment before death, being starved out. Could your magic remove these antlers, Master Wizard?"

"I can try, Khalon, but...."

"*I* will do it, Master Sarto," Isabel interrupted. "You're still recovering from your broken ribs. You rest a moment." Sitting on a nearby barrel, Sarto watched wordlessly as Isabel took charge. Placing one hand at the base of each antler, she muttered, "*Navosh.*" The antlers twisted free of Damerley's skull without a sound. Isabel handed the antlers to Khalon.

Raising his clawed hand, Khalon stated, "No, Lady Isabel. The antlers are for you and your master. Is there a spell to make it seem as though the antlers are attached to your own heads? 'Twould be the most convincing façade to those we may pass as we leave the city."

Isabel withdrew her hand, still clutching the antlers and looked puzzlingly at her Master. "Is there such a spell Master Sarto? I do not know it yet."

Sarto scratched his head briefly, searching his fragmented memory for the words. A moment later, he snapped his finger, pointing at Isabel. "'*Fraya mor het cranos'*.... yes, that's how it goes. Just a warning Isabel, this spell will be....*discomforting*. Only use one antler; the spell will grow a duplicate second to match the first."

Holding the first antler close to the top of her own head, she repeated the spell. Isabel grimaced in pain as the base of the antler melded to the top of her skull, spreading out to replicate a second antler. She breathed hard into the elbow of her robes to stifle the screams threatening to burst from her. Moments later, the spell was complete. Isabel was immediately aware of the extra weight atop her skull, trying to topple her forward. She hurried to Master Sarto with the second antler. Before commencing the grafting spell, she placed one hand over Sarto's mouth, whispering, '*nix.*' Then she began the grafting spell on her Master. She was pleased with herself for using the silence spell prior to starting. Isabel was certain- given his recent bouts of pain and fatigue- her master would be unable to remain silent as the grafting spell worked its magic; it turned out she was correct. When the grafting spell finished, he was sweating hard and rasping from his silent screaming fit. Isabel placed her hand briefly over his mouth again, muttering, '*yamba.*'

Sarto gasped, "Excellent thinking, using a muting spell before beginning. You are *assuredly* on your way to becoming one of the greatest sorceresses Kalnay has seen in *many* years."

Khalon stepped forward, an impatient look on his face. "I don't mean to intrude, but we *must* go. The night is young, but there is a shift change in a couple hours. Can we set Damerley's body back in the earth, Master gnomes?"

Eimar jumped in the hole, where Damerley's feet still rested, and said, "Back in a flash." Within seconds, Damerley's corpse disappeared. The hole he came out of was entirely gone.

"Excellent work, Master Eimar; truly, gnomes are a swift species."

"Where's my staff," Sarto interrupted. "Has anyone seen my staff? I lost it after I was knocked out."

Eimar and Tibelde looked at each other worriedly. "We....uh, we don't know, Master Sarto. One of the guards took it. We're not sure where it is."

"*Sptoch*," Sarto hissed. "I think I remember part of why I never returned to Lec'tair Forest: wendygos have a larger penchant for thievery than even gnomes." Eimar and Tibelde glared bitterly at him. Sarto quickly corrected himself. "I mean the *bad* kind of thievery: stealing heirlooms like wizard's staffs and spell books; not thievery of baubles and shiny things. I cry your pardon for the confusion, Master Gnomes." Thinking about it, Sarto amended, "I suppose I can recall the staff to me once we're safely outside the city."

Khalon stepped forward impatiently, interjecting, "Master Sarto, we really *must* be going. If we find your staff, we will retrieve it. Enemies are everywhere. The night presses relentlessly onward. Before we leave, we need to find some cloaks to shield us from unfriendly eyes."

Tibelde and Eimar reached into their rucksacks, pulling out two bundled cloaks. "Here," Tibelde said, handing one to Sarto, while Eimar handed the other to

Isabel. Tibelde glared disdainfully at Khalon, "You can find your own. Now, which way, *flesh-eater*?"

Khalon flinched at being called flesh-eater. He desired to escape more than fight over slanderous names. Nodding his head forward, Khalon replied, "It's this way. Follow me and stay close. If anyone stops us, or asks any questions, let me do the talking."

Eimar sank into the ground, prepared to follow below the streets. Tibelde stared hard at Khalon for a long moment, then snarled, "If *any* harm befalls my friends, you and I will have words at the end of my knife, *flesh-eater*. Understood?"

Khalon bowed deferentially, replying, "I promise you Tibelde, daughter of earth, no harm shall befall your friends by my hand. Now, let us move."

Tibelde sank into the ground. Isabel and Sarto slung their rucksacks over their backs, donned their cloaks and covered their heads. Scrounging a tattered cloak from a nearby rubbish bin, Khalon briefly inspected the two disguised Prezla. Satisfied they would pass scrutiny, he said, "Come, follow me."

To everyone's surprise, they escaped Hann'Lec with relative ease, though it took a couple hours of slow, careful moving. The city was massive and walled in; so they were forced to proceed through the main gate. The light guard detail at the city gates was satisfied with their scents and their declaration that they were setting out on an early morning hunt to collect sacrifices for tomorrow's executions. They were on the worn earthen road just beyond the gates when a guard changing shift bumped headlong into Isabel. "*Hey*," he growled, knocking her to the ground, "watch where you're going, *svanth*!"

Khalon helped Isabel to her feet. Sarto turned to the guard to rebuke him for his rudeness, then noticed his staff in the guard's hand. With a growl, he seethed, "That belongs to *me*." In one swift motion he lunged forward, gripped the staff firmly with his left hand, extending his right towards the guard's chest. "*Avia resh*," the wizard growled. The stunned guard flew thirty feet, crashing into an old birch tree across the road. Above, on the battlements, growls and cries were heard from guards who witnessed the commotion below. The off-key bell knolled its eerie cry; within the city dozens more wendygos began to bellow and holler. Facing the large oaken gate, Sarto hollered, '*Corvai*'. In moments, the thick city gate slammed shut against the wendygos rushing to meet them. Spinning to Khalon, Sarto spat, "Which way is south?"

Khalon wordlessly pointed a clawed finger through the trees to their left.

Sarto hollered, "Come on then! We have to run!"

Chapter Five: The Gates of Volcros

Though neither Abel nor Nairadj particularly relished captivity, there was a certain degree of rest in this circumstance. Big decisions were, presently, not their concern. Hearne and his 'Night Patrol' were in charge. Abel's curiosity burned within him: he wished to inquire after Queen Sigourney, about daily life in the Nightstalker Wastes, even the city of Volcros itself. He knew if he asked anything, he would promptly be told to 'shut his gob' by one of Hearne's eleven patrolmen, as he had already been told at least twice. So- with a measure of difficulty- Abel held his tongue, oddly relishing their silent, swift march over the two days twixt where they had been rescued by the Night Patrol and the fabled city of Volcros. When they drew up before the city gates early the next morning, Abel was unprepared for Volcros' massive size. He'd only ever seen one true city in his lifetime, when he was six years old. He didn't recall much detail regarding Marister; for it was long ago and in, what seemed, another lifetime. He recalled vaguely that Marister had seemed quite large. Granted, Abel knew that to a child of six, *everything* was much larger. Despite that vague knowledge, Volcros was larger still. He had first spotted the city as a blob on the horizon the day before. Standing before Volcros' massive wooden gate, upon an enormous drawbridge, spanning a moat thicker than the narrowest point on the Inaratu River, Abel knew with certainty Volcros was the single largest city in Kalnay.

Hearne called over his shoulder, "Under Queen Sigourney, Volcros has grown dramatically in size over the past ten years. Where once dwelt fewer than a thousand tribesmen, now resides over one hundred thousand souls. All are from different, scattered tribes of Wildmen in the Wastes."

Nairadj marvelled, "That is indeed a mighty feat, Captain Hearne. Even amongst dyre bears, it is difficult to find such singular unity with that many souls under one leader's governance. It seems Queen Sigourney is a greater leader than I hear tell of."

Hearne snorted, "While I appreciate the compliment on behalf of my lady, the Queen, you should know flattery will *not* curry you favour with her ladyship. She did not rise to take her father's crown by heeding flattery."

Nairadj was unsure of how to respond to Hearne's curt remark, so she held her tongue. As the Night Patrol passed through the gates, a deafening roar went up from inside the mammoth walls. Abel and Nairadj were startled by the ruckus. Drawing closer to Nairadj, Abel shouted over the din, "What is it, Master?! Why do the people cheer so?!"

Leaning close Nairadj shouted back, "The men and women of the Night Patrol are being honored! They have braved the Wastes for two weeks, returning to the land of the living; with a pair of prizes no less! There will be a feast tonight to celebrate!"

The companions were marched to the centre of Volcros. Abel expected the wild folk to hurl spoiled fruit, or rotten vegetables or jeer at them. They did not. Rather, they stared in bewildered awe at the statuesque Nairadj and Abel following alongside. The walk from the gate to the city centre was educational. All his life, Abel believed all Northerners were like their former foe,

Straker: cruel, sneaky, untrustworthy and savage. He observed none of that as they approached the city square. Upon arriving in the square, Hearne and the Night Patrol bent the knee before a sizeable, elevated wooden stage with a small flight of steps running up the front and on either side. Abel and Nairadj followed Hearne's cue and knelt. The members of the Night Patrol thumped their right hands on their breastplates, raised their right hands closed in fists toward their queen on the platform, shouting, "Hail Sigourney, madam saviour of the Nightstalker Wastes, and our Queen! Hail the Queen! Kill the nightstalkers! Hail and kill!"

Atop the platform, was an elegantly carved mahogany throne, with tribal runes and pictograms-depicting the reign of Sigourney over the past twenty years. Sitting upon the throne was a lanky woman with high cheek bones, long intricately braided chestnut hair and a pair of chestnut eyes to match. Upon her head sat a simple, hand-carved, mahogany crown, set with a single red ruby in the center. The Queen wore an elegant, yet simple, red linen dress. Covering her torso was a steel breastplate, lending her the appearance of a lady at court ready to do battle. Reinforcing that image, she had a sheathed longsword leaning against the left side of her throne; ready to be drawn and used at a moment's notice. Rising, the Northerner Queen strode gracefully down the platform steps towards Abel and Nairadj. She stopped to Hearne's left, soaking up the details of her captives. *What a* curious *pairing*, Sigourney mused to herself, *not since the ancient days have dyre bears and mankind traveled together in peace.* Sigourney spoke with a deep, yet smooth voice. "Hail to you she-bear and son of the Five Sisters. What has brought you together before me here in the Nightstalker Wastes? Speak freely, without fear of penalty."

Abel glanced sidelong at Nairadj, his eyes asking, *now what?* Nairadj cleared her throat, as she rose. She remained slightly bowed, her eyes lowered in deference. "Hail to you Sigourney, daughter of Ridley the Bold, Queen of the Nightstalker Wastes. My name is Nairadj, daughter of Yenoor the Wise." At the mention of Nairadj's name, a great gasp went up from the crowd. Abel was confused by the recognition of Nairadj's name, making a note to inquire about it later.

Indicating the kneeling Abel, Nairadj continued, "This is my apprentice, Abel. He is the sole son of Sir Aldrich of house Farthen, who served young King Alaster in the days of your father's rule. He has been named by the diviner, Pallas the Peaceful, as a warrior of the way of the Light."

At the mention of Abel's father and the deceased king Alaster, the crowd reacted with angry shouts and shocked gasps. Sigourney herself cast a quizzical eye upon Abel. *How* interesting. *The son of one of my father's greatest enemies is brought before me. I must not act in haste. I will hear them out before passing judgment.*

Abel rose to his feet when Nairadj mentioned his name, keeping his head bowed. When she mentioned his father and Alaster, Abel's eyes grew large. He glanced furtively about, half-expecting the crowd to surge forward and string him up from the nearest eaves by his own innards. Though many cried in anger and shock, none attacked him. Abel directed his gaze to Nairadj, his eyes shouting, *what are you* doing*?!*

Nairadj glanced at him briefly before finishing her address to Sigourney. "My apprentice has a plan to defeat Lilith and the Overlord. He will present that plan to you now." Saying thus, Nairadj knelt again, leaving Abel standing alone before Sigourney and the crowd. Looking the Queen of the Wastes square in the eye, Abel spoke loudly and clearly for all to hear, "Hail to your worship, Queen Sigourney. 'Tis true, I *am* the son of Sir Aldrich Farthen who served King Alaster in his campaign on the Crossroad of Kings these years past. There exists now in Kalnay a blight greater than *anything* known in this land's long memory. I speak of the Dark Witch, Lilith and the Overlord Malikh. My master Pallas believed that, despite old grievances twixt the North and the rest of Kalnay......he believed we could begin *healing* that rift by banding together to defeat the Overlord and his witch. He believed this unto his dying breath, just these couple months past.

"I intend to fulfill my prophesied destiny: kill the usurper Malikh, and Lilith. Yet, I cannot do it alone. *Together* we may begin setting right the scales of harmony, justice and peace. I have naught to offer you, save a promise: I will work closely with the new ruler of Kalnay- whosoever that may be- to provide the people of the north with lands and homes free of the dangers of the Wastes in territory and towns *south* of the Shavatnu Mountains; should you so desire." Kneeling then, Abel stated, "I would see the wrongs of the past- whether committed by my father, my Master, or even King Alaster- made right. I would see a *true* era of peace and prosperity return to *all* Kalnay. I beseech you then, Sigourney, Queen of the North, journey south with my master and I to overthrow Malıkh and his witch. Together we may begin restoring peace to this troubled realm." As Abel finished, the crowd grew tumultuous. Bitter cries rose for Abel and Nairadj's heads. Some hollered agreement for the march south.

Sigourney permitted her people to vent for a minute, before raising her hand for silence. The moment her hand rose, the entire throng fell silent, awaiting their queen's word. "My people," she called authoritatively, "long has it been since such an opportunity has presented itself here. A march south could prove to be a most *rewarding* experience, 'tis true. *However*, there are but *two* warriors here to pledge this alliance. It is well known that if a supplicating party has not the numbers to match the magnitude of the request there must be......" Here, Sigourney paused, staring directly at Nairadj and Abel before finishing, "a test of *worth*." Sweeping back up the steps to her throne, she sat gracefully, nodding to Hearne.

The Captain rose. His Night Patrol followed suit. Collectively they seized Abel and Nairadj, yanking them roughly to their feet. The companions were marched to the base of the central stairs, spun to face the audience, and forced to kneel again.

"Before I pledge my army to follow these brave warriors south, *one* must triumph in a trial by combat. They may choose amongst themselves who will be their champion." Looking down, Sigourney asked, "Which of you accepts this challenge?"

Abel began to rise, thinking, *this is* my *quest. I must see it through.* Before he had risen even a few inches, Nairadj shot to her feet, shoving Abel back to his knees. "*I* accept your challenge, o Queen of the Wastes. I, Nairadj, once the Princess of the Red-Ditch dyre bear clan, do stand ready to face trial by combat."

Abel looked up in shock. *Nairadj is a* princess*!? Why has she never mentioned this? Why does she* *mention it* now? Many of the throng surged forward, forced back by Sigourney's assembled guards. Abel heard shouts of, "Disgrace on your name!" "You are no *true* dyre bear!" "You murderous *svanth*!" "The gods *damn* you for your misdeed!" Through all the hurled insults, Nairadj stood tall, unmoved by the mob's harsh words. Abel's mind raced, anger stirring within his breast against the Northerners hurling these slanders. *Disgrace....?* Murderer......? *What could she* possibly *have done to earn such disdain? I must, if we are both still alive later, ask her the meaning of all this.*

Sigourney bowed her head, in acceptance of Nairadj's decision. Once again, the Queen raised her hand, instantly obtaining silence from her subjects. "It has been decided! Princess Nairadj of the Red-Ditch clan has accepted the trial by combat. Now, who wilt be *my* champion in this test of worth against the Lady Nairadj?"

For a whole minute, none spoke or moved. Abel thought, *typical: everyone cries for blood and punishment. Yet none step forward to dirty their hands with the deed.* When the minute was up, one of the Night Patrol strode up beside Nairadj. Facing the audience, the man declared, "I am Duncan, son of Edward, brother of Imre! You all know me. You know my grievance with the bear folk. My father Edward was *killed* by one such creature five years past. Long I have desired justice for his death. Today, I receive that justice! I accept the responsibility of Queen's champion in this trial by combat!"

Duncan and Nairadj spun to face the Queen, kneeling in tandem, as a deafening cheer arose from the crowd. As the she-bear turned, she quickly marked her opponent's features. Duncan had long, sandy brown hair, piercing blue eyes and the determination of a seasoned champion. When they rose, Nairadj noted he was under six feet tall. *It's always the smaller ones who fight fiercest,* Nairadj thought bemusedly to herself.

Sigourney rose, stating, "Behold, my people: our combatants in this test of worth!" To Duncan and Nairadj, Sigourney spoke, "Here are the terms of contest. You will disrobe to your basic raiment: no armor, furs, footwear or padded garments are permitted; tunics and trousers only. You are permitted *no* weapons: knives, swords, dirks, shields or any other form of armed defense is strictly prohibited. You will fight within the circle of honor here in the square. Should you leave the circle, or be forced out, you forfeit the contest. *Two* enter the circle; only *one* shall leave. Now, prepare yourselves."

Abel was released to help his master prepare. On the opposite side of the ring, Duncan's older brother Imre- a graying man of forty-five years- and Captain Hearne assisted Duncan in shedding his armor and weapons. As both parties stripped to their basic garments, the remaining Night Patrol made show of collecting weapons and garments from both sides; demonstrating to the crowd that the champions honored the Queen's decree. Their belongings were placed at either side of the central stairs leading up to the throne. The crowd drew closer to witness the contest. The Queen's guards stood along the edge of the crowd, ensuring none interfered with the combatants.

Abel removed Nairadj's sword belt, and her sheathed dagger, while she removed her furs and boots. "So," Abel began awkwardly, "what happens to me if you're killed, Master?"

Nairadj glanced to her apprentice, as she stripped to her tunic and trousers. "Either Sigourney will permit you to live....or she will not. Beyond that I cannot say."

"Well, *that's* comforting."

Looking him in the eye, she declared, "It *won't* come to that. I can beat Duncan. Anger blinds him to his true strength. I *shall* win. Then we will have an army to march south with *and* a new ally besides. *That* is made possible by Pallas....and yourself."

Abel fought back hot tears threatening to spill down his cheeks. "You're forgetting yourself in that statement, my Lady. You are the one about to enter trial by combat. You....you should have let *me*...."

Nairadj gripped his shoulders firmly in her large, slender hands. "Your survival is *essential* to this quest's success. I could not permit you to risk your life in a paltry show such as this. Besides, I am hopeful I may use this opportunity to set right bad blood twixt my people and the Northerners. Like Sarto, I seek to do right where I may. I too have stains tainting my past."

Abel hazarded the next question meekly, "Do these....*stains* have anything to do with your being a princess, Mi'lady?"

The bear lady sighed, stared solemnly into the youth's eyes, nodding faintly, once. "*Aye* Abel. Regrettably, they do."

Trying to conceal the hurt in his voice, Abel asked, "Did you *ever* intend to tell me of your past? Or were you planning to take your secrets to the grave?"

She drew Abel into a firm, loving embrace. "You have faced *so* much grief and carry *such* a great burden....I did not wish to add to your worries, by having you fret about *me* as well. Clearly, I was wrong in withholding that information." Withdrawing from the embrace, Nairadj declared, "When this is over, I shall tell you whatever you desire to know of my past. I trust you Abel. I am sorry for not telling you sooner."

With a great voice, Sigourney called out, "Let the contestants draw to the center of the circle of honor!"

Nairadj turned to face Duncan. Before she could enter the ring, Abel spun her back around, pulling her face close to his. "My true name is *Hamish*, Princess Nairadj," he whispered in her ear. "I trust you to keep my secret: as my master, my friend....and the woman I *love*."

The Princess was both deeply honored and surprised. As she withdrew from his whispered secret, she beamed fondly at him. Quickly, she leaned down, planting a kiss on his forehead. When she withdrew, she whispered, "Thank you Abel, for your trust *and* your love. I take them both with me into this contest. They will be my strength. I *will* win; for you and our friends, wherever they may be." Nairadj turned, striding to the centre of the circle, to face Duncan. They faced the Queen, bowing deeply. Sigourney nodded. The combatants then faced each other, bowing slightly. Then Sigourney cried, "Let the trial by combat commence!"

Nairadj had been in enough fights to know stature meant little if one didn't know how to use it effectively. She knew she could not intimidate this little man into surrendering or fleeing. She drew her hands up defensively, protecting her face, simultaneously widening her stance, so she was crouched lower to the ground. *The smaller I am, the less of me he can attack. I'll let him make the first move.* She held her stance, waiting.

Duncan circled the large she-bear, noting how she drew herself low, bringing her hands up to protect her face. *Smart bear; shrink your stature so I have less bulk to attack. She wants me to make the first move, so I will oblige her.* Like lightning, he dashed forward, faking to punch her with a right hook. She raised her right hand to block the attack. As she did, he slid to his knees, slipping twixt her legs on the thin layer of mud within the ring. As he slid beneath her, he wound his right arm up, striking her in the crook of her right knee. Having done so, he rose to one knee behind her.

Nairadj dropped to her right knee, throwing her hands out to break her fall. On her knee, she swung her arm about to catch Duncan's sneak attack from behind. Her foe raised his forearms blocking the sidelong, pivoting swipe. Batting her arm away, he swung his left elbow hard into her right temple, knocking her sideways across the ring. Nairadj's right ear was ringing. *This tiny man is* very *good.* She rolled to her feet as Duncan leapt at her, bringing his knee down where her head had been moments before. As he landed, Nairadj spun a tight circle, bringing her right foot up in a rear cross kick. Her large, mud-covered foot connected fiercely with his forehead, knocking him flat on his back.

Nairadj bent to pick him up. Duncan's feet scissored about her own, tumbling her face first into the mud. Quick as a hare, the little man was on her back. The lanky bear lady rose to her knees, struggling to throw him off. His arms were wrapped tightly about her throat, locking her in a chokehold. She knew blacking out would end the contest for certain, so she thrust her head back and was rewarded with a satisfying crunch as her skull connected with his nose. To her surprise, he did not let go; rather he tightened his grip around her neck. Nairadj thought, *I must get him off me, lest I pass out and he kills me.* With great effort, she found her feet. Then, with a rasping yell, she leapt in the air to plummet groundward on her back.

As the bear lady threw herself backwards, Duncan thought, *gods above, this is going to hurt. Whatever you do,* don't *let go.* Despite his mental warning, he couldn't help but release the she-bear as the air was flattened out of him by her plummeting weight. In a flash, she rolled to her knees, wrapping her left hand firmly around Duncan's throat, holding him down in the mud. With her right fist, she punched him swiftly in the face three times. The first blow was to his right eye, to cloud his vision, should he escape her grasp. The second strike was to the nose, to stir afresh the pain she had just inflicted. On the third strike, she punched him in the forehead, disorienting him. Despite his best efforts to the contrary, the little man could not shoulder all that pain and disorientation at once. He barked harshly in pain. Nairadj drew him close to her face by his throat, rasping hoarsely, "Do you *yield* Duncan? I have *no* desire to kill you. I ask again: will you *yield*?!"

Duncan knew his next move was foolhardy, and could very well knock him out, but he did it anyway.

"*No*," he hissed through clenched teeth. Then he savagely
head-butted the she-bear. His aim was true, despite his
swiftly puffing right eye. His forehead connected solidly
with Nairadj's nose. Duncan was rewarded with the
crunch of cartilage. Nairadj released hold on his throat as
she staggered back, cradling her broken nose. By now,
both combatants were weary with injury and fatigue.
Duncan was determined not to lose. Regaining his feet,
he dashed at the doubled over Nairadj. He leapt into the
air, his right knee jutting out to catch her square in the
jaw and end this contest.

       Abel saw the end coming. In desperation he
cried out, "Master, look out!"

       Had Nairadj not experienced how dangerous
tiny men's knees were- as when she was blindsided by
Straker before- she may not have reacted swiftly enough.
However, she knew *exactly* how to end this. Leaning
back as she rose, the she-bear dodged Duncan's savage
knee kick. At the same time, she pivoted her right arm in
a swift, circular arc towards her airborne foe. Her
decision was correct. Her arm flew up, catching Duncan
squarely in the chest. The downward arc of her strike
thrust him at high speed into the muddy earth of the
combat circle.

       Duncan had no chance. It was only after his
knee missed the she-bear's face, that he saw her massive
arm swinging towards him; the force of the blow robbing
him of air. It reminded him of the time, as a child, when
he ran a horse between two small trees with a clothesline
strung on it. The taut, thick clothesline threw him hard
from the horse, hurtling him groundward. *This*, in
retrospect, was a *much* harder blow than that. The
instant he hit the ground he flew painfully into blackness.

Nairadj knelt over the unconscious Duncan to ensure he was still breathing. Satisfied, she rose, standing over her fallen foe. In a loud, cracking voice, she hollered, "People of Volcros! I, Nairadj, Princess of the Red-Ditch bear clan, stand victorious over your queen's champion, Duncan. The brave lad is *not* dead, for I have *no* desire to kill him. He fought hard and valiantly and should be honored for his bravery at facing a dyre bear in unarmed combat! By the words of your queen, you are *sworn* to honor young Abel's proposed pact! I desire we may become friends, marching with common purpose to crush the usurper Malikh and his dark witch Lilith! As added incentive and a sign of friendship in this new accord, my apprentice Abel and I offer unto you fair people a great gift: a sack of ivory dragon's teeth."

The crowd gasped at this revelation. Even Sigourney started at this (for it had been many a long year since any but a wizard or Sir Brock Clegane had slain a dragon and lived to tell the tale).

Nairadj continued, "That is correct: my apprentice Abel *single-handedly* defeated Ulgnar the Grey who plagued the Voshkarna these many, countless years. We bring, as a token of friendship these teeth to provide protection against the nightstalkers of the north, or great wealth should you elect to sell them. Both myself, and my apprentice have slain *many* nightstalkers on our journey here. Accept the teeth as the gifts they are and honor the pact to march south with us!" Then she fell silent, staring at the Queen, awaiting her answer.

A moment later, the Queen of the Wastes rose to her feet. The assembled Northerners fell silent immediately. She looked from Nairadj to Abel, then finally to her people. *The she-bear is resourceful. She*

mentions no gifts until claiming victory. If I refuse, the
people perceive me as dishonorable and foolish for
rejecting such a rare and valuable gift as dragon's teeth.
I have no *guarantee of retaining the throne of Regalias,*
should we triumph against Malikh's forces......However, if
we do not *challenge the Overlord, how long before he*
decides to march north and conquer me before my own
gates? Already, I have achieved more in these past two
decades as queen than my father Ridley did in his entire
lifetime. I would be foolish to refuse this allegiance, frail
though it seems. So too is pottery frail, when first the
clay is set on the wheel. 'Tis only with skilled hands that
the clay becomes a thing of beauty.

        "My people," Sigourney spoke, "as the princess
has remarked, I have pledged my oath to aid her and her
apprentice on their quest, if she be the victor within the
circle of honor. We *all* behold proof that she is indeed
victorious. Furthermore, she reveals herself honorable
and merciful, for she spares the valiant Duncan's life-
which is hers to take as the victor. This gift of dragon's
teeth is both unrequested and gratefully received." To
Hearne, Sigourney called, "Captain."

        Kneeling before the queen, Hearne replied, "Aye,
my Lady."

        "Please, restore Princess Nairadj's belongings to
her person; her courageous apprentice Abel '*Drakt'vansh*'
Farthen's things as well. They are now our guests of
honor. Have Cort tend to Duncan's injuries."

        Placing his hand on his breastplate, Hearne
replied, "As you command my Queen, so it shall be done."

To her people, Sigourney added, "Let a great feast be prepared to celebrate this pact with our new friends. We shall celebrate three days and nights. At dawn, five days hence, we march south with an army of fifty-five thousand strong to overthrow Malikh and his dark witch Lilith. For the North! For Kalnay!" As Sigourney finished, the assembled Northerners unleashed a roar of approval. Abel feels a renewed sense of hope for the outcome of the quest.

Chapter Six: Blaze

Khalon took the lead, followed closely by Tibelde and Eimar as the fugitives from Hann'Lec crashed through the brush and scrub of Lec'tair Forest. The Shadow Twins were still leery of the young wendygo, fearing he may yet lead them into a trap. Sarto was behind them, running slower as his newly mended ribs cried in constant, silent protest. He dug deep for the strength to continue, leaning on his trusty staff. Bringing up the rear was Isabel, running onward but keeping a fearful eye behind them. She searched intently for the wendygo Sarto had sent flying but saw no sign. That didn't entirely comfort her; having no sign is how they were caught in the first place. As she ran, Isabel thought furiously, *I will* not *be some demon's meal.* That thought was followed closely by another: *I wish I had my* own *staff. Sarto never told me how, let alone* when*, I would get or forge my own staff.*

Far behind came the ghostly clanging of the off-key bell, rallying the wendygos to action. She knew it would be awhile yet, before they finally managed to force open the gate. Sarto's magic was strong; his desire not to be eaten reinforced his spell perfectly. Other thoughts clambered around Isabel's mind as well. *Why did master Sarto permit that* abomination, *Khalon, to join us? The Twins are right, distrusting him. His king ordered us served up for breaking fast. Everyone knows wendygos only eat human flesh, per the curse laid upon Wendaros the Mighty. I hope we outrun these monsters; elsewise we are doomed. It must be at* least *another day and a half before we reach Hesketh. Sptoch! Gods, keep us safe until then.* Behind her in the distance she heard a great bellowing; as if every moose, elk, and caribou was

THE CROSSROAD OF KINGS   PG. 100

crying in animalistic rage. She knew it was the wendygos. That did naught to ease the chills coursing through her body at the monstrous sounds. *We must move faster. I wonder if there is a spell that could help us outrun these beasts for good.*

Suddenly, Sarto's voice ripped through her head. *No! Don't attempt that sort of spell, child! It requires time to gauge and calibrate. Without preparation, we would run until we died of exhaustion, or thundered into Andalmere Bay to drown.*

A furious thought ripped across the mental link that Isabel and Sarto shared. *What would you have us do, Master?! Be killed in the dark of Lec'tair Forest?*

I would have you trust Khalon to lead us to safety, with the Twins assistance. All we need do is keep our pursuers at bay until we reach Hesketh. Will you obey me in this, Isabel? Our group is in danger of splintering over Khalon's presence as it is. If the Shadow Twins see us clashing amongst ourselves, they may turn on Khalon outright. We will make it, my child. I promise you.

Though her heart was reluctant, she agreed. *Aye, Master Sarto; I will obey and trust your judgment.*

My thanks, Isabel; now let us, focus our energies on escape.

As you say Master Sarto, so I shall obey.

They had run for two and a half hours strong, but their energy was flagging. Particularly, Sarto and Isabel; Khalon and the Shadow Twins could have run without rest a further three hours- though they were polite enough not to say so. While Sarto sucked in a deep, ragged breath, Isabel asked Khalon bluntly, "How close are your people, *wendygo*?"

Khalon ignored the spite in her voice. He had grown accustomed to the scorn of others- including other wendygos. Scenting the air to the north, he listened momentarily to the sounds drifting through the twilight sky. Looking to Isabel he stated, "They are less than an hour behind, Lady Isabel."

Eimar threw his knife in the ground at his feet in frustration. "*Sptoch* on it all! How do they cover that much ground so quickly?" Plucking his knife from the ground, the gnome leveled it at Khalon. "Is it you, *flesh-eater*? Are you *aiding* your brethren; slowing us down, or the like?"

Khalon looked flatly at the diminutive Eimar, but his words were barbed. "Those....*creatures* are no more my brethren, than I am yours, *earth-dweller*. 'Tis this forest: Pimedus holds dominion over all...influencing those traversing it, be they on the side of good *or* of ill."

Placing her hand atop her brother's upheld knife hand, Tibelde calmed him with a look. To Khalon, she queried, "You mean to tell me, flesh-eater, that Lec'tair Forest is *evil*? That it's lending speed to our pursuers?"

Nodding faintly, Khalon replied, "Aye, Lady Tibelde. 'Tis also what slows our progress as our pursuers gain ground."

Eimar spat angrily, "You *lie*, monster! Forests don't halt beings in their tracks." He took a step towards Khalon, brandishing his knife. The young buck stood impassive; neither defending himself, nor preparing to attack.

From his resting spot against a nearby tree, Sarto bellowed, "*Enough*, Eimar!"

The gnome stopped dead in his tracks, glancing to the fatigued wizard. "Khalon speaks true. I was once a dark wizard. I know *too* well the signs of Pimedus and its wiles. 'Tis Pimedus sapping my strength. It senses the magic of the Light within me; within Isabel as well. You may not feel it my gnomish friend; for that, count yourself blessed. As a child of Bloomaya, you are born impervious to the workings of Pimedus." Sarto glanced curiously at Khalon then, asking, "But *you*, Khalon......*you* feel the leeching too, do you not? Tell me lad. There is no shame in it."

Khalon stared Sarto dead in the eyes, his pure golden eyes meeting the wizard's weathered grey ones. He released a frustrated huff of breath, confessing, "Aye, Master Sarto. I do not feel my full strength any longer. I feel, as you say, *leeched*. I know part of my weariness is hunger....but this is *deeper* than hunger. It feels......I can't rightly explain it......"

"It feels like someone, or *something*, is whittling your soul away from the inside, does it not?"

Khalon started, nodding quickly in surprise. "How do you know that, Master Sarto?"

Gripping his staff tightly as he rose wearily to his feet, Sarto replied, "I know because....I know."

For a fleeting moment, Isabel heard Pallas' last words to her before he died. As clearly as though the Diviner were present now, they darted first across Sarto's mind, then hers: *Nor are all things that were once of the Dark, black at heart.* Knowing Sarto was sometimes absent-minded, Isabel paid them no heed.

Khalon didn't question the wizard's cryptic answer. "As you say, Master Sarto; if you are rested enough, perhaps we should resume our flight?"

Sarto took one step forward, replying, "Quite right, Khalon. Let us...." Then he passed out stone cold, falling flat on his face. Isabel and the Twins rushed to check on him. Khalon stayed back, fearing his approach may stir their ire anew.

Isabel rolled her master over, listening to his heartbeat. She checked beneath his closed eyelids, finding them rolled far back into his head. She asked the Shadow Twins, "What is *wrong* with him?"

"It is the *forest*," interjected Khalon firmly, "as I said before. Pimedus has seized hold of his mind. He battles the Darkness within himself. We cannot *truly* help your friend lest we escape this forest's dark influence."

Eimar snapped, "How are we to do *that*, flesh-eater? He is *unconscious*!"

Stepping forward, Khalon stated evenly, "*I* will carry him." Here he looked to Isabel, adding, "If you will permit me to help."

Isabel stared hard at him, probing his golden gaze with her iolite eyes. Pallas' last words occurred to her again: *Nor are all things that were once of the Dark, black at heart.* She had a revelation then: *Could this....this wendygo have been sent to* aid *us in our quest? He seems unlike any other wendygo we have encountered....* When the moment passed, she stated authoritatively, "You may carry him....Khalon. You have my gratitude for your assistance."

The young buck nodded to her, bent and hoisted Sarto effortlessly over his shoulder. Isabel retrieved Sarto's staff and rose to her feet. Eimar and Tibelde both stared, dumbfounded at the young sorceress's decision. Gazing firmly at the twins, Isabel declared, "Khalon is *helping* us. In lieu of Sarto's leadership, *I* am leading this company now. If you would still help my master and I, as you have sworn, you *will* make peace with my decision. Do you accept, Master Eimar and Lady Tibelde?"

The Shadow Twins cast an uncertain glance in Khalon's direction, for he had already begun trotting southward. Then looking to Isabel, they placed their left hand over their hearts (for gnomes have two hearts, on the right side of their chests). In unison, Tibelde and Eimar echoed, "My Lady Isabel, you have our hearts and our sworn service to you, your master and your quest. We are at peace and continue to serve you faithfully."

Kneeling, Isabel set a hand on each of the Twins' shoulders, Sarto's staff leaning in the crook of her left shoulder. "Happy is my heart to hear it. Now, rise *'Un Riveth Duallis'*. Let us away from this place." All three found their feet, dashing after Khalon who was well over a hundred yards ahead.

After two more hours of intense running, it was clear that the wendygos were determined to re-capture their quarry. The flesh-eaters nipping ever closer at their heels would not turn back; they would hunt their fugitives until they were recaptured or killed. Isabel knew her friends would not be safe until they reached Hesketh; until they could be protected by The Phantom Queen's powerful magic. While that was a glimmer of comfort, it didn't change the fact that they were presently mired within the bleak, sunless realm of Lec'tair Forest.

Behind them, drawing ever nearer were the huffing, chuffing sounds of the wendygo horde pursuing them into the high morning hours beneath Lec'tair's tightly knit canopy. Khalon still lead the group southward; though his energy was flagging between the combined weight of Sarto, his lack of proper nourishment for several days, and the oppression of Pimedus, now treating him as an enemy. Eimar and Tibelde kept good pace with him, but Isabel began falling behind. Within ten minutes, she could clearly hear the wendygos clomping through the bracken fewer than fifty feet behind her. A righteous fury overtook her in that moment, and she seethed internally, *Enough of this nonsense!* Slamming her heels into the ground, she spun a hard one hundred eighty degrees, aiming Sarto's staff at the canopy above, crying aloud: "*Luma devros numa!*"

A great tremor rushed up the length of Sarto's intricately carved staff. Isabel felt it surge through her whole body. Her already magnificent, iolite eyes blazed brighter. An intense stream of firelight shot from the end of the staff. The wendygo barrelling down on her was immolated where he stood, shrieking like a distressed elk, rolling weakly on the ground trying to suppress the flames consuming his flesh, blood and bone. When the flames touched the black canopy above (for indeed it was black and not dark green as Isabel originally supposed) it trembled; moaning in loud, dissonant tones as the fire of the Light burnt and purged it away. As the canopy began to blaze, Isabel lowered the staff to burn the four nearest, charging wendygos.

When she at last saw the bright morning sky above and observed no more wendygos attacking, Isabel hissed at the staff, "*Etsa*". The fire jetting from the staff's end cut out with a loud '*foosh.*' Then she noticed a massive problem. She had terminated the fire jetting from the staff; however, the young Prezla had *no* control over the fire blazing in the damaged canopy. A great roar emanated from it as the blaze rampantly grew; the sound of the blaze became louder than the crash of the waves on the coast of Gwenovair.

Gods above....what have I done?! Frantically, Isabel pointed Sarto's staff at a nearby blazing tree, shrieking, "*Etsa*!" The tree continued to blaze, charring blacker than the canopy had been just moments before. *Gods be gracious, I have burnt down all Lec'tair Forest! What a gods' damned* fool *I have been!* The young Prezla had no time to lament her mistake for the fire seized a life of its own, racing towards her: a beast more alive and hungrier than any pack of wendygos in Lec'tair Forest. Turning, she fled like a deer, racing desperately to catch up to her party over a hundred yards ahead of her. As she ran, she heard the frightened, angry bellows of the wendygos, retreating west and northwards, fleeing from the all-consuming blaze back towards their fortress city of Hann'Lec. The young Prezla's mind raced with a thousand questions. *What happens when these monsters no longer have a forest sanctuary? Will they turn their foul, ravenous gaze upon the folk of the Kalnayan Riverlands for recompense? Have I damned both myself and my country with this rash deed?*

Again, her thoughts were interrupted as the roaring fire raced along her left side, a mere hundred feet away. She watched in horror as the wildfire raced further ahead, beginning to turn westward. *Gods be merciful, the fire is surrounding us! It means to consume us alive! IT! How can a fire have will and desire!? This cannot be my doing. I would never sew such rampant destruction. Someone or something works against us. Is this the will of Pimedus, or something else?* Her terror increased as she witnessed the fire cut off her friends' flight like a white-hot curtain; drawing an end to the act of a play. Khalon dug his hooves hard into the earth, grabbing tighter hold of Sarto upon his shoulder lest he unwittingly fling him into the wall of fire before him. Eimar and Tibelde huddled together at Khalon's feet (which, at any other time, Isabel would have found amusing). She dashed another thirty feet, narrowly avoiding getting singed by the fire threatening to separate her from the others. She drew up alongside Khalon, feeling the oppressive heat pressing in.

I must protect us from burning....but how to phrase the spell?

The fire drew closer about them- like a wolf pack circling for the kill. The Shadow Twins prayed to Bloomaya, the mother of nature, for deliverance. Khalon stared hopelessly around him as he watched his former homeland burn to ash. Isabel swiftly arranged the spell words in her mind; then slamming Sarto's staff into the earth, she shouted, "*Cofrath het un numa philans dos aquitane!*" In a surreal moment, a six-inch-thick water sphere grew around Isabel and her company, protruding outward from Sarto's staff. It grew to eight feet in height; with room for Khalon, hers and Sarto's antlers (for they had not the time to remove the spell yet) and grew outward in a radius of six feet. Instantly, each of the huddled companions felt the cool relief from the inferno blazing just beyond their watery shield. The fire drew closer. Within the sphere they could hear the water on the outside of the shield sizzle and evaporate. The sound reminded Isabel of freshly forged steel when Bishop doused it in a vat of cooling water. No one spoke, though everyone's minds raced with thoughts of home, family and friends. Isabel thought briefly, *I'm glad marmie's not here to see me burning down an entire forest. I hope Abel's quest goes better than mine has. But more than anything, I hope this shield does the trick; elsewise, we are dead.*

As though the fire had heard her very thoughts, it circled closer; a mere four feet from the water sphere. At that range, the heat became too much for Isabel's spell strength. The water bubble burst, dousing the company in its dispersed water. Isabel's eyes bugged in mortal fear. She knelt before the gnomes, looking from Tibelde, to Eimar, to Khalon. Isabel wept in a bitter voice, "I am so, *so* sorry my friends......I have doomed us all. Forgive my stupidity."

Eimar and Tibelde hugged Isabel fiercely, muttering, "'Tis alright, Lady. 'Twas a pleasure to travel and serve at your side."

Khalon knelt too, laying Sarto on the earth. Reaching out a tentative hand, he clasped Isabel's shoulder, stating, "You gave me a chance at life I would otherwise not have right now. For that I thank you, Lady Isabel. I'm sure your Master would be proud of you for getting us this far."

Smiling weakly, Isabel grasped the wendygo's claw-tipped hand, replying, "Thank you for saying so Khalon. I cry your pardon for being so harsh with you before. You are more a gentleman than most men of Kalnay. I pray Bloomaya reserves you a special place in paradise, where we may see each other often."

He was genuinely gladdened by Isabel's words, smiling his nightmare smile. "Your pardon is granted my lady. I look forward to our talks in the Nether-Realm."

The fire drew closer, causing the skin on their faces to stretch from the pulsing heat. They grasped each other tightly in a group hug: a Wendygo, two gnomes and two wizards. They waited fearfully for the fire to hungrily consume their flesh. Then, with a great gasping sound, the all-consuming fire surrounding them snuffed suddenly from existence. The group was blown onto their backs as a great wind forced the fire eastward towards the Nevartane, extinguishing it in a great huff. When the gale blew past, the company sat up, gazing about in dumbstruck wonder and curiosity. Khalon, Eimar, and Tibelde looked to Isabel in astonishment, believing this her handiwork. Isabel registered their amazed faces, stating numbly, "This was not *my* doing."

A second later a great light encircled the travelers. A high-pitched tone forced them all to cover their ears in pain. When the noise died and the light dissipated, they were no longer in the fire ravaged domain of Lec'tair Forest. There was a bounty of trees laden in rich green and gold leaves all about them. There was no smell of burning timber. There were, however, tiny green, golden and orange colored dragons perched in the branches around them in the clearing where they dazedly sat.

From behind a tree to their immediate right, appeared the woman Isabel had seen in her dreams: Morgana, The Phantom Queen. "*I* stopped the fire child. 'Tis *wonderful* to finally meet you, Isabel Farthen. I welcome you all to Hesketh."

At that moment Sarto sat bolt upright, leaves in his beard, a dazed look on his face. Looking around like a wonderstruck child, he asked, "What did I miss?"

Chapter Seven: An Unexpected Reunion

Following Nairadj's victory in the circle of honor, Abel learnt many things during the next two weeks marching south with Sigourney's Northerners. He learnt that nightstalkers do not attack if the group is larger than one hundred souls. According to the Wildmen Queen, they prefer picking off their prey like wolves, overwhelming small groups with stealth, speed and sheer numbers. Surprisingly, he learnt Ridley had nearly slain King Alaster; nearly two and a half years into the Northerners military campaign. Abel also learnt that his father, Sir Aldrich, had foiled his attempt to do so. That was when the tide began to turn in favor of the Southerners (as Sigourney called any Kalnayan who dwelt south of the Shavatnu Mountains). The Southerners had been in mid-battle when Sir Aldrich Farthen very publicly saved King Alaster's life and gave her father a very visible scar in the deed. She also informed Abel of the gathering of tribes after her father's death following their defeat at the Crossroad of Kings. She spoke at length of the construction of Volcros. Abel discovered too, that she had a daughter named Branwen. He had not seen her at the throne dais in Volcros' city square. The Princess, he learned, was little over eleven, battling Dragon Fever at home.

"Your majesty," Abel consoled, when she told him. "I am sorry to hear that. Will she be alright?"

Sigourney looked across at him, a strange glint in her eye. "Aye, Master Abel. She is being tended by my Magister, Cort. He will act as my daughter's advisor while I am away to war. A finer man, I could not entrust my daughter's care and education to...." Here she trailed off before asking, "Why would *you* apologize for my daughter's illness? You did not cause her to be sick."

Abel shrugged, "My sister, Isabel, had Dragon Fever when we were six. That is why I went to Marister with my father, Sir Aldrich: we needed to fetch medicines sold only there. My mother....Amina, also feared I might contract the disease myself- as twins can sometimes share the same patterns of health and ailment. She never directly told me of her fear, but I could see it in her eyes. It was frightening, thinking I would lose my twin sister. In retrospect......it seems rather silly now."

Sigourney shook her head gently. "Love for one's family is *never* silly. They are the reason we exist. If I didn't have my daughter, I would *never* have been as ambitious in building Volcros into what it has become."

Abel looked at the Queen in wonder. "You mean....all I have seen in your city: the defenses, the organization...."

She nodded, "All that and *more* have I done for my daughter. I want her to have everything I can give her while I live. If we are successful on this campaign....perhaps she can live in absolute peace and safety, *south* of the Shavatnu Mountains."

"What would become of Volcros, if that happens, my Lady?"

The Wildmen Queen pondered this query a moment, and then shrugged. "Only the gods know for certain. I suspect many of my people may choose to remain in the north."

Abel was surprised at this, "If we win, they would be free to live south of Shavatnu......why would anyone *choose* to stay in the Nightstalker Wastes, with danger all around?"

Sigourney chuckled, "Gods bless your innocence, Master Abel. You see this the wrong way. Instead, see this from *their* point of view. They follow me south, on an uncertain campaign to overthrow a usurper they have *never* met, to free a land they have *never* seen. That is an ideal: *freedom*. However, once the fighting is done, the land is freed, and the ideal is realized, what then drives them? What is their purpose when victory for the ideal has been attained? In the North they are *already* free. In the North lies the *only* home they have ever known, or could be at peace in. As a son of the Five Sisters, do you not feel homesick at times? Do you not secretly wish to return to all you have left behind, somewhere in your heart?"

At the mention of home, Abel remembered Nevar's cruel proclamation before his death: his mother and his step-father, slain mercilessly at the giant's hands. *I have no home now; my father, mother, step-father....*and *Master Pallas.... all dead. My sister Isabel heads east to further her Prezla training. I am truly alone, save for Nairadj.* Abel voiced none of these thoughts to the Queen. Instead he nodded curtly, replying, "Aye, my lady, I do."

She marked his hesitation but did not pursue it. Instead, she continued, "So it will be with many of my people. They fight for me, because I am much like their mother, though I rule over them. Eventually, all children must choose either to explore the world at large or remain close to home. Many will choose to stay in

Volcros, just as others will choose to begin anew in the south, per our accord. Of all the things I have learned as a leader the most important has been this: you must *always* present people a choice. If you do not...."

"....then you become the very evil you seek to defeat....like Malikh, or Lilith," Abel finished.

The Queen cast an impressed look to the young warrior. "You are precisely right, young Abel. *Choice* is what distinguishes a king, or queen, from a tyrant. My father Ridley strove to abide by this; though admittedly he faced more challenges than I. That is his legacy to me: without his attempted uprising to better life for his people, we would *still* be scattered, ignorant tribes fearing frequent attacks by nightstalkers. Choices create a world of difference."

Abel spotted Nairadj, who had scouted ahead with Sigourney's best trackers, galloping towards him. When she drew close enough, she nodded faintly to the Queen, saying, "Pardon me your majesty for the interruption. Might I steal my apprentice for a time?"

Sigourney swept her arm in an open gesture, replying, "Abel '*Drakt'vansh*' is your student Princess Nairadj '*Vaith'vansh*'. Do with him as you see fit." To Abel, she said, "We may talk later, young Master."

Abel nodded, spurring his horse forward. "My thanks, your Grace."

As Nairadj spun her horse about, she nodded again. "My lady."

When they had galloped some distance ahead, Abel glanced to Nairadj, asking, "What is it Master? Is something wrong?"

Staring absently ahead, down the shores of Djintani Lake past the scouts before them, she furrowed her brow, replying, "I am unsure yet, Abel. I detected something at the lake's southern shore. Something I have not encountered in......by the ancestors....I have *quite* forgotten how long since I last encountered it."

With a note of concern, Abel asked, "What is *it*, Master? Is it a monster? Is there another dragon?"

Grunting a repressed laugh, his master mused, "No....no I am afraid this is *worse* than a dragon, Abel."

His stomach knotted uncomfortably. "What's worse than another dragon, Master Nairadj? Pray, tell me."

The Princess cast a look of weariness and sadness, co-mingled, to her pupil. "It is my kin: The Red-Ditch clan of the Djintani Riverlands."

They rode back to inform Sigourney of the dyre bears' presence south of Djintani Lake. Then Nairadj and Abel rode ahead as envoys on behalf of the Wildmen Queen to determine their intentions. As they rode, Abel bombarded his master with questions; questions that by his reckoning, he *required* answers for, before meeting her people. "Master Nairadj, at the risk of impertinence, or outright rudeness, I *need* to know about your past *now.* I can't defend you, if I don't know what I am defending you against....or for."

His master slowed her horse that they may have more time to speak before meeting her people. With a great sigh, she began, "You know now I am the princess....well, *former* princess, of my clan, yes?"

Bluntly, Abel replied, "You *know* I do....though why you waited until we faced the possibility of *death* before I heard about it from strangers, I'm still unclear on."

Nairadj sighed again, snapping, "Abel, I *know* you are upset with me for not telling you sooner. If, however, you're going to *insist* on being childish, I will be unable to proceed."

He sighed, responding submissively, "Apologies, Master. Please, continue."

The she-bear was silent for a long moment, then began. "My mother Yenoor, whom I've mentioned before, is Queen. My father, Ragnar, was king. Borne unto them were myself....and....my elder brother, *Jelani.*"

Abel looked sidelong at his master in surprise but held his tongue. *She has a princeling brother. Wonders never cease....*

Nairadj halted, a lump rising in her throat. "Jelani and I, though he was five years my senior, were *inseparable* as cubs. We went everywhere, did everything, together. We were the happiest cubs that ever were. The fact we were descendants of a bear king was something our young minds did not fathom in those days. As we grew, he became more aware of his future responsibilities both as prince and heir to the throne of the Red-Ditch clan. He grew more sombre in his ways, though he always found time for me. Our skills as hunters, trackers and leaders grew as well. One unfortunate day, our father Ragnar *died*...." Here, she halted, choking back unbidden tears. Abel drew alongside, placing a comforting hand on her forearm. She gripped his hand briefly, continuing "The ironic part was my father died from consuming ill-prepared sea bass. The strongest bear I ever knew....and he succumbed to poorly-cooked *fish*. Sometimes....sometimes I think the ancestors laugh at us when they grow bored......Anyways, our father's death meant Jelani was to become king. Though he prepared for it all his life, he never wanted it: as any great king *should* be. It unnerved him such that, three days before the next full moon, when he would be crowned king, he fled west in solitude, to sort out his thoughts. Being the over-protective little sister....well, I followed him.

"Now, normally, nightstalkers do *not* attack dyre bears. They know instinctually we are a force to be reckoned with. Alas....the same night my brother fled into solitude, he was attacked in desperation by a lone, starving nightstalker. Jelani slew it....but not before being bitten himself......It's ironic really: something *so* trivial holding so much sway over life and death; the same as my mighty father being felled by a tainted fish. As you know any creature bitten but not killed, by a Stalker is cursed to become one. When the prey is deliberately killed to be turned, they are *true* nightstalkers. In Jelani's case, being bitten but not slain, he would have turned into a ghoul. A ghoul has the same hunger for blood as a nightstalker but is mindless, roaming alone to devour flesh, blood and bone of whatever species may cross its path. Never in all my years before that night, had I *ever* heard of a nightstalker biting a dyre bear." Here, she paused again, preparing emotionally for the end of the story.

Abel had a sick feeling he knew how this ended. His heart stirred in grief for his master. *She has borne this pain unspoken, for years. How childish I feel for being so petulant with her about her concealed grief.*

"The next morning," Nairadj resumed tearfully, "I discovered my brother, a mere day's walk from our village of Bishtu. Jelani was still alive. He showed me the bite on his forearm. I told him I would take him to the village healer. Of course, he was already turning and we both knew it. We could smell it on the wound; yet we hoped against hope we could set things right. When night fell that evening, he was racked with pain and our progress halted. By the next evening, just before sunset, we were on the outskirts of Bishtu. However, 'twas also the night of the full moon. As the moon rose, Jelani and I began transforming into our bear forms. When the change was complete, I was horrified to discover my brother had been transformed into a grotesque amalgamation. He had stalker fangs; his eyes had gone a horrid, dead yellow color. He could no longer speak; for nightstalkers have no use for speech......

"I pled with him to regain his senses, but my brother......my cherished Jelani, was gone. He attacked then, trying to kill me and drink my blood. For several minutes, I evaded him, refusing to kill him. I knew if he injured me, I would become as he: a ghoul. When I could no longer avoid him, we fought. The battle was swift. I managed to get behind him, plunging my claws through his back, ripping out his heart." Here, she paused for a long moment, reluctant to revisit such a painful moment in her life.

"I stood over him, his *heart* in my right paw. Jelani shrank back to his human form. Though it should have been impossible, I....I heard him whisper, '*Thank you for saving me, sister. I go to join father now.*' Then my brother....my closest friend *died*, passing into the realm of the ancestors. The grief was unbearable, and I howled my pain loud and long into the night. Presently, several of the village sentinels arrived, hearing my cries. They beheld Jelani, dead, face-down on the ground in human form, with his heart in my paw. The sentinels assumed treachery, attempting to subdue me. In my grief, I fled; fearing death for the wrongly perceived murder of my brother. From *that* moment, I became an exile. I fled for weeks, running as far, and as fast, as I could: from my grief, and the fear of persecution. It was not until I reached the southern sand flats that I finally felt I had run far enough, settling there in isolation. Now you know the *whole* truth, young cub."

Tears clouded both Abel and Nairadj's eyes, as they drew closer to the encamped bear clan. Wiping tears from his eyes, Abel reached over, taking Nairadj's right hand in his left. He brought her hand up to his lips, kissing it once, deeply. "My Lady....*Princess* Nairadj, I mean....I am so *terribly* sorry for your loss. I know better than most the pain of loss....I cannot imagine losing Isabel; or having to personally deliver her to the Nether-Realm. Thank you for sharing this with me. I swear, as a warrior of the Light, your student, friend and companion, I will *never* betray your confidence in this matter." Looking ahead, to the bear encampment, he concluded, "I promise you, my Princess, to stand by your side, whatever may befall us here. You are *innocent* of murder. What you did for Jelani was *mercy*; even he knew that. You hold your head high when we enter the camp."

Squeezing his hand in return, Nairadj wiped her tears with her left hand. "My *deepest* thanks to you....*Hamish*. You are *indeed* mature beyond your years, as Master Pallas knew. As *I* know. Fear not; I *shall* hold my head high. I have had years to reflect on that fateful night. Uttering the words aloud....sharing with another, has purged me of the guilt gnawing on my conscience for *so* long. Thank you, ever so much." Then, they drew themselves upright in their saddles, spurring their horses on towards the dyre bears camp.

You could hear a stone drop in the silence enveloping Nairadj and Abel as they rode into the camp. Abel and Nairadj unsheathed their swords, holding them horizontally in the air with both hands in a gesture of peace. The further they rode into the encampment, the more they noticed a new sound: a wave of rising murmurs. By the time they reached the camp's center, the whole area sounded like a large hive of bees. At the center of the camp Nairadj dismounted her horse; Abel followed suit. She thrust her sword, blade first, into the hardpan at her feet, raising her arms again; Abel did likewise. She spun a slow, deliberate circle, declaring in a loud voice, "I am Nairadj: former princess of the Red-Ditch clan; daughter of King Ragnar and Queen Yenoor; sister to Prince Jelani! I am here as emissary to Sigourney, Queen of the Nightstalker Wastes. She marches south to challenge the usurper of Kalnay, the Overlord Malikh. We desire *no* conflict with the bear folk, and humbly request passage to the Drake's Maw Pass."

The murmuring ceased when Nairadj began speaking, the crowd listening intently to her words. When she finished, the crowd parted and there approached a column of twelve, armed guards. Abel glanced questioningly at his master, casting his eyes briefly to their swords. She shook her head faintly, watching the guards' approach, mentally preparing for whatever may come next. As the troops drew into the center of the camp, they fanned out in a circle, creating a barricade twixt the crowd and the two warriors. From where the crowd had parted, emerged a thirteenth figure.

Abel watched tensely as this lanky, cloaked figure slowly approached Nairadj. The cloak was rough red linen, bejeweled with a line of emeralds along the hood's hem. The wearer's face was shrouded by the hood; yet Nairadj sucked in a shaky breath, stemming a flood of tears threatening to burst forth. Abel looked measuredly from Nairadj to the shrouded figure, realizing: *Lady Nairadj* knows *this person.* The wearer drew the hood down. Young Farthen had to stifle an audible gasp. The figure beneath the hood was a spitting image of his master; but with more lines about her face, and short kempt, gray hair. The emerald eyes and lanky stature were the same, though the elder version of Nairadj was slightly stooped. *Gods above, this is Nairadj's mother, Queen Yenoor!* Realizing he still stood, while the entire crowd had knelt, Abel swiftly took a knee.

Daughter and mother stood in silence a long moment, both on the verge of tears. Nairadj lowered her head, dropped to her knees, grabbing her mother's hand and kissing it fiercely. "*Madriga*," she fumbled through thick tears, "I return to you to answer for Jelani's death. I did *not* kill him out of spite or jealousy......but 'twas still *my* hand that stole his life. I accept whatever punishment...."

The Queen dropped to her knees before her long-lost daughter, tears welling in her own eyes. With a firm hand, she elevated Nairadj's downcast face to gaze into her own. With her other hand, she stroked her daughter's face before whispering, "My daughter....my beautiful, *radiant* Nairadj, there is *no* need to explain. I, and all bear kind, know your innocence. I smelt the turgid scent of nightstalker on your brother's body the night we discovered him; but you had already fled. I wept hard that night, and *many* more nights after. My husband perished. A nightstalker stole my only son from me. Finally, a misunderstanding robbed me of my daughter; all in one fell swoop. I prayed and pleaded for the ancestors to restore you to me; never once did they answer. Then, three weeks back, one of our hunters caught your scent here by the lake. I fervently hoped you would return this way, and so you *have*. Oh, my *precious* Nairadj, your return greatly gladdens my heart. Now arise, beloved daughter. Be restored unto your people." Saying thus, the Queen arose, her emerald eyes brimming with tears of joy. Yenoor boomed joyously to the assembly, "*Behold*, my people! The lost princess of the Red-Ditch clan, Nairadj White-Fur, has returned at long last! Let the celebration commence! Have the finest mead filling our cups! The richest cuts of meat prepared in honor of my daughter's return!"

There arose from the bear-people a roar so great and glad, Abel forgot temporarily about their quest. He couldn't stifle the tears of joy welling in his eyes at the unexpected jubilation erupting around him. Seeing Nairadj reunited with her mother also stung his heart, causing his tears to turn bitterly painful as he reflected again on the loss of his own mother, Amina. *Sometimes the gods seem cruel,* Abel thought, mourning his lost mother anew. *Then again, the gods also restore joy from time to time.* Sheathing his sword, Abel busied himself with assisting the festivity preparations.

By nightfall, Sigourney's forces reached the dyre bears' camp, pitched their tents, joining in the celebration of the restored Princess Nairadj. The feast turned into a dual celebration, for the dyre bears willingly agreed to fight alongside Sigourney's forces against Malikh and Lilith.

As Abel observed Nairadj joyfully feasting, drinking and laughing across the fire beside her mother and people, he reflected silently on his feelings for her. *Can I even think of her romantically now? She is a dyre bear, my master, and now a princess, restored to her people. Who am I but a son of the sea, raised as a fisherman, and revealed as a warrior of the Light?* Surely *there will be suitors amongst her people; better matches with more to offer than I. Still,* he thought to himself, downing a pint of mead, *I cannot deny that I love her. I have loved her from that first night on the sand flats where she rescued us from the sea wulf, transforming before my eyes. She is unlike any woman I have known or heard tell of.......bah! Enough with these foolish thoughts. We have quite a way to go yet. Who knows if we'll even* survive *to ponder the notion of romance?* With that, Abel rose shakily (for the mead was wreaking havoc on his balance), stumbled alone to his tent and fell fast asleep. He found himself dreamily thinking of Nairadj: the beauty of her milky white skin in the full moonlight, the beautiful curves of her silhouette, and the intense beauty of her piercing emerald eyes. His sleep-fogged mind turned to his and Nairadj's shared triumph over Ulgnar the Grey. He dreamily anticipated the vengeance to soon be meted out upon Malikh and Lilith when they marched on the gates of Regalias, changing everything in Kalnay forever. After a time, he slipped deeper into a dreamless rest, wondering passingly what other challenges would mark their path.

Chapter Eight: Matters of Urgency

Regalias was closer to Lec'tair Forest than anyone cared to admit; Master Scribe Clarke included. So, the morning the forest erupted into flames from within, Clarke was extremely worried. He hurried to the top of the eastern ramparts. Huffing and groaning, he felt his age in the joints of his aching knees and the burning sensation in his lungs. While he hurried, his mind raced with a plethora of questions. How *did the forest catch fire? Is there not a dark magic shielding the forest from such things? Has something dire occurred within those cursed woods? Are the gods raining final judgment upon the wendygos? Where will they go, without Lec'tair Forest for shelter? What of the simple folk in the towns along the Inaratu River?*

When he burst through the door at the top of the rampart, he nearly collided with one of Overlord Malikh's Red Guards, dashing for the stairs. The guard was a scruffy, middle-aged captain with a dirt-stained jerkin, grubby black trousers, a spear, a shield, and a sheathed sword on his hip. Both his and the Master Scribe's reflexes were quite good, and they ground to a halt before coming to injury.

"What is it, Captain," Clarke queried. "Why do you flee?"

The captain responded gruffly, "In case you hadn't noticed, Master Scribe, Lec'tair Forest is *burning*! Wendygos flood from the woods like rats deserting a sinking ship! I must inform the Overlord. We need men out there to defend the people of the Riverland villages. I have family in Pankirsh, and I'll be thrice gods' damned if

I'm going to let them become wendygo nourishment. Now, step aside." With a rough shove, the Captain barged past, hurrying down the steps to the throne room.

Clarke grew more concerned. *I suppose I had better see this for myself.* With a souring stomach, he scales the steps to the lookout spot on the rampart, gazing east. Cold fear grips the old man's heart as his eyes fall on the terrifying spectacle to the east. White hot swaths of fire sweep through the heart of the forest to the southeast. The fire burns *outwards* in a circular pattern; as if some fiery stone had been dropped in a sea of woods, rippling outward in a hungry, flaming wave. *There is* surely *magic involved, or I am not the Master Scribe.* Though they were leagues from the blaze, he could make out a thick stream of silvery-black dots emerging from the tree line. Clarke's mind raced in mounting horror as he realized what those dots were. *Gods be gracious, the wendygos are being burnt out! The captain was right. I must inform the Overlord immediately.*

The elderly Scribe turns to descend the eastern tower's spiral staircase, when a gale sweeps up suddenly with thunderous noise. The gale strikes him as odd; there is no rain or lightning (which usually accompanies such gale force winds). In addition, it *only* blows through Lec'tair Forest. As quickly as the gust arrives, it vanishes east toward the Nevartane. The fires raging through Lec'tair Forest are snuffed out in a heartbeat. Had Clarke not witnessed it himself, he may not have believed it. *This is devilry, this wind. These events* reek *of magic. I cannot decide which is more terrifying: that somewhere in Lec'tair Forest is a Prezla strong enough to raze a forest; or that another Prezla has the power to snuff a firestorm with a single spell....or is it the work of the* same *Prezla? In any case, this news bodes ill for the realm.*

As if to punctuate his ruminations, further south from where the suppressed fire originated, there arose a pillar of blinding white light. A high-pitched tone accompanies the flash, forcing Clarke to cover his ears with a wince. A moment later, the light vanishes, and the pitch ceases. He marks no obvious changes in the landscape- aside from the newly charred southern region of Lec'tair Forest- yet the Master Scribe feels a difference in the air. *Something great and terrifying has transpired......though* what, *I cannot say.*

Clutching absently at the pendant of his patron god, K'colrehs, the god of wisdom and reason, Clarke prays in his head. *O merciful Godrich All-father, hear my prayer: cast your protective hand over this land. Keep a watchful eye on the Prezla who have spurred these events onward. In your wisdom, judge them for the deeds done against this realm. To you I also pray, K'colrehs: guide my words and thoughts as I advise Overlord Malikh on the best course of action. Finally, merciful and kind Bronwyn-Aetha and Jutlann: protect the citizenry and children of the Riverlands in the face of the emerging wendygo threat.* Finishing his prayer, the old man rushes down the tower steps as fast as his age permits, to recount what he has witnessed.

Despite his zealous attitude, the Master Scribe *was* getting older; that was something he could no longer deny. When he reached the bottom of the tower stairs, he rested. *Gods preserve me, I miss my youth.* After catching his breath, he hurried to the throne room at a more measured pace. Drawing into the courtyard outside the throne room, he observed the Captain he encountered on the wall briskly leaving, closing the doors behind him. The Scribe noticed him summon the two guards stationed outside the throne room to follow. Clarke wondered if the problem with the wendygos was more serious than he first suspected. He was about to enter the throne room, cracking the door open to announce himself. Until he heard Malikh shout, "Gods above, why do you *hate* me so!?"

Clarke froze. *Should I enter with his lordship in such a state? No, I will wait and listen. If his mood sours further, I will withdraw and wait awhile.* So, he stands there silently, his ear cocked to the crack in the door, and he listens.

"I abandon Ackreth on *Lilith's* freckaying advice! I gain a throne within weeks of landing here! We take Regalias in a *day*, with *no* loss of life to my men! I *finally* obtain what is owed to me: my destined kingdom! First, she says, I must kill King Alaster, his queen and their brood. Lilith......always *Lilith* whispering in my ear: 'You *must end the lives of the royal family.*' I take up my sword, setting to task. One by one, they perish beneath *my* blade...." Malikh pauses then.

The Scribe holds his breath, not daring to move. Within the throne room comes a great crash. Malikh roars in frustration, "Until....*until* I get to the youngest....Until I get to little Arya...."

Clarke covers his mouth with his left hand, stifling the gasp threatening to escape his lips. *Gods above, what is this about Princess Arya? Perhaps Lord*

Malikh is unwell. The Master Scribe listens more intently.

A moment later, Malikh resumes his musings, his voice sounding choked. "I get to Princess Arya....my sword poised *inches* above her tiny chest....and I *freeze.* I've slaughtered her entire family: mother, father, two older sisters, and yet....my hand is stayed by the stare of a tiny, blue-eyed infant....as if her eyes pierced my very *soul.* Her sapphire blue eyes.... *so* much like my sweet *Helena*...." Here, another pause; longer than the one before.

The Master Scribe wonders what is happening within the throne room. As he listens, his mind races in confusion. *Merciful gods above, is Arya....the Princess* Adelaide*?*

Then the Overlord speaks again, his voice tinged with sorrow. "*Helena*....my lovely, *wonderful* daughter....I plead your forgiveness for abandoning you. *Gods*! *Why* must I remember?! I spared Arya, took her as my daughter in atonement for abandoning Helena! Is that not recompense enough?!"

Clarke's mind reels at this revelation. Suddenly, Malikh's sword pierces the door a foot to the left of his head; for he'd hurled it in rage over his ruminations. The stunned Scribe is caught off guard as the door slams shut from the force of the Overlord's throw. He is struck in the head by the closing door, tumbling hard to the ground. He knows there are mere moments before Malikh discovers him spying. If that happens, he deigns think what may befall him. With a limberness that surprises himself, he rolls to one knee, rising quickly to his feet. He adjusts his leather truss forward, covering the mottled bruise on his forehead. Clarke hastens his breathing to falsely seem like he had just run some distance.

Seconds later, Malikh yanks his sword free, flinging the door open inward. His eyes are wild and suspicious as he observes Clarke's bent frame, huffing and puffing, before him. The Overlord flits his eyes about the courtyard, searching. "Master Clarke," Malikh begins cautiously, "how long have you been there?"

Carefully now, Clarke thinks. Heaving another exaggerated breath, he bows, sputtering, "I have just arrived, my lord. I come with news of wendygos and the fire in Lec'tair Forest."

Malikh stares harder, searching for lies in Clarke's face. "You are rather late with that news, Master Scribe. Captain Cillian of the Red Guard has been and gone awhile now. He is marching a legion of Red Guards upon the beasts, even as we speak. What took you so long to bring word of this....*aged* news?"

Use your age; play the doddering old man. The Master Scribe hunches, favoring his usually sore right knee (though it did not hurt presently). "My deepest apologies, Lord Malikh for my untimely arrival; at my age, speed is not my ally. Particularly, when traversing the eastern tower." Upon hearing this, Malikh's stern, distrusting expression softened. *Now,* Clarke thought, *distract his attentions.* "Did the captain mention the blaze was tamped shortly after erupting, my lord?"

Malikh's piercing gaze was replaced by surprise and curiosity. "*How*, Master Scribe, was the fire extinguished?"

Clarke stared levelly at Malikh, answering, "With *magic*, my lord. A great gale arose which snuffed the fire like one blowing out a candle. I believe magic started the blaze as well, though I know not why."

Malikh's eyes widened. *Magic*, his mind roared. *A gale* snuffed the fire?! Unbidden, Malikh's mind returned to the storm which destroyed several of his ships while crossing the Chakti from Ackreth. He recalled vividly his suspicion of magical treachery obstructing him from his destiny. *Gods'* damn *this mysterious Prezla! The point of hunting down all Prezla, was to* remove *obstacles such as this....master of winds. This same person* must *have tried sinking my fleet! This Prezla should be enslaved in my dungeons; working on my vision from the gods! The* impudence *of this Prezla, defying my will!*

Though Malikh spoke nothing aloud, the Scribe noted his eyes swirled with rage. He knew he was safe from discovery of spying. Aloud, Clarke ventured, "Shall we send a scouting party to investigate the fire's origin, my lord?"

Malikh's swirling eyes calmed as he regained focus. With a dismissive wave of his hand, the Overlord whirled away. "*No!* That would mean entering Lec'tair. I will *not* risk lives needlessly. We must protect the people of the Riverlands; Cillian and Markus have that in hand. No....I will inform Queen Lilith. *She* will investigate the forest with her Ravensight later."

The old man bowed to Malikh, replying, "As you say, my liege, so it shall be." He turned to leave. Before he had taken two steps, Malikh spoke flatly, "Master Clarke."

He froze in place, his heart thundering in his chest. *Be calm. He knows naught.* Clarke turns slowly, favoring his right knee. *Keep up appearances, old chap.* "Yes, mi' lord," Clarke calmly replies, "what would you have of me?"

Malikh stared at him impassively, declaring, "Next time you have *urgent* news, be it forest fires or wendygos, send a raven: the news may *actually* reach me in a timely fashion. Am I understood?"

Clarke bowed deeply, rose, touching his forehead and lips in the traditional fashion. "Of *course*, your lordship; I cry your pardon again for my delayed arrival."

Issuing a skeptical grunt, Malikh said, "That will *do*, Master Scribe. You may go now."

Bowing again, Clarke turned, hurrying off (with his exaggerated limp) for his study in the western keeps.

Jabesh was protected by Clarke's position as Master Scribe and considered his manservant. He wasn't noticed often by anyone in the castle; part of that could be attributed to some subtle magic as a Prezla and a Name Diviner. When Clarke rushed into the overcrowded study in the western keep, he found his friend nose down in a dusty tome: *Wondrous Fables of the Bold Sir Brock Clegane.* Despite Clarke's pressing news, it always brought him joy to see Jabesh relaxing with a book. He usually chose more serious literature during his tutoring with Adelaide. Clumsily knocking over a haphazard stack of history volumes with a thud, the Master Scribe slams the weighty door, locking it with a skeleton key strung about his neck, alongside his pendant of K'colrehs. Looking up from his book of tales, Jabesh asked, "What is it, old friend? You look....*disheveled*."

Once the door was locked, Clarke leaned hard against it; as if bracing the door against a giant. Jabesh set aside his book, rising swiftly to his feet and resting a gentle hand on the elder man's shoulder. "Clarke speak to me. What is it? What has you so stirred up?" He noticed something peculiar in his friend's countenance: the old man didn't appear frightened. If anything, he seemed oddly overjoyed.

Grasping his friend in a relieved hug, Clarke whispered, "The gods are *good*, dear Jabesh; *very* good indeed. The Princess Arya *lives*. She walks among us."

Jabesh searched the old scribe's face for any trace of madness, or cruel jest. There was none. Unbidden, tears sprang to his eyes as he asked, "How came you by this information, my friend?"

"From the *mouth* of the Overlord, I heard this." Quickly, he recounted the events which found him unattended outside the throne room, as Malikh raved to himself.

Jabesh's eyes were radiant with joy. "This is too much to hope for....the daughter of my former liege....*alive!* I have been her tutor for *years* and did not know her!" The diviner clapped his hands over his mouth to stifle overjoyed laughter threatening to burst from his lips.

Clarke patted Jabesh firmly on the shoulder, digging his fingers in slightly as he stated, "Now that *we* know, we are in *danger*; the *princess* too. If Lilith or the Overlord suspects we know, they may kill us."

Jabesh asks in shock, "You can't think they would harm Arya....*Adelaide*, I mean....could you?"

Clarke scratches his stubbly chin in deep, irritated motions. "I can't say for certain. I would ask you this in return, old friend: would Malikh's affection for the girl stay *Lilith's* hand against Adelaide, if she felt *threatened* by the Princess' presence?"

Jabesh's whirling mind saw scenario after scenario of what Lilith may do if she discovered they knew the truth. He conceded Clarke's point with a troubled sigh. "What do we do then? We cannot keep this to ourselves. 'Tis too crucial to hide."

Clarke had already considered this on his hurried return. Grinning like a mischievous child, he replied slyly, "We are *not* keeping this to ourselves. We will let all Kalnay know that the young Princess Arya lives; but we shall announce it discreetly."

Knowledge dawned on Jabesh as he saw the plan unfolding. "You mean for us to pass the word via the Name Diviners, don't you?"

"*Aye* Jabesh, I do; before Malikh and Lilith know it, there will be a *different* fire for them to fear: a fire of rebellion....of uprising."

Jabesh queried, "Where do we begin, my friend?"

"First, we get word to the diviners; have them stoke fire in the hearts of the populace. Then we plot our escape with Arya. When the time is right, remove the Princess from her gilded prison here in Regalias."

They clasped hands in accord. Then Jabesh stated, "I shall send word *immediately*. My brothers and sisters will be *eager* to aid in this endeavor. Draw the curtains; I require darkness and stillness to focus." Finding a clear spot on the study floor, the Diviner prepared for the journey his mind was about to take. Clarke hurriedly shut the curtains, plunging the room into darkness. Having done so, he silently took a seat, producing a loaf of bread and a skin of mead from one of his desk drawers; leaving them ready for Jabesh once he finished sending word. Enveloped in darkness, Jabesh tilted his head back, drawing on the magic of the secret, shared mind link twixt diviners. He sent word to Cheyanne, Diviner of Albion and, with that, word of the lost princess Arya began spreading silently and swiftly throughout Kalnay.

Chapter Nine: The Shadow Wood

The instant Sarto and his friends appeared in Hesketh, they all felt sick to their stomachs. This was a side effect of the transportation spell Morgana employed to rescue them from Lec'tair Forest and bring them swiftly to Hesketh. Though none mentioned how they ill they felt, they all certainly looked it.

After presenting herself to the group, Morgana informed them, "Regrettably, I am not here in body, my honored guests. I am a simple astral projection, here to welcome you to my realm of Messara. I have sent my eldest daughter, Ezri, to escort you all to Castle Endelheim. Once you arrive and settle in, we will begin your training, Lady Isabel." To the rest of the company, she added, "The rest of you may relax safely within Endelheim's walls, for you have traveled long and far to get here. I look forward to meeting you all in person soon." Then, without warning, her projection vanished.

For a moment, no one moved or spoke. Nothing could be heard but the reptilian rustling of tiny dragons' wings and the tree leaves whistling in the breeze. They were all still quite dumbfounded by the events that transpired of late: their escape from Hann'Lec; their near immolation in Lec'tair Forest; their unexpected and swift arrival in Hesketh. Sarto was first to break the silence. "Well, whether her daughter is coming or not, we should move. I am not sure about the rest of you, but I couldn't *possibly* sit, waiting for a journey's end to come to me." Rising wearily to his feet and brushing himself off, Sarto grabbed his staff and rucksack. Casually, he asked the fatigued company, "Shall we go then?" Without awaiting an answer, he turned east and began walking. The others glanced briefly at one another, seeing naught but deep-seated weariness and an unspoken desire to finish this trek. Wordlessly, the others hurried to their feet, gathered their sparse belongings and dashed to catch up to the aged wizard.

Shortly after re-embarking, the company found a sparkling, clear brook. Sarto and Isabel washed themselves clean of the wendygo scent they had smeared on themselves prior to escaping. Once they were clean, Sarto used a reversal spell, removing the antlers Isabel had grafted to their skulls. Both hollered in pain as the grafted antlers detached from their skulls. The ruckus caused a group of nearby miniature dragons to launch up through the sunlit canopy in fright. By now, the company seemed happier, more at ease, as they finally grasped that they had utterly escaped the wendygos and the unnatural forest fire. The travelers moved at a leisurely pace, enjoying the lush scenery, watching with rapt interest as the tiny green, orange and golden dragons glided care-free twixt the trees about them. At one point, the Shadow Twins gathered some apples hanging from a particularly aged tree.

As Isabel bit into the sweet flesh of the maroon red apple, she wondered aloud, "Does anyone know the name of this particular apple? It's the best I've *ever* tasted."

Eimar took a bite of his apple, rolling it around in his mouth, mulling the palette of this unknown fruit. After a moment he paused, looked her in the face and stated, "Lady Isabel.... I do not know this apple's taste either. Highly unusual, for I can determine a fruit or vegetable's name by a single taste; right down to the orchard or garden it came from. In this case, all I can determine is that it grows exclusively within the borders of Hesketh."

Tibelde punched Eimar hard in the shoulder, snatching his apple at the same time. Chomping off a sizeable bite, she spoke around the apple chunk in her mouth, "Such a *braggart*, brother. If you're trying to impress her, it's *not* working."

Nursing his already bruised shoulder, he snapped, "Very well sister of mine. If you're so smart what kind is it then? Pray tell, how many apples have maroon skin and *golden* insides?"

Tibelde glanced at it, noting the peculiar golden flesh. Curious, she bit the apple again; rolling the chunk of golden apple around on her tongue, searching for its history. In another minute, she still looked as flummoxed as Eimar had. "Well," she mused whimsically, "isn't that a peculiar thing?" She turned dreamily to Khalon, offering him the half-eaten apple. "Try this and tell me what you think, flesh-eater."

The young buck sniffed the apple, shaking his head with a chuffing noise. "Lady Tibelde, regrettably I *cannot* eat it. Wendygos are cursed to hate the fruits of the earth." Though it pained him to do so, he took the apple firmly in his grasp, adding, "Nor *would* I eat it, my friend. I scent *bad* magic on this fruit."

Sarto shot a curious look at the fruit clutched in Khalon's right hand; noting his hand sizzling gently like a side of beef on a skillet where the golden fruit touched his greyish skin. He plucked it from Khalon with a rag; cautious to avoid touching the apple's skin or flesh. Pointing his staff at the partially consumed apple, the

Prezla intoned, "*Iluminus mor identum*." The spell used should have permitted him to identify the apple's origins, ending the mystery.

Instead, the apple audibly screeched, emanating a wave of silvery grey light from within itself. Then it launched from the wizard's grasp into the nearest tree, destroying itself wholly. Sarto was knocked painfully onto his backside. He saw stars and heard ringing in his ears from the apple's high-pitched screech. Regaining his senses, he couldn't believe what he beheld. Khalon was dodging knife jabs from Tibelde. The lady gnome had drawn her knife, furiously and inexplicably slashing at the wendygo buck. She was screaming, "Filthy *flesh-eater*! Steal *my* apple will you!? Let me show you how we deal with monsters in Othros!"

Eimar evaded Isabel's loop-handled knives as she flung them. Between each fling, she bellowed, "I will *nary* be your bride, vile imp! If *that* is why you came on this quest, you had best leave, lest my knives find you!"

Sarto realized with shock what was happening. A whisper of a memory focused keenly in his mind.... *He is in Casteray, on the northern bank of the Quorontis River. A young man is infected with a strange madness. He tried killing his father for supposed infidelity with a young woman at the Red House in Casteray. The boy's mother discovered the lad had eaten a peculiar apple, plucked from the borders of Hesketh. Consuming it incited the murderous and accusatory behavior- for his father and mother both declared him innocent of any suspected unfaithfulness.*

In a flash, the wizened wizard recalled the spell to end the madness gripping his comrades. Slamming his staff into the earth, Sarto shouted authoritatively, "*Etsa mor glatza furiosa, het philans!*" From where he struck his staff into the earth, there emanated a bright white, thick ring of light rippling outward. As soon as the light touched them, the quarreling companions ceased fighting; dropping their weapons in terror, as though the blades were responsible for the madness. Tibelde, Eimar and Isabel stared in horror at each other. Tibelde glanced ashamedly at Khalon. Finally, they all gazed dumbstruck at Sarto for an explanation.

Leaning upon his staff- for the spell required much energy- he explained, "You three were the unwitting victims of something I have only encountered once before in my life as Sarto the Mender. The condition is termed the '*Golden Madness*'. It causes anyone consuming these apples to fall prey to hallucinations of enmity and suspicion; even among friends. If it is not cured early, the person afflicted may fall to permanent madness and develop a *nasty* murderous streak. Thankfully, the gods were with me. I recalled my previous encounter with this affliction and the spell to undo it."

Kneeling before Sarto, Tibelde, Eimar and Isabel each offered their personal thanks for his quick reaction. Tibelde turned to Khalon- placing her hand on her forehead and lips, as was tradition- and wept, "I cry your deepest, *sincerest* pardons, young Khalon. I hope you can forgive my ill behaviour just now. You have been an uncommon help and friend since our meeting in Hann'Lec. Please know I *truly* bear you no ill will."

Bending to take the gnome's hand, Khalon answered, "You have *naught* to cry pardon for, Lady Tibelde. You were not yourself, and we both know it.

Still, if it will ease your mind, I accept your offered apology, as my friend and ally." Saying thus, he helped her to her feet.

From behind a tree on their right, came a lilting but firm voice. "Now *that* is something one does not see every day: a wendygo aiding a gnome. I *must* tell my sisters of this. They will scarcely believe it."

Everyone in the company wheeled to the right, weapons and skills at the ready. None were prepared for the beauty that gazed curiously at them. Before them stood a tall, young woman of five and twenty with waist-length, raven black hair. Her skin was porcelain white, which drew focus to her radiant hair and shining brown eyes. She watched them amusedly, like they were children at play. If she was shocked by Khalon's presence, she concealed it well. The young lady curtsied deeply, greeting them properly.

"Welcome all. I am Ezri, eldest of the Five Daughters of Morgana the White, Queen of Endelheim, guardian of Messara. Welcome to you, Sarto and Isabel of Gwenovair: long have my mother, my sisters and I desired to meet you. I am glad the honor of first meetings is mine to cherish. Welcome unto you, '*Un Riveth Duallis*': 'tis an honor to meet such valiant protectors from legendary Othros. Whatever resources and pleasures we have in Endelheim, we are glad to share with you all." Settling her eye on Khalon, she queried, "I am afraid I do not know your name, Master Wendygo. Pray tell, what title do you go by?"

Khalon bowed to her, responding, "Lady Ezri, 'tis a pleasure to meet you. Thank you for granting me passage. I know wendygos are not traditionally permitted beyond the bounds of Lec'tair Forest. They call me Khalon in Hann'Lec, where I was raised after my....*conversion*. If I may be of service, you have but to ask."

Ezri nodded. "Thank you for your generosity, Master Khalon. You are rather an *odd* wendygo, if I may say so."

"You may indeed, Lady Ezri. My parents never ceased reminding me of my odd nature as a child....*before* I became a wendygo."

A surprised look drew across Ezri's face. She laughed aloud, covering her mouth as she did so. "I cry your pardon, Master Khalon. I am not laughing at *you*. I just....I was taught wendygos were mindless, flesh-eating *brutes*. Clearly, I was misinformed; you are quite the witty young buck."

Shrugging, Khalon responded, "There is *much* wrong with the world around us. I, for my part, strive to set a different example from my......*kind*. To show the world we are not all 'mindless, flesh-eating brutes', as you say."

"Interesting...." Ezri mused. Turning to Sarto, she declared, "You have assembled *quite* the diverse party on your journey Master Wizard. You *must* tell me and my sisters of it when we reach Endelheim."

Bowing faintly, Sarto replied, "I would be happy to regale your sisters and mother of our travels once we reach Endelheim, Lady Ezri. And please, just call me Sarto. I am not your master, and openly being a Prezla is a dangerous path to tread, as I am sure you are aware."

Ezri nodded, deferentially. "Of course, Sarto. Being a Prezla myself, I understand the risks of publicly revealing our powers." Then she turned, calling, "Let us be off then. The castle is a half days' walk to the east. If we hurry, we may make it home in time for supper. I am told our cook, Eben, is preparing quite the feast in honor of your arrival." An unspoken ripple of hunger ran through the weary travelers as they followed her eastwards.

Sarto inquired, "How did you know where we would be, Lady Ezri? For that matter, how did you know to be here so soon after our arrival?"

In a coy voice, she called over her shoulder, "My sisters and I share a mental bond with our mother, Morgana the White. She has marked your progress through dreams and the mental link with Lady Isabel."

Sarto nodded to himself, rolling her words around in his mind. "So....the *link* is how Morgana knew Isabel was in danger in Lec'tair Forest, then?"

Nodding, Ezri called back, "That would be correct, Sarto. Now, let us save our breath for the journey onward. You must be tired. We don't want you passing out before reaching Endelheim."

Behind Sarto, Isabel chuckled at Ezri's words. "She has a point, Master. We don't want Khalon have to carry you all the way to Endelheim." At this, the company burst into weary laughter. Shortly, they emerged from the eastern edge of Hesketh, gazing across the massive, green fields of Messara towards the distant castle of Endelheim. To himself, Sarto thought, *Gods be praised. We are almost to safety.*

Then, over his shoulder, he heard a faint whisper. *Sarto my friend, can you hear me?*

An odd mix of fear and relief touched the Prezla's aching, ancient heart. *Pallas, my old friend, is that you?*

Chapter Ten: Antlers and Steel

Cillian didn't have time to burden himself with stragglers. The first hundred ready men-at-arms were whipped into formation and marched double time to Pankirsh to protect the villagers who were, even now, in danger from the invading wendygos. Before marching, he sent a messenger boy to notify General Markus of the wendygos attack on the Riverlands. He quickly presented his troops the news, including their destination and what to do when they arrived there. "If it's got antlers and isn't human, you are to kill it where it stands, or die trying. Watch the claws and antlers: those are their primary weapons. If you're unfortunate enough to be gored or slashed by one these monsters, do yourselves a favor: cut your own throat. It's better than becoming a living meal to those bastards; or worse, being turned into one yourself. Any questions?" There were none; only looks of determination co-mingled with fear on the legions' faces. "That's what I like to see," Cillian stated. "Move out men. Pray the gods smile on us in battle."

The Captain's words had sufficiently roused his men's spirits. Before noon they reached the outskirts of Pankirsh. Had they judged the village's well-being on mere appearances, Pankirsh *appeared* fine. Then they heard the blood-curdling battle cries of the wendygos: the eerie growls and bellows of men mixed with bucks, elk and caribou. Cillian ordered a halt, listening intently before turning to his men. "We march for town square! Close ranks, weapons at the ready! Watch our flanks for ambush and press forward! Now, march!"

The legion marched unopposed through the mud and cobblestone streets towards the square. Every so often, they passed a dead wendygo in the street; impaled through the heart with a pitchfork or shot through the eye with an arrow. Though the sight of these monstrosities was repellant to some of the men, it brought the captain a modicum of relief. *Pankirsh does not wish to lie down and die, gods be praised. I only hope my wife and children are still safe.*

In another couple minutes, the legion entered the square. Merchants' booths were overturned and smashed; wares scattered about, broken or trampled. A handful of locals lay about the square; blood pooling around their dead, mangled bodies. The sight of the dead villagers stirred Cillian's blood hot with rage. He was somewhat heartened to see several more dead wendygos; but this didn't hold his attention long. What drew he and his men's attention were the six dozen or so wendygos swarming about the temple of Bloomaya; braying and bellowing in their demonic animal tongue.

The townsfolk must be within. That's smart: wendygos can't enter the temple, because of the goddess's curse. Bloomaya, please keep Amelia, Samuel and Elizabeth safe. Then he turned his attention to his men. "Let's make it clear to these demons now and *forever* that they are unwelcome here! Forward to victory! May the gods protect you all!"

With a collective roar, Cillian and his legion charged the wendygos. The beasts had marked the humans' arrival and were already past the large fountain in the center of the square before the legion crossed a quarter of that distance. The captain brought his oak shield up on his left, his broadsword ready in his right hand. In another moment, the legion closed with the charging band of wendygos. Chaos erupted as antlers and steel clashed in a fantastic cacophony of noise and fury.

As the Red Guards charged the wendygo horde, Cillian's lieutenant, Roland, thought eagerly, *I've been waiting for a battle like this.* He was one of the few children permitted to cross the Chakti with Malikh's forces. His father was Ivar the Furious: one of Malikh's mightiest warriors in Ackreth. With Roland's mother dead- for she had passed to the Nether-Realm giving birth to him- and his father departing with Malikh, an exception permitted the boy to remain with his father. Once Regalias was taken, Ivar traveled to Igraine to help round up the children, as Lilith had decreed. During the raid, he was felled by Sallari, the diviner of Igraine. No further battles of note had occurred since then.

This did not prevent Roland from practicing frequently with his knives- gifts from his father for each celebration day of Roland's young life until Ivar perished. As the boy practiced, he pictured the straw dummies as the unknown diviner who slew his father. The angry young man grew proficient with knives of all sorts. He made a vow to kill any and *every* diviner he found when he grew up, in vengeance for his father (though he never discovered any, for they drifted into secrecy to hide their magic from Lilith). By the time Roland was in his twentieth year, he was a corporal in the Red Guard. At five and twenty, he was a lieutenant in the Red Guard. Whispers persisted that his promotions were tied to the previous occupant meeting the sharp end of his knives in an alleyway. He had gotten thus far with his knives and determination to honor his father's memory; he would continue in the same manner.

When Cillian assembled his legion to march to Pankirsh, Roland leapt at the chance to finally taste battle. He'd earned a reputation as the best knifeman in Regalias and the Riverlands and he was eager to prove it. As he charged the wendygos, he thought, *these bastards are just burlier versions of deer. Remember your skills. Kill to honor your father's name.* He drew two knives of differing lengths from his belt, charging the largest buck he could find. *Take down a big one, frighten the smaller ones.*

Ten feet before him was a buck over seven and a half feet tall- not including its pointed, thick antlers. The buck caught Roland's stare, altering its course to intercept him; it bellowed a loud elk call, attempting to frighten him. The Lieutenant bellowed back hoarsely, putting on a final burst of speed. The buck lowered his antlers to gore his opponent. Dropping to his knees, Roland slid on a mud patch under the buck's legs; leaning back to avoid being gored in the face. As he slid, his hands were a flurry of activity. The longer knife in his right hand he thrust upwards, stabbing the buck through its left lung. The mid-length knife in his left he slashed sideways across its right hamstring, toppling the beast to one knee.

He rolled right as he emerged behind the downed creature, finding his feet and dashing back towards it. The wounded monstrosity spun right, despite his crippled leg, slashing its long claws forward, trying to catch the young knifeman in the chest. Drawing another long knife from his belt, Roland dodged right, slashing the blade downward, severing its right forearm off onto the cobbled street. In a single, smooth motion, he drove the knife up and forward, into the wendygo's face; killing it instantly. He clutched the knife planted in the beast's chest, as he kicked its torso, freeing both blades from the mutilated monster's body.

His guess was correct: the wendygos running with the buck froze, staring uncertainly at this dangerous human. Roland didn't hesitate. He hurled a small knife straight into the right eye of the nearest wendygo, killing it where it indecisively stood. Three of the remaining seven beasts shrieked their demon cries, turned tail and ran. The other four brayed louder and charged. *This is the* loveliest *day of my life,* the lieutenant mused euphorically. Then his blades and foes danced their dance of death.

Not everyone in the legion was as skilled or fortunate as young Roland. The captain admired their valiant efforts, nonetheless. Pressing his attack, Cillian beheld five of his troops on the left flank gored, slashed and fatally bitten. He himself had downed three smaller wendygos while the lieutenant downed the large buck and his followers. *Keep pushing,* he thought as his blade bathed in the silver blood of the wendygos before him. One by one they fell. As they did, Cillian led a small band of twenty men up the middle of the attacking wendygos, cutting a swath as they went. As Roland finished downing the four wendygos that ganged up on him, the captain advanced on the left side of the central fountain. With his twenty guards protecting him, he mounted the two-foot-tall lip of the fount, to survey the bloody battlefield of the square. He noted with admiration some of the Pankirsh citizenry emerging from Bloomaya's temple to combat the wendygo invaders, armed with bows and farming implements; shooting them with arrows and slicing smaller ones down with scythes and Kaiser blades.

Turning to Roland, who had downed another two mid-sized wendygos, Cillian hollered, "Lieutenant! Get to the temple! Organize their fighters! Press our advantage from that side of the square!"

The lieutenant snapped a quick salute, shouting, "Aye, Captain! On my way!" Then he was off, dodging, weaving and slashing as he dashed along the wendygos' right flank to Bloomaya's temple.

Watching him go, Cillian felt relief. *Good. My family will be safe with Roland nearby.* Below, his guards were being pressed hard by a dozen wendygos. Two of his men fell with strangled cries as a wendygo breached their shield defenses, slashing their throats. Two men on the same side impaled that wendygo with their spears. The captain knew he only had another moment to survey the field before being drawn back into the fray. He searched determinedly for something specific. *Where is the* leader *of this pack? If he dies, the rest may break rank and return to Lec'tair Forest.*

Cillian felt foolish for not spotting him sooner: the bastard was over nine feet tall, with antlers standing another two feet tall atop his skull. The brute was goring and slashing a passage right towards the fountain. Jumping down, the captain skewered a wendygo who had separated him from his men. As the gigantic brute closed on him, he offered up a quick prayer: *Bloomaya*

protect me. Lend me strength to defeat my foe, that
these creatures may lose heart and flee.

The brute was swift, grabbing a lone, dazed Red
Guard by the face with a massive, clawed hand. With a
chuff the monster crushed the guard's head like an
overripe melon; a wet squelching sound popping in its
ferocious grasp. Pounding his large clawed hands upon
his chest, he bellowed louder than the remaining
wendygos, numbering about three dozen now. The
fighting in the square ground to a halt at the magnitude
of the noise. The wendygos disengaged the weary Red
Guards (who now numbered roughly forty) at the
commanding holler of the buck. He turned a tight circle,
bellowing again; his arms outstretched to his kind,
gathered behind him.

He's determining if any will challenge his claim,
Cillian decided.

The Red Guards regrouped behind the captain,
nursing their wounds and gazing in horror at the
enormous beast rallying the others attention. The
Lieutenant ushered the fighting people of Pankirsh back
inside Bloomaya's temple, waiting watchfully inside the
entrance. Once the brute was confident that he would
remain unchallenged, he returned his attention to Cillian.
Pointing a long, deadly claw, the brute rumbled, "*You*,
tiny man! I challenge you to single combat! The victor
shall possess this town, and *all* within it, as prize. The
loser's followers will flee or perish at the hands of the
victors! Concede now, little man; there is no shame in it.
No one to face Runihura the Crusher has lived to tell the
tale. I grant you your life, but *only* if you withdraw *now*.
What say you, little man!?"

Cillian's heart thundered within his ribcage. *This is a smart devil. If we retreat, we give these demons license to destroy this, and other, towns. If we stay, we may all perish. There is no choice. I know what I must do.* Stepping forward, his head high, the captain of the Red Guard retorted. "Tis easy for you to demand retreat when my men triumph over your dwindling forces, *monster*! I, Cillian of house Duchesne, Captain of the Red Guard of Regalias, will *not* surrender! I accept your challenge of single combat to determine the victor, Runihura!"

A great call of elk, bucks, and caribou went up from the wendygo ranks as the Crusher strode forth.

As the captain stepped forth, one of his guards seized Cillian by his cape, hissing in his ear, "You *cannot* go, sir. To face this monster is to court death."

He spun to face the man, shedding his cape as he did so. "What is your name, soldier?"

The frightened young man stammered, "My name is....is Clancy, Captain."

Cillian nodded, mentally storing the name away. "Do you have family, Clancy?"

"Aye, Captain. I have a wife and a little boy, sir."

Gripping Clancy's shoulder, he asked, "Would you watch a wendygo eat your son like a crisped apple?"

The question shocked the young soldier, a look of horror spreading across his face. "Gods above Captain, *no*!"

The captain nodded, expecting this answer. Looking to where Runihura stood at the left of the fountain, pounding his chest, Cillian replied, "So 'tis with me, Clancy. *That* is why I must fight him: for *your* family and *mine*; for *every* honest man of Kalnay protecting their loved ones. If I fall, all you gathered here: you *fight*. You fight these cannibalistic bastards until *they* are dead, or *you* are." Then he spun, striding towards the mammoth Runihura, his shield raised and his sword at the ready.

For a moment, Runihura and Cillian stared wordlessly at one another, sizing each other up. Then the Crusher's silver eyes assumed a cold, calculating demeanor and the captain knew the contest had begun. The monster charged, lowering his antlers to gore him. Cillian raised his shield and was promptly bashed backwards as Runihura's antlers scraped fiercely against the oaken surface. He regained his footing, attempting to gain ground while hacking at Runihura's massive antlers. With a hard backhand, the brute sent the captain flying toward the fountain. He landed atop his shield, miraculously breaking no bones upon the elevated fountain ledge. He was distinctly disadvantaged now, with his shield under him. The Crusher barreled straight at him.

Rolling hard to his right, the captain found his feet, raising his shield in time to block a left claw slash from Runihura. Unfortunately, it was not a single attack; the first slash was merely a distraction, a cover for the second strike. The wendygo firmly gripped the edge of the shield in his right hand, whipping it and its owner to the left. The shield flew from Cillian's arm and he landed hard on his left; his shoulder jarring out of joint as he struck the cobblestones. Despite the pain in his shoulder, he rose rapidly to his feet. Runihura leapt, bearing his antlers down where the captain had been moments previous. Desperate to land a blow, the captain pivoted away on his right foot, spun and brought his broadsword down in a fierce slash.

The Crusher's antlers bounced off the unyielding cobblestones when he landed. As his head came up, Cillian's sword came down. The wendygo bellowed in pain as the captain lopped the tips off several of its right antlers, the pieces clattering onto the cobblestones. Runihura batted the captain into the fountain, slamming him hard into the statue at the center of it before Cillian splashed into the water. The wendygo rose slowly to his feet, staring furiously at his nine-inch antler prongs scattered uselessly on the ground. Cillian rose painfully from the water, sopping wet. He planted his feet on the lip of the fountain, his sword still firmly in hand.

Runihura locked eyes with the little man, seething, "How *dare* you defile my glorious antlers, you puny, no-horns! Your body will be my *personal* feast tonight, *after* we slaughter the rest of your pathetic Red Guards and the people of this village!"

The captain glanced at the lip of the fountain and had an epiphany. Placing his sword point down in front of him on the wide stones of the ledge, Cillian jeered, "You talk too much, o Crusher! Perhaps you should be called Runihura the Posturer! Come and get me if you're so hungry, ye dainty little *Doe*!"

Runihura's eyes bugged in rage. He dashed several paces before lunging towards Cillian, his antlers aimed down to skewer the puny man where he stood. The captain held his ground until the last possible second, when it would be too late for Runihura to realize his error. Captain Duchesne took an enormous risk on his plan working, yet there were no other choices left. He stood where the circular fount edge curved; where a slight crack lay between the improperly mortared stones. Nimbly sidestepping half a dozen paces to the left, he raised his sword, point down, and waited.

The massive wendygo could neither slow his descent, nor the trajectory of his landing. He landed hard, his unsliced antlers sinking deeply into the crack between the curved stones where Cillian had just stood, lodging his head firmly in place. Runihura placed his hands on either side of the ledge, attempting to free his trapped antlers. Then he felt a sharp pain at the base of his skull before everything disappeared in all-consuming darkness. Runihura the Crusher was slain.

Standing over the dead brute, Cillian stomped his right foot hard on the creature's shoulder, yanking his sword free from the base of its skull. He then spun, slicing Runihura's head off in one clean slash. Jerking the antlers free from between the stones, he hoisted Runihura's severed head in his left hand. The champion shouted at the terror-stricken wendygos, "See here you demons, the head of your champion, Runihura the Crusher! Return to Lec'tair Forest or suffer the same fate that has befallen him! Flee, and remember the name of the man who vanquished your hero: *Cillian Antler-Cleaver!*"

For another moment, the wendygos stood in shocked silence at what had transpired; unable to fully comprehend Runihura's defeat. From the Red Guard's ranks, Clancy dashed forward growling loudly, brandishing his sword and shield, charging directly at the wendygo line. Under normal circumstances, such actions would have been his death. These, however, were not normal circumstances. Clancy's actions were the catalyst that spurred the wendygos retreat, as they bellowed in terror at their defeat. In another moment, the remainder of Cillian's men took up the chase, joining Clancy as he cut down any stragglers unlucky enough to trip or look back. The monsters fled in a stampede of hooves out the eastern end of Pankirsh, leaving the bodies of their slain behind.

Captain Duchesne tossed Runihura's putrid head away, leapt down from the fountain edge and wandered wearily to where the severed antler tips lay on the cobblestone street. He bent carefully, wincing at the pain settling in his bones, and scooped them up: his mementos of an astounding victory. He beheld with joy, his children, Samuel and Elizabeth, running across the square towards him with outstretched arms. His wife, Amelia, followed close behind with a half full quiver of arrows slung over her shoulder, a bow ready in her hands. She joined her children, wrapping her husband, in a large, loving embrace. Cillian sucked in a pained breath as they squeezed his aching body, but he did not withdraw. "I love you all *so* much," he wheezed. "I am overjoyed to see you all safe. Bloomaya *truly* smiles on our family this day."

He gave both of his children and his wife one of Runihura's antler tips. "Never forget how much I love you all. Let these antler prongs remind you that I would face *any* enemy to see you safely back at my side."

With tears in her eyes, Amelia whispered, "I will, brave husband; forever and always."

Samuel looked at his sister's memento and whined, "Why does Elizabeth get the bigger one, papa?"

Despite the pain of it, Cillian chuckled aloud at his son's observation. Reaching into the back of his belt, he pulled out his own, larger chunk of Runihura's antler. To his daughter, he asked, "Do you mind if I give Samuel the bigger piece, Beth?"

Elizabeth looked at the three antler pieces, measuring them. Then she smiled and cooed, "No, papa, I don't mind. Besides, if it's *too* big, I can't put it on a necklace."

Cillian chuckled at her observations, conceding, "Right you are Beth; very right *indeed.*"

To Samuel, he presented his larger chunk of antler, stating, "You have a *truly* gracious sister, Sammy. What do you say for her generosity, son?"

Taking his father's larger antler piece, returning the smaller one to his father, Samuel beamed broadly at his sister and exuberantly replied, "Thanks Beth! You are the best sister of ever and all time!"

Lieutenant Roland came dashing across from the temple just then, beaming broadly and breathing hard. He held out a small piece of parchment to the

Captain while he caught his breath. Opening the parchment, Cillian asked, "What's the news, lieutenant?"

"A raven bore this from General Markus," Roland rasped excitedly. "His troops have successfully driven the wendygo invaders from Gilbesh and Frathmer, Captain."

Cillian looked stunned by the good news on the parchment, staring at his wife. "We've done it. We've repelled those creatures, Amelia." To Roland, he ordered, "Round up the men, lieutenant. Prepare to march back to Regalias."

Roland nodded, dashing off to rally the troops.

To Amelia, Cillian stated, "You and the children gather your belongings. You're coming back to Regalias with me. 'Twill be safer there."

Chapter Eleven: Lady of Endelheim

The name Endelheim means '*The Sapphire City*' in the ancient tongue of the long extinct Elduri. Sarto couldn't remember where he heard or read that, but he knew it was true. He knew it, because the '*Other*' knew it too. He found it troublesome that Apollos was lurking in his thoughts more frequently of late. He didn't trouble the others for they could do nothing for him, save worry. The last thing he wanted, particularly for Isabel, was for them to fret needlessly. They had, all of them, earned reprieve from strife in this sparkling, wondrous place.

Clamping down firmly on Apollos' dark presence, Sarto mentally beat him into submission; until the whispers of his former, devilish self were extinguished once again. It didn't help his state of mind to have Pallas now rattling around his fragmented mind either. Truthfully though, Sarto was relieved to have him back- even if he was a disembodied voice in his mind. Pallas had always been Sarto's balancing point. It seemed he found his way back from the Nether-Realm; though *why*, Sarto could not discern, and Pallas had not offered. Unlike Apollos, Pallas knew when to be quiet and listen.

The exhausted company plodded through the ornate brass gates into the castle courtyard. Seated on an elegant maple bench was the woman whom Isabel and Sarto had traveled all this way to meet. She appeared every bit as radiant as her projected persona in Hesketh. To her right, his hand on the hilt of a short sword, was a middle-aged man of average height. His sharp, brown eyes settled an uncomfortably long time on Khalon, who wisely stood at the company's rear.

For a moment, nothing happened. Then Isabel curtsied deeply, saying, "Hail to you Morgana, Lady of Endelheim. Long has my journey been, but I am relieved to finally meet you in person." Taking their cue from Isabel, Sarto, Khalon and the Shadow Twins all bowed to her. Morgana arose gracefully from the bench, strolling towards the bowed travellers, the hem of her scarlet satin dress dragging through the mud.

The scruffy, red-headed guard stepped closer to Morgana, his eye still warily eye on Khalon, hissing into her ear, "My lady, we don't *know* these people. The *flesh-eater* could be a spy for the freckaying Screech Owl. If he does anything here, there's no guarantee I can protect you."

Placing a smooth, reassuring hand on the tense man's shoulder, the Lady smiled, replying for all to hear, "There is *nothing* to fear, good Iolo. You are my truest protector but sometimes you worry *far* too much. Stand down; all will be well." Casting a final distrustful glance at Khalon, Iolo bowed deferentially to his liege lady. To Khalon, the Lady asked, "What say you, Master Wendygo? Need I fear coming to harm at your hands?"

With his head still bowed the young wendygo stated, "No, Lady Morgana, you have naught to fear from me." Then he locked his golden eyes with her faded blue ones, as he added, "Unless you mean me or my friends unwarranted harm. Their safety and well-being are my primary concern. I owe them my very life."

The Lady of Endelheim was surprised by the buck's intelligence and code of honor. She unleashed a peal of merry laughter, as though he had uttered a joke. Khalon was confused by her laughter but said nothing.

Collecting her composure, Morgana stated, "Forgive my outburst. I had all but forgotten wendygos possessed even a modicum of *intelligence*, never mind honor. Happy is my heart to see my assumptions disproven by such as yourself. Truly, you are *most* welcome here Master Khalon; as are you all. You must be unimaginably weary, so I will be brief. I wish to introduce my daughters to you. They are the only other residents of Endelheim Castle, save me, Iolo, Eben the cook, and Master Scribe Frodi. Isabel, since you will spend much time with them in training, it is good to know your fellow sorceresses and, gods willing, your newest friends."

Indicating a set of double doors on the western edge of the courtyard, Morgana mouthed, "*Corva.*" The doors swung open on rusty hinges, screaming a weathered cry. Emerging from within the cordoned room were five girls of varying ages. At the head of the line, taking her place beside her mother was the raven-haired Ezri, who now wore a rich green velvet dress and a simple jet necklace. She curtsied to Sarto's company. Next entering was a tall, brown haired, blue eyed, girl of twenty and one in a simple lily purple dress. She curtsied, saying, "I am Delja, second daughter of Morgana the White. Welcome, honored guests, to our home."

Following her, came Sena: a girl of eighteen years, wearing an elegant, cream-colored velvet dress, which highlighted her burnished orange hair and blue eyes. She too curtsied and introduced herself. Finally, entered a pair of blonde girls of fifteen and fourteen years, respectively. Aside from the slight difference in height, the girls looked nearly identical. Sarto mentally noted these two most resembled their mother Morgana, though he said nothing. The blondes, dressed in identical silver-colored silk dresses, curtsied simultaneously before

Sarto and his company, eerily echoing each other as they introduced themselves. "Greetings to you Master Wizard Sarto, Lady Isabel and other honored guests."

"I am Aloisa," the older one announced, before stepping back. The youngest stepped forward as her older sister stepped back. "I am Allegra, the Far-seer. Together, we are known as the Five Sisters. We welcome you, one and all to our home of Endelheim. What is ours is yours also. While you are here, you shall want for nothing. Here you shall know rest and safety."

Isabel was jolted when Allegra mentioned the Five Sisters. It reminded her of Birosh on Gwenovair; of her mother, Amina and her step-father, Bishop. Suddenly and inexplicably, her heart yearned for her far-flung home. Thinking of her mother also brought a pang of heartache at her brother's notable absence.

Abel, my dear brother, Isabel thought with a note of sadness, *how I wish I could tell you I have arrived safely in Endelheim. I swear to the gods, I will learn the self-projection spell first. I miss you dearly. I hope you are as fortunate on your quest as I have been. Goddess Sharlto, keep my brother safe, and Lady Nairadj as well. Guide them safely on, and usher their footsteps my way with haste; that I may regain my brother and a dear friend.* When Isabel returned to the moment, Morgana had shooed her daughters to their chambers to prepare for dinner. While she daydreamed, a short, middle-aged man in scribe raiment had entered and introduced himself. He led the company to their rooms on the second floor of the east wing of the castle. On the way up, Isabel asked Sarto who the scribe was.

"His name is Frodi, child. He is Keeper of the Tomes of Light, preserved here in the great Messaran library. Did you not catch that before?"

Isabel flushed a deep red color, muttering sheepishly, "I....I'm afraid my attentions were otherwise occupied, Master Sarto...."

Instead of berating her, Sarto nodded understandingly. "Thinking of Abel and Nairadj, I assume?"

Isabel nodded, whispering, "I *must* learn the self-projection spell, Master Sarto. It is tearing me up not knowing what is happening to them, or whether they are in danger...."

Sarto placed a reassuring hand atop hers, answering, "Isabel, I promise you, at the first available opportunity, I will guide you through the successful and *safe* completion of the self-projection spell, so you may contact Abel. We must be cautious though. Lilith can detect self-projection, at times. Do you believe me?"

Through the trickle of tears, Isabel replied, "Aye Master Sarto; you know I do."

Nudging her gently on the chin, Sarto whispered, "Now, what say we get ready for supper? I am anxious to learn more of our hostess."

Morgana certainly does know how to prepare a spread. That was the first thing Isabel thought when Frodi ushered her into the feast hall and she witnessed the innumerable dishes on the overlong banquet table. The second thing she thought was, *Eben must have been cooking since* sunrise *to prepare this much food.* The seating arrangement at the feast table saw Morgana at the head, as the hostess. Isabel was seated to her right; Sarto to her left. Down the right side of the table, beside Isabel, sat Morgana's daughters. On the left side of the table beside Sarto sat the Shadow Twins, Khalon and Scribe Frodi. Scribe Frodi did his best at concealing his excitement being seated next to a real, live wendygo; Khalon noted it, but did not indulge the Scribe's visible inquisitiveness. Iolo stood to Morgana's left, watching Khalon like a hawk.

Eben, a burly man of six feet, with short-cropped black hair, and salt and pepper stubble, served each course himself. The man possessed an air of class that (had he not personally served the food, describing its exact ingredients, textures and aromas) Isabel would not have believed him capable of. Pallas' final words echoed in the corner of her mind again: *'Not all things that shine are that of the Light. Nor are all things that were once of the Dark, black at heart.'*

Isabel finished a bite of her first ever roasted duck (which she found exquisitely delicious), when Pallas' words occurred to her. Instinctively, she glanced to where Khalon sat. She took another bite of duck, to avoid unwanted attention, but she busily rolled those words around her mind. *I wonder if Pallas knew we would meet Khalon when he uttered those words to me. Or....perhaps he was challenging me to see beyond the surface of a person's appearance. I mean....to look at Eben one wouldn't think he could prepare anything more complex than baked beans and a side of bacon. Yet....he is the Cook of Endelheim and possesses a broad, detailed culinary palette. Even Pallas himself was challenged on his notions regarding dyre bears when we first met Nairadj. Khalon has proven to be a truly unique member of his species, as well as a steadfast friend. I wish Iolo could see him how my friends and I do. I fear he may act rashly, stirring up trouble twixt our company and his lady's household.*

Morgana, running a moistened fingertip over the rim of her wine goblet, drew Isabel out of her musings. Clearing her throat, she raised her goblet, proclaiming, "I wish to propose a toast: to our new friends' safe arrival. There is much we can learn from one another. Through shared knowledge we can end the reign of Malikh and Lilith. A toast, to new alliances and friends!"

All gathered, raised their goblets, clanking them together, echoing, "To new alliances and friends!" Everyone seated drank deeply of the mead in their goblets. As the mead passed her lips, Isabel thought self-consciously: *If marmie could see me now....*

Setting her glass down, Morgana declared, "That was a *truly* splendid meal, Eben. My compliments on what may be the *finest* meal I have had beneath this roof." Eben bowed, taking his cue to exit. The Lady of Endelheim smiled, reiterating to Isabel and Sarto, "It is so *wonderful* to have you here, safe and ready to join our collective powers; ridding this once *glorious* land of the pretenders to the throne." Leaning back in her elegantly carved chair, she grinned an inebriated grin, querying, "Shall I confess something *wicked* to you, Lady Isabel?"

Isabel raised her eyebrows curiously, venturing, "Pray tell, Lady Morgana. What is this wicked deed?"

Smiling devilishly, she countered, "Have you not wondered....have you not *all* wondered, exactly *who* snuffed out the wildfire in Lec'tair Forest?" She leaned back, nursing her goblet of mead, watching for the company's reactions. The Shadow Twins' eyes widened in wonderment. Isabel was dumbstruck, pondering the implied magnitude of Morgana's power. A measured fear and shielded sense of concern dawned on both Khalon and Sarto. They both knew, in their own ways, anyone with power great enough to snuff out a wildfire was a power not to be trifled with.

Morgana drank in their gazes as she did her mead: slowly, savoring the diverse boutique of flavor. To herself, she thought, *Good. They know how powerful I am. With me, my daughters, Isabel and the might of Sarto the Mender, we shall rid this kingdom of its diseased heart.*

A short while later, the decadent feast concluded. All gathered retired to their chambers seeking rest from the eventful day. Tomorrow would find Isabel hard at work learning the ways of Morgana and her daughters. The Farthen girl was the first to fall into the welcome, comforting arms of a deep, restful sleep. The Shadow Twins requested Morgana's permission to sleep in her magnificent courtyard gardens; for gnomes do not sleep in human beds. Morgana happily obliged.

Khalon requested a stall in an isolated, empty stable at the north end of the castle. He explained that wendygos do not sleep in traditional human rooms due to their size. He was readily granted his request. He was secretly overjoyed; doing so denied Iolo the satisfaction of inventing some reason why he endangered everyone. The young wendygo had consumed nothing but fresh animal flesh since joining Isabel and Sarto's company. In truth, it had been at least two years since Khalon had consumed human flesh. He had successfully kept it secret from his wendygo brethren, but when it came out that he had broken tradition, he was labeled a traitor by King Fenyang. Hence, his starving punishment prior to his foiled execution.

Khalon knew if Iolo even suspected he would revert to his cannibalistic ways, that Morgana's young bodyguard would seek to put him down like a rabid dog. Being so far from the other occupants of Endelheim Castle removed all possible arguments regarding safety. Satisfied he would be undisturbed, Khalon curled up in his stall, dreaming of a day when he could live amongst the sons and daughters of men without fear of being reviled as a monster.

Sarto did not have such an easy time finding rest. Apollos lurked in the dark corners of his mind again, waiting to strike. He inspected his mental barricades with mounting worry. *Why is Apollos returned? Did not the diviners and the gods purge this monster from my being? Am I being brought to account for my sins?*

From beyond Sarto's mental barricades, came the sibilant, disembodied voice of who he had once been. *Oh, my mad, pathetic fellow, how foolish you are. You speak as if I were dead. Even when gods and diviners purge Pimedus from someone's soul, it is never entirely cleansed. Spots and stains remain that do not scrub clean. It's not that the gods don't want it clean. It's more that they can't clean it. The Light cannot exist without the Darkness. I'm afraid, old man, you are stuck with me.* Suddenly a barrage of fierce blows erupted against the mental barricades. Had Sarto been more exhausted, or less cautious, Apollos would have burst through, seizing control of his mind and body right then. With mounting fear, the old herbalist realized Apollos was extremely strong; stronger than expected. He also realized his dark half had been returned for some time, quietly amassing power in the shadows of his fragmented mind. Hearing the rending sounds of the barricades, Sarto hurled his mind hard against the unexpected power of Apollos. *'Vish un Rivaith, Apollos!'*

On the other side of the barricade, Apollos laughed cruelly at Sarto's attempted banishment spell. *'You can't banish me wizard. We are one and the same.'*

From behind Sarto, erupted a magnificent, blinding light. The Light pierced the cracks and gaps Apollos had created in the barricades. The dark wizard cried in pain and rage at the raw strength of it. A voice emerged from the Light, and deep relief flooded Sarto's weary mind; for the voice was that of Pallas. "*Apollos,*" the diviner's voice boomed authoritatively, "*you are unwelcomed here! I am Pallas, diviner and warrior of the Way of the Light. 'Twas I who banished you from Sarto's mind! While you may not be forced to leave his mind, I forbid you access to your body of old! Be gone, poisonous wraith!*" The diviner's light burned brighter, until Sarto felt Apollos' talons release the barricades protecting his mind. The wraith's cries faded, but before he was completely silenced, Apollos shrilled, *'I will be back, old man! Next time, I will reclaim what is rightfully mine!'* Then he was gone.

Pallas passed a ghostly hand left to right, up and down, wordlessly fortifying Sarto's mental barricades. The ghostly diviner declared gravely, "*We* must *speak, old friend. All is* not *right here in Endelheim.*"

Chapter Twelve: Dark Secrets

Malikh found himself more frequently spending time within his own mind. The firestorm in Lec'tair Forest; the wendygo attacks on the Riverland townships; these things and more disturbed him greatly. He could not speak to Lilith of these matters, for she had sequestered herself within her black tower- determinedly searching Pimedus for solutions to these debacles by other means.

I must visit the dungeon; inspect how my creation progresses, Malikh thought worriedly. Seizing a large, lit candelabra, he hurried through a secret exit behind a large tapestry to the left of his throne. The door groaned loudly. The Overlord darted a paranoid look about the barren throne room, before proceeding swiftly into the darkness.

After a long moment, a different secret entrance (one Malikh was unaware of) on the right side of the throne room, swung silently open outward; and Master Clarke emerged. He glanced furtively about for any sign of guards before proceeding to where Malikh had crept away. He silently searched the sunken doorjamb for the lone displaced stone to open the entrance. Finding it, he pushed, grabbing the edge as it opened to avoid its creaking. He did not wish to alert the Overlord to his presence. Clarke stared uncertainly into the darkness of the spiraling staircase, proceeding carefully downward without light, running his hand along the left wall.

Too long I have stood by idly, hiding behind Jabesh. It is time I did something. Lord Malikh is not himself these days. If I may guide him through a tough decision, I shall do it. Now, get you onward, old man.

The closer Malikh drew to the dungeon, the better he felt. With each step, he increasingly heard metal and smithy work. The sound of hammer and tongs echoed in harmony, as his captive Prezla worked tirelessly on his machinations. The heat increased as he drew nearer the base of the stairs. The Overlord found it comforting. In the throne room, it was cold and lonely. Down here- where he had secretly built a large-scale blacksmith shop after seizing power- things were sultry.

He emerged through a hidden door at the rear of the guards' empty dining chamber, proceeding into the dungeon hallway. The hall itself was sparsely lit with torches. As he proceeded down the left hall, the world became brighter and warmer. At the hall's end was a set of large, maple double doors, which the Overlord shoved open firmly. Behind them was a veritable hive of activity.

The smithy hall was more massive than three throne rooms combined. Masses of men, women and children, shackled with a single iron bracelet- marking them as captive Prezla- bustled to and fro with buckets of water, bronze plates, wood for ramps and other implements. There were over three dozen guards posted around the mammoth hall, supervising the shackled Prezla as they worked ceaselessly on the Overlord's secret project.

He stood just inside the open doors relishing the scene; like a father admiring the artwork of a dear child. *Not even Lilith could have devised something as magnificent as what the gods imparted through visions. My vision: the monster of metal. A time approaches when Kalnay will require my creation. I have utilized these Prezla's skills for better use in this unified endeavor. Magic is all but extinguished in Kalnay, thanks to me. Those who practice it are here, bringing my vision to life.*

Still, he pondered, striding to the center of the colossal workshop, *'tis wondrous strange......that fire in Lec'tair Forest. If all Prezla are here, building my metal beast....then* who *ignited that blaze? Perhaps 'twas Lilith......but if it was her, why not inform me? Is it possible there is* another *Prezla, besides the escaped old man, unbeknownst to me? If so, that is deeply unsettling.*

The Overlord now stood before what appeared to be a large, bronze-plated dragon's foot. Reaching out, he stroked the surface, relishing the cold, firm touch of the metal. He gazed upwards, vaguely glimpsing the almost complete skull of his sixty-foot bronze dragon. Through the din of hammer, tongs and the bellows all breathing the fire that was ushering his dream to completion, Malikh smiled in self-satisfaction. *Lilith does not rule the world. With the gods help I* shall *be Kalnay's savior. They decreed my creation shall protect this land from the fury of the Ancient Father. The gods look unfavorably upon Lilith. Upon* me *they shine their light; a sure sign that my rule shall last for years to come.*

He turned from the metal dragon and was nearly plowed into by an elderly man with a bundle of wood for the bellows. Malikh barked loudly in disgust, shoving him rudely backwards, sending the old man sprawling. Everyone present stopped what they were doing, watching in mute apprehension the scenario unfolding before them. The old man stared hatefully up at the Overlord.

Malikh stared back, intrigued to see what the old man might do. "Watch where you tread, elder, lest my men deliver you twenty lashes!"

The old man spat, "Twenty lashes, you say? That is a sweet reprieve from this slavery, o pretender to the throne."

The Overlord was unprepared for the insult. Impulsively, he kicked the old man in the face. He was morbidly pleased hearing the crunch of the fool's nose breaking; giddier still at the jet of blood squirting from his nose. The old man's eyes blazed with hatred, staring defiantly at Malikh with his jaw locked.

The Overlord leaned close, taunting, "You'd like to kill me with a spell right now *wouldn't* you, old one?"

The prisoner seethed wordless contempt through a mask of blood, breathing heavily through his bleeding nostrils.

This aged dunkla has spirit. I must give that to the stubborn old mule. Clanking his candlestick on the prisoner's iron bracelet, the Overlord smirked, jeering, "It's a pity these iron bracelets prevent you and your magic-abusing Prezla friends from retaliating. I would relish some combat right now. 'Twas *you* and your ilk who strove to keep me from my destined prize of the Kalnayan throne. How do you like your reward for your treachery, Prezla scum?"

The old man spat a thick mist of blood in Malikh's face, rasping, "I pray the gods *themselves* run a sword through your shriveled, black heart you freckaying *worm*!"

A blood rage seized Malikh then. Shrieking like a banshee, he brought the heavy candlestick down on the prisoner's head. The first blow cracked his skull. The second strike killed him. In the accompanying flurry of a dozen odd blows, the old man's head became pulp. By then, the Overlord struck him for pleasure's sake alone.

Rising to his feet, blood drenching his face, Malikh glared savagely at the rest of the gawking Prezla and guards in the workshop. No one dared move, for they were too frightened. Brandishing the bloodstained candlestick overhead, he shrilled, "What are you all staring at?! Get back to work or face the same fate as this fool!"

The prisoners bustled about, giving Malikh a wide berth as they resumed transporting iron and bronze plates to the nearly completed gear-work dragon.

Pointing to one of the nearby guards, Malikh cried, "*You*! Take this piece of *filth* away!"

The guard obliged with a quick bow and a rushed, "Aye, my lord; at once."

The Overlord gazed up to the face of the gear-work dragon. "*All* that I do, I do for the glory of the kingdom." Then he whirled about, storming from the shop. *I must see the prisoner. I must see Noshtain.* Reigniting his blood-soaked candelabra with a torch outside the double doors, he stalked furiously down the hallway, past the guards' breakroom- where he had first emerged- and down into the isolation cells in the sub-level of the dungeon.

Clarke had seen everything. He snuck down the hall to where Malikh had burst through the double doors. Thanks to his flamboyant entrance, all eyes had been drawn to the Overlord, permitting him to sneak right up outside the workshop unnoticed. He felt that old twinge in his right knee as he drew up silently outside. *Yes, my old husk, I know I'm too old for this sptoch. This is more important than old-age comfort, so cease your grumblings, by the gods.* The Master Scribe peeked around the corner, awestruck by what he beheld within the massive workshop. Numerous men, women and children- each wearing a single, iron bracelet- bustled about toting sheets of forged bronze and iron, bundles of firewood and buckets of water to and fro. *What is this madness? Who are all these people?*

That was when Clarke marked the dragon. He knew it wasn't real. Had it been, all within including Malikh, would have been singed to ash. Wary of being sighted, the Master Scribe inspected the dragon as best he could from beyond the doors. *Gods above, the dragon is made of metal! How long has this been here? Why does he build such a monstrosity? Again, who are these people? There is only one registered prisoner in the sub-dungeon, none registered on this level....so where did they all come from? No, confound that for now. The more pressing question is: what is the meaning behind this monstrosity? Surely, the Overlord does not mean to burn Kalnay as the fire lizards of old? That is madness beyond any I have seen!*

Just then Malikh and the old prisoner collided, snapping his attention back to the present. Clarke watched in growing dismay as the fallen man cursed the Overlord. Icy fingers of fear and revulsion gripped his heart as he understood what was about to happen. He bit his hand to muffle the scream threatening to burst from his mouth as he watched the prisoner beaten to death with the hefty bronze candelabra in the Overlord's hand. He stared numbly as a guard dragged the dead man away. *This is* not *why I came to Kalnay,* he fumed internally. *I came here to escape what tainted Ackreth: despair....oppression......death. Clearly, nothing has changed.* His reverie was interrupted as he watched Malikh storm towards the open doors. Clarke pressed himself into the darkness to the left of the door holding his breath as the Overlord stormed past, oblivious to his presence.

Clarke silently watched Malikh stride down the hallway, expecting him to return through the secret entrance in the guards' dining chamber. However, he kept marching down the hall, towards the stairs to the sub-level of the dungeon where the isolation cells were located. Once the guards closed the workshop doors, Clarke emerged from the shadows, hurrying quickly down the hall to the stairs on the far left. *Where are you going? What reason do you have for visiting the prisoner in the solitary cells?* He listened carefully at the top of the stairs, noting the distinct echoing rumble of Malikh's voice, and the weary, grating voice of the lone prisoner below. The Master Scribe leaned on the wall to the right, expertly descending the short flight of steps to the sub-dungeon level. At the corner where the stairs and hallway intersected, he listened for Malikh. His voice was loud, but distant. Clarke rounded the corner, following the dimly, torch-lit hall towards the sound of the

Overlord's voice. In another minute he could clearly hear the Overlord. He hid in an empty, open-doored cell within earshot of the ensuing conversation and listened attentively.

Standing before the barred window on the oak cell door, Malikh raised his candelabra to peer into the darkness. He heard the faint clanking of chains as the prisoner within shied from the light. Chuckling maliciously, he mocked, "Apologies, honored guest. I forgot you haven't seen sunlight, really *any* light for that matter, in a *very* long time. My *sincerest* apologies for my lapse of memory."

Within the pitch-black cell, a raspy, parched voice uttered, "Why do you do this? Why not kill me, and have done with this *charade?*"

Leaning close to the cell window, Malikh stated, "Quite simply: I do not *wish* to kill you. For a longer time than either of us cares to admit, I have desired you to *serve* as Commander of my Red Guard."

The voice in the cell seethed, "I say again what I *always* tell you: *never!* You destroyed my home. You killed people I loved. Why would I serve a monster like *you?*"

In a reasonable tone the Overlord declared, "Simply put: 'tis because I *wish* you to. As far as you're concerned that is *all.* Markus told me how valiantly you fought...."

"Many people have fought valiantly against you and your war dog. They are all equally as dead."

Malikh shrugged, replying, "What can I say? General Markus is persuasive. I trust his judgment intrinsically. If he says you can be turned, I believe him."

A weak laugh emitted from the cell, "Then you are *both* imbeciles. I will *never* join you." There was a shuffling sound as the prisoner rolled away from the light, ending the conversation.

The Overlord hissed, "*Fine!* Have it your way, you stupid *sptoch*! I have been reasonable. Negotiation won't work, so I will take....*alternate* steps. My Lady Lilith will be down here shortly to....*persuade* you. *Then* we will see if you don't have a change of heart, *Noshtain.*"

Within the cell, the prisoner shrilled in a cracked voice, "My name is *not* Noshtain! You tell that svanth of a trickster I will remain my own person, no matter what devilish spells she plies to my body! You tell her that, o usurper!"

Malikh clamped down on the rage that had earlier slain the old man in the dungeon workshop. *He wants me to kill him, free him from his torment. I will not give him that satisfaction!* Drawing a deep, measured breath, He responded, "You will not goad me into killing you. We will see how much of a trickster you find the Lady Lilith. For now, ponder your fate at her hands. Farewell, *Noshtain.*"

As he walked away, the prisoner barked again, "My name is *not* Noshtain!"

Returning to the throne room, Malikh thought, *very soon, you* will *see things my way. Mark my words.*

Clarke's mind whirled at the conversation he had overheard. *Noshtain? That means* 'Nameless'....*who is this prisoner? I desire to know. However, if he lets slip to Lilith under duress that I was here and spoke to him,* I *would be in danger. Princess Arya's safe escape is more crucial to me, though I wish to help this poor soul. I must commit a lesser evil to prevent a greater one. Gods forgive me.* The Master Scribe felt his way back along the hallway, returning cautiously to the main floor of the dungeons. Knowing Malikh was likely fuming in his throne room, Clarke took the main stairs up from the dungeons, his mind awhirl with these new revelations. *I* must *inform Jabesh of what I have learned here. This does not alter our escape plan; it is still something he should know, and perhaps he may shed some light on.*

Chapter Thirteen: A Dangerous Path

It had been two days since Nairadj rejoined her long-lost people. The bear clans and Sigourney's army continued south, marching towards the Drake's Maw Pass: their most direct path south to Regalias. Spirits were high amongst dyre bears and Wildmen alike. For the dyre bears, Princess Nairadj's return was the source of their joy. For many of the Northerners their joy came from the fact that they were moving beyond the harm of the nightstalkers; hopefully forever.

Abel found plenty of opportunity during their southbound trek to spar with Nairadj whenever they encamped; honing his skills with sword, knife, his hands and even his whole body as a weapon. He even attracted Captain Hearne's attention; the leader of the Night Patrol spent some time teaching Abel his own sword, knife and survival tricks that had served him well in the Nightstalker Wastes. He was glad of the tutelage, for he desired to be the best fighter he could. He did, after all, have an Overlord to depose. Things were proceeding better than either Abel or Nairadj would have anticipated; given how many obstacles they had faced since first meeting on the Southern Sand Flats. Of course, a saying exists in Kalnay that '*every good fortune must find its end.*'

On the second night of their march south from Djintani Lake, Abel and Nairadj were asleep in their pavilions. Like a cold wave, a sinister, enveloping voice washed over their minds. "*Greetings, Abel 'Drakt'vansh' and Princess Nairadj 'Vaith'vansh'; you two have become quite notorious of late amongst my kin. I am Melatharom the Burrower. I rule the under-realm of the*

Shavatnu Mountains. You both had a hand in the murder of my younger brood-mate, Ulgnar the Grey. I felt him die, when you severed his head from his body. Did you know we dragons share a mental link, tiny ones? 'Twas not a pleasant feeling; not at all. I demand justice. Present yourself before me for judgment. Fail to show your faces in the tunnel at the base of the peak you call 'Magna Spiro' three days' hence, and I will destroy the passage you and your allies seek to traverse. It shall be rubble if I will it. How then will you and the Northerner Queen overthrow Malikh the Usurper, I wonder?"

Melatharom chuckled cruelly as he sensed the companions' surprise regarding his knowledge of their plans. *"Aye, I see your plans through your dreams. You have three days......or find an alternate way south on your quest. The choice is yours but choose quickly; lest I decide for you."* Then, like a passing storm, Melatharom's presence left their minds.

They awoke abruptly once Melatharom's ultimatum was delivered. They dressed hurriedly, quietly gathered their belongings (including a week's worth of food, their weapons and clothes), hurrying to the camp line, where the central firepit was. Finding each other there, Abel and Nairadj knew the message from Melatharom was no dream. After quick discussion, they agreed to inform Sigourney and Yenoor of what had transpired before departing. They desired to be gone before daybreak, so they hurried to inform the Queens; they did not wish to dishearten the armed forces by simply vanishing.

While Sigourney loathed losing Abel's famed presence amongst her troops, she understood his current task was of greater import; both to him *and* the campaign. She knew if this rock drake caused a slide, the pass could be blocked indefinitely, forcing her to march over the mountains, or worse: marching through northern Lec'tair Forest. As she put it, "What good is having a famous warrior with us, if our passage south is blocked by a rockslide? Fame does not cut a path through stone." So, The Queen of the Wastes gave Abel her blessing, sending him hurriedly on his way.

Leaving for Nairadj was far more difficult. Queen Yenoor was sick at heart to hear of Melatharom's demand. *"No,"* the bear queen stated through a clenched jaw, "I *refuse*. You have *just* been restored to us.... to *me*, after *years* of separation! Now you would endanger yourself beneath Shavatnu?!"

Wrapping her grief-stricken mother in a fierce hug, Nairadj reassured, "Madriga, you will *not* lose me. I have already survived worse than this and...."

Yenoor shook free of her daughter's embrace and reassuring words, tears streaming down her face. "Do *not* attempt to diminish the dire nature of this....*Melatharom's* decree. He demands justice for his brother's death. Dragons are not *easily* killed Nairadj."

"*Abel* has already done so, mother! We will be *fine*, I swear it."

"Slaying a marsh drake is one thing, my daughter. They are prideful creatures with light armor, and a love of toying with their prey. Slaying a rock drake is another matter *entirely*. They are larger, craftier lizards, with thick armor. He knows the underbelly of the mountains better than anyone else. This monster means to *kill* you; the boy too! Do you not *see* that, my child!?"

Grabbing her mother firmly by the shoulders, Nairadj countered, "Madriga, if I do *not* go with Abel, the mountain snake *will* collapse the pass! The success of our venture southward depends on that pass being *open*. Sooner or later, Malikh will discover our intentions to invade. If Drake's Maw Pass is collapsed, he will remain unopposed, and be able to fortify the pass against invasion. If Abel and I do not *both* cede to this Melatharom's demands, he *will* collapse the mountains!

"Besides, Abel is my apprentice. I *promised* his master Pallas, diviner of Birosh, that I would protect and train him as a warrior of the Way of the Light. Pallas trusted me, as his *friend*, to watch over Abel in his absence. How would it look, dear Madriga, if the apprentice leaves to face danger and possible death while I, his master, remain behind? It would bring more shame to me than *any* possibility of death at the claws of a dragon. Pallas would forever look on me from the Nether-Realm with disdain and shame. Do you *understand*, Madriga? I *must* go."

Yenoor stared helplessly at her strong-willed daughter and wept. Clasping her in a deep embrace, the bear Queen whispered in her ear, "I understand, dearest Nairadj. Though it pains me deeply, I *do* understand. You promise me....you *swear* to me by the ancestors that you *will* return to lead your people. To lose you again after such a long absence would be far too much for my weary heart to tolerate."

Staring unblinkingly into her mother's brimming eyes, Nairadj uttered her promise in ancient Kalnese: '*Un compta, Madriga; bis vet lineas, un det vish.*' This translates to: 'I promise, Mother; by the ancestors, I shall return.' Promises uttered in the ancient tongue are considered sacred. If not honored, they bring shame upon the one who falsely uttered them.

Yenoor kissed her daughter once more on the forehead, declaring, "Before you leave, there is something I must give you. 'Twill bring you luck on your new mission; perhaps even aid you in triumphing over that *bastard* mountain snake." From a chest in the corner of her tent, she brought forth a necklace, a great oaken bow, and a quiver of thick-shafted arrows. The necklace was set with an ingot. Nairadj knew at once it was her Mere's (that is to say, 'grandmother's') necklace; a most precious heirloom. The bow and quiver she also recognized, though it choked her up to set eyes upon it again. Presenting the bow, Yenoor queried, "You know to whom this quiver and bow once belonged, do you not, daughter of mine?"

With a lump clutching firmly at her throat and tears welling in her emerald eyes, Nairadj confirmed, "Aye. These belonged to....to Jelani." She extended her hand to refuse, stating, "I *cannot* accept these gifts, Madriga. They are too much, by far."

Pressing them firmly into her daughter's hands, Yenoor scowled. "On the contrary, they are not *nearly* enough. They are to remind you that your people, your *family*, have not forgotten you. The ingot protects against most magic you may encounter; even the hypnotizing stare of a dragon. Take these gifts, set my fretting heart at ease that you are as safe as you can be. I trust you have not forgotten how to fire a bow during your self-imposed exile in the Sand Flats?"

Expertly slinging the quiver and bow over her shoulder, Nairadj stated, "It is as fresh in my mind as the day I fled south." Touching her forehead, then her lips and bowing to her mother, the princess added, "My *deepest* thanks to you, Madriga, for your most generous gifts. I will cherish and use them to bring honor to she who has bestowed them upon me so graciously." Then she wrapped her mother in a final, firm hug, whispering, "Farewell." Then she darted from the tent before she could change her mind about leaving.

By the time Nairadj met Abel at the southern edge of the camp, he had acquired a pair of fresh, saddled horses. She nodded approval as she strapped her gear to the saddle. Abel noticed the bow and arrows but did not ask where she acquired them. He noted the dried tear tracks on her cheeks and knew intuitively that her goodbye had been difficult. When she was prepared, Abel asked, "Ready to ride, Master Nairadj?"

Gazing south towards the jutting tip of the distant 'Magna Spiro', she nodded. "Aye Abel, I believe we are."

"Then may the gods spur our steeds on and strengthen our spirits in the face of this new foe." Abel spurred his horse on, the rising sun catching him perfectly in a fiery orange, side profile of light.

Spurring her own horse into a gallop, Nairadj reflected, somewhat mournfully, *with every new foe we face and best, Abel becomes more hardened by the cruelty around him. This should not be. Until the world is more at peace, it will continue thus.*

Melatharom had given them three days to arrive at 'Magna Spiro'; the duo reached it in little over two days' time. On the afternoon of the second day, they halted the horses before the splendor of 'Magna Spiro'. The peak was an impassable spike of rock, jutting higher into the sky than any man-made tower ever beheld. Burrowed into the side of the wide mountain spire's base was a massive hole; easily over one hundred feet in diameter. Drawing up before it, Abel and Nairadj stared in mute disbelief at the unbelievable size of the entrance Melatharom had opened for them. Casting a sidelong glance, Abel asked, "Should we enter now, Master?"

Nairadj stared hard into the burrowed mountain passage in silent contemplation. Finally, she stated, "We wait until nightfall. We will have time to adjust to the darkness of the mountain's interior then, and we can rest now before we face whatever Melatharom has concocted for us. We should free the horses; though we are marked to die, I *refuse* to provide this rock drake a free meal in our horses."

Unsaddling himself, Abel set about gearing up for the night's travels; Nairadj did likewise. She remarked, "We should sleep now, while the sun is up. I doubt there are nightstalkers this far south, but one can't be too cautious. I also doubt that Melatharom will emerge from beneath Shavatnu; under the mountains, he holds advantage. Rest, Abel. I will wake you in several hours to take watch. At nightfall, we depart."

Before resting, he first prepared them both a light lunch of roasted sparrows, after downing the passing birds from the afternoon sky with his bow. While she kept watch, Nairadj ruminated on what they might encounter beneath the mountain; more importantly, how they would overcome their new opponent. She had some rough ideas; though if their encounter with Ulgnar taught her anything, it was this: dragons are rarely predictable. They will certainly not willingly permit you to slay them.

After four hours, Abel awoke to relieve Nairadj, so she could get some sleep before venturing onward. She agreed readily. His sword, Mediator, resting across his lap, young Farthen sat staring into the looming, perfectly burrowed entrance. Like his master, he pondered fiercely how to defeat Melatharom; all he could determine was how uncertain he felt. *I guess I must wait to discover an advantage over Melatharom. The key is to keep moving; stay on my toes, watch for claws, teeth and fire.* He stifled a chuckle threatening to disturb Nairadj's sleep. Had he uttered his thought aloud in Sigourney's presence, she would have laughed him from her presence as a simpleton.

His mind turned to Nairadj then. He glanced to his right, watching this gorgeous, lanky woman breathe as she slept. He was captivated by the rise and fall of the curves of her side as she dozed. So much had happened recently, Abel scarcely had time to reflect on her personal revelations. *I barely know what to call her anymore......Lady? Master? Princess? Despite all I know of her.......I still feel drawn to her. This is not mere infatuation. I genuinely find myself intrigued, and perplexed, by her. She has promised to give us a chance should we survive what is to come......* Here, Abel gazed absently into the oppressive darkness of the mammoth entrance, before resuming his thought. *Try though I might, I fear we may not survive to reach Regalias. I suppose we will do our damnedest at defying the odds.*

*Pallas was right......I must wait on the quest's outcome
before pursuing the mysteries of the fairer sex.*

Four hours later darkness overtook the sky.
Abel awoke Nairadj and they gathered their belongings.
The boy almost lit a torch but thought better of it. He
knew a torch might encroach his ability to see and sense
his way through the mountain tunnel's darkness- if things
turned south. Additionally, he was unsure whether
Melatharom was blind or not, living chiefly underground.
If he was not, a blazing torch would make Abel an easy
target in the inky blackness under the mountains. Once
they were ready, master and apprentice gazed first at one
another, then the gargantuan entrance. With an uneasy
grin, Nairadj asked, "Shall we go, Abel?"

Sucking in a deep breath, he replied, "Lead the
way, Master Nairadj."

They strode into the blackness of the tunnel.
Nairadj shouted in a voice that was firmer and leveler
than she felt, "Melatharom the Burrower, we are here as
demanded! Reveal yourself, that we may discover who is
victorious: Abel 'Drakt'vansh' and Nairadj 'Vaith'vansh', or
yourself!" The abysmal chamber reverberated her voice
down the incalculable length of the tunnel corridor,
resonating richly in the space around them. Not awaiting
a reply, Nairadj and Abel strode boldly into the gloom of
the Shavatnu Mountains to face Melatharom the rock
drake's fury.

Chapter Fourteen: Grief and Other Lessons

The past three weeks seemed a blur to Isabel, for she had learned much since arriving in Endelheim. Morgana's daughters were extraordinarily powerful sorceresses. They had much to teach the young Prezla. Isabel observed little of Morgana during those three weeks. At most times the Lady Morgana was either sequestered within her chambers, Isabel was exploring the castle grounds or focused on her lessons with the Five Sisters.

Isabel learnt the self-projection spell from Sarto first, as she swore to her brother she would. The day after arriving, she pestered him ceaselessly to teach her how to properly cast the spell. She noted his look of fatigue: as though he had not slept all night. She decided not to mention it, for she knew he had issues he grappled with; even if he didn't outright say so.

After a hearty breakfast with Lady Morgana and her daughters, Sarto and Isabel strode to the field beyond the outer castle walls. None entered the domain of Messara, unless Morgana willed it so. As such, they felt no fear of attack as they relaxed to prepare the projection spell. None stopped them, for all understood how important contacting her twin brother was to Isabel. Iolo stood constant guard outside Lady Morgana's chambers as she rested within.

Sarto shed his outer cloak, spreading it on the grass before sitting on the ground. His staff set beside him, he gazed quizzically at his pupil, asking, "Will you join me or stand there all day, Isabel?"

Without retort, she sat obediently across from her master. She yearned to contact her brother, so she acted without argument. She feared that if she seemed contentious, Sarto may cancel the lesson. Since learning of the former existence of Apollos the Wrathful; moreover, *seeing* him that day in the river, she was extremely cautious of taunting the animal inside him. More than anything, she *needed* to reach her brother. She sat quietly, awaiting Sarto's command.

Gazing tranquilly at her- she, facing north; he, facing south- Sarto exhaled a deep breath before beginning. "The first thing about self-projection: your mind *must* be clear. Not simply with a clear picture of *whom* you wish to contact, but also a mind free of *clutter*: worries, fears, distractions. All of these *must* be erased. Do you understand, Isabel?"

Isabel pondered thoughtfully a moment before replying, "Aye, Master Sarto: a cluttered mind cannot clearly communicate across distance."

He nodded, satisfied at her explanation. "Secondly, particularly in the case of Abel and Nairadj, is this: their distance from us; beyond the Shavatnu Mountains, the spell *may* be prevented from reaching them. Like all magic, a self-projection spell can only travel so far. To push beyond that limit is to court danger; either of enemy discovery or perishing in the attempted contact. You will know *very* quickly, if the intended person is beyond range or not. You will feel a....*pressure*, within your mind. Or hear a sound like the ocean through a conch. Both are important signs *not* to be ignored. If you do, your mind may lose itself in the dreamscape: for that is how we travel in self-projection. This is also why you should not communicate too long in self-projection: magical enemies, such as Lilith, may track your whereabouts. As much as you desire contacting Abel or Nairadj, you must keep both them and your person safe from discovery. We are shielded by the Lady Morgana within Messara. Once your mind ventures beyond the boundaries of Hesketh, you *will* be vulnerable to attack. Is this making sense so far?"

Isabel nodded, her mind keenly devouring the information Sarto poured forth.

The old wizard nodded, scratched his head, and mumbled a couple of seconds as he recalled where he left off. "Right now you are unknown to Lilith in your powers. This is advantageous. She doesn't know how your Prezla mind *feels*. Yes, she is aware of your existence, but she has never felt your magic's presence. In the dreamscape, our minds are mirrors: they reflect whom they belong to. Your advantage is that, should Lilith sense you, your face will be to her as one gazing through a grimy window. In other words, she will know you are there, but not who you are. It is *crucial*, should you sense her, to *immediately* sever the connection. I say this not solely for your benefit, but Abel and Nairadj's as well. If Lilith cannot track *your* whereabouts, she *will* seek those you contact. Even in the north, that will not take her long...... Now, I think I have rambled enough about *how* it works. Are you ready to attempt it for yourself, Isabel?"

She nodded eagerly, replying, "Aye, Master Sarto. I certainly am."

He gazed into Isabel's iolite eyes, answering, "Very well. The words to free your mind from your body and commit to self-projection are: '*Vesh et Tirvish*', followed by the name of the person you wish to contact. When you finish, you sever the bond with *'Vish het un corpus.'* That spell will return your mind to your body. Remember, don't be too long, and don't be discouraged if you don't reach Abel on the first attempt."

Isabel exhaled slowly, uttering the words: *'Vesh et Tirvish Abel Farthen.'* Instantly, Sarto vanished before her eyes; her mind whisked away faster than the swiftest falcon. Northward she raced over the ethereal grey version of Kalnay that was the dreamscape. She was stunned at how the world blurred about her while her mind sought Abel. Suddenly, the blurring, grey landscape ground to a sharp halt. She gazed with her mind's eye, beholding the vast expanse of the Shavatnu Mountains before her: an immovable, unforgiving sentinel. She stared at the mountains before her, trying to push beyond. *Gods be gracious to me! I only desire to see my brother! To know if he is alright; Nairadj as well. After all I have endured, you would deny me a few minutes with him!?*

Just as her master warned, she felt a pressure mounting in her head: as though she were squeezing her head through a narrow crevice. With reluctance, she blurted, *'Vish het un corpus!'* If the journey north felt like flying, the return felt like plummeting from a clifftop. Half her mind prepared to meet the ground, while the other half screamed for control of her senses. When her mind rejoined her body, the force of reconnection slammed her backwards into the grass. Isabel lay there breathing heavily, struggling for breath robbed from her by the force of re-entering her body. The young witch stared thunderstruck at the bright blue morning sky, slowly regaining her senses, as spots danced before her eyes.

A moment later, a shadow appeared over her, obstructing the sun. "I should probably have mentioned," Sarto ventured, "the greater the distance twixt body and mind, the swifter and more forceful the return is. Next time, add '*despat*' to the spell phrasing to slow your return."

With a frustrated sigh, Isabel jeered, "You might have mentioned that *before*, Master Sarto. I'm going to have a lump on my head from that blow."

Sarto ignored her jab, querying, "I take it you were unable to reach Abel, based on your swift return?"

Brushing him aside, she sat up, tenderly nursing the back of her head. "Correct, Master. I reached the base of the Shavatnu Mountains and could go no further."

Placing a firm hand on Isabel's shoulder, he declared, "That's not necessarily a *bad* thing, Isabel. Abel and Nairadj are on a mission to reach Queen Sigourney. The mountains obstructing your path are a sign that they *live*; that they have either evaded the brutish Nevar or vanquished him."

With a handful of tears trickling hotly down her cheek, Isabel snapped, "How are the mountains obstructing me a *good* thing, Master Sarto?"

Here, her master's face fell grimly serious. "If he were dead, your mind would not have flown to seek him out. The dead have not the same mind as the living. So, wipe away your tears, dear child, and take comfort. Abel and Nairadj are where they are *supposed* to be. Do not be troubled. We *shall* see them again: either through self-projection or in person. Now, I believe Lady Ezri has some new skills for you to ply your hand at. Head to the gardens. I believe she mentioned she would meet you there."

Wiping the tears from her eyes, Isabel rose without argument and proceeded reluctantly to the gardens. Her concern for Abel grew, rather than diminished, knowing he was north of the Shavatnu Mountains. Often had her father regaled them with the tale of Wagnar the Bloodstained and the horrors north of Shavatnu: nightstalkers, marsh drakes and Wildmen. Offering a quick prayer for Abel and Nairadj's continued safety, Isabel re-entered the castle to locate Ezri.

Morgana's eldest daughter was a skilled horticulturalist. She knew many tricks to aid in the better, richer growth of vegetables and herbs: how to properly till the soil, how to leave seeds for the next planting, and how to gain more growth from the current crop (with some gentle, magical coaxing). Isabel knew instinctively that, had Sarto taught her, she may have forgotten or ignored these things. Caring for the earth, working with her hands beside a fellow woman gave her a closer sense of kinship to Ezri. As her tutor demonstrated how to properly clip a sampling of greenwood mint without damaging the plant, Isabel was reminded of her mother. She grew curious how her mother fared; whether she missed her daughter as much as Isabel missed her.

After her gardening lessons on the fifth day, Isabel excused herself, setting in the field outside the castle. This had become her most comforting, relaxing spot in the entirety of Endelheim. She sat on the grass, clearing her mind. Then with a calm exhalation of breath, Isabel whispered, "*Vesh et Tirvish, Amina Farthen.*" The usual rush of flight did not seize Isabel's mind, and her eyes started open. Closing them tightly again, Isabel focused her thoughts. "*Vesh et Tirvish, Amina Farthen.*" As before, nothing happened. A cold spike of fear jabbed her heart, as she recalled her master's words regarding the living and the dead. *Keep calm*, she commanded herself. *Perhaps....perhaps she has fallen ill. Perhaps she is too weak to communicate mentally. I shall search out Bishop. I will ask him what has happened to mother.*

Clearing her mind again she whispered fervently, "*Vesh et Tirvish, Bishop.*" As before, nothing happened. With a sinking feeling in the pit of her stomach, Isabel kept her eyes squeezed tightly shut, tears springing up. Gritting her teeth, she shouted desperately, "*Vesh et Tirvish, Amina Farthen!*" As with her previous attempts, nothing happened. Her mind whirled in confusion, anger and hopelessness. *What has happened? What could have* possibly *happened to both mother and Bishop? We left Gwenovair immediately. No one knew where we lived. No one knew......* In dawning horror, she recalled Straker and the surprise attack that had cost Pallas his life. A fragment of memory from her father's lessons rang clearly in her head: '*Northerners are* extremely *keen trackers. They can track scents over a month old, back to their origin.*'

In that sickening moment, Isabel knew the cold, stark truth: her mother and step-father were dead. Grief pierced her heart like a barbed arrow, ripping and tearing as it punched through her emotional defenses. At first, she could not give voice to her grief; she simply trembled violently in place, seated on the breeze-cooled grass outside Endelheim's castle walls.

When she felt the first hot tears course down her face, Isabel unleashed a shrill, broken cry of grief, shredding the serenity of the surrounding countryside. She struggled to stand, but the will to rise had fled her stricken soul. All she could do was roll onto her side, curl into a ball, wrapping her arms about her as tightly as possible; as though by hugging so fiercely, she could undo this cruel twist of fate. How *did this happen?* When *did it happen? Does* Abel *know?* Her overburdened mind raced in circles with unanswerable questions, crippling her with the weight of horrendous grief.

Moments later, Sarto dashed through the open castle gate, his staff ready. Beholding his student curled on the ground, he rushed to her side, dropping to his knees. "Whatever is the matter, dear one? I heard your cries and believed you to be in mortal peril."

In one swift motion she bolted upright, locked her arms about his neck in a deep embrace and shrieked through her veil of tears, "My mother and step-father are *dead*, Master Sarto!" Then her sorrow stirred anew, and she cried like a wounded beast on the verge of death.

Sarto was stunned. Numbly, he wrapped his arms about his grief-stricken apprentice. *'Mina and Bishop are* dead*? How can that be?* In another moment, he realized, as Isabel had, that Straker had led his repugnant friends to them. He clutched her firmly, while she sobbed openly against his shoulder. Silently, he attempted the projection spell. His stomach turned sour when nothing happened. His anger swelled thinking of Amina and Bishop, the friendliest souls he had ever known, murdered by the same brigands who had caused Pallas' death.

The Mender felt Apollos scratching at the boundaries in his mind, shoving his old demon down with anger. *Now is not the time to test me, Apollos. I have within me a rage that surpasses all caution. If you force me, I will do my best to destroy you utterly. Be gone back to Pimedus!* Sarto felt Apollos' dark presence retreat into the recesses of his mind. The ancient wizard knew he must be strong for Isabel now, as her master. He supressed his tears, planting a delicate kiss on her forehead. "This is a truly *terrible* discovery, dear Isabel. I will not tell you not to grieve, but....you must not let these ill tidings cripple you...."

Isabel stated coldly into her master's ear, "Teach me to *kill* with magic. I don't *care* what it costs me; even my very *soul!* I want to ensure things like this *never* happen again! My mother and step-father did *not* deserve death at the hands of those murderous *swine!*"

Sarto withdrew from the embrace, gazing mournfully at his pupil as she seethed. "*Isabel....*"

"Will you teach me to kill with magic, yes or no?"

He gripped Isabel's chin firmly in his left hand, staring sternly into her eyes. "I will *not*, Isabel. I have been there, as Apollos the Wrathful. In a manner of speaking, I am *still* there. If you willfully kill with magic, you become no better than Lilith....you may *become* the very evil you despise- selling your magical talent for money. Is *that* what you want?"

Isabel's face fell into a mask of ill-concealed rage. She pummelled Sarto's chest, shrieking, "I want *retribution!* I want my step-father back, Master Sarto! I want my freckaying *mother* back, gods *damn* it!" After this last, she broke down again, burying her face against his chest.

The old man scooped his pupil up in his arms, returning to the gate. A moment before he entered, Ezri and Delja came running out, looks of alarm on their faces. They were closest and had heard Isabel's grief-stricken cries from within the courtyard. Sarto solemnly shook his head. The look on his face told them something dreadful had occurred. The sisters hurried to prepare her chamber, and warm her some tea. Sarto kissed Isabel's forehead, whispering, "It will be alright my child. It will take time, but everything will be alright. I am with you, no matter what. We stick together until the end. I swear this on my life."

Isabel spent the next three days in bed: not eating, barely sleeping and crying often. Sarto never left her side. He could do naught, but he desired that she knew she was not alone. He too had known Amina and Bishop; the shock of their unexpected deaths hung heavy on his fractured mind. He thought too of Abel and Nairadj; hoping against hope that, had the boy learnt of his family's deaths, Nairadj was providing him strength to carry on. *Gods above and below, how* cruel *you are sometimes.*

On the fourth day after discovering her parents' deaths, Isabel arose of her own accord, eating breakfast in her chamber. She looked haggard and felt doubly so. After eating, she went to the field to contact Abel. She hoped against hope she might reach him, to discover if he knew of their mother's death, and how it happened. She

hoarsely uttered the projection spell, instantly flying
north; stopping once again before the mountains.
Despite that, she was relieved her mind had gone
somewhere. Now she understood: 'twas better to have
one's mind go forth and be obstructed by distance, then
not be sent at all. She cancelled the spell, slowing her
mind as she returned. *I* must *go on. If I stop now, their
loss is for naught. Then those freckaying* bastards *will
have well and truly won. I will show them; Farthens do
not surrender easily.* Picking herself up, she strode with
determination back through the castle gate to seek out
Delja, whom she was to sail and fish with today.

Isabel found her easily and together they strode
sombrely down to Andalmere Bay at the base of an
intricate set of a hundred stone steps carved into the cliff
face to the southeast of Endelheim. Delja had a small
fishing vessel stocked with supplies for the day waiting
for them at the old, rickety docks. The second eldest
daughter of Lady Morgana was dressed simply: her hair
wrapped in a white linen head scarf, a pair of long shorts
stopping just below her knees, and a simple, cream-
colored lace-up tunic, billowing gently in the sea breeze.
To Isabel, she appeared like the fabled pirate Prince
Baltus; or Zuberi, Rover of the Chakti of whom she had
read of in '*Legends of Kalnay*' as a child.

Delja glanced quizzically towards Isabel as they
descended the stairs, for the Prezla's cracking smile
betrayed her thoughts. "What's so funny?"

Young Farthen covered her mouth a moment,
regaining her composure. "I cry your pardon, Delja. It's
just....the only people I ever heard of dressing thus were

in pirate myths. It's....*odd*, seeing someone dressed like a pirate in real life, that's all." She gazed at her own apparel- a dress, trousers and boots beneath (for she still disliked being without trousers or boots). The young witch sheepishly resumed, "It seems I dressed incorrectly for today's outing....my apologies."

Delja raised a hand, halting the apology. "Nothing to fret over; I didn't explain we would be fishing on the bay, rather than from shore, so that is *my* error." Glancing mischievously back up the stairs for any sign of others, she whispered conspiratorially, "You know....*if* you brought your knives today, you could *modify* your dress into more....seaworthy apparel....if you so desired."

Young Farthen stopped in place, staring briefly at her friend before casting a mortified look at her radiant dress. It was a beautiful green silk dress with a bodice beneath. "Delja, I....I *couldn't*. This is *your* dress and...."

"As such," she interjected, "it is *mine* to do with as I see fit. Alter it to suit your needs, please. I shall deal with mother....assuming she even finds out. A lady should be comfortable at all times, wouldn't you agree?" At this last, she smiled devilishly.

Isabel decided, in that moment, she and Delja were going to be superb friends. Nodding agreement, she inquired, "Is there somewhere private I can make my....*alterations* to this dress? I'd feel horrible if your mother saw me butchering this fine dress right here on the docks."

Delja pointed down the stairs to the end of the pier, at a shack nestled against the cliff face. "That is the boat house. It will serve adequately as your impromptu tailor's suite. Come, let us go. I will ready the skiff while you change."

Isabel chuckled. *Why do I feel so good about this? I shouldn't wreck this dress, yet I can already feel the sweet liberation of doing so. It's true, Delja has given permission. I still feel somewhat* wicked *doing this. She did say a lady should always be comfortable. You don't see men wearing bodices while they harpoon swordfish.*

As they reached the bottom of the stairs, Isabel was impressed by the scope of her surroundings. The docks running the length of the shore were large enough for a frigate. However, nothing was anchored there save a skiff. The young witch excused herself, heading to the boat shack to alter her garments. Shutting the door, she stood in the quasi-darkness of the shack, faint light glimmering off the water beneath the shack door. Slipping off the dress, Isabel exposed her painfully constricting bodice. Plucking one of her knives deftly from her trousers' belt, she muttered, "Fare thee well," sliding the knife carefully down the front of her tight-laced prison. The flimsy strings were no match for the edge of her blade, and they burst with a faint snap.

In an odd moment of reflection, as her breasts were exposed to the chilly sea air, freed from the torture of the bodice, she mused, *I wonder if Khalon's claws would do such a swift and* thorough *job freeing a lady from her bodice....* As her distracted, young mind finished the thought, she blushed deeply.

The rational part of her mind nattered: *Just what do you think you are doing, nursing thoughts like that?! Get dressed! Focus on your lessons! Khalon is a* wendygo. *You are a sorceress; not exactly a gods' made match.*

Refocusing on the task at hand, she swiftly cut the dress below the waistline and lopped the arms off at the shoulders. Having done so, Isabel slipped on her newly created, sleeveless tunic. Then, the youthful part of her mind returned to arguing with the nattering old bitty. *Khalon may be a wendygo, but he is also* unique. *The more time our company has spent with him....that I have spent with him, the more I see not a monster. What I see is a young man discontent to remain what fate has made him; he is an aberration of an abomination. His own kind condemned him to die for retaining his individuality rather than succumbing to predatory instinct. I would not say that I love him, not yet anyways. But he....*intrigues *me. He has been a truer friend, than most boys or men I have ever met.*

The nag piped in. *What boys and men have you* met? *You grew up on Gwenovair, you silly, love-struck waif! The* boys' *there were less than sixteen years of age. Most* 'men' *were already married, or into their ripe, olden years. Your experience with* 'men' *is all but non-existent!*

Isabel mentally brushed the nag away, as she transformed the one sleeve into a head scarf to keep her hair out of her face as she sailed. *Be that as it may, I know how the world is; how* cruel *it can be. Even if I don't know many men, I see how they are, and can be, in the larger world: savage brutes who take* what *they want, when* they *want it and discard the rest. The Red Houses of the Mainland wouldn't be in such perpetual business if more men acted differently.*

You are not entirely wrong, the rational part of her brain conceded, *but you* must *know that men are raised first as children. Without proper upbringing, then yes, they become brutish thugs. If they are raised properly....well, they can become more like Pallas, or Bishop or your brother Abel....*

Please, Isabel interjected with a tone of sadness, *please don't mention them. Two of them are dead, and Abel....I cannot reach him, though I* desperately *desire to know how he fares......to discover if he knows aught of our mother or Bishop's ill fates. Now....if you are done chittering in my ear like an insect, I must go sailing.* The old woman took her cue, drifting elsewhere in Isabel's mind. With her newly adjusted wardrobe, Isabel opened the shack door, re-emerging into the sunlight.

Down the dock, Delja stood patiently, waiting for Isabel. When she observed Isabel's modifications, she looked pleasantly surprised at the changes. "My *goodness,*" she began, "you vastly improved that old dress's look; not to mention its functionality. Well done, sister."

Isabel gazed at the dock in embarrassment at the compliment, then back to Delja in surprise at being called sister. This lifted her heart indescribably. In return she offered, "My thanks, Delja; both for the dress *and* the compliment. My mother....*Amina* was her name.....she was the seamstress for Birosh, my hometown on Gwenovair. I learned tricks like this from her- though these sorts of alterations would *never* be done to a lady's garments there. In truth....it was the one thing she did that I *truly* loved sharing with her. I was never much interested in cleaning or cooking. Alteration and creating clothes filled many cold hours in winter twixt us with joy and laughter...."

Reaching out, Delja took Isabel's hand. "Amina seems an amazing woman, and a *wonderful* mother. I wish I could have met her. She and I would have gotten along splendidly."

Smiling, despite the tears threatening to pour, Isabel responded, "Aye....*sister*, I believe she would agree." Wishing to change the topic, Isabel asked, "What of *your* mother, Morgana? What do you two have in common?"

Here, a peculiar look crossed Delja's face. She paused a long moment as she considered Isabel's question. "Well....I....*we* possess magical abilities- though hers *far* exceed my own. We both enjoy reading....though lately, I haven't seen her much. She has taken to her chambers oft....though she *does* maintain the magic shrouding Messara from unfriendly eyes, as well as the defense spells cast over Hesketh. She also likes taking long walks in the gardens. That is another thing all of us share a passion for: things growing in the garden......" At that, Delja shook her head, as though clearing her mind, before smiling absently at Isabel. "Enough about my mother. Let us get this vessel into the bay. See what we can bring home for supper."

They climbed aboard, happy in the freedom of Andalmere Bay; listening to the gulls cawing, feeling the sea breeze, and hearing the gentle lapping of the water at the prow. Isabel and Delja sailed the entirety of the bay, never venturing past where it opened into the Nevartane (the ancient Kalnayan name for 'The Ever Misty Sea'). Delja showed Isabel some new knots to try on the skiff's rigging, providing their nets better hold against larger, heavier fish. She also showed Isabel spells to summon fish to the surface for easy catching; though she cautioned against overusing that spell. If it were, the small fish would eventually vanish- for no fish can resist the call of the summoning spell. The trouble became, she explained, that if all the small fish disappeared, the next thing summoned would be larger fish: swordfish and even sharks. Isabel understood the implication: if you summoned a shark, the skiff would likely lose. Additionally, if the balance of nature was too far off kilter, life in the bay could be drastically affected.

By day's end, the two of them had caught over two dozen sea bass. Isabel's heart felt happier than it had been since before learning of her mother and step-father's deaths. Sharing memories of them with Delja made her heart hurt less, which was an odd sensation to feel. Returning to the castle late that afternoon, Isabel offered a thankful prayer to Trytos for their bounty; another to Bauer for such a fine friend in Delja.

Over the next week, Isabel spent time separately with both Sena and Aloisa. With Sena, Isabel learnt several new spells. Among them was the spell of multiplication- '*brothsa*'; a useful spell when short on supplies or creating more weapons for defense. She also taught Isabel the spell for short-distance teleportation- '*dizva het*'; this is how Ezri arrived so swiftly to fetch Isabel and her companions from Hesketh. The toughest spell for her to master was the spell of illusion- '*breksa lokis*'. The spell required focus and imagination while shielding oneself from discovery. The point was to convince the observer that the party they sought had vanished; replaced instead by an illusory bear, or a solid rock wall. Isabel was proficient at one or the other, but she found dividing her focus to two separate tasks was both exhausting and frustrating. After two solid days of dedicated practice, she finally accomplished in her task.

The last several days of that week were spent exclusively with Aloisa, as they ventured forth on a three-day respite to Hesketh with Lady Morgana's blessing. Though there was not much to hunt- as the area was magically shielded by Morgana, from seemingly everything both predatorial and prey- they relished the chance to depart the castle. On the second day of trekking, Isabel killed two rabbits with a single, magically guided arrow. The kills were clean: the arrow punching through the rabbits' necks, planting itself in the ground just beyond the second jackrabbit. Aloisa scooped up the farther one, as Isabel grabbed up the first one. Had they missed, the miniature green and orange dragons in the trees above (which, Aloisa informed Isabel, were known as 'Draconias Minimus': or, dwarf dragons) would have swooped down and snatched the unattended food. "The last thing you want to do," Aloisa advised, "is stave off a brood of hungry dwarf dragons."

Isabel chuckled, asking, "Are you speaking from personal experience, my sister?"

Aloisa smiled slyly, wagging a finger, answering, "It's merely common sense, my sister. One should *never* let an opponent's size deceive you, regarding their abilities. I remember as a child, being out here with Sena. We witnessed a wolf ripped apart by a brood of the dwarf dragons. The beast snapped one out of the air, for it tried flying off with his dinner......a badger as I recall it. It is something I have *never* forgotten."

Casting a wary look at the foot-long dragons rustling their tiny wings in the trees above, Isabel stated, "My thanks for the warning; gods know *that* would be a disappointing end to my story: devoured by angry dwarf dragons."

Hearing that out loud caused the girls to burst out laughing. Above them the dwarf dragons scattered skyward, landing again after a moment's startled flight. When the dragons resettled, they collectively stared curiously at the humans, perplexed by the noise.

Aloisa stifled a second bout of laughter, nudging Isabel to a clearing a short distance away. "Let us set camp here for the night. We can discuss hunting stories over these rabbits, once they're cooked. Maybe we can do like the men do in the old legends and show off our hunting scars."

Isabel shook her head. "I'm afraid you may win by default. I have never encountered anything more dangerous than jackrabbits on Gwenovair. Though, I *did* battle a sea wulf my first night off the island."

Aloisa stopped dead in her tracks, looking shocked into Isabel's iolite eyes, searching for the hint of a lie. "Are you *serious*? You fought an honest to gods' *sea wulf*, and are alive to tell the tale? This, I *must* hear."

Isabel shrugged, adding, "Well....I *did* have help from Abel, his master Pallas and our new dyre bear friend Nairadj......though truthfully, had she not stepped in when she did, we would surely have all perished that night."

Aloisa waved off Isabel's minimizations and pressed, "Isabel, you were in a *battle* with a sea wulf and *survived.* I joke with Delja to beware of sea wulves on Andalmere Bay, but you have *genuinely* laid eyes upon one. That *alone* bears retelling; I want to hear *everything*, even the parts where the wulf was winning."

Isabel shrugged again, pointing at Aloisa and countering, "Fair enough. But first, you must tell me how and why you and Sena were out here as little girls all by yourself." Chuckling, Isabel jested, "Were you running away from home or something?"

Aloisa's face fell stone flat, save her eyes: those darted to and fro, as though frantically struggling to recall a memory, long since forgotten. Isabel had an odd sense of déjà vu to her time out with Delja these several days past as she watched Aloisa's contorting face.

A moment later, the conflicting emotions on her face fell away and Aloisa's face brightened again. She answered with a shrug, "Not much to tell I'm afraid. We were playing in the fields. We chased a rabbit into Hesketh, got turned around. We found the wolf; saw it attacked by the dragons. Half a day later, Iolo found and returned us home to mother." Aloisa laughed then (though to Isabel it seemed contrived). "See, that's why you *must* tell me of the sea wulf, I need a new story to tell my sisters. Come, let us get those rabbits cooked before the meat spoils." Then she sprinted to the clearing, bustling about to gather wood for a fire.

Isabel returned to camp, measuredly watching Aloisa and her behaviour. *There is something she is not saying.... but* what? The young Prezla knew that asking her friend anything right now would be a waste of energy, and possibly tainted with half truths. So, she let it rest for the time being, though she never truly forgot it.

The next morning at sunrise, Aloisa and Isabel returned to Endelheim, refreshed and happy. Isabel informed Aloisa that she was going to search for Abel with the projection spell before returning to her studies. Her friend bid her farewell and continued inside the castle.

Settling in the accustomed spot, facing north, the young witch once again used the projection spell to seek out her brother. As before, she arrived at the base of the Shavatnu mountains, the rockface pressing close in to where her astral presence halted. It seemed to her, this time, that the mountain was *different* than the one she had first stood before three weeks past. She would have sworn it was further east than previously, and that wasn't even the strangest part. What was strange to her, was Abel's presence didn't seem to be on the opposite side of the mountain. Rather, his presence felt *strangely* as though he were *beneath* the mountain. Since she could not explain it, she dismissed it as misinterpretation. Still, it nagged at the back of her mind. Since she could do nothing about it presently, she readied herself to see Allegra on this, the first day of the fourth week since she and her friends arrived in Endelheim.

Allegra requested her presence just before the mid-day meal, within her chambers. Isabel found this peculiar, but not overtly so. She was made aware of the girl's gift as a 'Far-Seer' by Aloisa while they were on their trek in Hesketh. Naturally, when Allegra requested her presence, Isabel felt a knot of uncertainty tangle in her stomach. *What could she possibly want to see me for? I haven't had anyone prophesy about me since my naming ceremony. That seems so long ago now. I wonder what one as young as Allegra could wish to share with me.*

Several minutes later, Isabel stood before the young girl's chambers. She noted all candles leading to the chamber were extinguished; plunging the hallway into a gloomy, rock and mortar tunnel of blackness. She raised her hand to knock on the door. Before she could, Allegra's soft voice lilted, "Enter, Isabel of House Farthen."

Her hand froze in mid-air as Allegra spoke. Swallowing the sizable lump forming in her throat, she pushed open the door. Within the chamber all candles were also snuffed, the shutters closed, and the room was cast into a deeper dark than the hallway. Allegra's voice emerged from the opposite side of the chamber, saying, "Please, sit with me Isabel and we shall begin."

It took a long moment for Isabel to feel her way across the room to where Allegra's voice came from. This instance felt strangely familiar; she felt as though she were back in Pallas' darkened hut on the day of her name divining. *Gods above, that feels like a lifetime ago*, she mused. In mild surprise, she found her way without incident and sat cross-legged on the floor across from where she sensed Allegra to be.

As if on cue, the young girl's voice emerged a mere three feet from the darkness before Isabel's face, "Like a divining ceremony, you must sit absolutely still and listen closely. Can you do that Isabel of house Farthen?"

Isabel nodded wordlessly, before realizing Allegra would not see her nod in the dark, so she rasped, "Yes, I understand."

Why is my throat suddenly dry?

Isabel heard a muted incantation from Allegra. Abruptly, a silvery light rose from a large water bowl on the floor twixt them. She flinched at the sudden light but did not move. She watched curiously as the silvery light rising from the bowl took on shape and form. Isabel drew a deep breath as a wispy, life-sized silvery figure turned towards her. It was her mother.

The silvery wraith of Amina echoed, *My dear, dear Isabel. Gods, it is good to see you. I'm sorry I cannot be there to hold you; more than anything I miss that. I have been permitted to see you, and to relay a crucial message. Would you hear it, Bell-flower?*

Isabel could not help the tears welling hotly in her eyes as she beheld this spectre of her mother. "Oh Madriga," Isabel grieved, "I am so, *so* sorry for what happened to you."

Amina interjected, S*weet one, it was* not *your fault. I did* not *go without a fight. I made those bastards feel it before they took my life, and Bishop's......but enough of that. Time is short. The gods have revealed a prophecy you are part of. I* must *relay it to you before I fade back to the Nether-Realm. Would you hear it?*

Isabel wiped tears from her face. "Aye, I would. Tell me what I must do."

It is 'the Prophecy of the Great Serpent', Amina's spectre declared. *It proceeds thus:*

> *When the Chosen overcomes the Serpent of Mirk,*
> *And Serpent of Stone is forever crushed beneath the Mountains,*
> *Then shall the Great Serpent of Mists be awoken.*
> *One of Divine Light must, with mind and spirit,*
> *Triumph o'er the will and wroth of the Great Serpent*
> *Else all is wrought to ash and fire.*

This the gods have decreed; this shall come to pass, in the fullness of time.

Isabel was confused at the prophecy, though she retained it. "Madriga, what does it mean? Who is the *Chosen*? Am *I* the one of Divine Light? What is the Great Serpent? I don't understand......"

Amina's silvery projection began to fade. Amina rushed on; *I am sorry Isabel. I can stay no longer. Your step-father beckons me return to the Nether-Realm. I will* always *be with you and Abel. Remember me fondly, Bell-flower.*

Isabel's heart broke anew, seeing her mother's ghostly visage dwindle. She reached to take her hand, watching in renewed sorrow as her mother's wraith disappeared. Then she was plunged into darkness, weeping softly to herself. *Gods be gracious. Thank you for the chance to see my Madriga again....but this pain....Freckaya, why must joy and pain walk hand in hand like moonlight lovers?*

A moment later, Allegra opened the shutters. She approached where Isabel sat bleary-eyed, wordlessly wrapping her in a gentle, sisterly hug. "I'm sorry," the Far-Seer offered simply.

Isabel gratefully hugged the young seer, whispering, "No, Allegra. Thank *you* for this gift. The prophecy itself....I do not yet fully grasp its meaning. I am sure, when the time is right, all will be revealed. Thank you for enabling me to see my mother one last time. That is a gift I can *never* repay. I shall do my best, regardless." Then she sighed deeply and seethed, "I just wish I could reach Abel; discover what he knows of mother's death, or *if* he knows of it at all. The *freckaying* Shavatnu Mountains keep obstructing me, though he felt closer when I last checked." Isabel sighed again, rubbing her temples and muttering, "I apologize, Allegra. You have been a *true* help, and I sit here, griping like a toddling infant."

Allegra rose, offering a hand and pulling Isabel to her feet. The Far-Seer gazed indistinctly out her window, her ear cocked like a dog listening for their master's return. With a faint smirk, she returned her gaze to Isabel, squeezed her hand and whispered, "I think....if you tried to contact Abel *now*, sister, you would find your chances *much* improved."

Isabel gazed wonderstruck at the implication of her words. The Seer beamed broadly now, nodding silent confirmation, watching her friend's face transform from disheartened to hopeful. Kissing Allegra sweetly on the cheek, Isabel turned, whipped open the chamber door and dashed down the stone steps, through the courtyard and out the castle gate. She raced to her spot in the field where she normally cast the self-projection spell, her heart beating like a drum.

Launching herself onto the grass, in a haphazard cross-legged pose, she spat, "*Vesh et Tirvish, Abel Farthen!*" As before, her mind flew free of her corporeal body, racing north across the vast expanse of Kalnay. Within moments, she drew up before the Shavatnu mountains. In another moment, she found herself rushing up the angled face of the mountain, to a rocky outcropping, with a crawlspace behind. Sitting on the outcropping, bruised and scratched, breathing hard from climbing and drinking from a water skin, was Abel. Nairadj was seated across from him, looking equally battered and weary; but they were *alive*. Isabel was so stunned at seeing her long-absent brother for the first time in over two months that she could not find the words to speak to him.

He saved her the trouble by wearily looking up as her ethereal, disembodied projection appeared, hovering before the outcropping. He started, shoved himself back towards the crawlspace, uttering a surprised, "*Gah!*"

Nairadj glanced at him, before turning her attention to where he looked and froze at the sight of Isabel. "Lady Isabel? Is that *you*?"

She beamed broadly at Nairadj, squealing joyfully, "*Yes!* Yes, my dear friend, 'tis me. I am in Endelheim with Sarto and....well, several new friends we picked up along the way who have helped us." Returning her attention to Abel, Isabel queried, "Are you just going to sit there like a cornered dormouse, or are you going to say hello to your sister, dunkla?"

Abel rose to his feet, surveying the ghostly projection of Isabel- for she did not realize how she appeared to him. He laughed a moment, before asking, "What took you so long? I began to think you'd forgotten me. Or worse, that you came to harm."

Isabel placed her hands on her hips, looking sourly at her twin. "*I've* been trying to reach you with this spell for the last *three* weeks. It was these confounded mountains blocking my projection from getting there." Indicating the crawlspace behind Abel, Isabel asked, "What were you doing *under* the mountain, anyways? Is there not a perfectly good pass but several leagues west of here you could have taken?"

Abel looked at Nairadj a moment, before bursting into a fit of raucous laughter, plunking onto his backside in joviality. Nairadj joined in the laughter, while Isabel stared in confusion, unsure of what was so funny. Once Abel gained his composure, he released a loud sigh, looked his sister's projection in the eye and stated, "That is one *long* story, sister of mine. Why don't you sit....or, *hover* while I will regale you with all the fun you have missed here in the north?"

Isabel listened keenly to the unfolding tale of Abel and Nairadj's journey north after Pallas' death.

Chapter Fifteen: A Touch of Darkness

With Pallas' aid, Sarto successfully supressed Apollos during the past three weeks. Now, he felt himself steadily slipping to Apollos' control. When Pallas informed Sarto of the ill feeling within Endelheim, they both wondered whether there was some cursed object, acting as a beacon for Apollos' attempted resurgence. As subtly as possible, he began searching Endelheim, using summoning and revealing spells; all to no avail.

He dared not ask Queen Morgana or her daughters. He wished to avoid seeming intrusive after being granted haven. He was also concerned by the possibility, remote though it was, that one or more residents of Endelheim may be under Lilith's dark influence. As someone who had experienced her....touch, the old herbalist knew it could run *very* deep. During his second week of careful searching, he casually asked Eben the cook what he knew of Endelheim. He asked after things like whether there had been any historic battles fought here, any dark wizards passing through who may have cursed the land or the castle.

Eben's face fell deeper into a blank stare the more Sarto pursued his questions. The old wizard believed Eben was straining himself too hard. *Clearly, he was hired for his culinary skills rather than his intellectual prowess,* he reflected dourly. In another moment, Eben's face resumed its usual lustre. The cook shrugged, chuckling, "Not so far as *I* know, Master Wizard. I'm more concerned with the day to day of culinary arts, recipes and spice blends to try. Perhaps ask Iolo or Scribe Frodi; they may be more helpful. Can I interest you in tasting this stew I am fixing for lunch?"

Raising a hand, Sarto politely declined, "Thank you Eben, but no. My deepest thanks for your advice." Sarto exited the kitchen, his staff clacking on the paving stones as he entered the courtyard. He felt Apollos brewing a storm within his discordant mind. Wincing, the troubled Prezla sat on the edge of the stone fountain at the courtyard's centre, while he and Pallas subdued his demon's antics.

This is becoming increasingly difficult, old friend. I feel him *gaining strength. I still have no idea who or what is fueling his rise. It is something rife with dark magic, whatever it is. Before too long, he will burst through my barricades and then......I don't even want to* imagine *what sort of danger the others will be in.*

Pallas offered: *Be* strong, *old friend. He is but a* wraith *in your mind. Together we can suppress him until we discover what transpires here. Perhaps you should ask Iolo? He has been in Morgana's service for years, it would seem. He may know the source of this disturbance....*

Sarto interrupted: *But what if....what if he is* so *loyal to her, he reports my queries? The last thing I need is to contend with our Prezla hostess for offending her* while *struggling to simultaneously repress Apollos.*

Well, Pallas searched, *that just leaves Frodi. Surely the Scribe of Endelheim will have records regarding the history of this place. Scribes are typically eager to share their knowledge with curious minds. There is no other soul in Kalnay more curious right now than yourself.*

Sarto snorted sarcastically and thought, *I'm choosing to take that as a compliment, Pallas; not as a critique of my rapidly decaying mind. But, aye, you're right. We will seek out Frodi; perhaps he will have some answers.*

As he crossed the courtyard to the library in the north wing, a disturbing thought occurred; more disturbing because, until this very moment, it had not crossed his mind. *Pallas....why are there so few people here? I mean, this castle could comfortably house at least two thousand people. There is a pier, plenty of grassland around for farming; even space to establish a small township or two......why then is this place so....empty?*

Sarto felt Pallas' presence grow still within his mind, as the ghostly diviner pondered the unsettling question. *That, old friend, I am unable to adequately answer. We must proceed cautiously; watch for signs to answer this quandary. Now, let us away to Scribe Frodi. Perhaps he may answer these questions.*

Let us hope so Pallas. The lack of answers in this place is beginning to unnerve me.

Shortly, Sarto entered the Messaran Library. He was surprised to realize he hadn't visited here sooner. It was quite *literally* the single most massive library he had ever beheld. It was larger than any he had visited in Ackreth, or even the Royal Regalias Library. Bustling about behind a central U-shaped counter space was Frodi, rooting through a pile of parchments, mumbling to himself.

As he entered Sarto waved, calling, "Good day to you Scribe Frodi! How are...."

"*Shhh*!" hissed the Scribe, popping up from behind the counter. "This is a *library* don't you know!? One must *always* observe silence in the library!"

Funny, Pallas noted sarcastically, he's *got no problem shouting.* Ignoring Frodi's abruptness and Pallas' remark on etiquette, Sarto whispered, "Apologies, Master Frodi. I merely seek information. I thought perhaps *you* could aid in my search."

Frodi perked up (reminding Sarto oddly of an excitable lap dog) replying, "*Well*, Master Wizard, you have *certainly* come to the right place! Information is one of my specialties!"

As is an overly-loud voice, Pallas jabbed. Sarto ignored his friend, responding cheerily, "That is *indeed* a happy coincidence. Perhaps you may help me answer some questions then, Master Frodi."

The Scribe's eyes grew large, his mouth agape in wonder. "You require *my* help, Master Wizard? Well....I would be honored to aid you however I may! What do you need help with?"

Sarto hesitated, recalling Eben's reaction when asked about Endelheim. *I must be delicate, if I am to get answers.* Smiling broadly, he ventured, "How long have you dwelt in Endelheim, Master Frodi?"

Pulling off his truss and scratching his thinning gray hair, the Scribe pondered a moment before answering, "Gods above....I must have come to

Endelheim......I think it was early in the reign of King
Alaster's father."

Sarto started in surprise. "Gods above that is
quite a time ago, Master Frodi. Tell me, if you can....in all
those years....has there ever been anything...? Gods, I'm
not entirely sure how to phrase this...."

Frodi uttered an impatient sigh, scoffing,
"Master Sarto, as my father Joel was fond of saying,
'Organize your thoughts *before* uttering them.' Though I
pour over books, tomes and parchments all day, my time
is *not* something I wish to waste on indecisiveness."

Sarto smiled, nodding deferentially. After a
theatrical show of organizing his thoughts, he exhaled
measuredly, asking, "Has anything....*odd* ever occurred in
either Messara or Endelheim, to the best of your
knowledge?" Upon uttering his question, Sarto observed
Frodi's face transform as Eben's had. Pallas noted the
change too. *This bodes ill for all dwelling here,* Sarto
thought. *Someone, or something, is controlling the
residents here....or this place is cursed.*

With a tinge of fear in his voice, Pallas inquired:
Could this be Lilith's *handiwork?*

No, Sarto stated flatly. *Lilith's interests are
accruing power for wanton destruction: all towards the
extinguishing of the Light. These signs we see....they are
more....*calculated, *subtle: two traits Lilith does* not
possess.

Well, there must be something *we can do.
Someone else we can talk to,* Pallas offered. The

conversation twixt Sarto and Pallas took space in a second.

Before the Prezla could respond, he watched Frodi's countenance visibly mutate; the dazed look on the scribe's face transformed into a grimace of struggle. The Scribe began visibly trembling as if emerging from a frozen lake. His voice took on a fierce, determined tone as he hissed through gritted teeth, "I have....a *key*....around my neck. Take it...! It opens....the restricted section of the library. The *truth* of Endelheim....of *what* controls this place....it is *there*. '*A Brief History of Endelheim*'....within its pages lies the truth......Take the key *now*, Master Wizard!"

Then Frodi seized fiercely, toppling to the ground. He knocked a stack of dusty, leather-bound tomes to the stone floor, bashing his head on the corner of the counter as he fell. Sarto dashed to assist him, only to discover Frodi unconscious. A large bruise mottled his right temple. The old wizard pressed two fingers to the side of Frodi's neck, feeling (with relief) a strong pulse. Satisfied he would live, Sarto felt around the scribe's neck, finding a thin leather strip brush his searching fingers. He tugged gently, drawing a large skeleton key from the folds of the scribe's robes. Carefully, he removed the necklace from around Frodi's neck. Doing so, he donned the necklace, concealing it deep within his robes. Then he took up his staff, hurriedly exiting the library.

Pallas spoke up. *Are you going to leave him like that, Sarto?*

The Prezla strode to the stables where Khalon was staying. *Don't be silly,* he scoffed. *Frodi is our best and* only *lead at this point. The* last *thing I desire is for Frodi to perish. I'm fetching Khalon to carry him to the infirmary. Once Frodi is on the road to recovery, I shall assist him in recovering his memories. I* must *know what has transpired here, if I'm to determine how to defeat Apollos.*

Presently, Sarto spotted the wendygo. The young buck was crouched at the edge of a vegetable garden with Eimar and Tibelde. The Shadow Twins laughed jovially as they taught him differences amongst the vegetables in the soil. Sarto was about to hail Khalon, when his limbs froze, and his vocal cords fell silent. He searched his mind frantically for Pallas but could not sense his friend's comforting presence. *Pallas, where* are *you?*

The voice that responded was the chilling, sibilant tone of Apollos. "*Sorry, old chum. I traded places with that dead diviner. Thank the* gods *you two built the barricades in your mind* so *strongly. That meddlesome buffoon can't help you now*, old man."

His mind turned to face the ghost of his dark past. As he made eye contact with the malicious former version of himself, Sarto felt an odd mixture of anger and sadness swell in his heart. He knew he was seeing himself. *Truly* seeing himself; possibly for the first time. He observed the emaciated, mad-eyed version of himself: long, matted brown hair, fiery steel eyes begging fools to challenge his might. He beheld exactly what he once was, or could be again, if he did not stop him now. *I don't want to fight Apollos,* Sarto stated.

Apollos laughed starkly That *is your best solution against me reclaiming the body your bedeviled*

friend and the gods stole from me? You try to call truce?
Truly disappointing. Pathetic, really. After all the years I
rattled around in your mind. Those scattered times you
almost *cut loose of your own freewill and rejoined*
me....Now, you plead neutrality? I would pity you....if I
knew what pity was.

        The old herbalist stared sympathetically at the
mad wraith before him, repeating, *I will* not *fight you*
Apollos. I'm a different man now. I am a healer, not a
destroyer.

        Teleporting directly before Sarto, Apollos
sneered: Bullsptoch, *old man! You* are *me! When you*
shed all Pallas' imposed self-righteousness and the gods'
fickle 'mercy' *all that remains is* me! Saying thus, Apollos
gripped Sarto's wrist, smiling maniacally.

        The Mender of Birosh did not struggle against
his grasp. *I forgive you Apollos*, Sarto stated evenly.

        Then he was hurled behind his own mental
barriers, into the darkest, loneliest corners of his mind.

        When his muscles unfroze ten seconds later- for
Apollos' and Sarto's internal diatribe had transpired
quickly- Apollos now gazed through Sarto's eyes; his fire
ringed, steel-colored eyes darted about, beholding the
first glimpse of real light in years. Apollos was so
overjoyed at the sudden plethora of sights, sounds and
smells around him that he laughed aloud; his crazed voice
booming in the courtyard, echoing through the empty
rooms and halls of Endelheim.

        Khalon and the Shadow Twins glanced up
curiously. They had never heard Sarto laugh thus. As

Apollos' gaze soaked up the open sky, the magnificent courtyard, his eyes settled on the curious trio at the garden's edge. Khalon rose, approaching Apollos, sensing a difference in the old healer's scent.

In his newly reclaimed mind, Apollos sneered, *Oh Sarto, you* sad, *lonely man. You've picked up* strays. *Since* when *does a wendygo smell flowers with Forest Children of Bloomaya? Is* this *what you have become, old fool: one who alters the very* nature *of those you encounter? How are* you *better than* me*? At least when I change something, there is no mistaking my intentions.*

Khalon slowed his approach, sniffing the air. "Master Wizard Sarto, what has transpired? You....smell different."

Smirking, Apollos replied coyly, "You are quite right, *flesh-eater*. I am *not* the same. *Behold*, Apollos the Wrathful, rightful master of this husk, which you know as Sarto!" Then with a loud cry, the dark wizard aimed his staff at the buck, bellowing, "*Furiosa Wendarosi!*"

As his words touched the air, Khalon felt a black cloud tumble over his thoughts, swallowing his conscience. Before he lost himself to the darkness descending upon his mind, the young wendygo felt that familiar, long dormant hunger for flesh surge from the depths of his heart to rumble, *I need flesh!*

He threw a desperate prayer up to Bloomaya, patron goddess of his gnomish friends, as the darkness of Pimedus blanketed his mind. *Bloomaya, protect my friends. If it will save them,* please, *take my life and shield them from my fury.* Then darkness crushed his mind; all swirled red and a deep bloodlust took him.

Eimar and Tibelde watched in mounting fear as Khalon froze in place once Apollos uttered his spell- for they knew the spell's meaning. *What should we do sister? In another moment Khalon will turn on us. We must act* now*!*

Agreed, brother; fetch Lady Isabel. She is in the field beyond the castle. We need her magic to counter this spell. I will remain, keep them distracted. Once you have notified Lady Isabel, fetch Iolo....

He will kill *him, sister! He has been eager for* any *excuse to put him down....*

Yes, brother. But he will not *dare if* we *keep him in check. Once you notify Lady Isabel and Iolo, return here. We must do our best to subdue Khalon without killing him. Now go!*

Eimar took off like quicksilver. Then it was just Tibelde and the madness-struck Khalon, facing one another. His golden eyes had turned milky white; a side effect of Apollos' spell. Though fear clutched her heart, she spoke. "Master Khalon? 'Tis I, Tibelde. Do you understand me? You *must* awaken."

The buck sniffed the air. His face crumpled into a mask of untethered rage. He bellowed an elk battle cry and charged, his head low to gore her with his antlers.

The gnome darted effortlessly to the side. "Khalon, come to your senses! You are not thinking clearly!"

The enraged buck whipped about, grunting in the base animal tongue of his kind, before charging Tibelde again. She dodged again, thinking: *He has taken total leave of his senses. Naught remains but the flesh-eating beast he was. Hurry, Eimar; I fear if this carries on too long, our friend will have to die.*

Isabel was still chatting with Abel and Nairadj, when she heard Khalon's elk-like bellow. The others noted the dismay on Isabel's ghostly, projected face- for they could hear naught of her surroundings. "What is it, Bell-flower," Abel asked, rising to his feet.

"Brother, I must go. Something is wrong. Khalon....he sounds *frightful.* I must investigate the matter."

Nairadj added, "Careful, Isabel. Even a reformed wendygo may suffer a moment of weakness."

Distractedly, she replied, "I will, Lady Nairadj. I will contact you both again soon. Be safe as you continue your quest. Farewell for now." Then Isabel uttered, "*Vish het un corpus*" and was returned to her body in Endelheim. As her mind slipped back to her body, she rose quickly, dashing through the open castle gate.

Before she made even a dozen paces, Eimar appeared. "Lady Isabel, Khalon has been struck by the bloodlust of his people. We need your help subduing him."

Isabel nodded somberly and resumed running. "How did it happen?"

Eimar's voice halted as he spoke. "It...it was Master *Sarto*."

Isabel hissed in disbelief, "What do you *mean* it was Master Sarto? He would *never* do something like that."

With fear in his eyes, Eimar added, "He is not himself. He proclaimed himself to be Apollos the Wrathful, and then drove Khalon into a blood rage. I saw it with mine *own* eyes my Lady; else I would not believe it either. I must warn Iolo, so he may help us supress Khalon."

"Do *not* let Iolo kill Khalon, Eimar," Isabel blurted. "You *promise* me. This is *not* Khalon's fault. I will not allow that spiteful little man to hurt our friend. If you can find them quickly, send for Morgana and her daughters as well. Together we may supress Apollos and perhaps aid Sarto in regaining control of his mind."

Eimar bowed, answering, "Aye Lady, I go with all haste." Then he darted off to spread the word.

Isabel's mind raced frantically. *How did Apollos rise? Sarto seemed in control....Something* must *have occurred....but* what*? Whatever the cause, I cannot face Apollos without a staff! His might is too expansive to survive without the magical aid of a staff. Gods* dammit, *Master Sarto, why didn't you help me forge a staff?!*

She was about to rush through the smaller entrance into the courtyard, when she spotted something from the corner of her eye; a pale glint of white off to her right. Turning her head, she beheld a small cluster of barren eight-foot-tall aspen trees in the darkened corner.

They were pale white and dead (for Kalnayan aspens cannot survive in shade). Still, something about this oddly placed copse of aspens drew Isabel's attention and she dashed instinctively towards them. As she drew nigh, she heard a whispering from the aspens.

Welcome, daughter of the Five Sisters. Long have we awaited your arrival.

Isabel shook her head. *I'm going mad.*

No, child. Your ears do not deceive you. We live, though the natural order would dictate otherwise. We have grown here, quietly in the dark, patiently awaiting your arrival. You have merely to touch one of us, then the one chosen shall become your destined sorceress staff, whispered the pale aspens in eerie unison.

What happens to the rest once I choose?

Why, we shall die *of course. Our purpose is served: to be* here *for when you discovered us. Such is sometimes the way of the world. The rest are happy to perish so long as one of us may assist you in your journeys, Isabel Farthen. Now, enough about us; your master and friends are in peril. They need you.* Then the trees fell silent.

Isabel gazed thoughtfully over the five aspens which had grown defiantly in darkness and isolation, awaiting her arrival. *This is utter* madness. *But I* need *a staff. Alright Isabel, focus and choose.* She closed her iolite eyes, passing her hand before each slender tree to sense the correct choice. With the first three, nothing happened. When her hand passed before the fourth aspen, she felt a tug in her mind. Her right hand jabbed out, firmly gripping the smooth, slender haft of the aspen.

The Lady has chosen, the trees whispered in unison.

She opened her eyes, watching as the rooted aspen she grasped shimmered with white light along its length. Then it transformed in her hand to a polished, ornately carven, white aspen staff; free of the roots that once held it. She observed her name (her *true* name, Mariana) emblazon itself in ancient Kalnese around the circumference where her hand gripped the staff. As her staff formed, she watched with a peculiar, measured sadness as the other aspens shriveled and died, turning to ash on the ground. Gazing at her newly created staff, Isabel asked, "What is your name?"

I am Toorg, my lady, whispered the staff. *I am your ally and servant from now until the day we are finally parted; be it by fire or death.*

"I am pleased to meet you Toorg. I thank you for your fealty. Now, let us go learn exactly what we are made of, together."

Lady Isabel, you lead the way.

Gripping Toorg firmly in hand, Isabel dashed through the courtyard entrance. Isabel was uncertain of what she may find, but felt better about her chances, now that she was properly equipped for a fight.

Apollos was enjoying himself entirely too much. The wendygo would not attack him, for he had willed it so. It was fascinating to observe the gnome dodging and evading the beast. He noted it was growing tougher for the female to evade the blood-mad buck- for he marked her movement patterns. A minute later, the male gnome re-emerged into the fray. The dark Prezla noted that, as the gnomes worked together, they were muddling the flesh-eater significantly.

Now, now little ones, Apollos thought mischievously, *that is not fair at* all. *Allow me to even the odds once more.* With a whispered word ('*zetarn*') and a point of his staff, Apollos cast the female to the ground in a deep, sudden slumber. The male was forced to alter his patterns to protect the female with dashes and sidesteps, keeping the wendygo focused on him, rather than his immobile kin. *There,* Apollos thought gleefully, much *better.*

Eimar felt he and his sister were doing rather well. *If we keep him moving and guessing, he may tire enough for Iolo to render him unconscious. Where* is *that slug of a human, anyways? He's* always *eager for a scrap with Khalon. The* one *time it's justified, he is nowhere to be seen. Typical human....*

Suddenly, to his left, Tibelde tumbled to the ground, unconscious but breathing. Khalon saw her fall, instantly shifting his attention her way, his claws grabbing for an easy meal.

Eimar dashed between Tibelde and the feral Khalon, flashing his knife at the deadly claws prying for his incapacitated sister. In one smooth move, he plucked her knife from the ground, pressing hard forward; struggling anxiously to drive the buck back. He nicked Khalon's long, clawed hands, causing him to grunt in discomfort. The gnome warrior was going to grab his sister and burrow into the safety of the earth, when Khalon made an unexpected move.

The buck sidestepped the gnome's lunging knives, spinning away. As a result, Eimar stepped forward several extra paces, tossing him off balance. Khalon finished his sidelong spin, rising behind Eimar and, with a great backhand blow, sent his quarry flying into the central water fountain. The gnome did not pass out, but he was thoroughly dazed from colliding with the fountain stones. He couldn't focus, blurrily watching the mad wendygo lumber towards him. Khalon grinned demonically at his assured victory.

Bloomaya, Eimar thought weakly, *Earth Mother, welcome my sister and I into the eternally green gardens of the Nether-Realm.* Then, through his foggy vision, he saw something peculiar. Khalon was becoming ensnared in writhing, creeping vines from neck to hoof. Wherever the vines touched his skin, smoke arose, and faint sizzling could be heard. *Bloomaya is with us,* Eimar thought hopefully. Then he slipped into the dark of unconsciousness.

As Isabel entered the courtyard with her staff, Toorg, in hand, she beheld a macabre scene. Sarto (*No, not Sarto,* Isabel corrected in her mind, *Apollos*) stood to one side of the yard. He leant on his staff, watching amusedly as Khalon knocked Eimar into the fountain.

Where is Tibelde? Isabel spotted her, several feet from Khalon, who was closing on Eimar. Gripping Toorg tightly, Isabel's iolite eyes burned brightly with righteous anger. Staring at the vines growing on the upper balcony she aimed her staff at Khalon and mouthed, "*Freya et tingrash, ripas.*" Isabel watched with a measure of pride as the vines grew and moved with astounding rapidity, darting down to coil about Khalon, hoof and claw. The young wendygo barked in pain as the foliage burned his skin.

I'm sorry Khalon, Isabel thought. Her heart broke with sorrow at the pain she was inflicting to save Eimar and Tibelde. Pointing her staff at his face, she mouthed, "*Etsa mor Wendarosi furiosa, het philas.*"

Khalon's head rocked back as though he had been struck hard in the face. His head lolled limply to the side as the spell rendered him unconscious. Pointing her staff near the entrance by which she stood, Isabel mouthed, "*Devarth het philas despar.*" The wendygo's unconscious form was set gently on the ground by the vines holding him in their grip. With another whispered word (*'Dopar'*), Isabel released him from the vines, glancing mournfully at the burned lines tracing across Khalon's flesh. She stifled hot tears, focusing her rage on Apollos.

Since Isabel had arrived, Apollos made no attempt to interfere with her spell work. Leaning his tall staff in the crook of his left arm, he clapped his hands slowly, three times. "Well *done*, child," he praised snidely, "it would seem Sarto has indeed trained you well."

"What have you done with him, *Apollos*?!"

Apollos beamed broadly to hear Isabel speak his name. "I see he has mentioned me. *Surely* you know you cannot defeat me, girl. Not without killing your precious master, as well. Are you prepared to do that? If not, you may as well lay your staff on the ground, kneel and pledge yourself as *my* apprentice. If not, I *will* kill you, and your friends, while your master watches helplessly from within. What say you to *that*, Isabel Farthen?"

Shedding her over cloak, Isabel whispered, "*Avia numa rysas.*" In a blur, her four knives drew themselves, flying across the courtyard towards Apollos.

"*Etsa,*" Apollos replied, bored. Isabel's forged blades stopped dead in the air. "*Artaz,*" Apollos added, chuckling as Isabel's knives clattered to the ground. "Apparently, you *are* as foolish as Sarto. I'm afraid my offer of apprenticeship is now rescinded. Pray to your gods if you wish, child. You shall join your ancestors momentarily." He pointed his staff at Isabel, forming a killing spell.

Ezri appeared on the balcony above, crying, "*Vesh mor het, tembre!*" Unprepared, Apollos crowed angrily as his staff was torn from his grip, flying to the young sorceress on the balcony.

"You little *svanth,*" he screeched, "Return my staff to me *now*! If you do, I promise to kill you quickly!"

Pointing Sarto's staff at Apollos, Ezri sneered, "I *refuse* your offer, o dark wizard; as will my *sisters*, including Isabel."

Whirling to face Isabel, Apollos cried, "*Avia numa rysas!*" In a flash, her blades spun on the ground, flying at her chest, whistling with the force of his anger.

Isabel countered, "*Etsa un Artaz!*" The blades clanked to the ground, inches from her chest. Before he could summon another spell, she aimed Toorg at him, bellowing, "*Vish un Rivaith, Apollos!*"

The dark wizard grunted loudly, dropping to one knee. He looked up, his face a grotesque mask of pain and mockery. "*Hah!* You do not have the *power* to force me back to the bosom of Pimedus, young Bell-flower!"

Isabel pursed her lips at the mockery, approaching him slowly. Toorg was leveled at the doubled over wizard. She repeated, "*Vish un Rivaith, Apollos!*"

He doubled over further, squealing in pain, as he felt the tug back to the darkness. "If you drive me away, *svanth*, I will *kill* your master! Do you want that?"

Nodding to Ezri, Isabel repeated the spell again, this time with Ezri bolstering her efforts. As Apollos grunted in pain again, Isabel replied, "You said so yourself: if Sarto dies, so do *you*. You love yourself too much to harm yourself. Now, do you go willingly, or must I continue?"

He spat in Isabel's direction, shrilling, "Do your worst, you simple, sleight artist *svanth*! I will *not* go quietly; not *ever*!"

Isabel spotted Delja entering from the eastern wing, nodding to her and Ezri. Together, they repeated the banishment spell, bolstered by the power of three voices, echoing within the courtyard. Apollos unleashed a blood-curdling howl as he was forced further into the darkness at the back of Sarto's mind. Still, he would not leave, laughing in mockery. "I'm still here, *girl.*"

Isabel glanced to Ezri and Delja, who were now joined by Sena from the kitchen. "Keep repeating the spell, my sisters. I am going to try something else."

Ezri, Delja and Sena all continued chanting, "*Vish un Rivaith, Apollos!*"

Isabel began chanting separately, "*Het tarthain, Sarto; vish un mor corpus*" (which translates: "I summon you, Sarto; return unto your body").

At the addition of this new summoning spell being chanted by Isabel- amidst the three sisters' simultaneous banishment chant- Apollos' eyes widened in pain. He felt Sarto emerging from behind the barricades with Pallas' assistance. He threw his mind against the barricades, trying to repress Sarto, as externally, he was forced back into the darkness. To his surprise, he was able to resist, despite being pummeled by two different spells under the command of four witches.

"No *woman* controls *my* comings and goings," Apollos grated through a clenched jaw, as he stared defiantly at the looming Isabel. Then he observed another two girls- blonde, both of them- appear from the western courtyard entrance. *Gods* dammit, Apollos thought furiously, *how many svanth sorceresses are there here!?*

One of the blondes, Allegra, joined Isabel in chanting the summoning spell. Aloisa, meanwhile, joined her other sisters in chanting the banishment spell. Apollos' arms gave out beneath him as he toppled sidelong on the courtyard ground, unleashing a jet of vomit. Within his skull, he could hear multiple, rending cracks of timber, as the barricades disintegrated. Sarto and Pallas flew out through the destroyed barricade. Apollos could no longer see the sky, or even the stones of the courtyard. *Those filthy witches have banished me from this body;* my *body! This is not* possible*!*

Grabbing Apollos within the recesses of his mind, Sarto hissed: *You are wrong, my old nemesis. It is entirely* possible*. Now,* 'nix un zetarn', *demon!* Saying thus he placed a hand on Apollos' forehead. The dark wizard's scream of pain was muted by the silence spell, moments before he passed into deep slumber. With Pallas' aid, they constructed a metal cage in the darkest corner of Sarto's mind, encasing Apollos' presence within. They then rebuilt the mental barricades, this time three layers deep. Inspecting their collective work, Sarto queried: *Will that hold him, Pallas?*

For now, it will suffice. You should return, let your apprentice know her plan worked, and that you are well.

Chortling, for he had forgotten about Isabel, Sarto replied with relief: *Yes....yes, I suppose I had better, hadn't I? Thank you, Pallas. You are* truly *an anchor in this mad world.*

Placing a hand on Sarto's shoulder, Pallas responded, *that is why I returned Sarto. I know that now. I will be here if you ever have need of me. After that....well, I suppose I will have to come to terms with being absent from this world. Now, enough stalling; get out there.* With a hard shove, Pallas thrust Sarto towards the light of the morning sky just past his closed eyelids.

When Apollos fell sick onto his side, Isabel thought, *this must be a trick.* She signalled for her sisters to keep chanting, watching Sarto's body language carefully for further sign of Apollos. After several minutes of stillness from her master, Isabel halted the chanting. She beckoned for her sisters to join her in the yard.

Sena- who was trained in medicine- checked his eyes, listened to his breathing and offered, "He is breathing normally, and his eyes appear their normal color. Apollos has been subdued."

Isabel looked from Sena to Sarto, asking, "Should we move him to the infirmary then? Why hasn't he awoken, if Apollos is subdued?"

Sena scratched her head, offering, "Perhaps....perhaps he is constructing mental barricades, reinforcing his mind against future attacks from within. Either that, or he is in a deeper slumber than I have ever seen." Noting the concern in Isabel's eyes, Sena reassured her, "No....he is likely reconstructing his mental defenses."

As if on cue, Sarto's eyes shot open, darting around at the six witches encircling him where he lay, as he uttered a raspy, "*Gah!*" The girls all jumped back, alarmed by Sarto's abrupt awakening. "Is anyone hurt," Sarto rasped, concern creasing his brow.

Isabel enveloped her Master in a hug, rambling, "Eimar and Tibelde need some rest and bandages. Khalon....he will need time to recover as well." To Sena, Isabel asked, "Do we have any salves? Khalon received many faint burns after I ensnared him in the creeping vines."

"Which was *ingenious*, Isabel," cut in Delja. "Without that to stay him, he may have hurt the others or himself far worse. You did the *right* thing. Yes, we have salves."

From behind them, Iolo's voice boomed, "I'm afraid, ladies, that if that....*monster* is to receive any care it will be within the prison cells! We are lucky he did not kill or harm anyone."

Shooting to her feet, Isabel stormed across the courtyard towards him. "Where *were* you?! Eimar fetched you *immediately* after he found me. So, where were you?!"

Iolo raised his nose, declaring, "I was doing my *job*, protecting the Lady Morgana. Had that wendygo found his way to her chambers, I would have dealt with him accordingly...."

"*Sptoch* on that, Iolo," Isabel spat, "admit it: you were cowering like a mewling *child*!"

Iolo's nostrils flared. He stepped forward three paces, hand on the hilt of his sword. "*Careful*, Lady Isabel. You tread upon *dangerous* ground here."

Isabel halted, half a dozen paces from him. "Then pray tell: if you were not hiding, what exactly *were* you doing?!"

From behind Iolo appeared Morgana. Isabel was shocked at her appearance, for she had not properly seen her since arriving in Endelheim. Morgana's lustrous platinum blonde hair was a dirty straw color. Her once sparkling dress was hemmed in a ring of mud. Her visage, once porcelain and shining, was graying, with deep, dark circles beneath her eyes. Her gorgeous sapphire eyes were faded blue like the water in Andalmere Bay. To Isabel, she appeared a totally different person, virtually unrecognizable.

When Morgana spoke, her voice was cracked and wispy. "Iolo speaks truth, dear Isabel. He *was* protecting me; more from myself than anyone. When that dark presence within Sarto awoke, he leeched my power. Iolo was with me, anchoring me to the real world whilst I mentally combatted Apollos' spells." Here, she chuckled mirthlessly. "As you can see, I did not fare so well. I owe you, my daughters, a debt of gratitude for halting his advance. Had you not done so....well, I shudder to ponder what may *still* be happening to me."

Isabel curtsied deeply, fumbling, "Lady Morgana....I am *so* sorry. I had no idea...."

Waving aside Isabel's apologies, Morgana interrupted, "Oh, 'tis quite alright, Isabel. You were occupied with your friends' well-beings....your master's as well. I commend you. However, Iolo is right: your friend Khalon *is* a danger. He *must* be contained....for a time, you understand? Until it can be safely determined that he will not be affected by any more.....*adverse* forces. Do you concur?"

Looking to where Khalon lay, still unconscious, Isabel reluctantly saw the wisdom in Morgana's words. With a trickle of tears in her eyes, she conceded. "Aye, my lady, you are right. I wish to tend to his wounds, since I inflicted them upon him."

Morgana returned the nod. "Aye, Isabel. Sena and Delja can assist in moving your friend to the cells. Aloisa and Allegra will take the gnomes to the infirmary for care..."

"My Lady," Sarto croaked intrusively, "I beg your pardon, but *I* have a request as well."

Morgana paused in mid-sentence, turning her attention to the weakened wizard. "Yes, Master Sarto? What would you have of me?"

"I must request you lock *me* up as well."

All eyes focused on Sarto as he spoke, shock and surprise on every face. Morgana spoke haltingly, "Why......Master Sarto....what reason have *you* to be locked up? You are yourself again, are you not?"

Nodding faintly, he replied, "Aye, my Lady I am....for now. I have reconstructed within my mind, mental barricades and a cage to contain the malice of Apollos. However, he slipped through before. Knowing him, he will do his damnedest to escape yet again. The only way to be *truly* safe is to lock me away. Until such a time I am certain I no longer pose a threat to the rest of you. I would not ask were it not vital."

Morgana considered this a long moment, the others watching with bated breath. Considering Sarto's eyes- seeing the shaded fear present therein- decided her mind. With a reluctant sigh, she conceded, "Aye, Master Sarto. As you request, so it shall be. Iolo, please escort the Master Wizard to the cells. See he is afforded *every* comfort."

Eyeing the unconscious Khalon, Iolo nodded. "Aye, my Lady, as you command. Come along, Master Wizard."

Sarto began following Iolo to the cells, when Isabel spoke up. "Lady Morgana, may *I* escort my Master to the cells? I wish to see he is settled in properly, and to discuss my training in his absence."

Morgana smiled, revealing several large gaps in her mouth where she was missing numerous teeth. "Of course, dear one, of course; he is your Master, after all. I would not come twixt a pupil and their master; especially after such an ordeal. Now, if you will all excuse me, I must retire for some much-needed rest. I fear today's ordeal has been rather taxing." Then she turned, gliding from the courtyard. Her daughters dispersed to aid the gnomes and Khalon.

Isabel and Sarto followed Iolo to the cells, walking closely together. They deliberately walked slower, creating a gap twixt Iolo and themselves, whispering amongst themselves.

"Isabel," Sarto breathed quietly, removing the key necklace he wore, "take this. It is a key to the restricted section of the library. Frodi gave it to me; *after* resisting a mind-control spell. He mentioned a tome: '*A*

Brief History of Endelheim.' He says it is key to understanding the strangeness transpiring here. Surely you have noticed something....*odd* about our circumstances, yes?"

Isabel nodded faintly as she hid the offered key. "Lady Morgana's appearance seems quite....*advanced* for an ordeal of only several minutes. She seemed *years* older to my eyes. She was even missing *teeth* when she smiled. It makes me think that....oh, I don't know how to phrase it. It feels like...."

"Like a *curse*," Sarto finished for her.

Her eyes snapped up to his. "*Yes*," she hissed in dismay, "as if this whole place is....*enchanted*. I asked Aloisa when we were out hunting last week about an experience she and Sena had as children. She stared at me blankly, answering with a contrived line of explanation. It felt....*rehearsed*, but *not* by her. Something similar happened with Delja on Andalmere Bay the week before. What could it *be*, Master; this secret dancing just beyond our sight?"

Sarto shrugged, sighing faintly, "I am unsure child. Whatever it is, you *must* be careful. I do not think Apollos' rising was accidental. There is something......some *force* striving to blind us to circumstances here in the Sapphire City. Be cautious, and all shall be well. Report what you find to me, if circumstances permit. Inform Eimar and Tibelde to be cautious as well."

Flicking her gaze back towards the courtyard, Isabel asked, "What of Khalon; should I inform him of my findings as well?"

"That is difficult to say right now. Apollos meddled with the deepest parts of Khalon's mind, returning him to a feral beast. How long those effects last, I do not know. Use your better judgment about what and when to tell him."

Ahead, Iolo stopped, opening a cell door. Looking back, he hollered, "Come, Master Sarto! We will have your meals brought to you. Your friends may visit, should you desire."

Sarto smiled broadly, replying, "My thanks, good Iolo. Allow me a moment to bid farewell to Isabel."

Iolo nodded deferentially. "As you say, Master Wizard."

Turning back to Isabel, Sarto mouthed, *do* not *trust Iolo. Whatever, or* whomever, *controls this curse has their hooks in him.* Aloud, Sarto bid Isabel a warm farewell, trundling down the hallway to his cell. She watched Iolo slam the door shut, turn the key and place the key ring on his hip.

Isabel returned the way she came, opening her closed palm to look at the key Sarto had entrusted to her. *Restricted section. 'A Brief History of Endelheim'. Key to the truth.* These points, Isabel chanted in her mind repeatedly until they were emblazoned on her memory. *I have some research to do....*

Chapter Sixteen: Ravensight

Lilith was enveloped in blackness. The cool, firm grip of Pimedus provided solace as she wallowed in her true master's presence. The only time she found comfort these days was drifting in Darkness within her Black Tower. The mercenaries had failed her horribly. Her prey's trail had gone cold. Four weeks ago, they resurfaced briefly, when the southwestern region of Lec'tair Forest burnt down. She was in her tower when the fire began.

Lilith had seen, through Pimedus, the bright Light which had ignited the blaze. She focused on that Light, for 'twas unfamiliar and exceedingly strong. Seizing control of a raven nested in the canopy of Lec'tair, Lilith was surprised to discover it was not the old man. Rather, it was the girl from the beach those months gone by now.

She observed in amusement as the little witch lost control of the blaze. *Oh dear, someone* else *has seized control of your spell. Who could that be....? What now will you do, little girl?* The Screech Owl watched the fire close in. She laughed to herself as she witnessed the little sorceress try to protect her friends in a flimsy water shield. *Oh no you don't, little Prezla. This ends* now.

Without warning, a great gust of wind blew north from the southeast. Lilith was physically batted across her chambers as the force of the spell threw her free of her Ravensight. She lost the girl and her friends. Crashing painfully against the wall, she shrieked in anger and pain. *impossible! Who could have countered the* might of that dark magic I felt?! Surely the girl can't be that *strong!*

Frantically, she scoured Lec'tair with her renewed Ravensight, where she had last seen the girl, and was distraught to discover the girl and her friends had disappeared. The Screech Owl panicked, broadening her search for any sign of the girl in the immediate area, finding naught of any of them.

Someone aids them! How *is there anyone else helping them!? Who commandeered the girl's fire spell?! Who snuffed the blaze?! Where did they freckaying go!? I have* every *other Prezla locked within my husband's dungeons working on....whatever fool's errand he has them slaving away on for the last eight years! Where did they go!?*

The Screech Owl raged within her chambers, destroying anything that displeased her. Not once did any guards enter (for word had spread quickly about the dead Northerner Master Talon had removed from the Tower recently). For the next two days, she employed Ravensight to scour Kalnay from coast to coast; from the Grymwulf Hills to the southern reaches of the Shavatnu Mountains. She found no trace of the girl, her master or the others.

People do not disappear*! Not unless* I *am the one making them do so! Who aids them? Perhaps the freckaying gods favor this girl. That would be typical: favor the young and foolish, and spit on the powerful and prestigious. Freckaying pretenders!*

On the third day after the fire, Lilith was summoned to the throne room on the promise of 'a thrilling venture'- or so the mewling guard who delivered the message conveyed to her. The Screech Owl was intrigued, for it had been several years since Malikh made a proposition worded in such fashion.

When she appeared, her husband approached, placing his hands firmly but gently upon her shoulders, and kissing her on the forehead. *What is this?* she wondered, smiling a broad, artificial smile.

Malikh withdrew, asking, "How goes the hunt for the escaped Prezla girl, my love?"

Lilith resisted the urge to bodily fling him across the throne room, for he was genuinely inquiring after her. With a frown, she hissed, "The trail is cold, my lord. Someone aids the fugitives. Whoever they are, their powers of concealment are greater than my tracking powers. Though *who* this party could be, I have not the faintest clue."

Wrapping her in a warm embrace, the Overlord whispered, "I am sorry to hear, my love. So....I have a proposition to brighten your disposition. Would you hear it?"

Gazing into Malikh's eyes, the dark witch smiled coolly. "Aye, husband, I would. What is your proposition?"

Wrapping his arm around her waist, he strolled with her around the edge of the court room. "You know of my prisoner in the cells, yes?"

"Of course, my lord," she replied evenly. *Where is this going?*

"I fear a time is fast coming when I will require his skills with a sword. I spoke with him the day of the fire. He refused to serve me willingly, as he always does. I have no more time or patience to waste trying to coax him. After the attacks on the Riverlands by the ghastly wendygos, I require a bodyguard who will kill anyone or anything I command."

"I *see*," the Screech Owl replied coyly, "how does that involve *me*, my Lord?"

Malikh chuckled, answering bluntly, "I need you to......*convert* him to serve me, my love. No one else could do it better."

"I see," she repeated. "What do I get from this 'thrilling venture', as your peon put it?"

Turning to face Lilith, he kissed her firmly on the lips. "Why, you may torture him into submission, my beloved. I know that *truly* thrills you. You need not deny it. I heard of the Northerner mess in your chambers some weeks back."

"As you wish my Lord; consider it done." Lilith strode gleefully towards the hidden dungeon entrance.

"There is *one* stipulation, darling wife," Malikh called brightly.

"*Oh*," Lilith called back. "What stipulation is *that*?"

"Do *not* kill him. Break his mind. Bend his will. Inflict physical pain. But you are *forbidden* from killing him. I need him at my side. Am I understood, Lilith?"

The dark witch nodded faintly. "Aye, my Lord; I understand you *perfectly*." Then Lilith glided down to convert Noshtain to Malikh's service.

The conversion took four days of slow, deliberate torture and breaking of both Noshtain's will and mind. Once Lilith controlled those things, the prisoner's body followed suit. When she was satisfied that he would obey her and Malikh's orders, she unchained him, leading him to the throne room.

The Overlord inspected his newly converted bodyguard. "He's too skinny. We must ensure he is fed and trained for duty. General Markus, approach!"

From the shadows behind the throne, General Markus stepped forward, his crimson red armor glinting in the torchlight. "My lord," Markus grated, bowing deferentially.

"Given how long our newly crafted Noshtain has been imprisoned in that cell," Malikh queried, "how long to have him in peak fighting condition?"

"My best guess, my lord, would be three weeks. That assumes we feed him three hearty meals a day, and train him twelve hours at a time. If we do *that*....he should be at his former level of swordsmanship and combat readiness within three weeks," Markus concluded.

Malikh looked from Markus to the grimy, long-haired Noshtain in surprise. "He can be ready in *three* weeks, General?"

The General nodded faintly. "Aye, my lord. As a soldier, I can tell you the muscles never *truly* forget the heft of a sword. Nor does the mind forget the motions and arc of the perfect cut of a blade. Based on the level of skill I beheld from this man....I would stake my reputation on three weeks being the correct amount of time to have Noshtain ready for service."

Malikh looked the scraggly prisoner in his blank eyes. "What say *you*, Noshtain? Will you be ready to serve at my side in three weeks?"

Noshtain rasped through his matted, salt and pepper beard, "The General speaks truth: the muscles and mind do *not* forget the feel of war and the heft of a sword. I shall be ready, Lord Malikh."

The Overlord chuckled cruelly. Beckoning Lilith, he wrapped her in a deep, warm embrace. In her ear he whispered, "You have *truly* outdone yourself, my precious Queen. Thank you for this gift."

Smiling slyly, she turned her black-eyed gaze to the empty, green eyes of Noshtain. "*No*, Lord Malikh," she hissed seductively in his ear, "my thanks to *you* for that 'thrilling venture'."

Over the next couple weeks, Lilith searched regularly for the sorceress girl and the old man, to no avail. Then, as the fourth week since the fire in the forest began, she sensed something. It felt like a projection spell. Where it came from, she could not pinpoint. *How is that possible? Surely, she hasn't gained so much power in so short a span of time that she can wholly conceal all traces of her magic and Light yet. I will follow and see where she leads.*

Gliding to a large bird cage near the southern window of the tower, the Screech Owl drew back a black draping sheet to reveal an unkindness of ravens within. They were all blind- their milky white eyes standing out starkly in the darkness of her chambers. Then she briefly opened the window- allowing a shard of sunlight into her room- followed by the cage door.

Extending her hand towards the cage, Lilith whispered, "*Corva mor lokis. Gata un tarvish het iras.*" The previously blind ravens' eyes all changed; the once milky eyes were now black as pitch, like Lilith's. In her mind's eye, she beheld herself reflected many times over through their eyes. The ravens stirred a cacophony of noise as numerous wings flapped and fluttered. They cawed a great, unified cry, flying out the open window. As soon as the last raven had flown, Lilith drew the window shut, returning to the safety and comfort of the pitch-dark chamber.

Through the ravens' eyes she swooped low, following an ethereal trail of light fragments winding north. The birds flew abnormally swifter with the aid of Lilith's magic, but it took time all the same. Forty minutes later, the ravens drew upon the lower, central-eastern Shavatnu Mountains; slowing their pace as they detected the light fragment trail ending. *What* possible *reason could the girl have to project herself to Shavatnu?*

As she spotted the destination of the girl's projection spell, she felt a great rippling disturbance within Pimedus. The tremor emanated from the far southeast, rattling the usual tranquility of Lilith's perfect Darkness to the core. *What devilry is* this *now?*

Dividing her mind- part of it maintaining her Ravensight, the other splitting into her own projection spell- she rushed southeast in moments to determine the source of the disturbance. As she drew closer, she realized why this tremor was so hard to track. *The girl is sheltered within a wood protected by Pimedus! The old man is there too! Who causes the disturbance then, I wonder...?*

A bizarre thought occurred to her then. *It's the old man!* He *emanates this ripple in Pimedus....but how? When I first encountered him, he emanated the Light....* Then like déjà vu, a startling scrap of memory returned to Lilith. *I know the Prezla bastard emanating this evil! I....I* taught *this man the ways of Pimedus! This man....was my* apprentice*! What, in the names of the freckaying gods, was his name?*

She wrestled within her mind to retrieve the name of this turncoat who defied her as the dark queen of Ackreth. His deeds against her returned first: tricking her into bestowing more power upon him; stealing her chief spell book; erasing her memories of him, allowing him to flee Ackreth......Finally, the name shot to the surface like dislodged driftwood hiding below a river's surface: Apollos! *Apollos the Wrathful! Apollos the Lying* Bastard *Turncoat! I have found you, my wayward apprentice!*

She had not actually discovered his specific location, just the region his dark signature pulsed from. *Messara? The Eastern Reach? I believed that place a Wasteland! A worthless lump of earth neighbored by wendygos to the north, and grymwulves to the southwest! You have grown strong, Apollos; to conceal yourself in this forgotten part of the world. But not strong enough, I fear. Now that I know, I shall not forget. I will repay you for your treachery, you feckless, ungrateful bastard.*

In her mind's eye, the ravens cawed loudly. Lilith returned her mind from Messara, focusing her Ravensight to discover the magic girl rushing back to Messara. To the ravens she commanded, "Draw near where she stopped. I must see who or what she observed." She watched in her mind as the ravens swooped a low spiraling circle. Lilith observed a tiny rock outcropping, but no visible sign of man or beast. The lack of sign troubled her; not knowing what the girl had seen or whom she may have spoken to was disquieting.

The Screech Owl commanded them higher into the sky to return to her castle tower; the ravens did as she instructed. As they climbed, wheeling gracefully to the west to find a rising wind, Lilith spotted something to the northwest. She commanded the ravens to fly northwest; her black eyes staring intently to see what had caught her eye. After another forty-five minutes of flight, she was close enough to see. Below her, like a massive black wave, was an army. This sizeable force was two days' march north of Drake's Maw Pass and showed no signs of stopping.

What madness is this*? Why are Northerners venturing* south*? I did not permit this!* She was so distraught at the sight of this massive force, she neglected to sight the scouting party south of the main army.

Without warning, the lead raven- whom Lilith dominated with her mind- was pierced through the heart with an arrow and plummeted to the ground, dead. While this did not kill the Screech Owl, it pained her deeply, for she and the raven were connected. She shrieked, withdrawing her mind from the remaining ravens. The Queen clutched her chest, feeling the echoed stab of pain from the raven's death.

How did this happen*!? Since when do Northerners think they can march south and invade* my kingdom*!? I must inform Malikh. We must mobilize the army at once. We* must *beat the Wildmen to the Crossroad of Kings. If they clear it, they will disperse and conquer Kalnay one valley and town at a time!*

Gathering her skirts, Lilith flung her chamber door open with a loud, "*Corva*!" She dashed down the steps as fast as she dared, for her kingdom's serenity in the perfection of Pimedus counted on it.

Chapter Seventeen: The Drake's Maw Pass

Hearne was glad he was still as keen-eyed as he'd been in his youth. Otherwise, he may not have noticed how uniform the ravens overhead seemed as they circled over Queen Sigourney and Yenoor's combined forces marching south towards Drake's Maw Pass. Notching an arrow, the Captain of the Night Patrol exhaled a long slow breath and loosed. His suspicions proved valid.

As the arrow pierced the heart of the lead raven, the rest of the birds cawed in panic, scattering. He marked where the raven fell, dashing the several yards to where it lay dead, with his arrow protruding from its feathery breast. Retrieving the arrow, Hearne gazed suspiciously at the bird. On instinct, he popped open its eyes and was half surprised to discover the bird's milky white eyes. *No way this bird flew so straight and true with blind eyes. Unless these eyes weren't blind before I killed it. I must show this to Lady Siggy.*

Sigourney considered the milky dead eye of the raven, before passing it to Yenoor. The bear Queen sniffed it, grunting in disgust, "This bird *stinks* of dark magic."

Sigourney stated coldly, "Lilith."

Yenoor nodded, looking ahead to where Drake's Maw Pass lay looming. "Aye, the Screech Owl has discovered us. How, I do not know, for she never spies near the Shavatnu. We must hurry through the Pass into central Kalnay."

To Hearne, Sigourney commanded, "Spread word through the ranks, Captain: we march double time south through the Pass. We do not stop until we clear it. We must suspect a double cross from Melatharom. If he collapses the Pass, it won't matter if we are swifter than Malikh when we are buried dead beneath tonnes of mountain rock."

"Agreed," Yenoor concurred. Summoning her own captain, Mikael the Short, she commanded, "Spread word to our people: we move doubly swift through the Pass. No stopping until we reach the Crossroad. We fear a double cross by Melatharom beneath these mountains."

Placing his right hand over his heart, and bowing quickly, Mikael replied, "As my queen commands, I will obey." Then he dashed back through the ranks to spread word, as Captain Hearne and his lieutenants were doing.

Staring again at the nearing mountain pass, Sigourney asked, "Do you think it's possible, Lady Yenoor?"

"Do I think *what* is possible, Lady Sigourney?"

"That Abel Farthen and Princess Nairadj can defeat a rock drake alone?"

Smiling broadly, Yenoor replied, "If anyone living in Kalnay *could* kill a rock drake, it would be that young man and my daughter."

Glancing sidelong at the bear Queen, Sigourney asked, "How can you be so certain? Our collective fate, and theirs, depends on them defeating that damned rock lizard."

"What you forget is they are both aware of the possibility of defeat. Melatharom, like Ulgnar before him, believes himself invincible due to size. When you are small, there's no pride puffing you up. You have determination of will- to not perish, to see the sun again....to return to your loved ones. *That* is why I feel they will succeed....if they haven't already."

Sigourney conceded the point. "Perhaps, Lady Yenoor....perhaps the smaller opponent *can* win......"

Yenoor indicated the Pass. "All the same, we should hurry." The queens spurred their horses onward, increasing the pace as their armies followed suit behind them.

"*What* did you say?!" Malikh was on his feet, storming towards Lilith, his eyes wide and a sneer on his face.

Lilith gazed demurely at the throne room floor, repeating softly, "The armies of the North march to the Drake's Maw Pass. They will be at the Pass two days' hence; in another two, three at most, they will be at the fabled Crossroad of Kings; in *our* kingdom, dear husband."

Hurling his goblet of cider across the throne room, Malikh fumed, "Who do those *freckaying* Northerners think they are! When have I *ever* given them cause to march on *my* kingdom so brazenly? Did I

conquer their pathetic Wastes and take their homes?!
No! I let them be, and *this* is how they repay me?!"

Rushing to his side, the Screech Owl placed a
cool, porcelain skinned hand on the nape of his neck.
The other she laced in his right hand. "Fear not these
rag-tag invaders, husband....not *yet*. If we act *now*, they
may be vanquished."

Malikh turned his troubled eyes to Lilith. "Do
you believe that? Or do you assuage my concerns in the
face of defeat, as when we fled Ackreth?"

Her countenance grew dark, and she withdrew
her hands. "Do you blame *me* for the Northerners
marching south? Did I not *just* bring you news of their
intentions?! There is time to act, but you must *stop* this
childish self-pity and act as a *king* would: bold and
decisive!"

Whirling on her, he clamped a large hand
around her thin neck, squeezing firmly. "Who do you
think you are talking to, *woman*!? *I* am Overlord of
Kalnay, and your husband besides! Were you not my
wife, I could have your *head* for such disrespect!" Malikh
breathed deeply, staring into Lilith's black eyes, asking for
an excuse to crush the life from her.

Gently, placing her petit hands around his thick
wrist, Lilith rasped, "*That* is what I wish to see: my lord
and husband seizing control." Unlatching his fingers
from her throat, she continued, "As I said, they are two
days' march from the Pass; another two days' march from
the Crossroad. Act *now*, and your troops can be
assembled within a days' time; marched north in another
two and a half days. You would arrive half a day ahead

of your foes, driving them back with the might of the Regalias Red Guard. It will be a close contest, but you *can* win." Stepping back three paces, she stared into Malikh's serene face. "If this is to be, you must act *now*....my lord."

For a moment, he stared hard into her eyes, searching for any hint of deceit. Finding none, he exhaled a long, measured breath. Over his shoulder, he called, "Noshtain! Summon General Markus. We must prepare our forces, with all haste. I have invaders to crush."

It was after midnight. Sigourney felt the fatigue of such a long ride. She knew she must appear strong for her people. Therefore, after sunset she had Hearne lash her legs to the saddle, in case she fell asleep during the march. In her head, she repeated, *we can triumph; we can change our fate; we can live free and happy in the south.*

On foot to her right was Yenoor, who gently called, "Queen Sigourney, a word, if you please?"

Sigourney snapped awake, looking around, disoriented by the dark. Then she yawned, replying, "I cry your pardon, Yenoor. I dozed off."

"There is naught to apologize for. Mortals do not normally travel such great distances all at once. One benefit of being half animal: we dyre bears can march three days before reaching a *true* state of fatigue."

Chuckling as she yawned again, Sigourney replied, "That must be a relief. You get more done with your time on this earth."

"To that end, I have a proposal."

"Oh," Sigourney queried, "and what is that?"

"By now, Lilith and Malikh know of our movements. If he acts quickly, he can have the bulk of his forces amassed within the next day. In another two, if he marches them hard, he could be at the Crossroad. If that be so, he will stand ready to repel our campaign."

Worry seized Sigourney's guts, twisting them into uncomfortable knots. "Are you saying we should turn back, Lady Yenoor?"

Shaking her head, Yenoor replied, "*No.* I suggest my people hurry ahead to secure *our* foothold at the Crossroad. It is three days hence until the full moon, when we shall take our ancestral bear forms. The closer it draws to the change, the faster we are and more animal-like we become. There are enough of us that, I believe, we could arrive *before* Malikh's forces and defend the Crossroad until your arrival."

Sigourney gazed at the Bear Queen, thinking: *How remarkable to find such courage amongst one's allies.* Aloud, she asked, "How many are you, Lady Yenoor?"

"My people number seven thousand, five hundred including myself."

"How many will Malikh's forces may be?"

Yenoor shrugged, "If I had to guess, perhaps sixty thousand soldiers stand at his command."

Sigourney cast a glance over her shoulder at her people. "My people only number twenty-five thousand. Even with your seventy-five hundred, we are well shy of rivaling Malikh's forces."

Yenoor scolded, "Have you so soon forgotten my words about the dragon and our champions, Lady Sigourney?"

Normally, Sigourney would be offended; but as Yenoor was queen in her own right, she simply replied, "What is that, Lady Yenoor?"

"Size or, in Malikh's case, numbers matter not when one is determined. Are *you* not determined to win a better life for your people?"

Sigourney gazed to the waning moon in the sky. For the first time in all her years on Kalnay, she did not view the moon as a foe- beckoning nightstalkers to terrorize and kill her people. Instead, it was a beacon of hope lighting the way to victory.

We can *defeat Malikh. We can have a better life, free of fear.*

With iron in her voice, she replied, "Aye, Lady Yenoor, I *am* determined."

"It is settled then. My kin and I will hurry on, holding the Crossroad against Malikh's forces until you arrive."

Reaching down with her right hand, Sigourney stated, "Until we meet at the Crossroad, Queen Yenoor."

Taking the Wildmen Queen's hand in farewell, the Bear Queen echoed, "Until we meet again, Queen Sigourney." Then Yenoor uttered a faint bird-like whistle. Throughout the marching masses, other whistles echoed in reply, rising into the night air. Sigourney watched Yenoor dash towards the Drake's Maw Pass; her people padding in near silence as they followed their queen to secure a foothold at the Crossroad of Kings.

Chapter Eighteen: Twixt a Draconias Petrificus and a Hard Place

Abel was becoming supremely disoriented within the darkness of Melatharom's burrowed tunnels beneath Shavatnu. It had been over a day since they had entered beneath *'Magna Spiro'*. They had seen neither tooth nor claw of Melatharom in that entire time. Nairadj took the lead once they lost the light of the sun a quarter of a day later, and her green eyes shone with their night vision luminescence.

After stumbling in the dark for a quarter of the first day, Abel could no longer take it. "Master Nairadj, we must stop a moment. I *need* to light a torch. I feel like a toddling infant on his feet for the first time, and I don't feel very helpful right now."

Ahead of him came the firm but gentle reply, "I know 'tis difficult Abel, but you must be patient. The longer you traverse the dark, the more your eyes will adjust to the gloom. If you light a torch, you make it easier for Melatharom to locate you when he reveals himself."

Grudgingly, Abel slung his rucksack over his shoulder, continuing in darkness. He strove to focus on Nairadj's lanky form, picking out details as he struggled to adjust to the ever-present darkness pressing in about him. After about half the day had passed, he found himself noticing jutting rocks in the dark around his feet and his frequent stumbling ceased.

"See," Nairadj whispered encouragingly, "you *can* see in the dark."

Smiling to himself, Abel replied, "Aye.... seems I can. Though, I will never see in the dark as perfectly as you, Master Nairadj."

Ahead, she chuckled, calling over her shoulder, "Well Abel, as they say: no one is perfect."

Abel and Nairadj journeyed another day and a half without impediment or delay. The further they proceeded within Melatharom's tunnels, the less at ease they felt. They were fatigued, and took furtive two-hour naps, alternating watches as they did so. Keeping watch was a relatively moot point, but it provided them a small measure of comfort. As they journeyed forth, they talked much; quietly at first and then steadily louder, until they carried on in their usual conversational tone. They knew Melatharom watched them- though how, they could not discern.

As they proceeded deeper into the heart of the mountains, they acknowledged that the rock drake was probably striving to dishearten them- make them believe they were lost or become lulled into a false sense of security. The real challenge about how to proceed occurred on the second day's trek, when they discovered a large, burrowed crossroad. Though there was no visible difference- for the travelers were still blanketed in stony darkness- they both concurred that the air flowed differently here. Nairadj scouted around with her heightened animal sense and night vision, confirming it was indeed a crossroads.

Concernedly, Abel asked, "What should we do Master? Should we forge onwards, or take the crossroad?"

Nairadj grunted, stating flatly, "We wait right here. If Melatharom *truly* wants us, he must meet us. If we press on, he could attack from behind. If we turn onto the crossroad, we may become lost. That could be a worse kind of death sentence- particularly if we do not find a way out. No, we wait. This burrowing Wyrm will have to work for its meal, young Abel- though we will deny him the privilege."

Abel swallowed a sizeable lump in his throat. "What should we do to draw him here, then?" Even as he uttered the words, he had an instinct about his master's response.

Though he could not see her face, he detected the devilish tone of her voice. "We are going to do something no sane creature should *ever* do around a dragon. We shall insult him, *loudly*, in his own domain. Dragons are prideful- as we learnt with Ulgnar. He will not sit by while we slander him, or his brother."

Before commencing their insults, Abel and Nairadj carefully and thoroughly trod the crossroads to survey for jutting outcroppings of rock, shallow spots in the excavated rock floor, and crevices they could hide in if things grew too dangerous. The ground seemed fairly level; there were no outcroppings to crack their heads upon, and there were no crevices in the walls of stone.

"Alright, listen closely Abel. Melatharom is likely a *much* larger dragon than Ulgnar, and better armored. His belly will probably be least armored, but most difficult to attack. He may breathe fire, so beware if you hear a sound like a bellows, or smell sulfur or oil. If the gods smile on us and we are lucky enough to be behind him, there is a sac behind his armored crest- above his jaw. That is where the fire mixes with the oil he naturally creates, before he launches a jet of flame. If that is punctured, his fire-breath should be disabled. That is a *highly* risky venture, so do not attempt it unless things are desperate. Keep moving, and whatever you do, don't let him push you further into the tunnels, or separate us. These things could spell our doom."

"Aye, Master Nairadj," Abel responded, trying to suppress the fear coiling in the pit of his stomach. He felt her slender hand firmly grip his shoulder in return.

"All shall be well, Abel. While we are watching out for each other, nothing bad can happen. Do you believe me?"

Reaching out with his right hand, he gripped her shoulder in return. "Aye, Master, I do."

"What is that quote from the '*Legends of Kalnay*' book you are fond of repeating? It escapes my memory."

In a level, firm voice, Abel proclaimed, "I have naught to fear...."

"....for my cause is just," Nairadj finished. "Yes, *that's* the one. I have found that reassuring on our journey together thus far. Who knows, perhaps it brings luck."

Chuckling, Abel teased, "Master Nairadj, are you looking to fairy tales for *luck* now? I would never have taken you for the superstitious type."

"Not superstitious, just....searching for hope. Melatharom is the greatest opponent we have faced thus far, and the situation is stacked heavily in his favor. Hope is the greatest weapon we have right now." There was a momentary pause when the silence and darkness fully enveloped the two warriors, master and apprentice alike. Then Nairadj exhaled a deep sigh. "Shall we get down to it then?"

"Aye, Master Nairadj. If we are marked by the gods to die, 'tis best to get it over with." Drawing his sword and dragon tooth dagger, Abel drew a large breath and shouted, "We are here Melatharom, you great, cowardly *Wyrm*! If you want our blood, you must come for it! Unless you are nothing but a big-winded, *braggart* of a rock snake, striking from the shadows! Face us! We have slain your water slug of a brother, Ulgnar the Grey! Come seek satisfaction, if you *can*!"

They did not wait long for their foe to answer the insults Abel hurled into the echoing tunnels. From the crisscrossing tunnel to the duo's right, came a terrifying, rumbling voice. "How dare you, *disrespectful*, mortal *murderer*! How dare you insult *me*, Melatharom the Burrower, in the sanctity of my own domain! You slew my brother! Apologize! Beg forgiveness, and I *may* offer you and the she-bear a quick, merciful death. Refuse, and I will rend your flesh and clean my teeth with your bones! What say you, son of man and daughter of bear? Do you own your misdeeds and accept my punishment of your actions?"

Abel's pride and honor had been provoked by the barbs of Melatharom's words. "Your brother Ulgnar, 'tis true, I slew. However, he was slain *after* he refused to grant us peaceful passage through the edge of Voshkarna on our journey north. He attacked *us*, unprovoked. I offer you my humblest apologies, O Melatharom, for slaying your kin.

"I will *not*, however, accept your punishment for defending myself and my master from certain death at the tooth and claw of your arrogant brother. Ulgnar believed himself mightier than he was and paid for that arrogance with his life. I beseech you, accept my apologies and grant us safe passage south through your mountains. If not, we shall deal with you as we did with Ulgnar."

Melatharom roared in rage. "*Insolence*! I decree, by the will of the Ancient Father, you shall both perish here within my burrowed halls! Your bones I will grind to dust! All memory of you shall be burnt away from Kalnay!"

Abel stood, Mediator in his right hand and his dragon tooth dagger at the ready in his left. Calmly, he stated, "I hear the family resemblance twixt you and your brother. You both love prattling. Let us get on with this."

"If you wish to die now, I will oblige your request," Melatharom hissed furiously. A sound like rumbling thunder rolled and before Abel's eyes, he witnessed a fireball grow in brightness and intensity, launching towards him.

Before Abel rolled right, the fire illuminated the horned, bony plate of Melatharom's crown, and part of his upper torso. The rock drake was indeed much thicker and larger than Ulgnar.

What have I gotten us into?

Rising to his feet, Abel jumped swiftly backwards, narrowly avoiding the bone shattering snap of Melatharom's enormous bite. He reflected concernedly; *He is too fast! Ulgnar did not move* nearly *this quick.*

Directly before him, for his backward motion had put him eye-to-eye with the dragon, he noticed something curious. Melatharom's eyes glowed orange in the dark, but the orange was hazy. Though the eye that Abel stared into moved back and forth, it did not settle on him. *He* is *blind,* his mind screamed in amazement. *He must detect us by sound then! That's why he didn't attack us sooner: he was familiarizing himself with our sounds! Our footfalls, grunts, breathing rhythms....who knows what else he perceives?*

Further ahead, down the left tunnel, Abel heard Nairadj's sword clank off the rock face. Melatharom snapped sidelong at Abel, who rolled to his right. As he did, he felt a large rush of air pass over him in the opposite direction and realized the dragon's great clawed foot passed overhead to propel him down the tunnel. Abel held his breath, laying flat on the ground until Melatharom completely passed him by. He heard the serpentine scrape and drag of the dragon's scaly hide and soft underbelly upon the granite rock surface.

I hope Master Nairadj is well. I must alter my sound, so I can sneak up on this brute. Down the left tunnel, Abel saw a fireball erupt as Melatharom strove to burn Nairadj. Instinctually, he ripped the arms from his shirt, wrapping them over his booted feet. Satisfied they were secure, he rose to his feet, testing the cloth-wrapped boots by taking several measured steps- listening for the usual '*clip, clop*' of his soles. Hearing nothing, he gave pursuit to Melatharom. Confident the strips would hold, he quickened his pace, hearing nothing but the soft shuffle of the cloth wrappings.

He gripped Mediator and his dagger tightly as he put on a burst of speed. Ahead, he heard Melatharom roar, saw another fireball erupt, and thought, *I'm on my way master. Hold on.*

When Melatharom launched his first fireball, Nairadj rolled left, turning as she did so. This put her in the center of the southward tunnel. Turning silently on the balls of her feet, she dashed to the right, into the east tunnel, directly across from the rock drake. Upon reaching it, she turned in search of Abel. She was dismayed to mark him crouched beside Melatharom's large, armor plated skull. Even with her night vision, she was unable to determine why her pupil was so near its mouth.

Move, *Abel! Gods, does he even know Melatharom is there?! I must get his attention, now!* Gripping her sword tightly, she thwacked it against the rock face to her left. She saw the drake cast a sidelong swipe at Abel. She observed Abel dodging right and flattening himself to the ground. Whether he was alright she could not determine, for she had drawn Melatharom's attention and he was now propelling himself towards her.

Pivoting on her right foot, she dashed briskly down the eastern tunnel, putting some distance twixt her and the rock drake. She paused, slowing and quieting her breath as she looked behind her. Rapidly dragging his thick, scaly hide along, the dragon slowly turned his head side-to-side.

She noticed then what Abel had previously discovered. *Melatharom is* blind. *He dwells exclusively beneath the mountains. He's probably not seen the sun in years. His eyes served no purpose here in the darkness, so they ceased working. He must track us by sound....maybe scent, too.*

Keeping a wary, luminescent eye on the steadily approaching beast, Nairadj delicately removed her boots. She could hear the flaring, sniffing rush of air through the dragon's nostrils as he crawled closer to her position. Crouching and hugging close to the tunnel wall, she raised one of her boots, tossing it down the tunnel until it clattered against the far wall some thirty feet further on.

Melatharom whipped his menacing, armored skull towards the sound of the boot striking the wall. Opening his powerful jaws, he spewed a jet of flame, aimed where the boot connected with the wall. As he did so, he resumed his crawling towards the sound. He passed within fifteen feet of where Nairadj pressed herself low against the tunnel wall and continued onward.

His sense of smell isn't that refined either, Nairadj observed. *He has evolved to rely mostly upon his*

*keen hearing to catch unsuspecting prey that stray
beneath his mountains.*

As he slithered and scraped his serpentine form
past her, she spotted the prize she hoped for: the large,
bulbous sac where the fire mixed, just behind the armor
plating above the right jaw. Nairadj raised her dragon
tooth dagger, quickly formulating her plot. *Ancestors be
with me, for I know not if this will work. Protect Abel,
should I fail.*

Like a striking cobra, Nairadj darted forward,
extending her dagger hand outward, and with bated
breath plunged the knife into the pulsing sac. What
happened next happened swiftly.

Melatharom roared in pain and fury, smashing
his head sideways, slamming the dyre bear into the
unyielding tunnel wall. The she-bear felt air rush from
her lungs as the dragon crushed her. She felt the heat of
its internal furnace through his skin and stabbed the sac
again. The dragon's neck vibrated with the surging fire
dying to boil forth. When she stabbed again, the beast
jerked his head away from the pain, freeing Nairadj from
between his thick, muscular neck and the tunnel wall. A
jet of flame burst upwards from the sac, scorching the
roof as he twisted his head away.

The she-bear didn't waste a moment. As she
dropped, she rolled left, gaining her feet and dashing
barefoot back to the crossroad. There was a ruckus
behind her as the enraged rock drake worked to spin his
lengthy, thick body about in several lithe, abnormal twists
of joints and limbs. She registered the repulsive sound of
him attempting to launch more jets of fire as several
squelchy, splattering chokes.

Melatharom roared furiously as he gave pursuit to Nairadj. "You foul, bear *svanth*! You have *ruined* my fire-breath! You will pay *dearly* for that offence!"

Calling loudly over her shoulder, the she-bear taunted, "First you must catch me, ye great *slug*. Then you may speak of offences given!" Her words further provoked her opponent.

He drew closer, putting on more speed. Nairadj looked ahead to the crossroads and saw something which distressed her greatly. Abel was dashing towards her and Melatharom without making a sound.

Gods above, this *wasn't part of my plan!* Aloud, she bellowed, "*Abel*! Turn back! Melatharom is coming!"

Abel dashed silently down the east tunnel towards Melatharom and Nairadj. A ball of corkscrewing fear wound into his belly. The sounds he heard moments before from the dragon's maw struck him as sounds of pain. This encouraged him, but only slightly.

I cannot help Lady Nairadj from here. Perhaps I can distract him.... Abel beheld a jet of flame propel straight upwards ahead of him, though it did not seem focused, as the previous fireballs. It twisted towards the roof a moment before extinguishing into nothingness. Further thoughts were interrupted by a mighty tremor in the granite rock surrounding him. His mind raced in trepidation. *A rockslide* under *the mountain?* He didn't realize Melatharom was worming around to give pursuit to Nairadj.

From down the tunnel about forty feet away, he heard Nairadj call out, "*Abel!* Turn back! Melatharom is coming!"

Without hesitation, he turned on his heels, fleeing back to the crossroad. She quickly overtook him, ushering him to hurry. Abel's mind raced faster still, striving to think of what to do next.

If we return to the crossroads, Melatharom has room to maneuver. If he outmaneuvers us, we perish. He could think of nothing helpful to defeat the enraged rock drake closing in behind. Distracted by his whirlwind thoughts, Abel drifted to his left......and fell flat into a three-and-a-half-foot deep depression in the rock floor.

Despite the surprise, he rolled into the fall, for he did not wish to tumble onto his sword. His left shoulder took the brunt of the force as he landed, his sword slapping him flat across his chest. He heard Melatharom closing and slowed his breathing. *He cannot see me. If the gods are merciful, he did not hear me fall either. I will wait and see if my fortune holds.*

Seconds turned into eons as he heard the scrape and slither of Melatharom's massive, scaled body racing closer. Then, the dragon was over him, his soft, fish white belly exposed and gliding mere feet above his face. Though he wanted to stab now, Abel was uncertain if he would successfully kill him, or merely rile the furious drake further. Calmly and quietly breathing through his nostrils, he thought, *I must wait. The moment is not right. Patience, Abel.*

Vaguely above and behind him he heard Nairadj's muffled cries beyond Melatharom's obstructive underbelly. He could not discern her words through the muffling thickness of the dragon's scaly hide, but Abel could tell she was furious and distraught. A thought occurred to him then, that concerned him greatly: *Does she believe me dead? She must not have seen me fall here.*

His suspicions were confirmed as Melatharom's shifting bulk lifted momentarily and he heard Nairadj cry, "For the Way of the Light!"

Abel realized she was charging the beast head on. *What is she thinking? She'll die!* Gripping Mediator firmly by the hilt, he rose to a crouched position, thrusting his sword upwards into the soft white flesh of Melatharom's belly. The rock drake was charging Nairadj as Abel did this. His momentum assisted Abel, turning the vertical puncture into a twenty-five-foot-long gash in the dragon's underbelly. From the enormous rent in its soft belly poured a thick stream of black blood, dousing the trapped young warrior from head to foot. Abel began to panic as oxygen was swiftly replaced with rank-smelling, foul-tasting dragon's blood.

Melatharom hissed loudly in pained surprise at the grave wound expanding in his underside, faltering in his charge as he struggled to grasp what was happening. Before the drake could move away, Abel slashed a wide horizontal line across the sizeable lengthwise one, creating a bloody cross pattern in the beast's belly.

As the slashes intersected, young Farthen was pummeled from above with over-warm dragon intestines. Already drowning in putrid, inky blood, he knew that, if he were to survive, he must escape from beneath Melatharom. Blindly seizing a coil of intestine, Abel ascended desperately from the blood-filled hole in the tunnel floor.

When Nairadj cleared the east tunnel, she whirled about to face Melatharom hoping to find Abel at her side. To her dismay, when she surveyed the tunnel, she did not see her pupil. *By the ancestors,* no*! Where* is *he?! Is he eaten?!* Her heart was greatly troubled at this.

Oddly enough, in those moments before she made her final stand, she had a revelation regarding her feelings for Abel. In this moment, she did not think of him as her pupil; or the misfortunate, curious boy against whom so many ill things had transpired in the past few months. Chiefly, she thought of him simply as Abel. She thought of him as a young man who genuinely- if not embarrassingly- declared his love for her in a Red House in Bogdan; blushing innocently in the presence of half-naked whores. She recalled him declaring his feelings would not change. How when their quest was over that, if *she* so desired, they could pursue a deeper relationship.

Witnessing Melatharom slithering closer, and seeing no sign of Abel, her heart felt heavier and angrier at this dreaded reptilian foe. Gripping her sword tightly, Nairadj stood her ground, shouting, "You *monster*! You killed him!"

The rock drake slowed, intrigued by her outburst. "Oh *really,*" he sneered. "What is it you think I have done, she-bear?"

"Is it not enough the boy lost his father and mother?! Or that his first master perished?! That he is separated from his sister and the life he knew in his hometown?! Now he has lost his life to a slimy, *despicable Wyrm* such as *you*!"

Melatharom chuckled cruelly at Nairadj's anger. "The bashing I gave you upon the rocks must have rattled your wits free. *I* have not killed the boy. You are attempting to distract me. Where is he, she-bear? Since he means *so* much to you, perhaps I *should* devour him live before your eyes, before ending *your* life. What think you of that?"

Leveling her sword at the rock drake, Nairadj seethed, "*One* of us shall perish here, but it will *not* be me." Raising her voice, she dashed towards Melatharom, screaming, "For Abel! For the Way of the Light!"

Melatharom smiled a malicious, toothy grin in the dark, snarling, "If you insist on rushing to your doom, I shall oblige you." He issued a mighty roar, resuming his speed. He opened wide his jaws, preparing to devour his foe whole.

Then....he felt something; a tugging discomfort in his mid-belly. It made him wince at first, but he did not stop running. The pain grew exponentially. He skidded to a distracted halt, wriggling uncomfortably to get away from the growing pain, but was rewarded with another, greater pain than before running side to side across his underbelly.

With this second peculiar wave of pain, he felt a great *rushing out* from within, causing him to feel weak. He felt something tugging on his innards. The extremity of the pain distracted him from the she-bear charging him. Feebly, he whipped his head to and fro, struggling to wriggle backwards or to the side, away from the pain. Still he felt stuck on something. The Burrower's senses began failing and he realized in dismay, *I have been grievously injured! But....how?! I am king under Shavatnu!* None *challenge me and live!*

He regained focus momentarily, spotting the bear lady closing on him. In a last-ditch effort to defend himself, he gaped open his great, fanged mouth, roaring in fury. It was only when he felt the she-bear wholly leap into his mouth, that he snapped shut his jaws with a mix of finality and confusion. Struggling to turn and investigate the searing pain he felt in his mid-riff, he realized, *the* boy*! The boy has wounded my belly! Well, he can join his master in my....* His thought broke off as he realized in cascading horror that the she-bear was still in his mouth. She had not slid down his gullet to be digested.

The deadly edge of the she-bear's sword punched up through the soft pallet in the roof of his mouth, piercing his brain. There were no final words or thoughts for the king under Shavatnu. Melatharom's world plummeted into eternal darkness, his great jaws tumbled open and he issued a wet vomiting sound as his armored head crashed hard to the rocky tunnel floor. Melatharom the Burrower was slain.

From his mouth emerged Nairadj, drenched in saliva, oil and mucus. She grasped firmly to her sword, rolling from his gaping, dead maw to the granite ground. Wiping the mucus from her face she stumbled down the length of the beast's corpse, searching desperately for Abel. About thirty-five feet down on the dragon's right side, Nairadj observed the scaly hide pulsing and rippling strangely outwards. Her heart leapt into her throat and she rasped, "*Abel!* Is that *you*?! Can you *hear* me?!"

As she drew alongside where her luminescent eyes had observed the pulsing scales, she heard a great, wet, rending sound. She watched in astonishment as Mediator pierced skyward from within the dragon's corpse, harshly ripping an opening twixt Melatharom's heavy scales from within. Seconds later, Abel's arms emerged, widening his gory exit. With a deep, frantic gasp, his blood-blackened face emerged from the dragon's corpse.

Stepping forward to pull the young warrior out, Nairadj cried in a mix of joy and relief. "I thought I lost you, Abel."

Sputtering a weak laugh, he replied, "Technically, Master....you did. Can you lend me a hand, please? These scales are tougher to move than you would think."

With great effort, Nairadj pulled Abel free of Melatharom's scaly side. As he wrestled his way free, he scraped his bare right forearm faintly on one of the dead dragon's scales. He didn't notice, given the gore he was caked in and the deep-seated weariness racking his body. The rock drake's black blood seeped into the faint cut.

Once free, young Farthen stumbled to the tunnel wall, slouched against it, sliding exhaustedly to the floor and breathing deeply of the fresh air. Nairadj huffed as she flopped down beside him. They sat in the darkness for a long minute not speaking; only breathing and relishing the feeling of being alive, and together.

In another minute, Abel fished in his rucksack; first for his water skin, taking a deep pull of the refreshing liquid, offering some to Nairadj. Then he drew his torch, lighting it and raising it to look at his master. He stared in ill-disguised repulsion as he observed the caked-on mucus crusting her hair, face, clothing and armor.

Nairadj stared at Abel, disgusted by the sight and smell of him drenched in drying, foul-smelling, black dragon blood. Then, smiles cracked on both their faces and they laughed loud and heartily.

"You....you look as though you just crawled from a dragon's snout, Master Nairadj," he gasped through a fit of laughter.

"*You're* one to judge, Abel; you look like a freshly hatched baby dragon, and smell about as pleasant as one too," she replied through a fit of laughter-induced tears.

"I *did* just crawl through dragon guts, you know. Which, by the way, is not something I *ever* recommend. Gods above, I'm going to smell like rotten dragon meat for *days.*"

They laughed for another solid minute before gaining control of themselves. Abel raised the torch, looking to his left. "I think we can get out of here if we head east down this corridor. What do you think, Master?" He was startled when he looked back in her direction, dropping the torch on the ground twixt them. Nairadj was leaning very close, her emerald green eyes brimming with tears, observing every detail on his face.

"Master Nairadj," Abel asked, "What is it? What's the matter?"

Raising her snot-crusted left hand, she stroked Abel's gore-splattered right cheek. "When I turned, and you were missing......I thought....I thought Melatharom had *devoured* you...."

Wrapping her hand in both of his, Abel soothed, "Oh....my lady, I am *so* sorry...."

Clasping her right hand over his hands, Nairadj continued, "It's alright Abel. It put things in perspective for me....fearing you had perished. I realized, in that moment, all the *goodness* within you. Not merely as a student, but as a *man*. You are a *good* man, Abel Farthen. I am happy to know you."

He smiled back. "I am happy to know you too, Master Nairadj."

Shaking her head, she interrupted, "No....no, I don't mean like *that*. I have never....I have never engaged in deep relations with *anyone*. When you proclaimed your love for me in Bogdan, I could not reciprocate. You were my student, and a mortal besides....I am beginning to see those things matter less than I thought. When I feared you dead, I felt a sharp pang of loss in my heart; like the death of my brother, but different...."

Abel glanced at her curiously, asking, "Master, what do you mean? What are you saying?"

"I *love* you," Nairadj blurted. "I've been denying it, making excuses, erecting barriers around my heart to defend me from being hurt, or disappointed. When I thought you died, those barriers crumbled; I realized they had kept out the *one* person who has stood by me through all the trials on this journey. I realized that......I didn't want to be *alone* anymore." Then she leaned in, planting a firm kiss on Abel's lips.

Abel was briefly surprised but heartily reciprocated. *Am I dead? Am I dreaming?* He knew he wasn't, but it felt so surreal to hear all this from Nairadj....especially after having just vanquished a *second* dragon together.

In another moment, she withdrew from the kiss. "Now, as agreed before, we finish our quest. *Then* we talk about deepening our relationship." Slowly, she rose to her feet, sore from battle. "I agree, by the way: we *should* take this eastern tunnel; there may be a way out. Come, Abel." Extending her snot-caked hand, Nairadj smiled, asking, "Unless......you'd rather stay here and watch this dragon rot?"

Chortling, Abel took her offered hand. "No, Master; I have had enough of dragons to last me *two* lifetimes." They shouldered their rucksacks and began walking down the east tunnel, the torch faintly lighting their way. "What are the chances, you think, of finding a spring down here, Master Nairadj?"

"With the luck we've been granted Abel, I say our chances are good."

"That's good enough for me."

They continued eastward for roughly a day; while the tunnel turned somewhat southward, they still traveled east. That day, they talked and laughed, relishing the unbelievable victory over their second dragon in as many months. Occasionally, Abel absently scratched at his right forearm, supressing an itch beneath his skin where he scraped against the drake's scales and its blood had co-mingled with his.

Near day's end, they found their way into a large cavern. Nairadj scouted ahead, while Abel kept watch; his torch a pinpoint in the cavernous dark. From the furthest southeastern corner of the cave arose a cry from Nairadj.

Abel rushed towards her voice, his dagger at the ready. "Lady Nairadj, what is it? Is something wrong?" As he drew upon her location, he was stunned to discover her up to her chin in water.

The she-bear laughed; the joyous, relieved sound echoing clearly off the stone walls, brightening the pitch-black space with the mirth of her laughter. Bobbing in the warm, spring water, Nairadj beamed broadly, saying, "It seems we *are* the two luckiest creatures in Kalnay. The water is *amazing*, Abel. Let us revel in this, our *second* victory in as many days."

He needed no further convincing. Propping the lit torch upright in a natural crevice in the rock floor, he shed his rucksack on the floor, backed up, and gleefully hollered, "Watch out, I'm coming in!"

Then he ran, leaping into the water. The relief he felt was beyond words as he felt the crusting, caked on dragon's blood, dissipate, washing from his skin and garments. He fully submerged when he struck the water with a mighty splash. When he surfaced from the refreshing depths, he floated on his back; his arms splayed, and he laughed, overjoyed.

Nairadj swam to him, calling, "Now, *here's* a side of you I've not seen since before the marketplace of Vosh. It does my heart good to see you laugh."

"I could say the same of you, Mi'lady."

Running her fingers through her wet, blonde hair, she spoke to the cavernous ceiling, "It is *so* good to be cleansed of dragon mucus and saliva. You have *no* idea."

Abel swam alongside her. "I have *some* idea. I used Melatharom's innards to climb from a blood-drenched hole in the ground. Though, I think you win. Given the choice, I'd rather be doused in blood and guts, than something's phlegm."

Splashing him, she replied, "I do not want your *pity*, cheeky cub."

Abel drew right up to Nairadj, raising a clean, wet hand to wipe a last crusty streak of saliva from her hair on the right side. "Not pity, my lady; sympathy from one who endured something similarly revolting." He held his hand there a moment, relishing the slick feel of her radiant blonde hair. Then he drew close, kissing her firmly, droplets of water running down his nose to drop onto her cheek.

Nairadj wrapped her arms about Abel, the water rippling around them and lapping at the lip of the spring as they clung to each other for a long minute. Nairadj released him from her grasp first, drifting backwards and speaking in hushed tones. "We must *not*. Not now, Abel. I love you, as I said....but we *must* see our task through to completion *first*."

Abel blushed red hot- hoping she could not see-clearing his throat. "No, you're right....we must defeat Malikh and Lilith first. I....I'm going to see if there is any wood to build a fire with to dry off...." He hoisted himself up onto the rocky cave floor, scooping up the torch to explore the cavern, drip drying as he went.

In her tumultuously conflicted mind, Nairadj thought, *what is* wrong *with me? Maybe I isolated myself too much in the Southern Sand Flats? No....it has naught to do with isolation. Perhaps 'tis all the shared grief and tribulations we have experienced together......Though he is younger than I, each challenge we encounter reveals more of his* true *self- the man he is becoming; the man he has been raised to be: a man of valor, honor and truth. This, these traits, are part of the whole that attracts me to him......But enough of that. I must help Abel set up camp.*

After exiting the spring, cleansed of Melatharom's dried gore, Abel scrounged some scrub brush for kindling; the only thing tough and stubborn enough to grow in the darkness of a dragon's den. As he knelt to cut free the thick, leafless branches with his dagger, Abel froze. In the torchlight, he saw something abnormal on his right forearm. Setting his dagger down and raising the torch with his left, he drew it close to his exposed right forearm, staring in dismay at something that was not there prior to battling Melatharom.

Running from the middle of his forearm to just below his elbow joint was a toughened patch of discolored, brown skin.

No, not skin, Abel's mind corrected numbly, *scales. Gods be gracious, what is this?*

He inspected the discolored area, noting that, faintly, in the middle of the growing scales, was the scrape he received while struggling free from Melatharom's guts. *What devilry is this?*

He did not want Nairadj discovering this. He desired her to be at peace, relishing their victory over Melatharom. *I cannot tell her....not now anyways. I will keep a wary eye on this.....if it worsens, then I will tell her. Does a cure even* exist *for something like this...? Whatever* this *is....* His mind turned unbidden to Sarto. The old herbalist had been around a very long time. He knew everything about potions, poultices and cures for obscure ailments. Abel suddenly, bitterly, wished the old coot were here right now. He would know *exactly* what to do.

Seizing his dagger with his right hand, he swiped the branches of the scrub brush free of its shallow roots and gathered them up. He returned to a spot near the spring, busying himself with preparing a fire. As the fire grew, Nairadj scrounged some food from the rucksacks. In a couple moments, she sat next to him, offering a shiny, crisp apple and several strips of jerky. They ate in comfortable silence, cherishing the gentle warmth of the fire, which slowly dried their sopping wet robes.

Staring into the flames, Abel ran his hand over his freshly covered right forearm- feeling the ridged, scaly skin gradually growing there. Absently, he reflected, "You know Master Nairadj....we really *are* the two luckiest creatures in Kalnay."

The next morning when Abel awoke, he held his left hand up to block sunlight prying at his closed eyelids. It took a moment to register, in his sleep-hazy mind, that it *was* sunlight. When he did realize, he sat bolt upright, staring amazedly past his shielding hand to gaze at the unexpected light. Forty feet up the rubble-strewn rock face, he saw a clear, thick ray of sunlight streaming through a large hole. Rising to his feet, he stared harder at that gods-sent ray of light.

We have a way out! Gods be praised! Kneeling beside Nairadj, Abel gently shook her shoulder, whispering, "Master, awaken. There is something you *must* see."

She rolled over, drawing her dagger in one smooth motion, looking wide-eyed around the cave. She froze, when she realized she could distinguish the features of the cavern; the light glinting off the water's surface on their right. Nairadj gazed wordlessly at Abel. He pointed towards the southern face of the cave, where the sun beam stabbed through. Her eyes grew wider and she beamed a broad smile. "The Ancestors and gods *truly* watch over us, Abel."

He smiled as well, already packing his rucksack. "It seems so. What say we rejoin the land of sun, and the living, Master Nairadj?"

Rising quickly to her feet, Nairadj scooped up her possessions, packing her rucksack hurriedly. Her eyes never left the glorious ray of sunlight. "Aye, Abel. That's a most agreeable idea."

They scaled the rubble slowly and carefully- as the pile of rocks was prone to sliding or dislodging from their temporary resting place. After forty-five minutes of careful ascent, the companions reached the opening. Abel glanced at Nairadj, gesturing towards the opening. "As my father Aldrich taught me in my youth, ladies first, Master."

Nairadj bowed faintly and replied, "My thanks Abel." Then she crawled through, scraping her sheathed sword on the rocky crawl space. He followed suit and they emerged into sunlight.

A short time later, Isabel appeared in her ghostly, projected form. Abel wanted desperately to ask her if Sarto knew any cures for a dragon-infected scratch. He held his tongue though, for he didn't want was his sister to worry needlessly, when she was so far away. He also didn't wish to suffer Nairadj's wrath when she learned of his incident. Instead, he savored the chance to catch up with his sister, learning of her new friends- the Shadow Twins and Khalon the wendygo.

After Isabel returned to her body in Endelheim, there came flying an ominous unkindness of ravens. The companions crawled quickly back into the mountain crawl space, watching warily until the birds altered course, wheeling northwesterly. When they re-emerged after the birds left, they surveyed the land below. In the distance, to the southwest, they discerned a handful of pin-prick structures jabbing towards the sky.

"There it is," Nairadj declared, pointing to the pin-pricks, "the fortress city of Regalias. Journey's end is within sight."

Abel stared, shielding his eyes from the sun. "It seems....*unreal*....doesn't it Master Nairadj?"

"What does, Abel?"

"Up to this instant, our quest has been about an *idea*. Suddenly......there is a landmark indicating the end. Part of me....part of me feels as though, even once we're there, things won't *really* be over....not until we are reunited with Isabel and Sarto...."

Resting a reassuring hand on his shoulder, Nairadj interjected, "A journey begins with a single step, young one. It ends the same way. By my estimation, we will arrive in about three days' time." *Assuming nothing untoward occurs twixt now and then,* she thought.

"Well," Abel replied, "I guess the only way to conclude this quest is to continue moving forward. Come on Master Nairadj, let us finish this." Subconsciously, he scratched his covered right forearm, wending his way down the gently sloping mountain face to the grasslands below. Nairadj followed close by.

Far northeast, across the mist-shrouded waters of Nevartane, upon the isle of Draconias Maxima, there issued forth an enraged dragon cry. Charridon felt the stabbing pains within his guts, where Abel had fatally slashed Melatharom's belly. He felt also, the cold jab of the she-bear's blade as she pierced his son's soft pallet. Before the touch reached his own brain, Charridon severed connection with Melatharom's conscious mind.

The Ancient Father's massive frame was still gradually awakening from his age-long slumber. His tail whipped furiously about his massive cavern dwelling, knocking pillars of rock to the ground, the spikes on his tail punching holes into the rocky walls enclosed about him. His mind roared in rage as he felt another of his sons perish to these two puny mortal creatures.

By the fires of the old world, I swear- *before gods and demons alike- for these foul, murderous deeds, all Kalnay shall feel my wrath! Were the Elduri yet alive today, they would rejoice. Their extermination was a* mercy *that shall be outmatched by the fatherly wroth stirring within my ancient heart!* None *shall live to write tale nor song of the immolation of Kalnay! I shall burn* all*: man, beast, field, castle, mountain, wood and lake alike!*

The word of Sir Brock Clegane is a hollow shell echoing the lies of mankind! He calls truce after killing my mate Jezreel, and yet his kind have flagrantly, and repeatedly, broken it! Now all shall feel the wrath of Charridon, the Ancient One!

Then he roared, unleashing a massive jet of fire that shot forth from his enormous cave, frightening the roosting seabirds perched along the rocky coast nearby. Though no one yet knew it, time was growing short for the realm of Kalnay.

Chapter Nineteen: Suspicion and Revelation

Malikh's forces marched north to halt the Wildmen advancing south through the Drake's Maw Pass a day and a half earlier. Clarke had watched from the northern ramparts as the swollen ranks of the Regalias Red Guard moved with haste. He was returning to his study when he was stopped outside the throne room by Lady Lilith.

"Greetings, Master Clarke," she began, "Lord Malikh wished you to know he will be leading the attack with General Markus. As such, he has charged me to safeguard the kingdom and capital in his absence."

Bowing, Clarke replied, "My Queen, thank you for informing me. It would be foolish to call upon the Overlord in his absence."

Lilith chuckled. "Indeed. I anticipate he will have no difficulty vanquishing these invaders. The Red Guard forces are closer than they to the Crossroad of Kings. I expect my Lord will return within three, four days' time, at most." She gazed hard into Clarke's eyes with her oily black ones and smiled. "If I were you, I would take this time to catch up on your favorite reading, Master Scribe. I anticipate when my husband returns victorious, there will be plentiful hangings and trials for any surviving prisoners. Additionally, you will have *many* exciting new pages to pen for the history tomes."

Clarke smiled, bowed briefly again, asking, "Should I take that as a command, my Lady? Or a recommendation?"

"I am Queen, so....consider it a recommendation. If I were to command you, Master Scribe, you would know it."

"As you say, majesty, so I will do." Raising his eyebrow quizzically, Clarke asked, "Perhaps I should devote these extra days of....revelry, to further expand the Princess A...."

He froze, with the name 'Arya' just behind his teeth. Adelaide, *you fool! Her name is Adelaide, not Arya! Utter* that *name and* everything *you are working towards will be dashed to pieces!* Shaking his head quickly, the Master Scribe chuckled, rapping his right temple with his right hand. "I cry your pardon, my Lady. For a moment there, I am embarrassed to admit, I forgot the young princess's name. It seems I am beginning to *act* my age, as well as feel it."

Lilith's eyes bored unblinkingly into the old man's soft blue ones, searching for any trace of a lie.

Stay calm, he thought, *she knows naught; as Malikh knew naught. You will be fine, if you remain calm.*

A moment later, the Screech Owl cracked a smile and laughed. "All is well, Master Scribe. Age catches up to everyone, eventually. And yes, to finish your thought, I concur that spending this time with Princess Adelaide is a wise investiture of resources. After all, the young must learn the nature of the world. Don't you agree?"

Cracking a measured smile, he nodded and replied, "I would, Lady Lilith. Children are the bright future of this world, while the old are the walking ghosts of the past."

She grinned at his word choice. "Well-spoken, Master Clarke; a well-spoken word, indeed." She gazed into his eyes, drew a measured breath and then clapped her hands together twice. The sound jolted Clarke, as if from a dream, though only a moment had passed.

"Well then," Lilith spoke cheerily, "I shall leave you to tend my daughter and her education. Good day to you, Master Clarke." She turned sharply, gliding eerily back to the throne room.

The old scribe rubbed his temple again, feeling a headache sprouting and mumbled, "Good day to you, Lady Lilith." Then he rushed to find Jabesh.

Clarke entered the aromatic, botanical gardens-heaving a deep breath, for he had rushed as swiftly as his old bones would permit. Regaining his composure, he strode towards the pond where Jabesh and Princess Adelaide were feeding breadcrumbs to ducks. She leapt up, running towards him, wrapping her arms about his slender waist. "Hello, Master Clarke! How are you this nice, sunny day?"

He smiled, returning Adelaide's hug. "I am fine, dear one; just fine, indeed. What of yourself? What have you been up to today, hmm?"

She smiled a broad, intelligent smile and began ranting- as only children can do- about everything. "*Well*, this morning, Master Jabesh and I stood on the upper northwestern ramparts and watched father's army march away for a *long* time. There were seventy-five thousand people marching. The ground shook as they marched, and it felt funny under our feet on the rampart stones.

"We talked about war, life, and death. We talked about what a good and wise ruler does when presented with a problem- such as invaders, or unexpected problems, like the fire in Lec'tair Forest. Then we went to the kitchen to bake honey cakes with Alfred for a mid-morning snack." Here, she leant conspiratorially towards her friend, shielding her mouth from sight as she whispered, "I ate *three* honey cakes all by myself, Master Clarke. They were *really* delicious."

"Well," he whispered back, beaming, "I don't blame you. Honey cakes are one of my *favorite* treats in the whole kingdom. Alfred bakes them *very* soft and sweet indeed."

Here, she smiled mischievously, reaching into the waist apron over her skirt and withdrew a cloth-wrapped parcel. Looking about warily, she drew back the cloth to reveal two perfect, fluffy, golden cakes inside. "I had Alfred make these two especially for *you,* Master Clarke. I knew you would want one after learning Jabesh and I already had some. Here." Finishing thus, she discreetly passed him the sweet, golden treasures, giggling.

Clarke chuckled back, bowing to Adelaide. "My sincerest thanks to you, princess. You are truly a gracious, thoughtful girl. I will be happy to serve as your Master Scribe when one day *you* are Queen of Kalnay." Taking a bite of the first cake, his eyes widened in playful surprise. "By the gods," he spoke between bites, "this *is* the most amazing honey cake I have *ever* tasted. Thank you for thinking of me. Be sure to thank Alfred for these, should you see him before I do. They are his best work ever."

Adelaide giggled again. "I *did* thank him, Master Clarke. If I thanked him again, he might think me crazy."

Clearing his throat playfully, the Master Scribe winked. "Well, we wouldn't want him thinking *that* now, would we? Otherwise, he may cut us off from honey cakes all together."

The Princess nodded, quickly finishing her account, "After we pilfered you some honey cakes, we came here with some old breadcrumbs from the kitchen. We've been feeding ducks, while Jabesh told me tales of his adventures as a young man."

"Hmm," Clarke mused, "nothing too boring I hope?"

"Oh *no*," Adelaide replied seriously, "Master Jabesh used to be a *warrior*, before coming here from Kiresh. We spoke of when he and his friends marched north against the Wildmen campaign led by their old King, Ridley. It was *very* exciting- full of battles, crazy odds and truly powerful enemies. I *like* Master Jabesh's stories."

"As do I child. As do I."

Adelaide asked, "Don't you get bored of writing down stories Master Clarke? I mean....Jabesh's stories must be exciting to write....but all those *boring* grown up stories about laws, and the number of cows each farmer has exchanged at market just seem so *dull*."

Licking his fingers clean of the drizzled honey from the first cake, the scribe knelt before the princess, ignoring his protesting joints, and explained. "At times it *is* boring. I readily confess that. Even so, 'tis important to mark the details, even when they bore us. Sometimes it is the small details which are the difference twixt guilt and innocence, truth and lies, or even right and wrong. Do you understand, Princess?"

Adelaide paused a moment, screwing her face into a perplexed knot. A moment later, it returned to normal and she answered simply, "*Yes*, Master Clarke."

He chuckled, patting her hand. "It's quite alright child. I am rambling, and you are young: that is a concoction that does *not* mix well." He pressed the last, cloth-wrapped cake into her petit hands, saying, "I want you to take this and head to the library. Master Jabesh and I must talk; more boring, adult talk. You enjoy that in the library with a nice book to read. We will check on you later, my Lady."

Placing the wrapped cake back into her apron pocket, Adelaide beamed innocently and responded, "Alright, Master Clarke, I will. Thank you for the extra honey cake."

"No, sweet Adelaide, thank *you* for your generosity. You did not have to save me those cakes, but you did. I happily return the second one to you as thanks for your kind-heartedness. Never lose that, Adelaide. Might is useful to a queen, but a kind heart will serve her better still."

Holding her head high, Adelaide happily proclaimed, "That is what I want to be known as, when I am queen: Adelaide the Kind."

Perhaps it was a trick of the light. Perhaps the old scribe caught a rare glimpse of the future. Whichever it was, in that exact moment, Adelaide's appearance seemed to be that of a stately, mature woman of twenty. Her shoulder length, blonde hair shimmered in the warm rays of the sun. Her radiant blue eyes seemed weighted with the knowledge and responsibility of her station and a strength that would hold fast through any trial presented to her. Then the moment passed, and Adelaide appeared as her sweet, childish self again.

Stifling tears of joy, Clarke answered proudly, "That is a most fitting title, Princess Adelaide; *truly*. Now, run along while I talk to Master Jabesh."

Without another word, she dashed off to enjoy her treat and the tales of Sir Brock Clegane. Clarke watched her disappear into the south wing. Then, over his right shoulder came Jabesh's smooth, bass voice. "She reminds me *so* much of her mother. It's hard to believe it took me so long to realize the truth."

In a measured tone, the old man replied mournfully, "I wish I had known Queen Rebecca....King Alaster as well."

Resting a reassuring hand on the old man's shoulder, Jabesh replied, "By knowing Arya, you know them, in a sense. In Kiresh, it was believed parents imbued their best characteristics to the child."

"That's a lovely notion. I hope in Arya's case, it's true," the Scribe mused.

"*I* believe it Clarke, my old friend. Ever have I held your confidence and trust; do not begin doubting now. After tonight, she will be free of both the Screech Owl and Malikh's clutches."

"Aye, that may be. But she will be a fugitive until she is safely under Sigourney's protection," the old man countered.

Jabesh chuckled softly, gazing into the clear blue sky, pondering secret thoughts.

Casting a curious glance at him, Clarke asked, "What amuses you, my friend? I don't see humor in what I said."

The Diviner shook his head in humorous disbelief as he explained. "It's just....if you told me twenty years ago that I would look to the daughter of King Ridley for sanctuary and aid....I would have laughed in your face. This feels....*unreal* to me."

Clarke offered, "Unreal or not, 'tis the only avenue available to us. Siding with Sigourney against a common enemy ensures Arya is restored unto her rightful throne and her family is avenged, in a way. If you have a better solution, I would hear it."

Jabesh shook his head, crossing his arms across his broad chest. "No, *this* is our best chance. We will sneak out through the northwest moat gate. There are at least two rowboats anchored out there for perimeter patrol. I will dispatch the guards, steal the boat and then we head north along the banks of the Lesser Inaratu River, until we find Sigourney's forces."

"You make it sound so simple," the scribe replied skeptically. "There will be numerous other problems, large and small to contend with...."

".... which we will deal with as they arise," Jabesh finished. "Honestly my friend, you shouldn't worry so much."

Clarke's brow furrowed in concern; like something just beyond thought eluded him. "I *know* I shouldn't worry; that doesn't prevent me from doing so." Without knowing why, a question emerged from his mouth. "How are your skills with the bow these days, Jabesh?"

With a quizzical look in his eye, the Diviner answered, "As good as ever, as you well know. Why do you ask?"

The Master Scribe's face was still a mask of worry. "I'm....not entirely sure. However, if it crosses my mind, perhaps you best bring it tonight." The cohorts then discussed their escape plan quickly in hushed tones before parting ways to ready themselves for the coming night.

Sunset came swiftly. Clarke had a rucksack of provisions prepared and slung over his back. He was shrouded in black, and bore a short sword sheathed on his hip beneath his black cloak. He moved without hindrance or suspicion- for he was one of five people

within the inner keep of Regalias who could do so
without question. The scribe was nervous, though he
concealed it well. He encountered only two guards as he
headed to Adelaide's chambers. They offered a cheerful,
guileless nod (for the Master Scribe was well-liked and
well-known) and then continued their rounds. He
returned the nod, but thought nervously: *Should there
not be more guards on duty?*

The officious part of his brain spoke up.
*Malikh's forces have journeyed north to combat the
Northerners. That is why we chose to execute this escape
plan* now. *Honestly, you are jumping at shadows like a
wee child.*

As he proceeded up the stairs to Adelaide's
chambers, he rebuked himself mentally. *'Tis one thing*
discussing *escape in private by the light of day. 'Tis
something else* entirely *to execute a plot under cover of
night. Now, focus.*

Presently, he stood before the princess's
chamber door, knocking faintly and waiting. He became
acutely aware of his surroundings in the long, broad
corridor stretching out on either side of him. The
torches along the walls were sparse, giving off little light.
The darkness twixt the torches seemed palpable, as if he
could reach out and feel resistance. Drafts of wind
moaned and whistled beneath the doors lining the hall.

After what felt a small eternity, the Master
Scribe heard Adelaide shuffle to the door and unlatch it.
As she opened it, he strove to compose himself in a
casual manner; as though being at her door this late after
dark were the most natural thing in the world. To his
relief, she was still dressed in daytime apparel. Had she

been dressed for bed it may have been tougher to get her ready to leave.

"Greetings, Lady Adelaide. How are you this lovely night?"

The Princess beamed at him. "Good evening Master Clarke. I am well. What brings you here at this hour?"

Hoping he sounded sincere, he smiled and replied, "Why, didn't I tell you earlier? We are going on an adventure. Something of a......late-night hike. Would you join me, Princess?"

Adelaide bounced up and down on her heels, wringing her hands in excitement. "Oh *yes*! Yes, I *would*, Master Clarke!"

The old man winced at the girl's sudden outburst and cast a furtive glance up and down the corridor for any sign of disturbance. Kneeling quickly, his joints creaking in protest, he took Adelaide's hand in his own. "I am glad to hear that. However, we *must* be quiet as we go. Think of it as....as a *game*."

Leaning in conspiratorially, Adelaide whispered, "I *love* games, Master Clarke. Should I bring anything with me?"

Smiling back, he indicated his rucksack. "I have some provisions already. All you need is a warm cloak and some comfortable boots. Grab them quickly and we will be on our way."

"Can I bring Sir Martin too? He doesn't like missing out on adventures."

Nodding quickly, he conceded. "Aye, dear one, Sir Martin can come too. Fetch him, your cloak and your boots and we will go."

Without a word, Adelaide darted back to her bed, plucking up a burlap bear doll with black, stitched eyes. Sir Martin securely clasped in her left hand, she dashed to her wardrobe, opening the squeaky elm door to retrieve her cloak and boots. In a matter of moments, she had them on and stood before her tutor, ready to go. "Okay, Master Clarke, can we go on our hike now?"

Offering his left hand, the old Scribe nodded. "Aye, dear one. Let us be off."

He did not encounter the guards he met on the way to Adelaide's room, and felt a modicum of relief. He may come and go about the inner keep as he wished. It would be harder to explain to any guards he might encounter why the young princess was out so late. They were over halfway across the courtyard, before it occurred again to Clarke that he had not seen any more guards.

At the very least, I should hear approaching patrols, or the clatter of sword and armor as the guards move. I don't hear a sound. As if reading his mind, there suddenly appeared on the upper balcony all around him, a dozen Regalias Red Guards with crossbows loaded and aimed at the Scribe. A dozen guardsmen dashed from the throne room, around the courtyard perimeter, spears at the ready.

The Master Scribe drew his short sword, ready to defend the princess. *Gods be gracious and spare the child for my folly.* How *did they know? I was so careful....Jabesh too.*

From the throne room appeared Lilith, followed by Malikh and the helmed Noshtain. When the old man noted the Overlord, he started in surprise. *I thought Malikh lead the campaign against the Northerners. How did he return so swiftly? Did he ever leave?* As he pondered this, he realized he had not seen Malikh leave. He was informed by Lilith. Gripping his sword tighter Clarke realized, *this was a set-up....a ruse! But how did they* know*?*

Chuckling cruelly, Lilith taunted. "I am guessing, Master Scribe, you are attempting to puzzle out exactly how we knew of your treachery. Would that be correct?"

Eyeing the guards on the balcony, the old man replied, "Aye, the thought had crossed my mind."

"It is so simple as to be laughable. You *told* me."

If he was surprised before, he was outright shocked at this revelation. *She could be lying,* his seething mind shouted. Laughing, despite how terrified he was, Clarke spat back, "*You lie*, Lilith. I told you naught."

Lilith laughed again, "Are you *certain*, Master Clarke? Think back earlier today. Did nothing feel....*odd*, after we spoke?"

He searched back through his memories. *We spoke. She stared into my eyes and....and then she clapped. She clapped and....and I got a headache......*

Something dawned on him then. His ill-feeling when he spoke with Jabesh, his nagging worry that something was off. His requesting Jabesh bring his bow tonight...... *Gods be merciful....she enchanted me and coaxed me to reveal my plans!*

His mind raced in furious circles. *Did I reveal Jabesh's part in this?* Bracing himself for whatever may happen next, Clarke did something most sane people of Regalias would never do; he laughed at Lilith. "Do you think me a clown, *Screech Owl*?! You expect me to reveal my secrets simply because you *infer* I have already done so? I think not. You must do better than inference. Those are the tricks of palm readers and *charlatans*!"

Around him, the guards nervously shifted their collective gaze to Lilith, afraid of what wrathful actions the scribe's words would provoke. The scribe sensed her tense and he braced himself for her reaction.

Levelly, Lilith pointed her right forefinger at the old man's lower, left leg and shouted, "*Burtsa despa rysa!*"

Crying in pain, Clarke toppled to his side, his sword clattering to the courtyard stones. He clutched his leg with tears welling in his eyes. He felt a slow, digging stab- like a dagger- being forced through the meat and bone of his already fragile leg.

Be strong, old man. She is not master of your senses. You control pain. You've done it for years. Get up! Grabbing his short sword, he rolled painfully to his right knee and pulled himself to his feet. "Is that the best you have, ye cut-rate *mountebank*?!"

The Screech Owl's black eyes grew large in shock at the scribe's audacity. "You *dare* insult me?! You fool! Kneel, beg mercy and you may just live out the rest of your days in a cell."

Wincing at the piercing pain in his left calf, Clarke spat a large globule of phlegm on the paving stones before her feet. "I will never beg, you murderous, mad *hag*!" Pointing at Adelaide, he bellowed, "Since we're airing soiled garments, why don't you tell this child how you murdered her *real* parents in cold blood eight and a half years ago, while she was a babe at arms! Tell her how you and your....puppet king robbed her of her *true* kin! The King Alaster, his Queen Rebecca, and her sisters: the princesses Tabitha and Brienne!"

In rage, Lilith, balled her fist, twisted her wrist to the right and hissed, "*Shetra marsan.*"

Like a lightning bolt, pain ripped up and down the length of his left leg as it buckled below the knee. He heard his femur shatter like so many dried twigs twisted within his leg. He barked sharply in pain, crumpling to the ground again, cold sweat cascading down his face, his heart racing.

Adelaide dropped Sir Martin and ran to her friend's side, staring at Lilith with a mix of confusion, hurt, fear and pleading. "Mother, stop this, *please*! You're hurting Master Clarke!"

Turning her hateful gaze on Adelaide, Lilith sneered in contempt, "I am *not* your mother, you putrid little *svanth*! Your precious friend is right: I *killed* your parents *and* your sisters! Unless you want me to kill *you* as well, back away from him *now*!"

With tears streaming down her face, Adelaide shielded the scribe's prone form with her own, smaller frame. "I will do *no* such thing! You are a *monster*! Demons and monsters from legends of old are kinder than you!"

Lilith's eyes shrank to pinpoints as she frowned loathsomely at the upstart princess defying her command. "Very well then, mewling, little brat!" She raised her hand, pointing her forefinger at Adelaide.

The Princess stared back defiantly; her jaw set, her eyes brimming with hot, angry tears at the distressing revelations about her false parents. "Come then, if you're so brave. Kill me! That is what you do, *isn't* it: kill girls, kings and old scribes?! Well come then! *Do it*!"

Lilith was forming a killing spell on her lips before she was wheeled hard to the right and backhanded so savagely that she toppled dazedly to the ground. When her vision cleared, she was outraged to see Malikh kneeling over her, his left hand gripping her throat, a dagger hovering inches before her face.

Who does this little man think he is*?! I am Lilith the Black, the most feared sorceress in* all *Ackreth! How* dare *he strike me?!*

With a mad look in his eye, the Overlord spat tendrils of saliva in Lilith's face as he ranted, "Are you *mad*, you crazy *svanth*!? That is my *daughter*! You raised your hand to kill *my* daughter! I should plunge this dagger through your eye, ye mad *whore*, for raising a finger against Adelaide! Do you *wish* to die!? Answer me!"

In a calm, controlled voice, the Screech Owl smiled through the spittle upon her pale face, replying, "Did you not hear the Master Scribe, husband? The girl, the dead king and queen's daughter, knows the *truth*. There is no need to pretend any more that you love her. In fact, why don't you tell her what her *real* name is, since we are sharing buried secrets?"

Malikh drew his face closer to her alabaster face and hissed, "I don't *care* what the truth is, Lilith! Adelaide *is* my daughter! She is all the family I have left! I will be gods' *damned* if I let you alienate my remaining family with your bewitched words!"

Raising her right hand, she firmly gripped the hand clutching her throat, and slowly removed his fingers from her neck. "If that is your wish, I will abide by it. You agree that your traitorous scribe must die though, yes? Perhaps you should channel your rage into *that* task. I am on your side, as ever. I cry your pardon for raising my hand towards Adelaide. Now let me up, or I will show you *true* anger."

The Overlord breathed heavily through flaring nostrils, the dagger still poised inches from Lilith's left eye, his hand shaking mildly as his rage subsided. After another tense moment he arose, gripping the dagger loosely at his right side.

Clarke had watched the whole scene unfold, gritting his teeth at the spiraling pain in his useless leg. Staring in rapt suspense as Malikh struck and pinned Lilith, Clarke thought, *there is hope yet for the Overlord. He did not allow her to kill the child. He seems ready to murder her should she raise her hand to the princess again.*

While Malikh seethed his threats, Clarke rolled onto his back, pulling himself into an upright seated position. He noticed in his peripheral vision, that the balcony appeared emptier; there were only three crossbowmen remaining. He marked briefly, the crouched form of Jabesh sneaking along the balcony. *Good man. Seize every chance.*

His sitting up drew the attention of the remaining crossbowmen. He was glad of; it meant they were unaware of Jabesh's presence. He tapped Adelaide faintly on the arm, signalling her to draw close. She needed no further prompt; the princess flung herself into his arms, weeping gently at the frightening things happening around her.

Caressing her soft, blonde hair, Clarke whispered, "Fear not child. You are *strong* and *brave*. You spoke back to Lilith and are alive to speak of it. I am not long for the land of the living now. They will *surely* kill me, but you will be safe if you stay near Malikh. Do you understand, Adelaide?"

Through a veil of tears, Adelaide whispered back, "Aye, Master Clarke, I understand. But I....I don't want to stay here anymore."

"I know child," the old scribe replied. "It will not be long. Master Jabesh will be your guardian in my absence."

"As you say, Master Clarke....but I don't want you to die." Unbidden, the princess cried into the crook of his shoulder, as she faced the hard truth of her tutor's imminent demise.

"Do not weep for me, child. I will see you someday in the Nether-Realm. In that place there is no war, or pain. Your family and I will be waiting for you."

"How will I recognize them? I do not know their faces."

"I will introduce you, when you get there." Clutching her in a tight hug, Clarke hissed in her ear, "Your *real* name is Arya, princess. Remember that name-recite it before going to bed, and when you awake in the morning. Before long, it will be as familiar to you as my name."

"*Arya*," Adelaide whispered. "I shall not forget it. Nor will I forget what you have done for me."

Malikh had just arisen, when he noticed his daughter and the traitorous scribe embracing. To his guards around the courtyard perimeter, he shouted, "Separate them! Two of you, return the princess to her chamber and keep guard. The rest of you, get this traitor on his feet!"

The guards set about their orders, dragging the screaming princess off the old fool and back to her chambers. The remaining guards rudely grabbed Clarke, dragging him painfully to his feet.

Malikh approached; his unsheathed dagger glinting in the moonlight. The Overlord stared contemptuously at the injured Master Scribe, who stood awkwardly on his right foot, his arms gripped firmly by the four guards. "I am *extremely* disappointed in you, Clarke. I brought you across the sea from Ackreth, because I *trusted* you. You stood by, while my forces took this city. What makes you think *your* hands are any less bloody than *mine*?"

"Penitent acts are a balm to a guilty soul. I do not deny my guilt. But I will be thrice gods' *damned* if I spend another minute pretending *that* girl deserves to be raised by a mad man like *you*, or that bedeviled *svanth* who has pulled your strings since before we departed Ackreth!"

At this declaration, Malikh backhanded the old man across the face, sending three teeth and a mouthful of blood flying. "How *dare* you speak to me thusly, you demented old *fool*?! I am *Overlord*: your *liege* and *master*!"

Spewing a mouthful of blood in the Overlord's face, the old man sneered, "You haven't properly been my liege or master since you decreed the death of children on Igraine all those years ago. The Malikh of Ackreth I knew would *never*, in his wildest moment, have ordered the death of children."

Malikh wiped the bloody spit from his face before head-butting the Scribe, shattering his nose, causing it to gush blood. "Traitorous *swine*! it was *you*!

Markus told me the people and many children had already prepared to flee before they arrived. For a long time, I figured it was divine intervention; that the cursed gods of Kalnay acted against my will to spare their champion.

"It is odd to think such a fool as yourself could be *capable* of treachery or maintain such a clever disguise for so long. You could not have accomplished this by yourself though. You had help. Who was it? Tell me, and I might spare your life; permit you to live your remaining years in the dungeons."

Clarke laughed through the mask of blood gushing down his face. "Are you negotiating, Malikh? You forget I *know* you: you don't negotiate, nor do you show mercy. Your only choice is to kill me. That, or appear weak. Word gets around swiftly about weakness. If *you* don't kill me, someone from your Red Guard will eventually challenge you for your throne....perhaps Markus...."

The Overlord punched the old man in the face again, rocking his head back hard. "Shut your mouth, you fool!"

With his left eye rapidly swelling shut, Clarke groaned and spat, "I've *seen* the General fight, Malikh. If I were a gambling man, I would wager on *Markus* emerging victorious in single combat against *you*."

Roaring in anger, Malikh gripped the dagger tightly in his right hand. In blind fury, he rammed it through the old scribe's heart repeatedly, marking with crazed satisfaction the crunch of bone and the squelch of blood as it forced its way between the old fool's ribs. As he did, he shrieked, "Shut your mouth! Blathering fool, shut your thrice gods' *damned* mouth!" After a dozen blows, he released the dagger's hilt; the blade still buried in the old man's ruined chest.

Despite the flood of pain and his life ebbing rapidly from him, the Master Scribe managed a bloody grin, sputtering, "I *win*, Malikh. My secrets are safe from your witch's prying claws. I die a happy man, knowing I defied you to my last breath." Then he spewed a large mouthful of blood, his head lolled to the side, and he toppled to the ground, dead. Malikh roared at the night sky in rage.

On the balcony, where all dozen of the crossbowmen now lay slain, Jabesh fiercely bit his left fist as he watched his friend die. He observed Noshtain standing immobile at Malikh's side, watching passively. He was almost tempted to shoot at them, but his thoughts turned to Arya.

Clarke passed to the Nether-Realm on his terms. He kept my involvement secret, granting me the chance to rescue the princess. I must not waste it. She must escape tonight, or Lilith will pour out her wrath on the child; Malikh's protection or not. Like a wraith, the diviner kept low, silently sneaking to Princess Arya's chamber.

Detained in her chamber, Adelaide wept openly into her furs and down-filled pillow. Her mind swirled at the horrible, shocking things that had just occurred.

My parents were Alaster *and* Rebecca. *My sisters were* Tabitha *and* Brienne. My *name is* Arya, *youngest daughter of Alaster and Rebecca. Master Jabesh* will *rescue me. Master Clarke is* dead. Over and over she repeated these revelations in her head, as she poured forth her grief and anger into her pillow.

She had not been detained long when she heard two muffled thuds outside her door. Arya stared at the closed door with bated breath. A moment later, it creaked open and her heart leapt into her throat. Standing before her, bow in hand, was Master Jabesh. Behind him, dead on the ground were the two guards. Extending his right hand, he whispered, "Lady Arya, you *must* come with me. You are no longer safe here."

The princess beamed broadly, running towards her deliverer. She threw her arms about the old diviner; her only true friend left in this world. "They killed him," she wept into his shoulder. "They killed Master Clarke."

Jabesh wrapped Arya in a brief protective embrace. "I know, Princess. 'Tis a *grievous* loss. Let us not waste the chance he gave us. I will protect you now, and always; until my dying breath. Do you believe me, *Arya*?"

She was still not accustomed to her true name. However, hearing it from her friend and protector gave her an odd sense of strength. Wordlessly, she nodded. Then she put on her cloak and boots. Following him into the moonlit night to the longboat and the world beyond Regalias, Arya repeated her family's names and Clarke's in her head, determined not to forget all she had learnt tonight.

Chapter Twenty: Quiet Before the Storm

Markus rode tall astride his russet-colored war horse at the centre of his legions. They were now a day's ride south of Drake's Maw Pass. By his judgment, his army was both well-prepared and well ahead of the northern invaders. He felt confident that when his forces reached the legendary Crossroad of Kings, there would be a swift and decisive victory by his forces.

Roland, one of the celebrated heroes of Pankirsh after the invasion by the wendygos, felt as General Markus did regarding their assured victory. During the Raid of Pankirsh, he learned something surprising about himself: not only was he *good* at killing things, he rather *enjoyed* it. In the time since then, he discovered quelling the thrill of killing was a greater challenge than the actual deed. He became a fervent, ferocious, underground bare-knuckle fighter in the past several weeks. Often, he had beaten his opponents to death with his bruised and bony fists. Since his foes in the ring were lowlife scum, no tears were shed over their deaths; for they were people whom none would miss.

When the call to arms was proclaimed, Lieutenant Roland prepared hastily for war. He had kept his knives sharp. He invested his paltry soldier's wage into buying light armor, providing protection without restricting his movement and speed. Between his bouts of fist-fighting, he continued dutifully training with his knives, lest he be unprepared. He needed to stoke his rage against his enemies.

Captain Cillian thought after defeating the wendygos at Pankirsh with naught but a legion of soldiers, he would feel relief in an army of seventy-five thousand strong. Instead, he felt unsettled. A legion is swifter to rally and control than assembled hordes. He knew this was an excuse his uneasy mind created to rationalize and control the fear he felt. Not that he was a coward; after all, the only other from his legion who had fought more determinedly and fiercely at Pankirsh had been Roland.

Young Roland fights for different reasons than I, Cillian reflected. *He fights for glory, advancement and some sort of......revenge. I fight to see Amelia, Samuel and Elizabeth again. I fight so they may be safe from wendygos, or Northern invaders....* Here, Cillian's mind turned to a question many of his men whispered as they marched north. The only question that *truly* mattered: *why do the Northerners march south* now*? What has changed since the defeat of King Ridley these twenty odd years now passed?*

Whatever the reasons, he knew in his bones his course of action: defeat the Northerners and protect his family. Nothing else- be they orders or prevailing circumstances- mattered to him; only his family mattered. Like Markus and Roland both, the captain felt confident in swiftly achieving victory. Reports indicated the Northerners were further from the Crossroad than the Red Guard.

Anxious to establish a foothold at the Crossroad, Cillian sought out General Markus, requesting to march his legion north double-time through the night. He wanted to establish a defensive line in advance of the central force's arrival. The General was impressed with

Cillian's initiative, agreeing to his request. He ordered another nine legions to follow and gave Cillian a field promotion to Commander.

He was flattered but made no show of celebration. His sole aim was to beat the Northerners to the Crossroad and establish their presence and await Markus' arrival. The Commander was not a cruel man, but he understood the importance of haste. His ten legions marched hard without complaint through the night, ignoring their sore feet and the twinge of hunger. He was glad of their strength and sensibility, proud of their determination to defend their homeland and families. By four in the morning, they drew near the Crossroad. The moon was full and bright in the sky above.

He marked something odd down at the Crossroad as his troops neared. The ground seemed to be moving....*churning* even. It appeared like the gentle ebb and flow of the tide lapping at the seashore. All present would have sworn there was a low, persistent rumble on the air; like an approaching storm, or the roar of surf crashing on rocky crags.

He summoned Roland and three others considered the fleetest of foot and keenest of eye to scout ahead and discover the true nature of this peculiar sight. Within an hour, they returned, blanched and their eyes bulging with terror. Only Roland seemed unshaken by what he witnessed.

Anxious for news, Cillian asked Roland, "What is it lieutenant? What has the others so terrified? I pray, speak."

Roland spoke with a strange smile upon his face, stating, "Commander there is something at the Crossroad I *never* thought I would see in my lifetime......I feel silly even saying it...."

Growing impatient, the Commander snapped, "For the love of the *gods* Lieutenant, what is down there?!"

The smile on Roland's face morphed into a grin. He stared directly into Cillian's eyes stating, ""The Crossroad is rife with bears, Commander. Bears of all sizes, colors and species. I believe they are dyre bears, sir."

The bear clans, under Yenoor's leadership, made excellent time to the Crossroad after leaving ahead of Sigourney's forces. The approaching full moon had been highly beneficial, as her people's animal traits took dominance. She glanced about at her people as they thundered south through Drake's Maw Pass; the ground shaking beneath their feet. In her mind churned many questions.

Will the might of my people be enough to stem the advance of Malikh's forces? Will I see any of these faces alive after the coming battle? Will I see my long-lost Nairadj again? Have she and Abel Farthen defeated the rock drake, or do we charge towards an obstructed path?

These questions needled at Yenoor's mind as she ran, holding nothing back. Though outwardly she appeared strong and determined, inwardly the bear queen felt fear and uncertainty gnaw at her heart. After a moment's allowance for the fear, Yenoor mentally squashed it, replacing it with the hope she held during the years Nairadj was gone. She recalled a memory of old then; a moment with her husband and king, Ragnar......

It was the year of the Cruel Winter, over a century ago. Food was in desperately short supply. Many of the elder bear folk and cubs had perished from sickness and starvation. Nairadj took ill with fever. Though the clan healer had done all they could, the princess was taking a turn for the worst.

She remembered staying awake through that terrifying night, never taking her eyes from her daughter's sickly, bed-ridden form. She sung snatches of old fairy rhymes, dabbing a cool cloth to her infant daughter's burning brow and held her when the babe cried in discomfort. As the night wore on, Yenoor felt reluctantly certain her cub would not survive to see the morning.

Late that night, Ragnar entered the tent where she kept vigil over their feverish daughter. Expertly, without making a sound or disturbing his fitfully resting daughter, the King scooped Nairadj into his burly arms, rocking her comfortingly. Were Nairadj not in danger of dying, Yenoor would have found the picture of this bearded, muscular bear king tenderly clutching a babe in his arms oddly humorous. Fatigue and looming grief struck her instead. She planted her face in her hands, weeping silently.

Ragnar placed a firm, comforting hand on his queen's shoulder, still cradling their daughter in his other arm. "Has there been any change, my queen? Do the ancestors yet favor our young she-cub?"

Lifting her gaze in the dim lantern light, Yenoor reached over her shoulder, gripping her husband's callused, bony hand. "Her temperature has been high all night, but she fights hard. In that regard, she is like her father: stubborn and tough to a fault."

Gently chuckling, the king countered, "I don't know about that, my love. I've thought she greater resembled her mother: fierce and determined, no matter the odds."

Yenoor barked a weak, mirthless laugh at her husband's comment. She ran her long, slender fingers through her hair. "Do you truly believe that Ragnar? Or do you merely seek to assuage my fears?"

Replacing the baby in her carved, birch cradle, the King knelt, wrapping his arms about his wife. Calmly, he whispered, "It's a smidge of the latter, and a vast portion of the former, my love. I feel it in my bones: our beautiful Nairadj will emerge victorious to take her place as the princess of our people. She and Jelani will grow into the best of friends and siblings. I need you to believe this too, my Queen. Our people follow me, but they sense the well-being of the tribe from you. If you are distraught, or show fear, it trickles into the people's hearts. You well know that tribes perceived to be weak or fearful are destroyed by the cruelty of the Wastes."

Whirling on Ragnar, Yenoor spat in hushed tones, "Do you not think I understand this!? Do you think me addle-brained, requiring frequent reminding of my duties?! I have not forgotten o king, my responsibilities as your wife and queen. I am also twice a mother. I would no sooner turn my back on Jelani or Nairadj than I would the lowest-born bear cub."

Gazing into the queen's blazing eyes her husband replied affectionately, "My wonderful, amazing wife, you mistake me. I am not telling you to turn your back on Nairadj. I would never do that."

With a mix of confusion and suspicion on her face, the queen asked, "What are you asking then, my Lord?"

Releasing a sigh, the king took his wife's hand, looking her directly in the eyes. "What I desire is for you to believe in our daughter's strength....but also, prepare yourself for the possibility of letting her go, should the ancestors call her to the Nether-Realm. Be strong for our people, though your heart may deeply mourn. Can you do that, my precious Yenoor? May the ancestors forbid it......but should it come to that....can you be Madriga to all your people should your own child be taken from you?"

For a long moment, Yenoor stared incredulously at him. She struggled to wrap her tangled, emotional thoughts around the frank terms her husband presented. Is he asking me to give up my only daughter? Would he have me put the needs of our people ahead of my needs as a mother? Can I do that? Do I possess that strength of character: to sacrifice feelings for my own blood in order to better guide my people?

After this moment of silent, swirling questions, she took a deep, calming breath. Leveling her gaze at her husband- patiently awaiting her reply- the queen spoke, "I will, *my love and lord, cling to your faith in our daughter's recovery. To believe otherwise is to tumble into a pit of sorrow; which I refuse to do. However, if Nairadj should not survive...."* Yenoor swallowed the lump threatening to strangle her words and continued, *"....should she not survive, I* will *be strong for you, Jelani and our people. I am no weepy she-bear unable to carry on when trials arise. This, my word, I pledge to you, Ragnar: both as my king and husband. I pray you accept it, as the promise it is."*

Smiling broadly, he kissed her first on the forehead, then each cheek and finally, tenderly, on her lips. He then enveloped her in a deep embrace. He whispered in her ear, "Aye, dear Yenoor: I do accept. I stand by my word from before: our little Nairadj shall overcome this fever and be whole again." Cradling her head to his chest, Ragnar concluded, "Fear not, my love. All shall be well."

All shall be well.

Yenoor heard Ragnar's simple, yet reassuring words at the back of her mind. Had any observed her countenance just then, they would have seen a peculiar transformation. Her furrowed brow- a well-known sign of the concern and worry she bore as their leader- was the most familiar expression most saw. This turned to surprise as she heard Ragnar's words in his voice, within her mind. The bear queen smiled, shedding a short spurt of tears; ones of joy and reassurance.

In her voice, she repeated the same phrase: *All shall be well.*

She reflected on how often those four simple words saved her from grief threatening to consume her- from Ragnar's death, to Jelani, then the overlong absence of her daughter. During it all, as she led her clan alone, her husband's words brought solace, confidence and strength to persevere despite the odds.

Glancing about at her people- loyal, brave and united in common purpose- she felt these words' power, as she had not for some time. She knew the dyre bears were equal to the task of defending the Crossroad until Sigourney's forces reinforced them. Gazing to the receding mountain tops, Yenoor suddenly realized they were almost free of the Pass. The Burrower had *not* sealed it. Though she had no tangible evidence of Nairadj and Abel surviving Melatharom's sworn vengeance, Yenoor believed it true in her heart. Had the rock drake slain them, he would have likely toppled the Pass out of spite. Dragons are well-known to carry a grudge for several generations against relations, friends or family of a party that is decreed a foe.

Another two hours run saw the dyre bears emerge free and clear of Drake's Maw Pass. It drew close to dark, so the Queen ordered a rest. In several hours, she and her people would undergo their ancestral transformation as dictated by the cycle of the moon. They had run hard and without complaint, for all knew how crucial victory was for this campaign. Her people rested and ate in preparation of the transformation and the forthcoming battle.

As midnight drew closer, the clan broke into smaller clusters of three dozen or so. History and experience had taught the dyre bears that transformation is accomplished with less risk of maiming or frenzied attacks from the animalistic side of their nature in smaller groups. Once the moon was at its highest, the strained cries, grunts and sounds of rent flesh and breaking bones filled the night like a macabre choir of the damned.

As the leader, Yenoor was considered the oldest and wisest of them. For countless years, she had undergone the change. Still, never in all those years since her 'Becoming Ceremony' at thirteen years, *never* had she gotten used to the sheer discomfort of it. The discomfort was familiar and temporary. It was the momentary loss of oneself to the animalistic side of herself that had always secretly terrified her. The legend of Mad King Kidrahs and his permanent transformation into the mad bear form he was renowned for, always hovered at the back of her mind. Though it concerned her, nothing ever became of those fears.

On this night- as with every full moon she ever witnessed- she and her people transformed into their terrifying, magnificent bear forms. None were harmed or afflicted with 'bear madness' as it was known among them. In her russet-red, fur covered body, Yenoor felt at harmony with nature. She lumbered through her people's ranks to check on their transformed states. Through the shared, psychic link with her people- as all dyre bears are capable of- she personally checked on their well-being. The bear queen turned her gaze northward, up the Pass where Sigourney's force approached from.

All shall be well, Yenoor thought again with a sliver of hope. *All we can do is wait for what happens next. Ancestors hear my prayer: guard Nairadj and Abel*

*Farthen beneath Shavatnu. Be with my people this day.
Lend our bodies' strength; our claws and teeth power;
and strike fear into our enemies' hearts. This I pray, in
humility and reverence to you, o ancient guardians.* Then
she turned her gaze south awaiting the arrival of Malikh's
army.

The Commander was shocked by Roland's news.
He felt his jaw drop open, like some churlish, dimwitted
jester. Drawing his mouth quickly shut, Cillian queried,
"I beg your pardon Lieutenant. Please *repeat* what you
just told me. I must be certain I heard you say......what I
think you said.

The Lieutenant held Cillian's gaze; all traces of
maniacal glee tamped. In a cool, even tone, Roland
repeated, "Bears of all sizes, colors and species occupy the
Crossroad. Dyre bears, *sir*."

Cillian bristled at the sarcasm in Roland's voice
as he uttered the word 'sir', though he didn't show it.
His mind raced at this unsettling news.

How can dyre bears be real? Have they aligned
*with Sigourney's hordes? Can we repel them from the
Crossroad without Markus' forces to back us? Their
appearance surely bodes ill......but, no....we* must *triumph,
or they will have their first foothold in central Kalnay.*
Coming back to himself, he heard one of the scouts, a
corporal, asking, "......your orders, Commander?"

Shaking the fog from his thoughts, he addressed
the corporal, "Pardons, my mind was occupied.... what did
you ask, soldier?"

The corporal repeated, "I asked what your orders are, Commander?"

Cillian spoke decisively, despite the uncertainty he felt, "We march against the bears at sunrise. For now, tell the men to rest. Roland, arrange perimeter watches along our flank. The last thing I want is to be snuck up on while we rest. Get to it men. We have mere hours before sunrise."

The Commander squinted north towards the Crossroad in the dawn sunlight and was unsettled to discover the bears were *still* bears. He strove to recall the tales of dyre bears he had read to Elizabeth and Samuel when they were tykes. He silently cursed himself for not being more attentive to the details of those stories.

It must be a twenty-four-hour transformation; not a twelve or six hour one before reversing. Damn! If I wait out the change, General Markus' forces should be here by then. We can then crush this vanguard of bear folk with ease. On the other hand, if I wait, General Markus may deem me an indecisive coward and strip me of my promotion....or worse. Moreover....if he is late to arrive, we could face the combined strength of the bear folk and *Sigourney's northerners. That is a confrontation we are* certain *to lose.*

He sighed, turning his war horse to trot along the front lines of his men- all of whom stood ready at arms, shifting nervously on their feet. The Commander took a deep breath and in a powerful voice, addressed his men. "You all know me! You know me as the hero of

Pankirsh, the town recently attacked by the wendygos of Lec'tair! Today, I am simply another soldier amongst brave fighting men in the Regalias Red Guard! Some of you, like me, crossed the Chakti! Others have spent your entire lives in this realm of Kalnay!"

Pointing toward the Crossroad with his unsheathed long sword, he continued, "Down there are *invaders* who wish to upset the peace we enjoy here! Who wish to *steal* the *freedom* we have *rightly* earned! You know by now our foes are dyre bears of legend! I will not conceal that from you. You should know what you face in battle! I *will* say this: though they may be legendary beings, they are *still* composed of flesh, blood and bone! They *can* be hurt and killed! The only thing to give them true dominion over us is will power! If they desire triumph *more* than we do, chances are they will win!"

At this remark, many men shifted uncomfortably, coughing and murmuring beneath their breath. The Commander raised his sword high and the men grew instantly silent.

"I am not finished! The only way we will *truly* defeat them is to crush their will beneath the strength and resolve of our *own* wills! So, I ask you men: do you want to win this battle *more* than the bear folk!?"

Like a swelling storm, a thundering war cry arose from the ranks of the Commander's ten legions. Swords, pikes, axes and spears jabbed skyward in testimony of the men's desire to crush their foes. Cillian joined the cry. Once the troops quieted down, he barked a final order, "Stay together! Defend your brothers in arms about you! Push the bears back, take the Crossroad and protect *your* homeland! Now, *charge!*"

With a thundering cry and a ground shaking stampede of thousands of feet, Cillian's legions charged down the gently sloping hill to engage the dyre bears. The Battle of the Crossroad had begun.

Chapter Twenty-One: The Battle of the Crossroad

At dawn, seventy-five hundred bears stood ready to defend the entrance to the Drake's Maw Pass in the Crossroad of Kings. All their attention was focused on a strong defensive position along the frontlines. Trundling to the front of the ranks as the sun rose, Yenoor turned, rose on her russet-colored haunches, growling in her animal tongue, relaying her orders to her people.

"We can repel this paltry force of men. The mountains shield us on the flanks and from behind. Sigourney approaches from the North. All we must do is hold our ground here at the Crossroad. If they push us back somewhat, fear not; they cannot flank us. Watch over your brothers and sisters and control your blows. If the Red Guards taunt you into the open, it could spell your doom. Be brave. Know that I will be with you *every* step of the way. Know too that the Ancestors watch from on high. They will lend us their strength in battle."

The ranks of bears- from grizzles, blacks and pandas, to browns, snow and sun bears- all roared their war cries. The southerners were charging down the hill to the Crossroad as the bears unleashed their cries; striking fear into the hearts of many men at the forefront. Turning to face the charging soldiers, Yenoor growled, "Front line, rise and prepare to strike!"

In another moment, the men at the front of the Red Guard charge were upon them, weapons ready. None, however, could withstand the might of the bears. The bears fell on them, swiping their savage claws as they did. They knocked many soldiers back into their own people; armor, leather and chests gashed open by flesh-rending claws. Red Guards shrilled in pain and death.

Yenoor pressed the advantage, preying on one who had fallen but not died, tearing his throat out with her puncturing teeth. Up and down the line, other bears did likewise: slashing with claws and biting throats with their powerful jaws. In a matter of minutes, the bears amassed a large pile of bodies before them; at least a hundred. Several Red Guard dodged the swiping claws and snapping jaws of the bear people and found themselves amongst the bears. The quick ones landed a few fatal blows upon the bears, before retreating to their own lines. The unlucky discovered themselves encircled by bears, with no means of escape and were quickly cut down.

Yenoor felt her blood run hot at the taste of human flesh. Her adrenaline surged, making her impervious to the meager nicks and gouges that landed on her furry hide. As she clamped onto one hapless spearman's arm, she thought, *by the Ancestors, we are doing it! We are holding them back!* Another spearman dashed towards her, his spearpoint down about to skewer her through the right shoulder.

Fortunately for Yenoor, one of her personal guards surged forward to cover her left flank. The bear slashed a mighty paw downward, breaking the spear in half. As he landed, he turned his head, puncturing the attacking spearman's jugular vein with powerful, clamping jaws. The assailant rasped a surprised, gurgling death cry and dropped to the ground, dead.

Yenoor turned from the mangled spearman at her feet, to face the approaching hordes of red garbed soldiers. She admired them for openly engaging her people. *Many men fear encountering a single, ordinary bear in the woods, yet* still *these men charge. They are a credit to their kind for that courage. I wonder who their commander is, and whether I shall meet him on the field? He must have stirred their courage well.*

Suddenly, the bear who defended Yenoor from the spearman issued a pained growl. Her attention spun his way, concerned. She watched in disbelief as a single little man with naught but long knives raced about her guard, expertly slashing the hamstrings on all four legs. He tumbled hard to the ground as the little man leapt onto his back. Before she could react, the little man with the knives had buried his longest knife deep into the bear's neck.

Her guard issued a brief grunt and tumbled dead to the ground. The little man with the knives leapt deftly off the dead bear, dashing towards Yenoor, bellowing in a voice half-cracked with madness. Of the men that had fallen thus far, none were as swift or bloodthirsty as this little man with the knives. The bear queen snarled in anger as he charged her, calling to her kin along the frontlines: *we must take down this little man! He is dangerous and fleet of foot.* Then he closed on Yenoor, his knives flashing as brightly as his overly broad, blood-stained grin.

Roland "Ghost Blades" (as he quickly became known after Pankirsh), was a quarter of the way back in the wave of troops charging the bears lines. He watched angrily as row after row of his fellow troops fell to the claws and teeth of the bears. Commander Cillian was halfway back in the lines, watching in horror astride his horse as four dozen men fell in what seemed like moments. On the ground, Roland thought furiously, *I must find the leader. Slay the leader, the others may lose heart and break rank; as with the wendygos in Pankirsh.*

Drawing closer, the Lieutenant watched the bears closely, looking for signs. After another two dozen men fell, he spotted one who might be the leader. It was an enormous, eleven-foot-tall monster with russet-colored fur. When things lagged on the bears' lines, the russet one bellowed in its bear tongue and others responded.

I must know for certain before I attack. If I'm wrong, I may perish before turning the tide for our soldiers. Shouting above the din to a spearman ahead on his left, he pointed at the russet bear. "Hey! That one is the leader! Run it through, and you could turn the tide for us!"

Excited by the adrenaline coursing through his veins, the spearman gripped his weapon tight and charged the russet bear- who already had another spearman's arm in its mouth. Roland watched as the second spearman charged the big bear. In an odd moment of fear, Roland thought, *by the gods....what if he does kill the bear? Did I just hand him my glory?!*

He was measuredly relieved when he saw a grizzly bound at the charging spearman. He watched in grim satisfaction as it swiftly rose on its rear haunches, before slashing the spearman's weapon in half. In another quick movement the grizzly clamped its teeth on the poor fool's throat.

My guess is correct then, Roland reflected. *They protect the russet bear. If it's not their leader, it's certainly a bear of considerable authority.* He raced around the unawares grizzly, slashing its heels, dropping it to the ground. The beast bellowed in animalistic pain.

Morbidly he thought, *I hate to see an animal suffer. I will relieve your misery, friend.* Then, he leapt onto the downed grizzly's back, skewering it through the neck, killing it instantly. Leaping from its back, he charged the russet bear, bellowing a war cry in his loud, cracking voice.

Then, he was before the massive russet bear. The creature slashed at his face. He rolled safely to the left. Rising, he saw another bear (this one a black) plummeting towards him, claws swiping. He spun right, between the russet bear and the black. As he spun, he brought his long knife up in a curved arc, slashing savagely through the artery under the black's armpit. The black fell heavily to its left; for Roland had also severed the tendons. Finishing his spin, he plunged his right-hand knife into the bear's right eye, killing it instantly.

The russet pivoted on its forelegs, trying to snap him in its jaws. The Lieutenant rolled backwards, deftly drawing another knife from his belt as he did. Around him, more Red Guards clashed with the bears along the line; his sights were fixed firmly on the russet. Finding his feet, he dashed forward again, trying to get inside the russet's defenses. He feinted left, came in on the right with a knife extended to slash the bear across the face. The russet saw this and ducked, avoiding the attack.

He rolled again, coming face-to-face with a snow bear to the russet's right. Without hesitation, he plunged his left-handed knife up through the soft tissue below its jaw, punching into its brain and killing it instantly. The russet side-stepped, knocking Roland off-balance, turning quickly to slash with its right forepaw. He didn't fight the momentum, but rolled with it, like water in a stream doesn't fight the flow.

Roland heard the russet's claws slash another soldier who had the misfortune of getting between the two combatants. He heard the fool's death cry behind him but felt no pity. Seizing the chance to gain advantage on the russet, Roland clambered up onto the dead snow bear's hide. Shoving off with his feet, he launched at the russet, bellowing savagely.

The russet was swift for such a large bear, but still too slow for the nimble lieutenant. Another bear, this one a Kodiak, saw Roland leaping at the Queen with two knives drawn. It rose on its haunches twixt the little man and her. Roland knew this Kodiak spelt his doom if he didn't kill it. With a flick of his right wrist, he flung his blade into the Kodiak's exposed chest, mortally wounding it.

He had no time to draw another blade, so he simply drew both hands together around the hilt of the short knife in his left, plunging it home with tremendous force. Roland's aim was true. As he slammed bodily into the russet's furry backside, he felt the knife bury itself up to the hilt in its mid-back.

The bear growled in pain and anger, rising to its haunches. Lieutenant Deschene did not expect such a strong reaction; he was almost certain he had punctured its lung. With a bark of dismay, he was flung from the its back to land amongst the second line of bears. He toppled on his back, unable to draw his remaining knives sheathed at the back of his belt.

All about him Pandas, Kodiaks, Sun bears, and more descended on him with speed and ferocity. His last word, before he was rent to blood-drenched pieces was simply, "*Sptoch*."

Yenoor was impressed at the skill of the determined little man. The fact that he had killed three dyre bears already was shocking to her. Each death grieved her, for she knew each bear he slew. The first, Baltar, the grizzly, was one of her bravest personal guards. The second, Zepora, the Snow bear, grew up playing with Nairadj and Jelani; now she too was dead. The third, Wallace, the Kodiak, was a member of the clan council. None of these would be easily forgotten or replaced, nor should they be. Right now, however, she could not dwell on those things.

She felt the blade buried in her back, and the blood seeping out around it. *That sptoch of a little man has hurt me, grievously.* Part of her was determined to keep fighting, but she began feeling light-headed and could not focus her vision.

The panda that set the other bears on the puddle which had been Lieutenant Roland "Ghost Blades" Deschene drew up alongside the Queen, declaring over the psychic link, "Majesty, you are injured! You *must* fall back and seek aid from our healers."

Yenoor protested, "I am *fine* Han-Chu! I must keep fighting."

Han-Chu summoned another; a Sun bear named Jorry. Together they escorted their liege safely back through the ranks to find the healer near the rear. "Nonsense, my lady," He rebuked, "You've been badly injured. That little man knew his way around a knife. We must ensure you live to lead us."

Under normal circumstances, Yenoor would have protested. However, her vision blurred further, and she noticed she no longer walked a straight path. "Very well, Han-Chu. *You* must lead the people against the southerners. Whatever happens, we must *not* let them push us back into the Pass. Am I understood?"

"Aye, my queen, I will hold the line. Jorry, please ensure the Queen finds her way to Talia."

"As you say, Captain, so it shall be done," he replied, guiding Yenoor through the ranks.

Han-Chu turned and lumbered back to the front. When he arrived, he noticed two things immediately. The first was the pile of dead red garbed men had become a small hill. This brought him a moment of encouragement, for the queen's plan was working. The second thing he noticed caused his stomach to jump into his throat. On the nearby hilltop where the one thousand little men had previously been, now stood a large line of horsemen. General Markus and his Regalias Red Guard had arrived.

From the hilltop Markus looked down in disbelief at what he beheld. The majority of Cillian's one thousand troops lay dead in a mound at the mouth of the Pass. He made a mental note that should he find Cillian alive, he would personally end his pathetic life.

He ordered two thousand horsemen to punch a hole in the bears' seemingly impenetrable frontline. He ordered a further one thousand to follow, removing the bodies annoyingly obstructing the Crossroad- as those would obstruct their forces from pushing further into the Pass to drive back the invaders.

Markus watched as the horsemen charged, slowly but surely pushing the bears back into the Pass. The men moving the corpses did so fearfully, but less so with the horsemen standing between them and the bears. *It won't be long now,* Markus thought smugly, as he watched from his saddle near the back of the battlefield.

In the Pass entrance, Han-Chu bolstered the bear folk as best he could. Too many had seen Queen Yenoor wounded and feared the worst. He was a valiant fighter, and a good captain, but he was not a leader of an entire army.

"My people, listen," he cried across the psychic link, "we have conquered the odds thus far. We *must* stay strong, and *not* yield ground. The queen is injured, 'tis true, but she lives! What would she think if we balked *now*?! Sigourney comes soon to provide aid; we *must* hold until then. Now, forward and hold the line! When the horsemen close with us, eliminate their steeds. A horseman without a horse is simply a swordsman.

Swordsmen can be easily vanquished! Are you with me?!"

A weary, collective growl went up from the bears as they pressed forward to combat the advancing horsemen.

With two thousand of them, each horse created a sizeable advantage. Markus did not have them charge recklessly, but rather concentrate their attack on the center; thus providing the footmen necessary cover to safely remove the corpses of Cillian's fallen men. Han-Chu realized dismally if the Red Guard cleared the bodies, their remaining forces could charge the dyre bears completely without hindrance.

The captain pushed his bears forward, focusing on the mass of horses, taking down many dozens here and there, but never enough to slow their advance. The one thousand soldiers moving corpses became twelve hundred, as Cillian redirected his surviving two hundred or so troops to aid moving the bodies, providing them reprieve from direct combat.

After several increasingly failed attempts to push back the horsemen and the soldiers moving corpses, Han-Chu realized they were rapidly losing ground. At least three hundred bears had been downed by the horsemen and only about half that number of horsemen had been overcome by his bear kin.

The bear captain reluctantly ordered a retreat from the mound of dead at the entrance to the Pass. The Crossroad of Kings was lost to the dyre bears, and Markus's army pressed steadily forward, gaining a stronger foothold in the mouth of the Pass.

Yenoor was ushered halfway back through the bears' ranks before they located Talia the healer. She busied herself, preparing a salve of healing herbs that was pressed firmly into the wound once Roland's cruel blade was removed. As a bear, being a healer is not easy-everything is done in their bear form with tooth and claw; hence 'tis not as gentle as human touch may be.

She had only been away from the frontline for a half-hour before word reached her of the reluctant retreat from the Crossroad. Word was the bulk of the Red Guard Army, under General Markus, had finally appeared. Between her reported injury and Markus' arrival, her people were losing heart and were falling back rapidly.

Ancestors' damn *that puny man who injured me! His display robbed the courage from my peoples' hearts. Han-Chu is a great leader, but he has inherited a weary batch of fighters disheartened by my injury.* Yenoor struggled to her feet, watching the sun-drenched world spin before her eyes, before crashing back to the ground.

Talia lumbered over and through the psychic link, scolded the queen. "Your highness, you have been *deeply* injured, or have you already forgotten? You must *rest.*"

Struggling to rise again, the Queen retorted, "Not when my people need my help."

"Han-Chu has control of the situation...."

"I can't just *sit* here Talia, while my people are murdered by cowardly little men astride their horses. Our forces *need* my presence."

"That makes *no* sense, my queen. How does your wounded, weary person bolster our warriors' courage? The *Ancestors* will provide if we are to be victorious. If not, we made a stand worthy of the histories. That is all that we can do."

"I just......I don't like...." Here, Yenoor trailed off as she felt a rising tremor in the earth. It came not from the south, but from the north. "Talia......do you feel that?"

The healer looked north, marking a great cloud of dust drawing closer by the second. "Aye, my queen; and I *see* it too. Look."

Yenoor's spirits lifted and she summoned Jorry. When he appeared, she relayed a message for Han-Chu. Jorry lumbered off at his swiftest pace to deliver the news, and a new plan of attack.

Han-Chu had blood in his left eye. He was constantly flicking his head, rubbing his sizeable paw across his forehead, where a lance had gashed it open during their last charge. Through the cascading blood, he observed the Red Guards continuing to remove their numerous fallen comrades from the mouth of the Pass. Another six dozen of the bears had fallen to the pressing horsemen. The bears slew a further four dozen horsemen in compensation for their fallen kin. The horsemen were warier in the mouth of the Pass; ensuring that they did not get isolated from their fellow troops, lest they fall to their animal foes.

Han-Chu and the dyre bears had fallen back about two hundred feet within the Pass entrance. The bear captain was determined not to lose any more ground to the little men. He was about to call another charge- his last, in all likelihood- when he heard the bear call of Jorry. The captain fell back, ordering his blood-stained and battle-weary people to hold the line, while he conferred with Jorry.

The Queen's messenger drew alongside the panda captain, his eyes wide in dismay at Han-Chu's bloodied state. "Are you alright, Captain?"

"Believe it or not, it isn't as bad as it looks. What brings you back to the front? Does the queen yet live?" The Captain braced himself for bad news.

"Yes sir, the queen lives. I come bearing news of Sigourney's army. They approach swiftly down the Pass as we speak."

Han-Chu's heart leapt with relief at the news. "That is *most* excellent, Jorry! Queen Yenoor has a plan then?"

"Aye, Captain. I think it will be a *most* welcome prospect." Jorry then relayed the Queen's orders.

Commander Cillian assumed command of the remaining horsemen- which still numbered close to twelve hundred fifty. The bears had fallen farther back into the mouth of the Pass. He seized initiative, ordering the horsemen to defend the northern side of the dwindling mound of bodies as the men on foot hurriedly moved the corpses to either side of the Pass entrance. The bears were smart enough not to directly charge the line, but they were also not retreating any further than they already had. He admired their fortitude.

These are truly remarkable *creatures, these dyre bears. It's a shame we must ride them down once the bodies are cleared. They would make* fantastic *allies in combat....I wonder if they will surrender?*

Looking over his shoulder, Cillian was encouraged to see the bodies almost completely cleared. To the soldier in charge of moving bodies, he asked, "How much longer until we can enter the Pass unhindered, corporal?"

Wiping his muddy, blood-stained brow free of sweat, the corporal stated, "We should be done in several minutes, Commander."

"Excellent," Cillian replied. To the men astride their steeds, he barked, "Prepare to charge, men. It won't be long now. We will drive these rogues back and live out the rest of our days in peace."

A rallying cry arose from the horsemen as they trotted towards the line of bears. Cillian was satisfied. There had not been as many deaths as he first feared. When he returned home to his family, he would be a war hero, tested in the field against not only wendygos, but against dyre bears as well; and at the legendary Crossroad of Kings at that.

The one thing he hadn't considered or noticed (given his limited vantage point) was the bears holding the line did so at a curve in the Pass. Indeed, Drake's Maw Pass is not straight, but winds serpentine, back and forth. It gets its name not just from the jagged stab of mountains comprising it, but also of the sidewinding nature of its path.

As the Commander and his sizeable line of horsemen drew confidently a mere fifty feet before the battle-weary bears, something peculiar happened. The bears before them parted cleanly and willingly down the middle, pressing themselves against the rocky barrier of the mountain walls on either side, leaving the central path of the Pass exposed.

Sound does not carry the same in the Pass either; due to the formation's natural twists and turns. Until something is directly around the bend, one does not hear it coming. Confusion at the bears' actions transformed into horror for Cillian. Immediately behind them appeared a large, thick rank of northerners, all astride horses. Each had weapons in hand and unleashed a savage, unified war cry as they laid eyes upon the paltry twelve hundred fifty horsemen.

Though the Commander was surprised, he was not so stunned as to stay idly gawking at the rapidly approaching northern hordes. In a fearful voice, he called, "*Retreat*! The Northerners are *here*! Flee or die where you stand you fools!" He swung his horse about to flee and was dismayed to see a vast number of Markus' own horsemen had ridden down the hill behind them.

His mind raced in fear. *If I get caught between my own forces and the Northerners, I will surely perish! I must evade the Red Guard and gain the hill. The Northerners cannot be stopped now, not with the dyre bears at their side. Together, their numbers rival ours. To stay is to die. I must survive for my family's sake.*

Like a force of doom in Cillian's path was General Markus, astride his russet war horse. The Commander almost galloped towards him but caught a murderous look in his eye. *By the gods, he means to murder me for losing the Pass! I will not be his scapegoat, by the Nether-Realm.*

Sharply altering his horse's path to the left of the Pass's opening, the Commander spurred his horse onward, leaping over the small remaining mound of bodies yet to be cleared. As he galloped hard for the hills, he heard Markus furiously bellow, "Cillian, you *coward!* I will *kill* you for this failure! I will have your family's lives for this! Do you *hear* me!?"

Anger seized Cillian's heart as he registered Markus' threat. *Over my dead body will you harm my family, monster,* he vowed silently. He raced up the hill, disappearing on a southward path to rescue his family from Markus' following vengeance.

Markus had not noticed, or known about, the curve of the Drake's Maw Pass. In the roughly eight years since landing in Kalnay, he never found occasion to venture north towards the Nightstalker Wastes. As such, he knew naught of the sound damping effect of the Pass. He was already down the hill, so he had also not sighted

the approaching plume of dust kicked up by the
Northerners' numerous, approaching horses. Indeed, he
only spotted the tide of Northerners after the
Commander and his horsemen turned tail, fleeing for the
safety of the central Red Guard forces.

Cillian, that bungling fool*! He has surrendered
a sure victory to save his own skin! I will* kill *him for this
disgrace!* He sought him out amongst the approaching
horsemen, spotted him and focused on him like a hawk.
Subtly, he drew a dagger from his belt and waited,
watching his approach- oblivious to all else around him.
He cursed under his breath a moment later, when Cillian
altered his course sharply to Markus' right.

*The fool is not as foolish as I thought. He
knows I mean to kill him.* Watching him gallop hard
away, Markus raised his voice, bellowing, "Cillian, you
coward! I will *kill* you for this failure! I will have your
family's lives for this! Do you *hear* me!?"

The fleeing commander pressed on harder,
galloping up the hill well wide of the Red Guards.
Markus redirected his gaze to the sizeable approaching
northerner force and cursed again. Wheeling his war
horse around, he bellowed to his troops, "*Retreat*! Fall
back, or perish you fools! We do not know how many
they are! The field is theirs! Flee or die!"

Without waiting for his troops to acknowledge,
he spurred his horse and fled up the hill beginning his
retreat to Regalias. *I* must *inform the Overlord of this.
We* must *recruit more troops to combat this horde.
That, or we are forced to flee Kalnay as we did from
Ackreth. I would rather* die *than leave.*

Behind him, he heard the clatter of armor and the thunder of hooves as his army followed him in retreat.

Sigourney's forces gave brief pursuit, slaying any stragglers who fell behind. With their victory assured, and no further contest from the fleeing Red Guards, the Northerners and dyre bears emerged from the Drake's Maw Pass; eager to leave behind the scene of battle. They established camp atop the hill up from the Crossroad of Kings, which opened onto a vast plain with the tributary of the Lesser Inaratu running gently alongside. There was much cause for celebration, as there was also much cause for mourning.

Queen Sigourney ordered her people to assist the dyre bears in collecting the dead for cremation, be they bear or Red Guard. Yenoor did not object, for northerners and dyre bears both believe strongly in cremation. In the Wastes, exposed or freshly buried corpses were temptation for Nightstalkers and other predators. Cremation ensured nothing ghoulish could return to torment the living.

The ensuing feast was equal parts mass funeral and victory celebration. The Northerners raided their stores for the best meats and the finest mead to drink- to honor the sacrifice the bear folk made in securing not just the Crossroad, but a chance at a different future for them and theirs.

The hour prior to midnight, the bears moved back to the Crossroad to transform safely back into their human selves when midnight struck. Once transformed, they rejoined their human comrades around the big, central bonfire of the conjoined camps. Sigourney found Yenoor, properly bandaged up, relaxed and recovering from her injury. The Queen of the Wildmen sat beside the Bear Queen, generously offering her a flagon of mead.

Politely declining, Yenoor indicated her shoulder. "Our healer, Talia, says liquor thins the blood. It would be embarrassing to survive that little man's attack only to die from drinking at the victory celebration. Thank you though, Queen Sigourney; another time, for certain."

Leaning back and pulling another swig on her flagon the Queen of the Wildmen replied, "I will hold you to that, Queen Yenoor. If there is *one* thing I know in life 'tis this: one should never drink alone."

Chuckling, and wincing in pain at doing so, the Bear Queen replied, "Wise words, my lady." Indicating the bear folk and mingling Wildmen, she added, "Though, by my count, you are *far* from drinking alone. One's subjects are as crucial to a successful kingdom, or military campaign, as any ruler or power."

Raising her flagon to Yenoor, Sigourney praised, "Wise words from *you*, my lady. I see why your people follow you. You command authority but bear the wisdom of the humble and learned."

"My thanks. You honor me. I like to think wisdom is accrued by observing much and listening even more."

Pulling another swig of mead, Sigourney replied, "You truly *are* a fountain of knowledge, Lady Yenoor. I wonder then......what think you of our chances seizing control of Regalias?"

The bear queen thought a minute before responding, "That depends on *many* things. It depends whether Nairadj and Abel Farthen have defeated Melatharom. It supposes whether they can successfully sneak into Regalias and murder the Overlord. To do that would destabilize the southerners' army; weaken their spirits. It depends whether the witch, Lilith, can be overcome. By what force, I cannot say, for dark magic is *quite* potent. It depends whether we encounter resistance from the locals of central Kalnay; for we *will* be considered invaders here by many citizens......as I said, our chances depend on many things."

"That's not incredibly encouraging. I hoped for a solid, dependable solution that I may present my captains and commanders with. If we must fight *every* step of the way to Regalias and, more broadly, our very *future* in central Kalnay......then our victory here at the Crossroad may be short lived."

Gazing at the starlit sky above, Yenoor breathed deeply of the fresh night air. "You worry too much, Lady Sigourney. I believe......"

Gazing half-drunkenly at the bear queen, Sigourney jibed, "*What*? What do you believe, Lady Yenoor?"

Turning her gaze from the sky to the blazing fire, she smiled, answering faintly, "I believe......all shall be well."

Chapter Twenty-Two: An Ally Revealed

Never in her young life had Arya travelled so long or far; *certainly* not on foot. She was used to dashing across the inner keep of Regalias from the gardens to the library, or from the library to the central feast hall. Always, hard running had been rewarded with a large meal or a treat (like candied chestnuts) from Master Clarke or Jabesh. To her nearly ten-year-old mind, it was quite shocking to traverse such distances she and Master Jabesh had already journeyed with nary a meal or treat. The young princess understood it was not punishment for some unknown transgression. Things had changed drastically in both their worlds in recent days.

Their fugitive status forced them to flee the familiarity of Regalias for concepts which, largely, were too complex to Arya's innocent mind to grasp. She understood what she had seen and heard in the courtyard these three nights past. Malikh, whom she once called 'father', had been savage with anger; fatally stabbing Master Clarke. Even now, through closed eyes, Arya could see his blood staining the moonlit courtyard stones.

It terrified and confused her: a man she trusted implicitly and loved unconditionally had *murdered* another man, one of her few friends, in a fit of rage. Compounding the confusion in her impressionable young mind was the discovery that not only was Malikh *not* her father, but Lilith was not her mother either. She always suspected as much.

Lilith was so unlike *any* woman she knew; particularly her unsettling, pitch black eyes, which spoke of things dark and mysterious. The butterflies in Arya's gut whirled more when she learned of her *real* parents' deaths; that the man who raised her had committed the deed. Perhaps the saddest revelation to Arya's sensitive conscience was discovering she once had sisters.

All her life, she contented herself with being an only child- silently praying to the gods for another sibling. Discovering she was the youngest of three sisters troubled her deeply; more than she would have initially guessed. *What kind of monster murders two innocent girls? What did my sisters do to deserve death? What of my mother and father? What did they do to deserve such a fate?*

These and other questions swirled around Arya's perplexed mind in the subsequent days since escaping Regalias. By nightfall the third day, she could neither satisfactorily answer these questions, nor stifle her curiosity regarding what she had learned. So, she asked Jabesh, as he cooked the four medium-sized hares he snared that afternoon, watching his face raptly.

For a long moment, her friend uttered not a word; he simply kept skinning and preparing to spit the rabbits. His face twitched and contorted as he strove to explain something complex as simply as possible; yet he struggled to find adequate words. Arya knew the look well. Seeing it was oddly comforting to her; as though all that had transpired could be stayed for a moment with that look. When Jabesh finally spoke, he gazed into Arya's face sombrely. "First will you tell me, Lady Arya, how much you understood from that night in the courtyard?"

The princess started at hearing her name; her *real* name. Adelaide, the fiction born of Malikh and Lilith, had died in Regalias with Master Clarke. It was three days, yet she was *still* surprised at hearing her true name. She made a mental note to continue familiarizing herself with it: *Arya*.

With reluctance, she recalled to her protector that fateful evening's events. "Master Clarke told me my real name, my *birth* name, is Arya. My father was King Alaster. My mother was Queen Rebecca. I had two older sisters....Tabitha and Brienne, both of whom were princesses, like me; both of whom were put to the sword...."

Jabesh nodded confirmation to what she unfolded, encouraging, "Aye, my lady. Please, continue."

Swallowing a lump in her throat, Adelaide (*No,* she thought in rebuke, *Arya. My name is* Arya*)* resumed her train of thought. "Mother......I mean, *Lilith*.... she said father......*Malikh*, killed my family with her help. They called Master Clarke a traitor, but I don't believe that at *all*. He was the kindest person I have ever known."

Pausing for an awkward moment, Arya's eyes widened as he eyed her curiously. "Oh....," she fumbled, "Not to say you're *not* kind, Master Jabesh. More that......Master Clarke was a *different* sort of kind....more playful...." She ceased talking, fiddling nervously with the edges of her tunic sleeves, dropping her eyes to the fire before her.

Jabesh chuckled softly, cracking a faint grin as he finished skewering the final rabbit and setting them over the fire to cook. "Do not worry, Lady Arya. I know what you mean. You are correct about Master Clarke: he had a better way with you than I could ever hope to. I was trained as a name diviner in my hometown of Kiresh. Part of my duties as teacher was not to draw too close to my students. A teacher who is too friendly loses some authority with his pupils. In that respect, I suppose, I excelled at my work."

He paused, smiled faintly to the princess before concluding, "My apologies, highness. I rant like an old hermit. I am sworn to protect you, both on Clarke's behalf and as a renewed filial obligation to your deceased kin. Any questions you have, feel free to ask. If there is anything you desire, you need only ask. I will fulfill your requests to the best of my abilities."

The young princess gazed steadily at the diviner, soaking up every detail of his time-worn face, as if seeing him well and truly for the first time. During her education at Regalias, Masters Jabesh and Clarke spoke of the different governing forces of Kalnay- from kings and generals, to healers and name diviners. Arya took name diviners for myth; much like dyre bears or sea wulves. To discover her mentor and guardian, was one of these fabled diviners confounded her young mind deeply.

Unaware of the words coming out of her mouth, or that it was her first question, she gazed sternly across the fire and asked, "Why didn't you save my family from Malikh and Lilith, Master? If diviners are sworn to serve and protect the king, why didn't you stop my family from dying?"

Jabesh stared remorsefully across the fire at the inquisitive young princess with a wounded look in his eyes. Sighing wearily, he rose, circled the fire and sat to her right. Arya watched his every move, waiting on him to speak.

He twiddled his thumbs a moment, gazing into the fire, searching for where to begin. As he stared, the diviner began slowly, "The first thing you must know is that your *true* father Alaster, was one of my *best* friends. He was one of the best men I've *ever* had the privilege of knowing. His death....and the deaths of your mother, Rebecca and your sisters, Tabitha and Brienne, are something that, could I reverse time, I would trade places in a heartbeat to prevent. You must understand, Lady Arya.... after Malikh landed in Kalnay, I was taken captive. I had *no* way of knowing, not then anyways, the extent of the Overlord's cruelty; or Lilith's level of control over him."

Here he paused, jabbing a stick into the pit to stoke the coals of the cooking fire. "*Clarke* saw it though; even then, he saw it. He saw the Screech Owl's madness. It changed him. He became......he became a *hero* shortly after that. Through *his* bravery, many children were saved from the Island of Igraine, almost nine years ago now. The man had no skill with blade or weapon, but his wisdom and wits saved *many* lives. Every time I think of what he risked saving those children....it stirs shame in my heart that I did *nothing* while my king....my *friend*, was slain.

"I was *there* in that city with him *before* he was murdered, and I did *nothing*. I think sometimes....maybe things would be different for the better if I had snuck into Malikh's chambers and slit his throat, the very night he took Regalias. You may still have your family. I would be resting in the Nether-Realm with my friends, Aldrich and Sallari......" Jabesh halted suddenly, his lips pursed.

Arya watched his face intently, waiting for him to continue. After another long, silent moment, she decided her master was done. Wordlessly, she snuggled close to him, leaning her head against his arm. Linking her arms around Jabesh's left arm, she replied, "I don't blame you. It's *not* your fault, Master Jabesh. Malikh and Lilith are to blame."

Unlinking his left arm from hers, he wrapped it around Arya, drawing her close to his side. She could hear the muffled *'thump, thump'* of his heart. Squeezing her upper arm gently, the diviner muttered, "Thank you for your understanding, majesty. You *truly* reflect wisdom beyond your years; an *excellent* quality in a future queen."

Looking up into his tired face, Arya asked, "Who are Aldrich and Sallari, Master Jabesh?"

The diviner started faintly at the mention of his dead friends, before settling again. "They are......they *were* two of my best friends when I was a younger man. Both are dead now. They died valiantly during the attack on Igraine. They are heroes, like Master Clarke, who will live on in my memory forever.

"According to the reports Clarke shared with me, between the two of them, they slew over seventy of Marcus' men defending the children of Igraine. Their sacrifice allowed many children and some of their families to escape the island. In our youth, Aldrich, Sallari and I all served your father alongside my other friends: Pallas, Barsayt and Sarto."

Her curiosity peaked, Arya asked, "Where are the others *now*, Master Jabesh? Are they still alive?"

"As far as I know child, they are. Pallas and Barsayt are both name diviners. Pallas dwells on the Island of Gwenovair. If memory serves, he is watching over that crazy old bat, Sarto. When I last heard, Barsayt lived in Kaldesh. I must admit, I have neither seen nor heard from them since I was kidnapped from Kiresh. They could be earls, or dukes, and I would never know."

Attempting to be encouraging, Arya offered, "Maybe...maybe we'll meet them on our journey north, Master Jabesh?"

Chuckling softly, he removed the spits from the fire, setting them across a smooth, angled stone to drain off the hot grease. "As much as that would cheer my heart, Lady Arya, it's highly unlikely. Their homes are far south and west of here. They have *no* reason to venture north. Thank you for the encouragement, though. You are truly thoughtful."

"You're welcome, Master," Arya replied, glancing hungrily at the cooked rabbits, dripping grease down the rock. "Could we eat now? I'm *really* hungry."

Blowing on the cooling rabbits, Jabesh began to answer, "Aye, Lady Arya, we can. Which....?"

Just then, he heard muted footfalls twenty feet behind him. In one deft motion, he spun to a standing position, drew his bow and notched an arrow, aiming into the darkness beyond the firelight. "I hear you there, *both* of you! Step forth and identify yourselves immediately or I *will* put this shaft through your heart!"

From the darkness, came a woman's voice and the sound of two swords slowly being drawn. "My name is Nairadj, daughter of Yenoor, queen of the Red-Ditch dyre bear clan. My companion and I are passing south to Regalias. We have disarmed ourselves and offer you our swords as a gesture of peace. May we approach and present ourselves, sir?"

Jabesh held his position for another moment, weighing her words. With a sigh, he lowered his aim, replacing the arrow in his quiver. "Aye. Approach Nairadj of the Red-Ditch bears; you and your friend both. I am....*Clarke* of house Christoph, originally from Kiresh, but more recently of Regalias. This is my......*niece*, Ava. Come sit and be welcome."

Though he welcomed them forth, he did not sit, nor did he shoulder his bow. He knew Malikh would have scout parties searching keenly for him and Arya. Until he laid eyes on these strangers, he couldn't be entirely sure who they were.

The woman stepped into the light. Jabesh was surprised, looking up over a foot in the air to meet her gaze. Her blonde hair shone in the firelight, as she stretched her hands before her, effortlessly holding an enormous great sword flat on her palms. Jabesh nodded curtly to her. She knelt, placing her sword on the ground near the fire, then rose, backing up several paces.

Jabesh searched the darkness past the giant woman, but could not discern her companion, for her physique obstructed much from sight. Indicating her shadowed companion, the diviner altered his stance, so he was a narrower target. He declared, "Now your friend; step forward and present your weapons. Otherwise things will turn *distinctly* unpleasant."

The woman stepped left several paces, allowing her companion to step forth. As the young man stepped into the light, the diviner felt a tremor run through his muscles, causing him to drop his bow in shock. The lad, standing just a few inches shorter than himself, gazed levelly across the fire at him with a familiar set of sea green eyes. The light and shadows traced the outline of a face Jabesh had not seen in many a year. Though this man was considerably younger, it was still eerily similar.

In a voice choked with a mix of confusion, grief and joy, Jabesh asked, "Aldrich, old friend, is that *you*? Are you a wraith, come to haunt me?"

If Jabesh was shocked beholding the ghost of an old friend, dead these nine years, Abel felt doubly afraid. Here was a man he had never met, who knew his father's name, and addressed him with it. The young warrior's gaze became a mistrustful scowl. He withdrew several paces, swiftly spinning his sword, Mediator, in his hands; the tip of it now pointed at the stranger across the fire. "How do you know that name, sir? Answer me quickly, or we will have harsh words, you and I!"

The man across the fire stared at the hilt of Abel's sword, recognition dawning on his face. In a shaky voice (which Abel mistook for fear) the stranger pointed at the sword, asking, "That is *'Mediator'*, is it not, my lad?"

The question shook Abel momentarily, the sword dipping groundward as confusion gripped his mind. "How do you know my sword's name? *How* do you know the name Aldrich?!"

With a voice of joyous sorrow, Jabesh stared at Abel, stating, "I knew a man, many years gone now, whose face you bear. I knew him, as I know the man whose sword you wield. Pray tell, are you the *son* of Sir Aldrich Farthen and dear Amina?"

Nairadj's eyes darted twixt the men's faces, seeking answers passing like wisps of smoke over the fire. *This is either an omen of great fortune, or great ill. I will observe carefully.*

Abel allowed his sword tip to touch the earth as he stared perplexedly at the stranger across the fire. In a dry, hushed voice, he answered, "Aye, stranger. I *am* Abel Farthen; son of Sir Aldrich and Lady Amina. The blade I bear is *indeed* named 'Mediator'. It belonged to my mentor, Pallas. He has been....*dead* a month now......possibly two. My track of time has been somewhat muddled during my recent travels."

The stranger tumbled onto his rump, tears welling in his eyes as he listened to Abel. Staring warily at the stranger, Abel asked, "Now sir, I have told you who *I* am. I pray you tell me who *you* are. I know no one named Clarke, nor did my parents. How do you know my father and mother?"

Jabesh couldn't help tumbling when he heard of Pallas' death. They were the closest of friends in the Peaceful Warriors. Aldrich and Pallas had a special relationship, of course; but Aldrich was not a diviner. Jabesh and Pallas had grown close during the campaign against King Ridley's northerners.

To Jabesh, Pallas was closer than a brother; someone whom he could rely on absolutely, regardless of the situation. Hearing news of his death from Abel's mouth was hard to accept. The old diviner cursed himself internally for not keeping in closer touch with his friends after going their separate ways. He cursed himself again for not fighting Malikh's invading forces in Kiresh. More and more, he began to wish he had died, for then he wouldn't have to continue discovering his friends passing. *First Aldrich and Sallari......now* Pallas*? Gods above, why are you so cruel?*

Regaining his composure as he rose to his feet, he introduced himself. "My real name, Abel Farthen, is not Clarke. It's Jabesh; of house Christoph. I am, or rather *was*, the diviner of Kiresh before Malikh landed upon these shores. I was one of the 'Peaceful Warriors', as we were called, during King Ridley's northerner campaign. Among my closest friends were Barsayt, Pallas, Sallari, Sir Aldrich and Sarto. I assume your father didn't get much chance to speak of the old days before he....before he passed. I know your face, for his is etched into yours. This is a *great* providence. I am overjoyed to finally meet the son of my dear friend." Saying thus, he extended his hand.

Cautiously, Abel approached, sheathing Mediator and taking the offered hand. The diviner drew the young warrior into a strong hug. Abel could hear him weeping with joy in his ear. "We have much to discuss Abel, my lad," Jabesh mumbled, regaining his composure.

"There is little time, I think, to do it in. Let us sit, share some food, paltry as it is, and learn of the others' adventures." So Jabesh, Arya, Nairadj and Abel sat around a small fire sharing a meal of cooked rabbit. Arya strove to stay up and listen but fell asleep shortly after finishing her rabbit. The three grown-ups recounted in detail the events that transpired to bring them together here.

Abel recounted, with Nairadj's assistance the major turning points of his revealed destiny in Pallas' hut: the flight from Gwenovair; the battle with the sea wulf; the attack by the mercenaries; the death of Pallas; the parting of ways with Isabel and Sarto shortly thereafter; finally of his mother Amina's passing. Jabesh wept quietly for Pallas and Amina as Arya slept, offering up a quick prayer to the gods for their rest.

The diviner asked, "Have you heard aught of Isabel and Sarto since you parted ways?"

With a frown, Abel responded, "Not until we emerged from the under-realm of Shavatnu." He then launched anew into the adventures he and Nairadj faced since entering Voshkarna. Jabesh could scarcely contain his wonder learning of the slaying of the marsh drake, Ulgnar the Grey. His incredulity grew as he learned of the treacherous crossing of the Nightstalker Wastes to reach Volcros, and the accord with Sigourney.

As Abel finished summing up the pact Sigourney, Nairadj and he had reached, the diviner shook his head, chuckling softly. "That sounds like Pallas alright. *Always* with the foolhardy plans....like when he purged Sarto of his old persona, Apollos the Wrathful." Here, Jabesh froze, darting a concerned look at Abel. "You *are* aware Sarto used to be....a different person, yes?"

Abel nodded faintly. "Pallas informed me. Isabel was the first to discover it. Pallas charged her with watching over Sarto before his death."

Jabesh grunted with relief. "That is good. Sarto is strong, but he needs someone to anchor him to the world. That was why Pallas and Sarto both left for Gwenovair after the war. Pallas needed peace and silence. Sarto needed a haven free from the temptations of his old life."

After a brief pause, he queried, "So, you managed to convince the northerners to mount *another* campaign against Regalias and Malikh? What happened next?"

Here, Nairadj took over the tale, explaining the unexpected reunion with her people, the Red-Ditch bears; the challenge from Melatharom the Burrower; the journey to his realm and the slaying of the rock drake.

Jabesh whistled in amazement at the triumph over Melatharom. He had heard tales as a young man regarding rock drakes and their ferocity. Absently, Abel scratched his forearm where the dragon scales continued growing on his skin, frowning. The diviner noted this but said nothing.

Nairadj finished her tale with the astral visit from Isabel, her update on reaching Endelheim in Messara, and the addition of the Shadow Twins and Khalon the wendygo to her company. "Then," Nairadj concluded worriedly, "Isabel was called away by some trouble on her end. She did not specify its nature, but it seemed disconcerting, whatever it was. I hope she and her newfound friends are alright."

Jabesh furrowed his brow at the mention of Endelheim and Messara- struggling to remember something important on the edge of memory, long since forgotten. In another moment, that something dissolved into mist.

Returning to the conversation at hand, the diviner regaled Abel and Nairadj with the crucial events of recent months. He touched on Clarke's discovery of Princess Arya's identity; the fire which scorched Lec'tair Forest; the village raids along the Inaratu River by the wendygos; the tamping of the fire by an unknown Prezla; Clarke's death and Jabesh's flight with Arya from Regalias.

Now, it was Abel and Nairadj's turn to be stunned. Much had happened of late. Turning to Nairadj, Abel asked, "Isabel told us she started the fire, but it quickly blazed beyond her control. Do you think *Lilith* may have tried killing her and the others? She mentioned Queen Morgana admitted snuffing out the fire......but who would have unleashed the inferno, and *why*?"

Nairadj crinkled her brow in thought. "This has troubled me too, Abel. Here's a better question: what does Lilith *gain* by burning out the wendygos? Every indication thus far is of someone who desires absolute control. Burning out the wendygos sews seeds of chaos and interrupts the control Lilith exerts over the land. Unless......unless Lilith was so pre-occupied with destroying Isabel and Sarto, she did not consider the consequences....or care about them.

"I think......I think we are searching for *another* foe; one concealing themselves utterly within the shadows. Maybe someone else within Regalias looks to seize power from Malikh and Lilith, using subterfuge to gain control."

For a moment, Jabesh's mind stuck on the name Nairadj uttered: *Morgana*. He felt there was something important about her he was forgetting. Suddenly, another name jumped to mind, and he forgot about her. "Noshtain," he blurted.

Nairadj and Abel turned their gazes towards the diviner. "Who is Noshtain, Jabesh? Is that who set fire to Lec'tair Forest?"

The old diviner shook his head fervently, answering, "No, not even remotely. I just remembered Malikh is using a prisoner from the dungeon whom Lilith broke with magic. Noshtain is Malikh's personal guard. He is tall, intimidating and, from what Clarke gleaned during his spying in the dungeons, a warrior of note. Whether Noshtain is his real name, I cannot say. I only saw him once, the night Clarke died. He was helmed and never left Malikh's side. Expect resistance from him, should you encounter him."

In a wary tone, Abel asked, "What makes you say that? Why would *we* encounter him?"

Looking slyly at the youth, Jabesh replied, "You head southward to aid Sigourney. I am a diviner, Abel. Sometimes, I glean things about people I meet. Though you have not stated it outright, I *know* you sojourn south to kill Malikh and Lilith. Am I wrong?"

The young warrior gawked in amazement at Jabesh. "Pallas never mentioned diviners could read minds."

Jabesh chuckled wryly, answering, "You assign me too much power, Abel. I merely *glean* things. It is my latent ability. For Pallas, 'twas the gift of prophecy. It was years ago, but I remember Pallas showed me his prophecy, for it scared him greatly. I have never forgotten it: '*The Prophecy of the Chosen*.'"

Abel locked eyes with the diviner, asking, "Do you believe it?"

Nodding, Jabesh replied, "I never doubted it. Gods do not reveal prophecies every day. Though we never know *when* they shall be fulfilled, there are always signs pointing *towards* fulfillment. It seems I have seen the fruition, at least in part, of this prophecy. As a diviner, and friend to your late master, it is my obligation to help you. You need a way into Regalias, do you not?"

Abel glanced to Nairadj for advice. She glanced from him to Jabesh, as if to say: *Well....are you going to ask or not?*

Looking back to the diviner, Abel asked hesitantly, "Why would you help us, Jabesh? You have just met us. Aside from what I tell you, you know nothing about us."

Jabesh stared bluntly at the young man. "Is that so? I am friend to your father and your former master, Pallas. I am a name diviner. I knew your father as a man of honor and, while he lived, he taught you the way a man ought to go. I know Pallas was *always* wise beyond his years. He made bold plays to bring peace with minimal bloodshed.

"I also know, *firsthand*, Malikh is a madman. Tyrants must be removed from the world whenever possible, as soon as possible. Who better than the son of a knight, trained by a diviner and accompanied by a dyre bear to execute the deed and restore justice to Kalnay? So, I will help you. The question is, Abel: do you *accept* my help?"

Abel's path, once muddled, was aligned anew to his destiny. To himself he thought, *I am* Hamish. *It is my destiny to supplant this tyrant and his dark witch. Here is aid in the form of another diviner and friend to my father and Pallas. To refuse would be folly of the highest order.*

With renewed determination, Abel gazed into Jabesh's strong, brown eyes. "How do we get into Regalias that I may kill Malikh?"

The diviner unfolded the way into Regalias. Abel and Nairadj listened keenly.

Chapter Twenty-Three: '*A Brief History of Endelheim*'

It had been two days since the incident in the gardens. Isabel had not yet found opportunity to visit the restricted section of the Messaran Library. Indecision on how to proceed consumed her mind the first day. Having no one to share her doubts with troubled her. After conferring with Master Sarto on the way to his cell, she began seeing everyone- from Lady Morgana, to her daughters, to Iolo- with suspicion.

She knew she could talk to Eimar or Tibelde but chose not to, for fear of burdening them with worry about something beyond their power to change. She contemplated talking with Scribe Frodi, as he was the one who pointed Master Sarto towards the answer of the mystery shrouding Endelheim. She chided herself as she recalled Sarto inferring Frodi combated a mind-control spell or curse when he passed Sarto the key. She feared discovery or, worse, causing Scribe Frodi to come to further harm.

On the second day, she visited Khalon in his cell to confirm he was healing, physically and mentally, from his ordeal. During her visit, she pondered asking his advice regarding the restricted section and the key. One look at his still weary face and Isabel decided she must keep this secret to herself.

In the afternoon, she retreated to the pier, listening to the water of Andalmere Bay lap at the dock moorings, carefully formulating her plot to infiltrate the library's restricted section. She returned to the gardens afterwards, seeking out Eimar and Tibelde. No matter her reservations, she could not execute this task alone. To no one's surprise, they accepted without question.

After a glorious spread prepared by Eben for supper- which included honey-glazed ham, cooked garden greens drizzled in melted cheese and a rich chocolate cake for dessert- Lady Morgana retreated to her chambers. She was still recovering from the attack by Apollos, though her appearance had returned to normal late the day before. Iolo escorted her through the dimly lit halls to her chambers, taking up his post outside her chamber door. Ezri and her sisters excused themselves from the table last, for they did not wish to leave Isabel alone so soon after the ordeal with Apollos.

The young Prezla was grateful for the company; yet as she looked around the table at each of the five sisters, she couldn't help but wonder whether one of them unleashed Apollos. She found her gaze settling on Allegra. *Allegra gave me the prophecy of the Great Serpent. She was* certainly *not herself. Though, enemies aren't prone to delivering prophecy, or aiding foes in accomplishing their aims.* Focus. *After tonight you will have the answers you seek. From there you can plot your course.*

Upon leaving the feasting hall, Isabel retreated to her chambers to change into her darkest clothes for her mission into the library. When she was ready, she checked on the Shadow Twins; for the gnomes would not dine within the confines of the stone hall. They protested they could not feel the earth of Bloomaya in there and had taken to dining outdoors.

Upon arriving, she settled on the bench near the tree they came to favor: a simple birch, whose bark they had utilized into a smooth, woven hilt grip on their respective knives. They bantered casually for a short time, ensuring no one may be spying on them. Satisfied they were alone and would remain undisturbed, the trio set to their task.

Eimar disappeared into the earth near the birch tree, re-emerging moments later with Isabel's newly acquired staff, Toorg. The young Prezla had grown increasingly paranoid that this unknown enemy entity would strive to destroy or steal her staff. So she entrusted it to the Shadow Twins for safe keeping early yesterday afternoon. Wrapping her hand about the polished, familiar staff which had revealed itself to her, she felt a measure of confidence and strength return to her. Touching the leather strap of Frodi's necklace, Isabel looked to both of her friends.

In a commanding, hushed tone she stated, "Let us go, my friends. We have questions to find answers for."

The only true benefit Isabel could discern from living in a large castle with so few occupants was this: sneaking where you shouldn't go became far easier. In minutes, the trio stood before the great, outer door of the Messaran Library. Eimar and Tibelde were nervous now, for they could not burrow through the stones of the hall floor (should escape become necessary).

In a voice that sounded more confident than she felt, Isabel smiled roguishly at the Shadow Twins and said, "*Relax*, you two. We're a little restless and decided to find a book to read in the library. That's all."

Then she faced the door, placed her left hand upon its grainy surface and pushed. With a moaning creak, the great door swung inward and the dark interior of the library became vaguely visible.

Isabel whispered, "*Luma*," to Toorg. A bright, clean light emanated from the top of the staff, piercing the veil of darkness within the library. Over her shoulder, Isabel whispered to the Shadow Twins, "Follow me and stay alert."

Eimar and Tibelde followed closely, their hands gripping the hilts of their knives as they proceeded into the blackness of the library. The gnomes' reluctance to enter the library was a cultural one. To gnomes, libraries are exceedingly unnerving; more than humans are aware of. To gnomes, the smell of musty parchment and paper is not soothing, as it is to humans. All gnomes smell in a library is the death of countless trees in the pages and sheaves of bound words. Though they are smart and cultured, theirs is an oral history, passed from the lips of the tribal Master of Stories.

These Masters of Stories verbally pass down the history of the gnomish people from the beginning of Kalnay to the present. Eimar and Tibelde pursed their lips, firmly gripped their knife hilts and pressed onward into the catacomb of books humans called 'library'.

Isabel knew the layout like the back of her hand. Often during her training she found her way here, researching the exact wording of obscure spells, or learning the proper way to tie a knot for her fishing or hunting expeditions. With the aid of Toorg's magnificent light, Isabel led the Shadow Twins confidently to the rear of the library.

When they reached the wrought-iron gates cordoning off the restricted section, Isabel pondered its contents briefly. There had been *so* many books to explore and study, she had never been afforded the opportunity to contemplate what knowledge lay beyond those uninviting iron bars. Now, however, the massive maple shelves lined up beyond the bars seemed to thrum and vibrate with knowledge, power and secrets regarding Endelheim.

Standing before the gate, Isabel quietly retrieved the key from the leather strip around her neck. Toorg's light pulsed and hummed as he illuminated the lock for Isabel. Before opening the lock, she turned to Eimar and Tibelde, whispering, "My friends, I *must* do this to help both Master Sarto and Khalon. I count you as my truest friends......but there is *no* need to endanger yourselves here. I know not what we will find in the tome Frodi mentioned, but....if you wish to leave now, I will bear you no ill feelings."

Despite their fear walking through the dead heart of the library and hearing no songs from the stilled pulp lungs of the books lining the numerous maple shelves around them, Eimar and Tibelde shook their heads once, curtly.

"Lady Isabel," Eimar chimed in, "we have faced *many* dangers together: wendygos, wildfires, Apollos......even Eben's ghastly take on garden salad. We have emerged victorious *every* time because we stuck together."

"To turn back now," Tibelde continued, "would bring us disgrace amongst our kin. To say nothing of leaving *you* to face the unknown by yourself. In the absence of Sarto or Khalon, that would be *wrong*."

Shrugging and speaking in unison, the Shadow Twins finished, "In short, my lady, you are stuck with us; until the very end."

Kneeling, Isabel kissed each of them on the forehead, wrapping her arms around them. "Thank you both, so very much. You are truly wondrous companions and ambassadors, both for your tribe and *all* gnomes. Your presence means a great deal to me."

Placing their hands over their hearts, Eimar and Tibelde bowed their heads. "Thank you, my lady. You honor us."

Rising with Toorg in her right hand and the key in her left, Isabel strode to the locked iron gates. With a deep exhalation, Isabel turned the key in the lock. She heard a weighty '*chlunk*' as the restricted section gate opened before her. Offering up a quick, silent prayer to Bronwyn-Aetha, goddess of the White and justice, she crept into the restricted section with Eimar and Tibelde close behind.

Under her breath Isabel whispered, "I have naught to fear for my cause is just."

Subconsciously aware of the danger of being discovered, the young Prezla could not help but be in awe of the magnificent tomes surrounding her. Behind her, the Shadow Twins could not get over how extremely murderous mankind was to everything around itself in the world. They marveled in horror at the size of some of the volumes they passed (subconsciously aware of exactly how many trees died to hold the breadth and volume of man's knowledge).

They searched up and down four massive aisles in search of 'A Brief History of Endelheim', without avail. Isabel was perplexed. She was an avid bibliophile and could ordinarily drum up what she sought in minutes. Now, however, all her usual guesses on where to find this elusive, 'revelatory' tome yielded no results. She also knew the Shadow Twins could not help her with this search (given their cultural reservations and how brave they had been to venture this far). On a whim she addressed her staff in a hushed voice. "Toorg, can you help me locate the book 'A Brief History of Endelheim'? We have been here too long."

In an even voice, Toorg responded within Isabel's mind, "Of course, mistress. Place the key atop of me. I shall divine the book's location."

Despite how silly she felt, Isabel obliged Toorg's request, resting the key atop him. For what seemed a small eternity, she stood stock still with Frodi's key resting atop Toorg, his clean light pulsing first brightly, then fading almost to a pinpoint before returning to brightness again. In another moment, he focused his light into a beam, shining before Isabel and the Shadow Twins to illuminate their path. "The volume you seek is this direction, mistress. Follow my light, and you will find it presently," Toorg stated simply.

To herself, Isabel thought: *How does he do that? He didn't utter any words of magic, yet is able to guide us to the tome we seek with a beam of light? I must ask him more of his capabilities later.*

Glancing behind to Eimar and Tibelde, she whispered, "Toorg will show us the way. Stay close and remain alert." Then she faced where the light pointed, walking swiftly towards this secret volume and the truths it contained.

Within minutes, Toorg had discovered the book. As Isabel removed it from the shelf- crammed unceremoniously twixt two ancient, leather-bound genealogy tomes- it struck her as peculiar. With all the secrecy and mystery surrounding it, the young Prezla expected something more grandiose: a hardcover book with small diamonds encrusted about the edges. Even a book with gold flake-etched wording on the cover. At the very least, she expected a clasp and lock, sealing the pages from being read.

Instead of diamonds, gold-etching or a lock, '*A Brief History of Endelheim*' was a simple brown, soft-leather volume with the title embossed by a leather press. The book appeared more like an over-sized personal journal than a book of precious secrets. The illusion of its being a simple journal disappeared once Isabel picked it up.

She observed concernedly a speckled maroon coloring on the edges of the parchment that comprised the pages. More splotches of maroon macabrely decorated the leather binding on the rear cover. For a moment, Isabel stood motionless, the long sought-after tome clutched tightly in her hands. The fingers on her right hand subconsciously wormed their way twixt the blood-splattered sheets of parchment. When she realized what her hand was doing, she halted herself.

Do I really want to know what lies within these pages? No one has discovered us yet. We could put it back, lock the restricted section again and return the key to Scribe Frodi in secret....

Before she could finish rationalizing a retreat, *'The Nag'* piped up. *You cowardly, little girl! Your Master needs help fending off Apollos! Khalon is locked up like a criminal for a deed Apollos forced him into! Your answer is to turn back?! To turn a blind eye, because you fear truth?! Your parents would be ashamed! Your brother Abel has slain two dragons and lived to tell the tale! What would he think of you balking at the truth within a simple book?!*

Find your courage, woman! Find the bold, powerful sorceress who battled a sea wulf when she was naught but an initiate beginning her training. Find the woman who battled beside her friends against a trio of cutthroat mercenaries and sent them fleeing into the night, like whipped pups. Open the book and remember....

"I have naught to fear, for my cause is just," Isabel finished in a whisper. As she uttered the words,

she opened the tome in her hands and began to read
quietly, so Eimar and Tibelde could hear......

---

*The twenty-ninth day of Ghoslan, in the year
3434 of the Third Age of Kalnay; the third year of the
reign of King Alaster:*

*I, Master Scribe Joel, servant to Duke Waldemar
the Compassionate, of Endelheim, have some unusual
news to transcribe today.*

*Prior to sunrise this morning, Yaltan the
fisherman happened upon a small skiff adrift at the
outermost southern fog bank where Andalmere Bay
opens onto the Nevartane. Within the skiff, he discovered
a lone woman curled up on the floorboards. She was
barely responsive to his questions, but he was able to
determine her name (Morgana) and where she hailed
from (the land of Xel'darth- far to the east, if I recall my
geography correctly).*

*If she knows why she was adrift, she will not
say. I fear her mind was broken by her ordeal. One can
hardly blame her, if that be so. It is whispered that
Nevartane's mists carry hallucinogenic and magical
properties (though, again, this is pure speculation. None
have ever coherently documented a journey into the mists
of Nevartane).*

*On an odd side note, Yaltan brings it to my
attention that not only did she have no food, or palatable
water; she was also without oars in the boat. It is
possible she threw them away in a hallucinatory fit, being
lost in the mists as she was....but it is peculiar. I wonder*

if she wasn't set adrift......possibly in punishment or banishment. Though, what crime such a frail creature could be capable of, I'm sure I don't know.

The thirty-first day of Ghoslan, in the year 3434 of the Third Age of Kalnay; the third year of the reign of King Alaster:

It's been two days since Yaltan retrieved the newcomer, Morgana, from the briny expanse of the Nevartane. Already, she seems <u>much</u> improved. She has her color back, and seems to have regained her appetite (which, for someone so diminutive, is considerable).

Duke Waldemar has been to call on our guest himself, inquiring how she came to be adrift. The lady refuses to speak of her time at sea; an understandable reaction, given what she's endured. After speaking with her, the Duke has instructed she be moved into the inner keep of Endelheim, to grant her better access to the Great Library and the gardens. He feels these comforts may aid her on the road to recovery. I am inclined to agree with his lordship: a good book and a little scenery can do <u>wonders</u> to rejuvenate the soul.

I must conclude here. Tomorrow is the Feast of Restful Spirits. The Duke has asked me to escort the young baronets- Ezri, Delja and Sena- to the festivities. Before concluding, it is worth remarking how strong his lordship has been since Duchess Diane passed from Wulfscales these two years gone. I am <u>overjoyed</u> that her daughters so <u>strongly</u> resemble her. It keeps his lordship from spiraling into sorrow and lends him strength to care for the subjects of Messara.

The next several pages were reflections on the Feast of Restful Spirits- newly engaged couples, infant dedications to the gods, sacrifices to the gods for a bountiful harvest and the like. Isabel skimmed the pages searching for the next passage where Morgana was mentioned. After a couple minutes search, Isabel found a passage that struck her, and she read aloud:

The twenty-first day of Craslan, in the year 3434 of the Third Age of Kalnay; the third year of the reign of King Alaster:

The increased number of disappearances reported in the villages of Tolbesh, Dunmouth and Sarsgall <u>still</u> remain unsolved. No bodies have been discovered, but that isn't the worst. The worst is how little effort is being made to search for <u>five dozen</u> missing souls.

Magister Waleigh seems......peculiar. Since I've known him, the well-being of <u>every</u> person in the Eastern Reach has <u>always</u> been chief in his mind; even as a child. Now he seems <u>unconcerned</u>....almost <u>flippant</u> regarding the shocking number of disappearances over a mere month and a half.

For as long as I've been Master Scribe of Endelheim, we have dealt with fewer than a <u>dozen</u> disappearances a <u>year</u>. Most times, it is due to drunken misbehavior: drowning in Andalmere Bay; falling into a ditch and breaking one's neck; even on occasion, a child disappearing into Hesketh for a day or two (though, thank the gods, they have always been found again, and alive).

I've taken my concerns to his lordship, Duke Waldemar. My hope is to stir him to action against both Waleigh's casual dismissal and the general lack of concern or action to search for the missing. His lordship was equally unmoved by my pleas regarding the disappeared villagers.

The Lady Morgana (as she has become _just_ this past fortnight) assures me she will speak with his lordship in private, regarding the missing populous. I thanked her (though more from perfunctory social etiquette than sincerity). Others call me paranoid, but _none_ of the numerous griefs of late, _ever_ befell Messara or Castle Endelheim within my long and detailed memory. Not until _that_ woman drifted into Andalmere Bay.

If you reading this doubt my words, consider this: in less than _two months' time_, Morgana ascended from a penniless castaway, on the verge of death in a drifting skiff, to the Duchess of the Eastern Reach. I even hear she is with child already, though I cannot confirm that with certainty at this time.

As a precaution against her potentially prying eyes or eavesdropping ears, I have gone to Tucker, the village Prezla to place a confounding charm on this book. The charm ensures that none who serve Pimedus- the demon Lord of Darkness- may ever lay eyes upon the contents of this book. I also had Tucker place a protective spell over both myself and my son, Frodi; that the Light may shield us from the Darkness worming its way deep into the heart of the Reach.

If Morgana truly is _'the Phantom'_: the secret evil ferreting away the citizenry (as the locals have begun calling the body thief), she will _not_ have me or my son, without a fight. I would die before willingly surrendering either my son or this volume to that enchantress.

The twelfth day of Winlan, in the year 3435 of the Third Age of Kalnay; the fourth year of the reign of King Alaster

Another _six souls_ have disappeared from Sarsgall. Where are they being taken? What happens to them that they never return? Why have we _never_ found a body, or even remains? I am the only one now who seeks answers to these ever-mounting questions.

I have lost _all_ influence with the Duke. When I last saw him, but three days hence, his countenance was gaunt, pale and distracted. Every time he sees the Duchess now, he mumbles incoherently about the future of Messara. If I only knew what he meant, I might help him.

Duchess Morgana is the Phantom. I am _certain_ of this now. Tucker has vanished, and he was a powerful Prezla. Who else, but another Prezla could make a Diviner disappear? She holds most of the power of Messara within her clutches. She is more powerful than anyone could have guessed.

Until she arrived, I believed Duke Waldemar to be the most powerful Prezla I had ever met. He did not use his powers much, for he walked a humble path (odd for a Duke, to say the least; more peculiar still for a Prezla). I begin to suspect why Morgana was cast adrift *from Xel'darth. The conclusion I have come to terrifies me.*

Why was she set adrift? Since she arrived here, that has been the biggest unanswered question on my mind. Why didn't the people of Xel'darth kill her? What if casting her adrift was the only choice presented to those who sentenced her to die of hunger and exposure upon the Nevartane? The implications are horrifying to consider at length......but I fear I must do it, for there are few who are safe from her wiles here in the Eastern Reach.

Perhaps the bigger question looming in my mind is this: why has there been no word or contact from beyond Hesketh? Surely someone in the vast expanse of central Kalnay has noticed the lack of commerce and communication with Messara....haven't they? Or are the lords and citizenry of Kalnay blind to the slowly-festering plight consuming Endelheim and the Reach like fungus tainting a healthy wheat field?

Isabel had to stop reading a moment, to get a grip on her whirling mind. In a peculiar sense of relief, she noted the fear on Eimar and Tibelde's faces.

"Hesketh...." Isabel fumbled, searching for the words, "....that forest is *cursed* with black magic. *That's* why we fought amongst ourselves after eating that golden apple. Morgana has blanketed Hesketh in a dark, protective series of spells and curses which stir anger, fear and confusion within any who enter the woods...."

"It's *impossible*," Eimar barked in disbelief. "Tibelde and I can *feel* the magic of a place in the very *soil*. The soil has a feeling of the White....of the freckaying *Light*! If Morgana were a dark witch....we'd have *known* it before *ever* setting foot in Endelheim!" Angrily, he turned and punched a nearby stack of leather-bound tomes, sending them flying.

With lightning alacrity, Isabel shot Toorg forward and whispered, "*Etsa*."

The tumbling volumes froze in mid-air, their yellowing pages and bindings holding their place in the air like a bizarre art spectacle. Pointing Toorg to where the tomes had been moments before, Isabel whispered, "*Vish un dopar*."

Without a sound, the displaced volumes returned to their original places. As soon as the books were reset, all three of them released a pent-up sigh of relief.

Out of nowhere, Tibelde cuffed Eimar up the backside of his head. He grunted in pain and surprise, rubbing where his sister smacked him. In an angry hiss, she spat, "Are you *trying* to get us caught, you *dunkla*?!"

Still rubbing the tender spot, Eimar glanced at Isabel. "Apologies, Lady Isabel; I did not mean to cause a scene...."

" 'Tis fine, Eimar. Though I must inquire after the *reason* for the outburst," she asked levelly.

Here, he turned to his sister, asking with his eyes for her to explain. With a sigh, Tibelde explained,

"My Lady, Eimar's outburst concerns pride; and rightfully so. We have a reputation amongst our kin as being *excellent* in detecting magic traps and evil places."

Following the implication, Isabel offered, "So....Eimar is upset because....he was fooled by the magical properties of the soil?"

"*Precisely*, my lady," Tibelde confirmed. "I too have been fooled, if that is the case. By ourselves, either of us may, on occasion, be fooled. No one can sense *all* dark magic or avoid it completely. Together, however, our individual abilities amplify the other's gifts. *If* Lady Morgana is a dark witch....then, quite simply, she is the *single* most powerful witch I ever heard of.

"This would mean we unwittingly walked into a place of great evil, and even *now* are in danger. To alter the latent magic within the earth takes tremendous skill and focus both to cast and maintain."

Scowling at the open tome on the table, Isabel replied, "This is a *dangerous* implication. We must learn more before acting. If we are wrong, we will create an enemy where none before existed."

To Toorg, she whispered, "Find me another relevant passage, my friend. I must know more, before passing final judgment."

Her staff pulsed in her hand, and the pages turned swiftly on their own, until settling on a passage, two thirds of the way into the slim book. Isabel read the entry aloud.

The fifteenth day of Draslan, in the year 3437 of the Third Age of Kalnay; the sixth year of the reign of King Alaster:

I don't know why I bother continuing to write in this old book. I would like to think that, whoever you are that has discovered this book....that perhaps you can, or will, right the wrongs that have transpired both in Messara and Endelheim, unchecked for the past two years. I'm probably fooling myself, but hope is all I have.

Hope, and my son Frodi- these are the only things I have left. He is so young. As a young man, it is hard for him to understand how such evil reigns unchecked. I don't know what to tell him, so I lie. I tell him someone will come and right things in the Reach again....but I distract myself. Where was I....?

The villages of Tolbesh, Dunmouth and Sarsgall all lay razed now. The smell of burnt flesh and scorched lumber permeate the air. The Phantom Queen, as Morgana now calls herself (malcontent, it seems, with being a mere duchess) has murdered all remaining in the villages. Granted, that isn't many souls. The remainder were ones like me, who had charms and protective spells over themselves and their families.

I heard from Judith the local rug merchant in Tolbesh, who followed Morgana one night to witness what happens to those who are taken. Her husband, Brantley, was taken from the street outside their home and drug off to the countryside by Iolo. By Judith's description, Morgana sacrificed Brantley in a field, by firelight. 'Tis hard to know if she was completely in her right senses since losing her husband, but she swears a great black cloud arose from the earth, dragging Brantley bodily down into the earth.

　　To anyone else, this may sound like madness, but to me, it makes sense. If what happened to him has happened to all the numerous others taken during the past two years, that explains why there have never been any bodies recovered. The Phantom Queen sacrifices the people of the Reach to the demon Lord of the Darkness! Pimedus, I tell you! It must be an exchange: for every person she sacrifices, she receives more power, or a longer life, or a younger visage from It....

　　Judith is gone now. There are only a few of us left. I write this from a burnt-out hut on the far northern border of Hesketh, near Lec'tair Forest. Frodi is with me, and he is mortally frightened. I assure him everything will be well, but I know I am not being entirely honest with him. I bequeath this book to him, should The Phantom Queen sacrifice me to Pimedus.

　　I am hopeful she will not be able to come for me herself. The young Lady Allegra was born within this past week. Morgana may be a powerful Prezla, but the strain of childbirth will take the energy out of any woman. Again, Morgana used her dark magic on Duke Waldemar to procure another child, securing her legacy as ruler.

　　No doubt, the svanth will send her young bodyguard, the boy Iolo, to collect my head. Despite his willing servitude to her, I cannot remain angry at him; he looked out for himself. What's to say that, were I not a

*father and only pre-occupied with my own survival that I
would not have done as he did?*

*Should Iolo come for me, I will plead for my
son, dear Frodi, to live. Iolo is not without conscience;
not yet, leastwise. I will entreat him to spare my son. If
the gods are with me, he will permit Frodi to keep the
book. If they are bountifully merciful, he will remain
ignorant of the damning contents of this book. Iolo is a
talented fighter, but he never gave much time to learning
his letters. This may be a faint blessing in an endless sea
of ill fortune.*

*I sense this is my last night on Kalnay, though I
will not burden Frodi with this knowledge. I want him to
retain one last shred of youthful innocence, even if only
for one more evening. I want so <u>desperately</u> to breathe
free, clean air one last time. Alas, the air in Messara is
choked with fumes of razed villages, burnt crop fields,
and the permeating stench of death.*

*Duke Waldemar is slain also. The Phantom
Queen ensured that herself, just two nights after Allegra's
birth. I mourn in silence for my lord and regret <u>deeply</u>
that I could not do more to help him escape the clutches
of that deceptive <u>svanth</u>. Of Lord Waldemar's daughters,
I know naught, for I fled with Frodi after hearing of the
Duke's death. Morgana may spare them, simply to gain
more power (for Ezri, Delja and Sena have already
demonstrated strong abilities towards becoming powerful
sorceresses, even at their young ages). I hope and pray
that, whether they live or die, they are spared the cruel,
leeching effect Morgana spreads to all around her,
whether they know it or not.*

Know this, you, reading this: Morgana's <u>true</u> <u>form</u> is how old Yaltan discovered her in the skiff. She is truly emaciated, missing many teeth. She has hollow, cold eyes and faded flaxen hair. The Phantom Queen gains her power by leeching off those more powerful than she, or by sacrificing to the Darkness of Pimedus. Her tongue is polished silver: you will desire to do as she says, but you <u>must</u> resist. If her honeyed words do not dull your defenses or senses, she will turn that same tongue into a deadly dirk, waiting to slip between your ribs and end you.

Your only choices when facing her are these:

1) *<u>Fight her</u>; tooth and nail, you must fight her until you are victorious or dead.*

2) *<u>Flee her</u> presence; flight will buy you time, but her power is far-reaching and vast in strength.*

3) *<u>Join her</u> in the Darkness; know that if you do this, there are powers greater than Morgana which may do worse to you than she is capable of.*

4) *<u>You die</u>. All things die- even she may (though I never learned the exact nature of her tentative demise). You have a choice in this though: either die on your <u>feet</u>, or down on your <u>knees</u>. If you choose the former, at least you may die proud, knowing you have done so courageously.*

I grow tired now. I shall tell Frodi the tale of The Mighty Deeds of Sir Brock Clegane' *one last time, before he lays down to sleep. Perhaps I do this merely to bolster my own meager courage. I prefer to think I am telling him the story to remind him to be courageous in the coming days and years and, like Sir Clegane, to* <u>*never*</u> *stop fighting evils that plague this world.*

*   * <u>*I love you*</u> *Frodi, my son. My prayer for you is that long days and pleasant nights ever follow at your heels.*

The next page Isabel turned was discolored by a long-dried, and rather large, blood stain. None needed ask what happened. Master Scribe Joel had spoken enough on the circumstances leading to the splotch on the book's pages.

Numbly, Isabel closed the remaining pages, so that the rear book cover, stained with Joel's years' old blood, lay facing the ceiling; neither accusing, nor apologizing. Merely telling the blunt, bloody truth.

In a voice that sounded calmer and more collected than she felt, she stated, "Come my friends. Let us leave this place."

As Isabel replaced the book on the shelf between the two history tomes, Eimar inquired, "What would you have of us, my Lady? Whatever you will, we will obey."

Standing tall with Toorg grasped firmly in her right hand, Isabel declared, "We must free Master Sarto and Khalon. Then we *must* leave this accursed place, immediately."

Upon uttering these words, Isabel and the Shadow Twins began to see Endelheim- the *true*

Endelheim- through the veil of magic Morgana had woven about them. That had been woven into the very air, stone and soil of the long dead castle. The great bookshelves were rotting and decrepit; many windows were shattered, and entire stacks of books were dampened with mildew. The illusion faded rapidly.

Isabel and her friends knew in their bones it was time to leave the Eastern Reach.

Quiet as wraiths, the three cohorts exited the library, locking the restricted section behind them. Emerging into the hallway, the trio were disgusted anew as they observed the crumbling stones in the walls; rotten and crumbling support beams criss-crossing the roof and sizable patches of moss and lichen growing on the damp walls.

Try as they might, none could mask their disgust at having traversed these dead, ghostly halls so blindly for so long. They felt anger at having been deceived for so long. They also felt sorrow for the few inhabitants of Endelheim who were likely oblivious to the fact that they dwelt in this giant, entombing edifice.

Steeling herself against the rampant decay pressing in about her, Isabel strode with authority to the prison cells. When they emerged into the courtyard between the hall of cells and the library, the Shadow Twins were mortified by the new appearance of the gardens.

Where once lush, colorful flowers sprung radiantly from the rich, black soil, there was now naught but sickly, rotten stalks, drooping with death and decay. The noble birch, once healthy, was a gnarled, arthritic hand- hard, lifeless and hateful to gaze upon. The soil in the gardens was no longer rich black; rather it was a clumping, foul smelling fertilizer. Both Eimar and Tibelde clutched their dagger hilts deathly tight- channeling their silent rage at having been so thoroughly deceived by Morgana's dark magic. Not a word was spoken by any, for their demeanor conveyed their anguish at being so thoroughly deceived. Anger for never questioning the false friendship of Morgana, the Phantom Queen.

Within minutes they were in the prison cell corridor. Eimar and Tibelde drew their daggers, flanking Isabel as they drew close to Khalon's cell. Holding Toorg before her, Isabel focused on the lock and whispered, "*Nix et corva.*" Without a sound, the cell door swung inwards and she caught faint sight of Khalon in the dark of the cell.

"*Luma,*" she whispered. Toorg lit up, punching a hole in the darkness. Seeing Khalon, Isabel was taken aback by his scars- standing out in an inflamed pink against the grey of his skin. She felt a tinge of regret as she recalled what she had done. Approaching the wendygo curled uncomfortably on his too short, plank bed against the right wall, she gently placed a hand on his upper left arm, whispering in his ear, "*Khalon*? You *must* awaken."

In a smooth motion the young buck rolled onto his back, holding his slender, clawed fingers up to shield his silver eyes against Toorg's light. "Lady *Isabel*? What are you doing here? What time is it?"

She whispered sternly, "Khalon, my friend....I am sure you have questions, but we have no time right now. All I can tell you is I have learned something disturbing. We are, *all* of us, in danger of discovery and captivity. Do you believe me?"

Without hesitation, he replied, "Of course I believe you, my Lady. I do not understand right now, but you have nary led me astray since we've met. I am yours to command. When the time is right, you will tell me all, yes?"

Struggling to stifle tears, she answered, "Aye, Khalon, I *will*. For now, we must fetch Master Sarto and leave Endelheim....leave Messara all together, once and for all."

In a flash, the young wendygo was on his hooved feet, his head ducked to avoid scraping the low roof of the cell with his antlers. "Lead on, Lady Isabel. I will follow."

She exited, followed by Khalon and proceeded to Master Sarto's cell. As before, she uttered the spell '*nix et corva*', opening the door with ease.

"Master Sarto? It's Isabel. Can you find your feet, Master? We must leave this place."

Sarto woke quickly, but his reactions seemed sluggish to her. Looking dazedly at the light on Toorg's top, he slurred, "When did you get a staff? Or is that *my* staff? It's hard to think....so groggy."

After a moment's worried consideration, Isabel slapped Sarto hard. The crisp sound of the blow startled the Shadow Twins but succeeded in rousing her master's senses. Looking hard into his focusing eyes, Isabel asked, "Master Sarto, are you good to travel? We have *urgent* cause to leave Endelheim, and the Eastern Reach. I learnt the truth contained in Scribe Frodi's book, '*A Brief History of Endelheim*.'"

If the slap drew Sarto from his stupor, then mentioning Frodi's book was as a cup of cold water splashed in his face. He shot to his feet, and hissed, "*Vish mor het tass.*" In a flash his staff shot into the cell, found his hand, and he leaned heavily on it. "What have you discovered, my child?"

Isabel shook her head. "I will reveal *all*, but not now. Right now, we are in *danger*. Morgana is *not* who she seems. We believed we roosted amongst sparrows, when we actually squirmed amidst a pit of vipers."

Sarto's eyes grew large. Suddenly all the odd pieces of this convoluted puzzle began to fit. *Apollos' rising was* no *accident;* Morgana *channeled him. The odd behavior of Eben and Frodi......even the Five Sisters and their odd memories, or lack thereof....it* all *makes sense now. Morgana is a dark sorceress; a* powerful *one at that. Even Lilith could not achieve the level of deception Morgana has woven throughout the Eastern Reach, and upon everyone within it.*

Returning to himself, he nodded grimly, stating, "Lead the way Isabel. This is *your* task to see to completion. I will aid you if I may, but I fear Morgana has been leeching my powers quite deeply while I was confined to this cell. I may not be battle ready. I suggest caution and subterfuge to escape."

Nodding curtly, Isabel replied, "If all goes as I hope, Master Sarto, they will never know we have left."

Smiling faintly, despite the pain in his head and his general state of fatigue, he responded, "Let us be rid of this place, my pupil."

Isabel knew they were in trouble before entering the courtyard. For some reason she was not able to fully grasp, she sensed Morgana's presence in the courtyard. She also detected Iolo there; his beady eyes watchful and his sword drawn, waiting for them to emerge from the cells.

Cautiously, Isabel stepped into the courtyard. Fanning out about her, Khalon, Eimar and Tibelde began to flank Iolo and Morgana. Sarto remained near Isabel, ready to lend his magical strength to her reserves.

Rising from the bench beneath the gnarled, dead birch tree, Morgana clapped slowly. She looked radiant; as she had when she first appeared in Isabel's dreams. "Well *done*, Isabel. You have broken my confounding spell. No other Prezla to enter Endelheim in all these years has *ever* discovered the truth or broken through my charms. I am *impressed*."

Scowling, Isabel sneered, "I wish I could say the same of *you*, o Phantom Queen. All *you* have done in the past years is leech from others to sustain a false image of beauty, power and perfection. You are as false as a dragon oil mountebank in Marister."

Morgana's perfect smile dropped, her eyes darkening, swirling with orange fire in the irises. Wagging a single finger side to side, she hissed, "*Careful*, child. I admire your skill and intelligence. Provoke me however, and I will *destroy* you; as I have destroyed *every* other would-be Prezla ensnared in my domain."

Planting Toorg firmly in the ground at her feet, Isabel retorted, "Am I supposed to fear your words?! You could not contain Apollos when you leeched too deeply from my Master Sarto. I *saw* what it did to you then. How you reverted to your *true* self. Just as Yaltan found you in that skiff all those years ago. I know the *truth*."

At the mention of Yaltan, Morgana's left eye twitched. For a moment, her composure crumpled. "I *see*.... you have found that meddlesome Scribe Joel's rantings. How you did so, I couldn't guess....However, knowing the truth will not save you. Your only choice is to join me as my apprentice."

Spitting on the ground at her feet, Isabel snapped, "I would rather *die* than join you!" Here, she directed her ire towards Iolo, sneering, "I would rather die now, than live a coward's existence as a lap dog like Iolo chose!"

Unaware that anyone knew of his past, Iolo stumbled, "I....you don't know *me*, Isabel Farthen! You don't know what choices, what *impossible* choices, I faced! You don't know *why* I did what I did!"

Whipping her gaze in Iolo's direction, Morgana shouted, "Shut your cur mouth! The girl is baiting you to fight. A foolish idea regardless, for I could destroy her, her master and her....*repulsive* friends with a single spell."

Isabel laughed involuntarily. "You sound like the Red Giant in the tales of Sir Brock: talking large but doing little...."

In rage, Morgana pointed a finger at her, shouting, "*Luma devros, Isabel!*" Without warning, a large fireball shot from her fingertip, propelling towards the girl.

As one, Isabel and Sarto hollered, "*Cofrath dos aquitane!*" A large, thick ball of water appeared and quenched the flame; barely.

Pointing her finger in Khalon's direction, Morgana screeched, "You may be able to defend yourself with your paltry spells, but can you provide this *monster* an adequate defense spell from over there before my fires consume his flesh?!"

With mounting fear, Isabel realized their tactical error in fanning out: she could not adequately defend them all without a brief delay. She glanced fretfully towards Khalon. His eyes begged her not to concede. The young Prezla's compassion got the better of her.

I am willing to die to defeat Morgana. I will be thrice gods damned if I knowingly endanger my friends. Khalon is a wendygo- there is no denying that; but he's not just a wendygo. He is also my friend, someone I trust intrinsically to watch over me, as I would for him. I will not let him die for my pride; especially when I don't know the full extent of Morgana's powers.

With reluctance, she extended her staff horizontally, setting it on the ground. She indicated for Master Sarto to do the same, which he did (albeit

grudgingly). She was about to instruct Eimar and
Tibelde to place their daggers on the ground only to
discover they vanished; precisely when or where to, she
did not know.

Isabel declared, "Morgana, I concede. I wish no
harm to come to my friends, so I will do as you ask. Give
me your solemn promise that no harm will come to *any*
of them, and I......agree to become your apprentice."

Lowering her hand, Morgana smiled, revealing
the gaps where her teeth had fallen out on that long-ago
voyage upon the Nevartane. "*That*, my dear Isabel, is the
correct choice. Iolo! Be so kind as to relieve our....*guests*
of their weapons and escort them to their cells. Isabel
will be taking up residence in my tower, where I can keep
close watch over her and her......becoming."

As Iolo marched Sarto and Khalon back to their
cells, Morgana glided up beside Isabel, wrapping one
bony arm over her shoulder, guiding her to the tower.
Isabel cringed in disgust as Morgana unleashed a mad
cackle, tearing into the silence of the night. In their
chambers, the Five Sisters continued to sleep, though the
Phantom Queen's cackle wormed into each of their
dreams; causing them to shiver in fear as their dreams
warped into nightmares.

From the base of the dead copse of old ash
trees where Toorg had magically grown from, Eimar and
Tibelde watched in dismay as their friends were led into
captivity. They began to furiously, and wordlessly, form a
plan to rescue their distressed comrades- the stench of
the foul soil of Endelheim seeping into their nostrils.

Chapter Twenty-Four: The Court of the Overlord

Abel's heart pumped faster than usual. He hadn't been running; at least not recently. The diviner's information had been good (something both Abel and Nairadj had borne slivers of doubt about since parting from Jabesh and Princess Arya's company). Not only was the secret way into the castle good, but due to the army's absence to the Crossroad of Kings, there were only a handful of Red Guards patrolling the inner keep of the castle. The companions incapacitated the dozen or so guards they spotted as they infiltrated the keep from the moat entrance. Within several minutes of entering by the moat dock, they stood before the throne room door.

Abel placed his right hand on the door. He felt the rustle of the concealed, brown dragon scales growing slowly but steadily along the length of his right forearm. Before pushing on the door, he paused.

After such a long journey, it seems surreal to be here. The end is in sight, yet the story feels....unfinished. What happens after *I kill Malikh? Will all be well? Will the imbalanced scale of justice aright itself with the thrust of my blade? Or do I create new dilemmas through my actions?*

On his left, Nairadj adjusted her footing, snapping his mind back to the moment.

Focus, Abel; there will be time to reflect later. Right now, focus on Malikh. Focus on what he's taken from you: your father; your mother; your freedom to grow up without the burdens that rest on your mind and body. End his life. Find justice for your parents and regain a modicum of peace.

Releasing a large, pent up breath, Abel shoved open the great door to the throne room, entering the court of the Overlord. He half expected the door to groan loudly, giving away his presence and alerting Malikh to approaching danger. The door was silent.

The young warrior spotted Malikh in the far corner of the throne room, his back to them and wearing a hooded cloak. The intruders quickly surveyed the throne room, noting no one else present. Nairadj pivoted, shutting the door. With relative ease, she placed the heavy wooden beam behind the door in place, locking the Overlord in with them. As she did so, Abel silently drew Mediator, treading swiftly across the well-lit expanse of the throne room.

The hooded figure remained where they stood, facing the corner. As he drew closer, Abel heard muttering under their breath as they shifted from foot to foot; but they did not turn around.

In another moment, he was directly behind Malikh. He held Mediator low, intending to run him through the back. Then the hooded figure spoke reproachfully. "You would run a *lady* through the back, Abel '*Drakt'vansh*' Farthen? *That's* not very heroic for a warrior of the Light."

Abel froze, startled by the woman's voice, and the familiar way she addressed him. The momentary hesitation was all she needed. Whirling about, the woman with pitch black eyes shed her cloak, raised her hand and hissed, "*Avia.*"

Before he could react, Abel was propelled across the room. He was slammed hard into one of the pillars ringing the edge of the throne room and Mediator was flung free from his grasp. Hovering four feet above the ground and gripped fast by an invisible hand, Abel was rightfully terrified.

From behind the throne, three dozen Red Guards, the hulking, helmed Noshtain and the Overlord Malikh emerged through the secret dungeon entrance. The soldiers rushed Nairadj, pressing in around her with swords drawn, pinning her against the barricaded throne room door. Noshtain remained at Malikh's side as he strode cockily across the throne room to stare at the suspended Abel.

As he crossed the distance, Malikh slowly and loudly clapped his hands, the echo reverberating hollowly off the stone walls of the hall. "I am *impressed*, Abel. You've made it farther than I expected you to....once I learned you were coming. I've been fairly....*distracted* of late. First, there was the fire in Lec'tair Forest. Then, the march of the Wildmen to the Crossroad of Kings. Now, those dirty Northerners are continuing their march south. *Finally,* the disappearance of my daughter, Princess Adelaide; stolen by that weasel, Jabesh....I'm amazed I even heard about you before your sword ended up between my lungs!

"Lady Lilith caught wind of you when she followed your sister's ghostly projection spells north to the Shavatnu Mountains. I'm curious: what took you underground in the first place......? Ah, but that is something we may discuss later. Assuming, of course, there *is* a 'later' for you.

"For now, I want to know *how* you snuck into Regalias undetected. You *must* have had help......did you meet Jabesh, I wonder? You must have, because you snuck in almost as well as that *freckaying* thief snuck out with my *daughter!* But I forget myself." Malikh nodded then to Lilith.

With a word, the Screech Owl dropped Abel to the ground. All the air in the boy's lungs rushed from him in a large '*woomph'* as he crashed to the cold stone floor. Malikh strode forward, kicking him hard once in the mid-riff, flipping the young warrior onto his back.

Abel searched fruitlessly for Mediator, spying it resting over six feet away. Malikh rested a heavy, booted foot on his chest, pressing down hard on his sternum. Abel struggled to appear unfazed by the abuse his enemies inflicted, but he could feel the pinch in his lungs as he labored to breathe beneath the Overlord's boot. Malikh noted his discomfort, pressing down harder with his foot as he leaned close to Abel's face. "What's the matter, *dragon slayer*? Do I cause you discomfort? Why don't you *make* me stop?"

Despite the pressure, Abel smirked. "Should I ask *you* to stop....or should I ask your *master* to stop you?" He indicated Lilith as he said '*master.'*

Malikh glanced at Lilith, before returning his furious gaze to Abel. "She is *not* my master! That is my wife and queen, you *whelp*!" Saying thus, he struck Abel with a fierce backhand, rocking the boy's head hard to the left.

The young warrior felt a thick, warm spray of blood fly from his mouth to patter onto the floor.

Smiling around his torn lip, Abel jibed, "How about you let me up and we fight on even terms, Malikh? Or do you fear a sixteen-year-old *whelp* may claim your life, ridding Kalnay of your tainted memory once and for all?" Then, Abel spat a mist of blood in Malikh's face, causing him to stumble back in disgust.

Noshtain stepped forward, punching Abel hard in the face. The force of the blow broke his nose, causing his head to bounce faintly off the stone floor. A burst of stars dazzled before his eyes momentarily.

"Noshtain, *desist*," Malikh barked. Like a trained dog, he arose, standing like a great, flesh-bound statue at Malikh's left.

Running a hand over his blood-splattered face, Malikh knelt beside Abel and hissed, "You *really* want to meddle in my affairs, *boy*? So *be* it. You wish to battle? I shall provide you with a battle. When you die, you die with the knowledge that I have taken *everything* from you."

Snapping his fingers as he rose, the Overlord turned, marching to his throne and sitting. The two closest Red Guards' yanked Abel unceremoniously to his feet, shoving him rudely to the center of the throne room. One retrieved Mediator, sliding it across the stone floor, then stepped back.

Malikh snapped his fingers again, and the guards boxing Nairadj against the door surged forward, overpowering the she-bear and relieving her of weapons. It took six of them to shackle her hands. They drug her to the throne, where she was chained to the left leg. Lilith had quietly taken her seat in her throne to her husband's left, smiling devilishly the entire time. With Nairadj chained to the throne, the Red Guards formed an armed perimeter around the edge of the throne room, twixt the pillars, swords drawn and at the ready.

Abel watched the guards' bustle about. He marked Malikh settling into his throne, as if preparing to witness a bout at a feast. The young warrior noted Noshtain had not moved from where he stood. He got a sick, angry feeling in his stomach as he realized what was happening.

"You cowardly *bastard*," Abel seethed through clenched teeth, "I challenge you to armed combat and you send another to fight in your stead? How did you *ever* seize control of Kalnay? You won't even face a sixteen-year-old in single, armed combat. You are no king, *Malikh*. You are a *pretender*, hiding like an infant behind your witch's skirts, and the sword of a mindless brute."

Pointing a finger at Abel, the Overlord spat, "You are *wrong*, Abel Farthen! *Everything* I have, I freckaying *earned*! I may not have done so honestly, but who, in this entire *cursed* world, ever got where I am by being honest?"

"King *Alaster* and Queen *Rebecca* did," Abel retorted angrily.

"Ah yes....and look where *that* got them."

Abel clenched his fists in growing anger, as he stared loathingly at the pretender king.

Malikh matched the furious youth's stare for a moment, before bellowing, "Come, enough of this self-righteous preaching! You promised me a fight. Now, fight! Prepare to die, Abel Farthen!"

Abel raised Mediator, assuming a defensive stance, and shifting his focus to the helmed Noshtain. He searched quickly for weaknesses in his armor, his weaponry or his stature. He detected none.

With an evil smile, Malikh barked, "*Noshtain*, remove your helmet. Then kill this whelp who threatened your Overlord. I *command* it."

Noshtain removed his helmet.

Abel's heart sank. His mind simultaneously whirled with confusion, love, relief and sorrow. Though it had been many years since that night on the beach of Igraine, he could *never* forget the face staring back at him with these familiar sea green eyes, now hollow and emotionless.

Gods above, be merciful, Abel prayed in silent desperation. *This cannot be happening....* His mind trailed off then, for he literally knew of nothing else to pray or think.

Standing before him, more haggard than he had been eight years ago, stood his father, Sir Aldrich. There was no love in his eyes, nor was there hate. There was simply obedience to the word of Malikh.

Noshtain drew his great sword, stating in a monotonous voice, "As you command, Lord Malikh, so shall I do." Then the enchanted Sir Aldrich Farthen closed on Abel. Like legends of the old world, father and son began to battle for the amusement of a mad tyrant.

Epilogue: A Dark Bargain

It was night in Endelheim. The moon shone overhead with a waxy yellow sheen. Morgana, the Phantom Queen of Messara, had just rejuvenated her appearance by sapping some of Sarto's strength. She felt *fantastic*. With Iolo standing guard outside, she closed her chamber doors, instantly enveloped by darkness.

Muttering a spell under her breath, she stared into the center of the chamber. As she muttered, a dirty ball of light began growing- slowly at first, then faster as she repeated the words. In moments, a dark-tinged orb of light levitated in the center of the chamber. Through it, she clearly saw the face of Fenyang, the wendygo king seated at Hann'Lec.

When he beheld her, Fenyang dropped his gaze; partially in deference, partially in disgust. "Lady Morgana, good evening," he intoned half-heartedly.

Beaming broadly at the wendygo king, Morgana replied cheerily, "Lord *Fenyang*, good evening to you. I *hope* you have given my proposal careful consideration, as you promised."

With a buck-like snort, Fenyang retorted, "*What* proposal, O Phantom Queen? If you mean your *order* to subjugate my people into your army or risk your razing the *rest* of Lec'tair Forest....I think you *know* my response to your....*offer*."

Morgana chuckled maliciously, shaking her head. "Whether I know it or not, you *must* say it. That is the foundation of bargains: the verbal exchange of promises and services on mutual terms of understanding. I am afraid I *must* hear you say the words......or I will be forced to *finish* what I started when that wildfire burnt out southwestern Lec'tair Forest. As I said before, the choice is *yours*, Lord Fenyang."

For a moment, the king's reflected image did naught but scowl nightmarishly, snorting a loud, angry elk snort. Then his fierce, golden eyes dropped. With a sigh, he answered, "I swear, Lady Morgana, that my people, the wendygos of Lec'tair Forest, will fight at *your* command against all mankind residing in Kalnay. This we will do until we are dead, or victorious." With great personal difficulty, Fenyang knelt to Morgana's projected image, placing his hand over his heart. "This I do swear, as King of Hann'Lec and Lec'tair Forest.......and your faithful servant."

The Phantom Queen's smile widened further, revealing two missing teeth at the back of her mouth. "*Excellent*, Lord Fenyang. You have chosen wisely, both for you *and* your people. Now, issue an emissary to the Grymwulves in the southern hills and recruit them to our cause. If they refuse, remind them of what I have done to Lec'tair Forest. Inform them that I can wreak *similar* havoc upon their homes and people should they refuse me."

"As you command, Lady Morgana, so I shall do, with all haste," Fenyang grumbled.

"My thanks. When I rule Kalnay from Regalias, you and your people shall have not only the lands of Lec'tair Forest, but also those of the Golden West Wood *and* the woodlands of Hesketh. You will learn I am a generous queen....once I have my rightful throne."

Bowing awkwardly, Fenyang began, "My thanks for the generous gift. The wendygos will...."

Closing her fist mid-air, Morgana severed the connection. To herself she thought: *How foolish the wendygos are. Once I rule Kalnay, I will finish the blaze I began. Monsters have no place in my kingdom. Only fools believe liars.*

With a peal of laughter, Morgana thought: *Everything I have striven towards, for......I don't even remember how long......everything is finally coming together! Prepare yourselves, Kalnay. I, Morgana, the Phantom Queen will have my throne. You may join me or perish under the thunderous footfalls of my nightmare army!*

Outside, Iolo shifted uncomfortably on his feet as he heard Morgana's maniacal laughter rend the night's silence.

The End

The adventure will continue in Book Three of
'The Legends of Kalnay' Series:
Pimedus Rising

Appendices: Kalnayan Spells and their Meanings

Artaz- 'drop'

Avia- 'fly'

Avia Briesa- 'fly fire'

Avia numa rysas- 'Fly, all blades'

Avia resh- 'fly far'

Avia rysa- 'fly blade'

Breksa lokis- 'confound the eye'

Brothsa- 'multiply'

Burtsa- 'dig'

Burtsa despat rysa- 'dig slowly, blade'

Burtsa rysa- 'dig blade'

Cofrath het un numa philans dos aquitane- 'Shield me and all my friends with water'

Cofraith numa philans- 'Cover all friends'

Corva- 'open; part'

Corva aquitane imor het- 'Part the waters for me'

Corva mor lokis. Gata un tarvish het iras. - 'Open your eyes. See and follow my sight.'

Corvai- 'close'

Despa- 'slow'

Devarth het philas despar- 'Lower my friend slowly'

Dizva het- 'transport me'

Dopar- 'release'

Etsa- 'stop'

Etsa mor glatza furiosa het philans- 'Stop your Golden Madness, my friends'

Etsa mor Wendarosi, furiosa, het philas- Stop your Wendygo Madness, my friend'

Fraya mor het cranos- 'attach to my skull'

Freya et tingrash, ripas- 'Grow and ensnare, quickly'

Furiosa Wendarosi- 'Madness of the Wendygo'

Het tarthain, Sarto. Vish un mor corpus- 'I summon you, mender. Return to your body.'

Iluminus mor identum- 'Reveal your identity'
Luma- 'Light'
Luma devros numa- 'Light consume all'
Nix- 'Silence'
Nix et corva- 'silence and open'
Nix un zetarn- 'silence and sleep'
Reksla terra- 'rise earth'
Shetra marsan- 'shatter bone'
Vesh mor het, tembre- 'Come to me, staff'
Vis marsane- 'reset bones'
Vish et Tirvish- Depart and locate
Vish het un corpus- "Return me to my body"
Vish mor het tass- 'Return to me, Staff'
Vish un dopar- 'Return and release'
Vish un Rivaith, Apollos- Return to the Shadow,
Destroyer'
Yamba- 'sound'
Zetarn- 'sleep'

Appendices: Ancient Kalnayan Dialect and Curse Words

Drakt'vansh- 'Dragon Slayer'
Dunkla- idiot
Freckaya- 'F**k'
Freckaying- 'F**king'
Madriga- 'Mother'
Magna Spiro- 'Great Spire'; a steep, distinct mountain peak on the northern side of the Shavatnu Mountains
Nevartane- 'The Ever Misty Sea'; the large eastern ocean of Kalnay, which no one has traversed upon in aeons; the mists from Nevartane shield the location of Draconias Maxima- home of Charridon, the Ancient Father
Othros- 'Golden West Wood'; a geographic location in the west central region of Kalnay; home to the fabled gnome tribes
Shavatnu- 'Drake Mountains'; a geographic location in the north central region of Kalnay; contains the Drake's Maw Pass (i.e. The Crossroad of Kings); the border marking the end of the Nightstalker Wastes; below the mountains lives Melatharom the Burrower
Sptoch- 'S**t'
Sptoches- S**ts
Svanth- 'B***h'
Un compta, Madriga; bis vet lineas, un det vish.- 'I promise, Mother; by the ancestors, I shall return.'
Un Rivaith Duallis- 'The Shadow Twins'
Vaith'vansh- 'Shade Slayer'
Vish mor Rivaith, gotsmer- 'Return to the Shadow, demon'

Appendices: Character Name Meanings

Abel- Breath

Abrafo- warrior; executioner

Adelaide- noble; nobility

Alaster- defender of men

Allegra- Joyous

Aloisa- renowned warrior

Amelia- Industrious; striving

Apollos- one who destroys; Destroyer

Arya- honored; noble

Baltar- regal; stately

Bertram- knight

Brantley- firebrand

Branwen- blessed raven

Brienne- Strong; she ascends

Charridon- Fire on the Land

Cheyanne- an Algonquin tribe

Clancy- ruddy warrior

Cillian- war

Cort- brave

Clarke- Cleric; secretary

Delja- daughter of the sea

Diane- fertile; divine

Duncan- dark warrior

Eben- stone

Eimar- swift

Elizabeth- My God is bountiful

Ezri- helper; strong

Fenyang- victory

Frodi- wise; learned

Hearne- mythical hunter

Imre- great king

Iolo- wealthy guardian

Jabesh- Sorrow; trouble

Jelani- mighty; powerful

Jezreel- God scatters

Joel- Jehovah is God; strong-willed

Jorry- God will uplift

Judith- She will be praised

Khalon- strong warrior

Laran- clear

Lilith- Night monster; screech owl

Malikh- Lord; Master

Markus- Mars; god of War; manly; virile

Melatharom- render of stone

Mikael- Gift from God

Morgana- Phantom Queen

Nairadj- Precious Present; great

Noshtain- Unnamed

Ragnar- warrior of judgment
Rebecca- captivating; a knotted cord
Ridley- cleared wood
Roland- famous land; renowned in the land
Runihura- destroyer
Samuel- told by God
Sarto- mender
Sena- bringing heaven to earth
Shomari- Warrior
Sigourney- the Conqueror
Straker- the descendant of Stracian; to stroke
Tabitha- Gazelle
Talia- Dew of Heaven
Talon- Claw of the bird of prey
Tibelde- boldest
Toorg- rooted sentinel
Tucker- to torment
Waldemar- famous ruler
Waleigh- teacher
Wallace- foreigner
Yaltan- adventurer
Yenoor- red-haired
Zepora- beauty

Appendices: Gods of Kalnay

Bauer- god of mirth and merriment
Bloomaya- goddess of nature and growth
Bronwyn-Aetha- goddess of the white and justice
Eaitunim- god of time and order
Godrich- father of all gods, and supreme protector of
Kalnay
Hannibal- god of the hunt and strength
Jutlann- goddess of youth, innocence and children
K'colrehs- god of wisdom and reason
Sharlto- goddess of travellers and safety
Trytos- god of the sea and of salt

Appendices: Legendary Creatures of Kalnay

Dragons- Dragons live in a variety of locations, including:
the swamps and marshes of Voshkarna (the Kalnayan Bog
Lands); beneath the Shavatnu Mountains, and; within
Hesketh (the Shadow Wood). They are rarely seen by
mankind but are engraved upon the golden coin currency
of Kalnay- the most valuable coin currency in the land.

Dyre Bears- A once thriving and prevalent species in
Kalnay have gone into hiding and seek solitude since the
fabled 'Massacre of the Light' by the Mad Bear King,
Kidrahs. Dyre Bears share a magical bond with the cycle
of the moon, like Grymwulves. Unlike Grymwulves, the
Dyre Bears retain their human conscience, and hunt only
wildlife, and leave humans be. Because of their solitary
and secret lifestyle- residing in the Nightstalker Wastes
parts of the Shavatnu Mountains and the Southern Sand
Flats- they have faded into the realm of myth in modern
Kalnay. Few people in Kalnay have ever seen a Dyre Bear.

Elduri- the Elven People of Ancient Kalnay has not existed
in Kalnay since eons ago when they stirred the wroth of
the Dragons. In reprisal for offending the dragons, the
Elduri were all destroyed in a great fire. This extinction
event became a legend: 'The Great Fall of the Elduri of
Kalnay'.

Gnomes- Magical beings who have a love of nature-
plants, birds and small game; they are tribal by nature
but can work with other tribes in time of collective need.
They are fleet of foot, superb pickpockets, have a
weakness for shiny objects- metals, gems, coins, jewelry.
They have magical dominion and partnership with small
game- a variety of birds, burrowing mammals, and tree

critters. They reside exclusively in cities below the earth of Othros (The Golden West Wood) and, like the Dyre Bear, are widely considered myth in modern Kalnay.

Grymwulves- Werewolves who live in tribal villages of the Grymwulf Hills; also known as: Bludwulves. Grymwulves are also engraved upon the silver coin currency of Kalnay- the second most valuable coin currency in the land.

Nightstalkers- Vampires who reside in the Nightstalker Wastes of North Kalnay; also known as: Fanged Shades; Blud Devyls.

Wendygos- half demon, half human cannibals who plague Lec'tair Forest in Eastern Kalnay; distinguished by their pale gray skin, black eyes and stag antlers (of varying size to denote age). Wendygos are also engraved upon the bronze coin currency of Kalnay- the lowest coin in value.

Appendices: The Kalnayan Calendar

Months of the Year in Kalnay
Froslan- The Month of Cold
Winlan- The Month of Wind
Berlan- The Month of Vigilance
Sedlan- The Month of Planting
Tharslan- The Month of Faith
Woldlan- The Month of Love
Hetlan- The Month of Heat
Draslan- The Month of Rains
Kreslan- The Month of Harvest
Ghoslan- The Month of Spirits
Rexlan- The Month of Healing
Craslan- The Month of Festivity

Made in the USA
Columbia, SC
11 October 2020